RUMORS

BY

PHIL M. WILLIAMS

Printed in the United States of America.
First Printing, 2018.

Phil W Books.
www.PhilWBooks.com

ISBN: 978-1-943894-49-9

Cover design and interior formatting by Tugboat Design

A NOTE FROM PHIL

Dear Reader,

If you're interested in receiving my novel *Against the Grain* for free and/or reading my other titles for free or .99 cents, go to the following link: http://www.PhilWBooks.com.

You're probably thinking, *What's the catch?* There is no catch.

Sincerely,
Phil M. Williams

CONTENTS

CHAPTER 1

Gwen and the End of the Beginning

Gwen sat on a plastic and metal chair, waiting with a diverse group of people. The seats were set up in strict rows and columns. An elderly couple chatted quietly. A mother bounced her son on her knee, trying to keep him entertained. Several women tapped their feet, wishing they could tap their phones. Everyone's cell phones had already been confiscated. Two young men wore long-sleeved shirts to cover their tattoos. One had a large bandage on his neck. Displaying gang tatts or wearing revealing clothing would likely result in a denial of visitation. Gwen glanced at one of the women. She was busty, her blouse low-cut. Despite the August heat, Gwen had worn a long sundress with a conservative neckline.

An officer entered the waiting area. The patch on his shoulder read, Philadelphia Department of Prisons. "Group seven," he said.

Gwen and her unknown compatriots stood in unison, making their way to the officer. They'd be the seventh group of visitors that Saturday. The officer looked them over, narrowing his eyes at the busty woman.

"You got a sweatshirt?" he asked.

She frowned, putting one hand on her cocked hip. "It's damn near a hundred outside. *Whatch* you think?"

He swallowed, his Adam's apple bobbing up and down. "I think you're not gettin' in."

"I done signed in. They ain't said nothin'."

"They don't check dress at sign-in. Just your ID."

"That's stupid."

The officer nodded. "You got thirty seconds to find a shirt, or you're not gettin' in."

The woman looked around at the group, hoping someone would or could rescue her. One of the young men took off his long-sleeved T-shirt, revealing a white tank top and tattoos covering every inch of his caramel skin. He handed her his shirt.

"Thank you," she said, barely audible.

"Sir, it's against the dress code to display tattoos," the corrections officer said.

The man nodded to the officer, his expression resigned. "I know." Then he addressed his friend. "I'll wait in the car."

The other young man lifted his chin in acknowledgment.

The corrections officer checked IDs again and led them in a single-file line to the metal detectors. When no one set off any alarms, he led them through double doors, where inmates waited at stainless steel tables. The group separated, everyone finding their person and their table.

Gwen spotted Brian toward the back of the beige room. He stood from the table, his shoulders slumped. Despite his posture and baggy orange jumpsuit, he was handsome and well-built—naturally athletic and muscular from three years of pumping iron at the prison gym. They hugged for two seconds and sat across from each other. There was an envelope in front of him, turned facedown.

Brian forced a smile, his hazel eyes still. He opened his mouth to speak but nothing came out.

Gwen searched his face. He had a strong jaw, high cheekbones, and a long thin nose. Tears welled in her eyes.

He reached across the table. "I know."

She wiped her eyes with the side of her index finger and placed her hands in his. "What do we do now?"

Brian took a deep breath. "It's time to let go."

Gwen shook her head. "I'll save everything I make from my new job. I'll rebuild our credit. I'll hire another lawyer."

He squeezed her hands. "Gwen, no. It's over. I don't want you throwing good money after bad."

"Then what? I just sit around and hope for the best over the next twenty-two years? I won't give up."

"I've been thinking a lot. Especially now with the rejection of the appeal." He exhaled heavily and paused. "We can't go on like this."

"We can't go on like what? You're not making any sense."

"I'll be fifty-seven years old when I have my first shot at parole. You'll be fifty-four. We'll never have kids." His voice wavered. "We'll miss our best years. You never know. I may not make it out of here alive."

"Don't talk like that. If it's the last thing I do, I'm getting you out of here."

"I want you to stop."

She removed her hands from his. "Stop what?"

"Everything. No more appeals. No more letters. No more phone calls. No more visits."

"What are you talking about?"

Brian clenched his jaw. A tear slipped down his face. He slid the envelope across the table. "I want a divorce."

Gwen flipped over the envelope, her mouth hanging open. It was addressed to a Virginia law office and already stamped.

"Just sign where I highlighted," he said.

She sniffled, her eyes glassy. "You don't love me?"

He looked away for a moment. "You're everything to me, … everything. But … I can't be the reason you're not living your life. This is my punishment, not yours."

"Please don't do this."

A tear snaked along the side of his nose. "I'm sorry, Gwen. I'm sorry for everything."

CHAPTER 2

Caleb and Worthless

Cleats click-clacked on the concrete floor. Metal lockers opened and slammed shut. The mood was jovial and raucous—everyone happy for the last practice of football camp. Two-a-days had been grueling, the temperature unusually hot for West Lake, Pennsylvania. Teenage boys were in different stages of dress. Caleb Miles worked the combination lock and opened his locker. He removed his shoes and placed them on the bottom of his locker. He stripped off his T-shirt, exposing his slight upper body. He glanced to his right, then to his left. The starting quarterback, Shane Wilcox, stood in front of his locker, wearing only a diamond stud in each earlobe. Caleb's eyes swept over his tall, athletic frame. For a moment, he settled on Shane's flaccid penis.

"You lookin' at my dick?" Shane said.

Caleb looked forward. He rummaged in his locker, pretending not to hear Shane.

Shane stepped closer, still naked, and now within striking distance. "I asked you a *fuckin'* question."

Caleb turned toward the tall boy. Shane had ice-blue eyes, dark hair, and a pencil-thin beard.

"I'm sorry. ... I, uh, didn't hear you," Caleb said.

4

"You were lookin' at my dick, weren't you?"

A group of football players in various stages of dress surrounded the scene.

"I, I wasn't," Caleb said.

"Faggot-ass faggot." Shane looked around at his audience with a crooked grin, then zeroed in on Caleb again. "Don't fuckin' lie. I saw your bitch-ass lookin'."

"I'm sorry. I didn't mean to." Caleb dipped his head in deference, accidentally catching another glimpse of Shane's penis.

"Dude, he did it again," Lance said, pointing and laughing at Caleb.

The rest of the crowd laughed in unison, and someone said, "What a fag."

Lance moved closer, standing next to Shane. Lance wore his football pants and no shirt. He was the star receiver and Shane's favorite passing target. "You're outta the closet now. You might as well look at his junk. You know you want to."

The crowd laughed. "You know you want to," they echoed.

Caleb turned back to his locker, rummaging through his things again.

"You ain't gettin' off that easy," Shane said.

Lance sidled up to Caleb and put his arm around him, turning him toward Shane. "Go on, Caleb. Check it out."

Shane widened his legs and put one bare foot on the bench, his penis and scrotum on full display for Caleb.

Caleb held his gaze upward.

Lance grabbed Caleb's head and forced his gaze toward Shane's crotch. "Go on, faggot. You know you want to."

Caleb's gaze followed the trail of hair leading from Shane's belly button to the nest of dark hair and Shane's circumcised penis.

The crowd hooted and hollered, providing a running commentary.

"Look at him."

"He wants your junk."

"Dick-slap him."

A dark-skinned boy pushed through the crowd. "Let him go," Jamar said.

Lance smiled at Jamar. "Or what?"

"I said, *let him go.*"

"Who are you, his black boyfriend?" Shane said, laughing.

"Ten minutes," Coach Bob Schneider said, entering the locker room. "Move your asses."

As the burly, bearded coach walked past, Lance let Caleb go. Shane hurried back to his locker to get dressed. Caleb spent the next ten minutes arranging and rearranging his locker, afraid to face anyone. With the last player gone to the practice field, Caleb sat on the bench, put his chin to his chest, and cried. After a few minutes, he sniffled and wiped his face with his T-shirt. He put on his football gear, exited the locker room, and jogged to the practice field.

Head Coach Rick Barnett stood at the edge of the practice field next to his Offensive Coordinator Bob Schneider, while the team warmed up on the fifty-yard line. The summer sun beat down on the coaches. They wore hats with intertwined initials WL, which stood for West Lake. Coach Schneider had sweat rings under the arms of his WL Wolf Pack T-shirt.

Coach Barnett frowned and glanced at his watch as Caleb jogged closer. Coach Barnett was tall and well-built, with a stubbly beard. "You're eight minutes late. That's eight laps. Get moving."

As Caleb started to jog, he heard Coach Schneider say, "If it wasn't for his hot mom, he'd be worthless."

CHAPTER 3

Rick and Controversy Brewing

Coach Rick Barnett frowned at Coach Schneider.

Bob Schneider chuckled, his hands on his gut, as if he were trying to hold it in place. "Come on. You know it's true. What I wouldn't give for one night with her."

"What I wouldn't give for a family like yours."

"I can look. I just can't touch. You can though. Then you can gimme the details."

"That's not happening."

"Why not? Shit, I saw her checkin' you out at the parents meetin'."

Rick shook his head and walked away from Bob, toward the team. As soon as the team finished warm-ups, Coach Rick Barnett said, "First O, on the ball. Second D."

Shane lined up in the shotgun. On "Go," the center snapped the ball. Shane caught the snap, faked the handoff to the running back, reared back, and threw a bomb to Lance. Shane's favorite target caught the pass for a touchdown. It went on like this for half an hour. The first-string offense scored at will, asserting their dominance over the smaller and slower second-string defense.

After the drubbing, Rick said, "First D. Second O, on the ball."

The cycle began in reverse. This time the defense was bigger, faster, and stronger, leading to defensive linemen tackling the running back in the backfield several times. The second-string quarterback, Jamar Burris, dropped back to pass, but, before he could throw, three defenders planted him to the turf.

The next play, Jamar dropped back to pass again, this time sprinting out of the pocket to avoid the pass rush. Caleb Miles was wide open fifty yards downfield. Jamar threw a rocket right on the money. The football hit Caleb in the hands, but he dropped it.

The defensive back that Caleb had gotten behind laughed. "Butterfingers."

Coach Rick Barnett approached the defensive end that Jamar had run around. "Do not let the quarterback get outside of you. You do that next Friday, and we're gonna get killed. You understand me?"

The boy nodded.

The next play, Jamar had the pass rush in his face again. He scrambled to his left to find a wall of defenders. Jamar reversed course, giving ground, and sprinted to his right. Another wall of defenders but with a small seam up the middle. Jamar stuck his cleat in the turf and streaked through the opening, leaving the entire defense in the dust. Touchdown.

Rick shook his head, a crooked grin on his face.

* * *

After practice, the players carried their helmets and walked to the locker room, joking and laughing as they went. Head Coach Rick Barnett stood on the practice field with his Offensive Coordinator, Bob Schneider.

"Jamar's pretty good, huh?" Rick said.

"He'll be good next year," Bob replied.

"He might be better than Shane now. And he has a much bigger upside."

"He doesn't know the offense."

"He's a smart kid. If he was getting the reps, I'm sure he'd pick it up."

"What are you sayin'?"

"If Shane falters, we shouldn't be afraid to go with Jamar."

"It'd be a mistake. He's only a sophomore. We have a proven commodity with Shane. It'll split the team. The seniors'll be pissed. Shit, Shane's mother'll be pissed. You know how she is."

Rick blew out a breath. "I don't give a shit about who's gonna be butthurt. The best kid plays, period."

"And you think that's Jamar?"

"Maybe. We'll see how they do in the scrimmage tomorrow."

CHAPTER 4

Janet and the Connection

Janet paced in the kitchen, her bare feet on the tile floor, her cell phone to her ear. She wore yoga pants and a tank top, her sports bra stretching to contain her ample bust.

"It's an old boys' club," Janet said into her phone. "I'm tired of it. The district deserves better."

"It's been that way for as long as I can remember," Cliff replied.

"Your apathy is part of the problem."

"Come on, Janet. I'm one of the good guys. Things'll get better. You just need to wait your turn."

"Pruitt needs to go now. He does nothing. *Absolutely nothing.* I've been doing his job for years."

"And you think you should be his replacement?"

"Damn right I should. I've been vice principal for ten years, and I've done an excellent job under difficult circumstances. Plus I live in the district. I care about this community. Pruitt doesn't even live here. He lives in Palmyra."

"I heard he's planning to retire in five years," Cliff replied through the phone. "You'll be a shoo-in then."

"Matthews is retiring in three years. If Pruitt's still the high school principal when Matthews retires, and the school board members don't change, they'll hire another one of their cronies to be superintendent, and we'll be stuck with this same shit. Now's the time to make a change. The school board doesn't even have to fire Pruitt. Just force him to retire early."

Cliff sighed. "It's happy hour, honey. How about you and I go out for a few drinks?"

"Don't you *honey* me."

Cliff chuckled.

"This is serious, Cliff. We're one board member away from a majority. If we can break the old boys' club, we can get rid of Pruitt, and we can turn this district around. Don't you care that we have the third-lowest test scores in the county?"

"The five have a strong base in the community. They've been on the school board for damn near twenty years. Who's up for reelection in November?"

"Daub and Pastor Goode."

Cliff paused. "They'll be tough to beat."

Janet stopped in her tracks. "You hesitated. You know something about them, don't you?"

Cliff chuckled again. "I've known these men my whole life."

"Then you must know how to beat them."

"I might."

"I'm listening."

"I'm not *that* easy. I could be persuaded to talk about it in person. It is sensitive information. What do you think, beautiful?"

Janet pursed her lips. "Where?"

"Days Inn in Hershey."

Janet giggled, but her laughter faded with Cliff's silence. "Are you serious?"

"As a heart attack."

"Would this be a friendly meeting … or a more-than-friendly meeting?"

"What do you think?"

Janet sat at the kitchen table, her forehead creased. "Seriously, Cliff?"

"I have friends and *good* friends. My good friends do things for me, and I do things for them. That's the way of the world."

Janet cringed, imagining Cliff's hands all over her. "I don't know."

"You let me know when you do." Cliff's tone became much more upbeat. "So, what do you think of the team this year? Think they'll win the district title?"

"I think they'll win state. Shane's excited," Janet said.

"So's Lance. They make one helluva connection."

CHAPTER 5

Gwen and the Leprechaun

Gwen sat at her desk, reviewing her lesson plans on her laptop. Her mind wandered to Brian. It had only been six days since he'd produced the divorce papers. She'd signed because he was right. Intellectually, she knew he was right, but it didn't feel that way. Her life *had* been consumed by him and the appeals. But moving on felt worse. Even though he was in prison, at least she got to hear his voice, to see him, to hug him and to hold his hands. And now she was just supposed to let him go? Forget all about him?

She sniffled and grabbed a tissue from the box on her desktop. She dabbed the corners of her eyes. Gwen felt like she'd been fired by Brian, which was weird because she'd recently been hired, her first teaching job in almost four years. It had been her first week at her new school. No students yet. The teachers were expected to return a week before the students for trainings, orientations, and preparation. The only kids around campus were the student-athletes on the sports fields. Otherwise, Monday would be the first day of school for the kids.

A knock came from her open door. She looked up to find a short man with platinum-blond hair and reddish-white skin standing on the threshold. His face was smooth and youthful.

"Knock, knock," he said, smiling.

Gwen stood from her desk and returned his smile.

He approached with his hand held out. "I'm Lewis Phelps, across the hall from you—history."

Gwen shook his hand. "Gwen Townsend, ELA."

Lewis glanced around her colorful classroom, complete with a purple-carpeted reading area, beanbag chairs, motivational posters, and stacks of clear plastic containers filled with books and organized by genre. "Your room looks great. You must've been an elementary teacher."

"I taught third grade right out of college."

"I can tell. My room looks like a jail cell compared to yours."

"I think I may have overdone it. I guess I want to make a good first impression."

"Is this the first time you've taught high school?"

"No, I taught high school English at my last school."

"Where did you teach?"

"I was in Philly."

"Whoa." Lewis grinned. "The inner city. Now you're in this rural backwater. Talk about a change."

"I guess it was time." Gwen looked down for a moment.

"So, how was the new teacher orientation today? That was today, right?"

"Yes, today. It was good." Gwen didn't sound enthused.

Lewis grinned. "It was boring. You can say it."

"It was a bit bland."

"I'm pretty sure I fell asleep during mine. Principal Pruitt droned on for like five hours. He did capture my attention with his presentation on school shootings. He talked about improvised explosives and said we didn't have to worry about bombs because we don't have any Muslim students."

Gwen cringed. "He *didn't*."

"Oh, he did. Then he made a joke. He said something like, where do suicide bombers go after they die?" Lewis paused. "Everywhere."

Gwen covered her mouth, stifling her laughter. "That's unbelievable.

I'm surprised he still has a job."

"The school board and the administration still think it's 1955. We have teachers who still give the same worksheets from when I went here. Last year, I found a grammar worksheet left on the copier that referenced President Reagan."

Gwen giggled again.

"That was actually your predecessor."

"Those poor kids."

"I'm not sure the younger teachers are any better. Everyone's so apathetic around here." Lewis gestured to the classroom windows and the view of the parking lot. "Did you see the Indy 235?"

"The what?"

"Every day at contract time, the staff rushes out of here at 2:35. I call it the Indianapolis 235. It drives me crazy. Everyone loves to bitch, but they're not willing to put in the time to make things better."

"It *is* Friday."

"It's like that every day. You'll see."

Gwen nodded. "How long have you been teaching here?"

"This'll be my sixth year. I started here right after grad school. What about you? You look like you're about twenty?"

"That's why you're my new best friend. I'm thirty-two. You look pretty young yourself."

Lewis smirked. "Yeah, but, when you look young as a man, people disrespect you. It doesn't help that I'm as tall as a leprechaun."

"You don't look that short to me."

"You are too damn nice. I used to be nice too. This school will fix that. You'll be cynical like me by Christmas break."

"Now you're making me nervous."

"I'm just kidding … mostly. You'll be fine. Do you know who your evaluator is yet?"

"Principal Wilcox."

Lewis winced. "Janet, the Destroyer of Worlds."

"She seems okay."

"She's very political and very out for herself. If you fall in line and align yourself with her, she'll be your best friend. If you don't, watch out."

Gwen sighed. "I really don't like office politics. I just want to do my job."

"Just don't go out of your way to oppose her, and watch your back. Don't give her any information that she can twist and use against you."

Gwen chewed on her lower lip.

"Don't worry. You'll be fine, and, if you get into trouble, I'm right across the hall."

"Thanks, Lewis."

"That's what neighbors are for. Well, I just wanted to introduce myself. I'm about to head out. Looks like you're the last man standing."

CHAPTER 6

Caleb and Ragu

Shane and Lance cheered from the sideline, their helmets in hand. The first string of the West Lake Wolf Pack had dominated the Dauphin Rams during the first half of the scrimmage. Shane had played well, throwing two touchdown passes to Lance, but he'd also thrown an interception. The second string was in now, vying for positions as backups. Caleb had slipped to the third string, his red-and-white uniform still sparkling clean.

On the field, Jamar took the snap and fired a frozen rope, hitting a backup wide receiver for the first down. Caleb thought about how that should've been him. He'd been Jamar's favorite receiver when they were freshmen, but Caleb had dropped too many passes lately. For some reason, Caleb had been nervous. He had trouble concentrating, especially when it mattered the most.

On the next play, Jamar dropped back to pass. He sidestepped the rush and threw a bomb, a perfect arcing spiral into the outstretched hands of a West Lake receiver. Touchdown. The West Lake sideline and stands cheered.

Lance razzed Shane. "Nigger wants to take your position."

"Ain't gonna happen," Shane replied, shoving Lance.

The defense recovered a fumble, and Jamar took over again. This time he faked a handoff to the running back and sprinted around the left end, making a little jump cut that froze the defensive end just enough for Jamar to slip past. Two tacklers converged near the sideline, but Jamar planted and spun 360 degrees, leaving them grasping for air as Jamar galloped for a fifty-five-yard touchdown run.

The West Lake sideline erupted again, cheering and shouting. Judging by the level of excitement, Caleb's teammates were more impressed with Jamar's two touchdowns than Shane's pair. Judging from Shane's frown, he was fully aware of that fact.

Lance nudged Shane. "You gotta admit, that was badass."

"Big fuckin' deal," Shane replied. "He's playin' against the second string."

* * *

After the scrimmage, Caleb undressed and dressed quickly, not making eye contact with anyone and avoiding the shower altogether. He hurried from the locker room into the hot afternoon sun.

"Hey, Caleb," Jamar called out.

Caleb turned back toward the locker room door. Jamar stood just outside, still wearing his football pants and a sweaty T-shirt, his feet bare. Jamar was nearly six-feet tall, trim and wiry, nearly every muscle visible through his skin.

"Good game," Caleb said.

"Thanks, man. Why are you in such a rush?"

"I have some stuff to do at home."

"If you gimme a few minutes, I'll walk home with you."

"I really have to go, ... but thanks, Jamar."

"Check you later."

Caleb walked on the narrow shoulder of the asphalt road. He walked beyond the school, along cornfields with massive cornstalks. Sporadic traffic passed him—mostly pickup trucks. He heard the rumble of knobby tires on asphalt. Shane's lifted Chevy pickup approached close to the shoulder. Caleb stepped closer to the corn. A handful of guys stood in the truck bed. They pointed at Caleb and pounded on the roof of the cab as Shane drove past. Shane reversed the truck and stopped next to Caleb. Lance hung from the passenger window.

"Hey, you need a ride?" Lance asked.

Caleb shook his head. "No, … thanks."

"That's good, because we don't pick up faggots." Lance threw a mostly empty plastic bottle at Caleb, striking him on the top of his head.

The peanut gallery standing in the truck bed laughed and threw their beverages at Caleb. Soda cans and Gatorade bottles flew through the air. Caleb raised his forearm, shielding his face. Most of the bottles and cans bounced off him, impotent. One full can of soda hit him in the knee, causing Caleb to drop to the ground. The boys laughed, and Shane gunned the engine of his lifted truck, leaving Caleb in the exhaust.

Lesson learned; stay away from the road. Caleb picked up the full soda and cut through the cornfield. He limped a little, his knee already swelling. It was probably just a bruise. He walked between the cornstalks, invisible to the world, the world invisible to him. He was nothing. Nobody. Actually, he was less than nothing. If he was just nothing, they'd leave him alone. He stayed in one row, knowing if he stayed true, he'd eventually reach the end of the field.

Twenty minutes later, he made it to his neighborhood of vinyl-sided ramblers, double-wide trailers, and prefab colonials. His house was a double-wide trailer, with an attached carport, large enough for only one vehicle. His mother's car was gone, but Ashlee's Jeep was parked in the street. She'd gotten it a few months ago for her sixteenth birthday. Her dad wasn't around much, but he did buy her the Jeep, and his child support not only paid for Ashlee but most of the household bills. Caleb's father was another story entirely. Caleb pushed inside, walked past the living room and into the kitchen. He put his soda in the fridge, then stepped down the hall, toward the bedrooms and bathroom. He heard voices from his sister's room.

"You're not coming?" Ashlee asked.

"I can't, babe. I barely have time to talk," Ryan said through Ashlee's computer.

"You could come get me. We can spend the weekend in State College."

"If I barely have time to talk, what makes you think I can come pick you up? It's a three-hour drive one way."

"I guess I could drive up there."

"But I don't have time to hang out."

"Then we're never gonna see each other."

"I'll be home at Christmas, ... unless we have a bowl game."

"I have to go. I'm going out. I'm not gonna sit around waiting for you."

"Don't be like that."

Ashlee slammed shut her laptop. She opened her bedroom door. "What are you doing?"

"Uh, nothing," Caleb said. "I was just wondering where Mom is."

"She went out. Said she won't be home until tomorrow."

"With who?"

"I don't know. Probably some douchebag."

"Did she leave any money for food?"

Ashlee's mouth turned up for a split second. "No. She said to make spaghetti."

Caleb crossed his arms over his chest. "You took the money, didn't you?"

"It was only ten bucks. You can't buy pizza with that."

"That's not the point."

"I'm going out. I need it."

"I'm telling Mom."

"Go ahead. I'll tell her how you were listening to my *private* conversation."

"Whatever." Caleb started for the bathroom.

"There's pasta and half a jar of Ragu," Ashlee called out.

Caleb slammed the bathroom door behind him.

CHAPTER 7

Rick and His Dirty Little Secret

Coach Rick Barnett turned his pickup truck into his neighborhood, the afternoon sun shining in his eyes. He flipped down his visor. Boxy stone colonials and brick ramblers built in the fifties sat on quarter-acre lots, with mature trees that caused a leaf-removal apocalypse for the residents every fall. He parked in the driveway of his one-story brick home and cut the engine. His garage was too small for his full-size truck.

He stepped to the front door and pushed inside, into the foyer. Soft music played on the stereo in the living room. Perfume wafted in the air. Rick blew out a breath and walked into the living room. *I really need to start locking my door.*

Heather Miles stood in high heels, heavy makeup, and nothing else. She was tan and toned from head to toe. "I thought we could celebrate the big win."

"It was just a scrimmage," Rick said.

She sauntered toward him, her hips rocking back and forth. Heather was in her mid-thirties, petite, with curly brown hair to her shoulders. She was pretty but overdone, like an eighties' Glamour Shot.

"You can't come over here unannounced," Rick said. "How would it look if someone saw you? You know how people talk around here."

"Maybe it's time for the world to know."

Rick took a step back. "Did someone see you? One of the boys?"

She frowned. "No, I parked around the corner. Went through the backyard." She pressed out her lower lip. "Don't I look pretty?"

"Of course, but ..." Rick glanced at her clothes in a small pile on the couch.

"Don't you want me?"

Rick grabbed her thong and lacy bra, and handed them over. "We need to talk."

She snatched her underwear, then nearly toppled in her sky-high heels as she put on her thong. "I'm tired of being your *dirty* little secret." She kicked off her heels, grabbed her T-shirt and jeans from the couch, and dressed, not bothering with the bra. She stood with her hands on her hips, her brown eyes boring a hole through him.

"I told you from the beginning that I didn't want anything serious. And I told you that I didn't want this getting out."

Tears welled in her eyes. "You've always been ashamed of me."

"Come on, Heather. How would it look if people knew I was sleeping with a player's mother? How would Caleb feel? What do you think the other kids would say to him?"

She wiped her eyes with her index finger. "Nobody would say shit if we got engaged."

"I can't do this."

"Can't or won't?"

"Does it matter?"

"You're a fuckin' asshole, you know that?"

"I'm sorry. I was wrong."

She moved into his personal space, looking up at him. "Don't do this. Please. I can be whatever you want." She undid his belt.

He stepped back, but she moved forward, holding firm and unbuttoning his khaki shorts. Rick removed her hand, buttoned his shorts, and fastened his belt. She sat on the couch, put her head in her hands, and cried. He sat next to her but out of reach.

"Heather, I'm sorry. I'm really sorry. If I could take it all back, I would."

She turned to him, her eyeliner streaking down her face. "Don't you fuckin' say that. I'm not some mistake. You're just like every other man. You want what you want, but you don't wanna be serious."

"You came on to me. This was your idea."

"Fuck you." She stood from the couch and moved in front of him. Standing, she wasn't much taller than Rick seated. She reared back and slapped him across the face.

Rick stood, now towering over Heather. "You can leave now."

"You're gonna regret this."

"I already do."

She grabbed her bra and heels and glared at Rick. "You can't throw me away like fuckin' trash."

"That's not what this is," Rick said. "I'm trying to be straight with you. I don't love you."

"You don't know what love is." She stomped from the house, leaving the front door wide open in her wake.

CHAPTER 8

Janet and the Poison Apple

Janet sashayed down the empty hall, flanked by red lockers, classroom doors, and the occasional drinking fountain. Coach Rick Barnett exited the staff bathroom.

"How's my favorite coach?" Janet said as she approached.

Rick turned toward Janet.

He was a decade her junior but just her type: tall, like her; athletic; a strong jawline with a symmetrical face; and those ice-blue eyes.

"I'm all right," Rick said, his face impassive.

"The team looked good at the scrimmage. You guys ready for the Lions?"

"Not yet. That's why we practice all week."

She smiled wide. "Well, I'm sure you'll have them ready to go by Friday. Shane's really excited. His goal's a state title."

Rick nodded. "That would be nice, but we have to focus on the Lions first. One game at a time." He glanced down the hall. "I should get back to my class. Lewis is watching them for me."

"Of course. Me too. I need to check on one of the new teachers."

He turned to walk away.

"Rick?"

He turned back to Janet.

She bit the corner of her lower lip. "If you ever want to … get a drink or something, let me know."

Rick smiled with his mouth closed, his eyes still. "Thanks, Janet." He walked down the hall toward his classroom.

Janet followed for a bit, then stopped at room number 122, Ms. Townsend, English Language Arts. Raucous voices spilled into the hall. She opened the door and stepped inside without knocking. Janet's mouth hung open. The desks were arranged in a horseshoe. The room was awash in bright colors. Gwen Townsend and her twenty-seven students threw balled-up pieces of paper at each other, laughing, with huge smiles.

"*What* is going on in here?" Janet shouted over the insanity. A piece of paper ricocheted off her glasses. Janet glared at the culprit. Drew Fuller. The eighteen-year-old senior piece-of-trailer-trash. Big nose, beady eyes, and forehead acne.

"I'm sorry, Principal Wilcox. Total accident. I swear," Drew said, showing his palms, with a barely detectable trace of a smirk. He went back to throwing paper balls, ignoring her authority along with the rest of the class.

"That's enough," Gwen said, smiling and also ignoring Janet. The room quieted on Gwen's cue. "Everyone pick up the paper ball closest to you. Only take one. Read the five facts, and try to figure out the person behind the facts. Remember. Only yes and no questions, and the first ten who ID the person correctly get a treat. Ready? ... Go."

Janet narrowed her eyes at Gwen. She'd been hired by Principal Pruitt without Janet's input. Definitely not someone Janet would've hired. She could tell Gwen was all fluff and no substance. One of those teachers who was too damn nice to the students. Teachers like her made it hard for rigorous teachers and administrators like Janet. They did the hard work of instilling discipline, only to be undermined by teachers like Gwen.

The students chattered, going from person to person, asking yes/no questions. Gwen turned her attention to Janet. "I'm sorry about that, Janet—"

"Principal Wilcox."

"If you prefer."

"I'd like to talk to you outside … *now*."

Gwen turned to her class, holding up one hand. "Lovelies."

Her class laughed, then quieted.

Drew said, "*Lovelies?*"

Gwen smiled at the young man. "Yes, you are all my lovely students, so get used to it. I'll be right back, but please continue with the icebreaker. Drew, will you keep track of the first ten winners?"

"I got your back, Ms. Townsend."

Gwen followed Janet into the hall, shutting her door behind them. Gwen wore a pencil skirt and a loose blouse. She was fresh-faced, with milky skin, big blue eyes, and straight dark hair. A real-life Snow White. Janet thought, *Where's that poison apple?*

"Your classroom's out of control," Janet said.

"I'm sorry, Principal Wilcox. We're doing a first day icebreaker. It's called snowball fight. The kids love it, but it can get out of hand."

"Well, your class is making entirely too much noise. What if one of the classes next to you was taking a test?"

"On the first day of school?"

"That's not the point."

"I'll be more careful about the noise in the future."

"Consider this your first warning." Janet turned on her heels and marched back to the main office.

Principal Pruitt's administrative assistant sat at the reception desk, typing on her laptop. She looked up from her screen. "Good morning, *Vice* Principal Wilcox."

Janet glared at the old woman. She wondered if Grace's use of *Vice* Principal was purposely pejorative. Maybe to get under Janet's skin. "Good morning, *Secretary* Moyer."

Grace Moyer smiled at Janet.

Janet walked past reception to the back offices. Principal Pruitt's office door was open. Pruitt sat behind his desk, laughing into his phone receiver. Don Pruitt had a ruddy complexion, stocky build, and a big blocky head atop a nearly nonexistent neck. He looked like an aging Barney Rubble.

"All right now," Principal Pruitt said. "Tell that beautiful wife of yours that I said hello. Yep. Of course. Bye." He hung up the phone and looked at Janet. "Morning, Janet."

Janet stepped into his office, shutting the door behind her. "Hi, Don. How was your weekend?" Janet sat in one of the chairs in front of Pruitt's desk.

Principal Pruitt leaned back in his leather chair. "Nancy and I are officially empty nesters. We dropped off Mary at Penn State over the weekend. My back's killing me from helping her move in. I'm getting old with a capital O."

"How does Nancy feel about being an empty nester?"

He sighed. "She cried when we left State College, but that's Nance. She's emotional, but I wouldn't have it any other way." He paused for a moment. "Do you know how you can tell if you're suffering from empty-nester syndrome?"

"Depression?"

Pruitt shook his head with a grin. "You call the power company and ask them to check your meter because the hot-water bill's way too low." He slapped his knee and laughed.

Janet forced a smile. "You guys can have sex all over the house now."

Pruitt laughed again, his barrel chest moving up and down. "I'm not sure my old back's ready for that. I just hope the good Lord'll grant us good health for the duration."

"You and me both."

"You're still a young woman. No need to worry about that yet."

Janet smiled at her boss. "Thank you, but I'm not that young."

"You're a spring chicken compared to me. I'm an old rooster, too tough and gnarled even for the Crock-Pot." He chuckled.

"All right, you old rooster. When are you going to retire and live the good life with Nancy?"

"Oh, I don't know. I need five years for full retirement. I'd rather not take a pay cut until Mary's out of college."

Janet nodded. "There's more to life than money."

"You're right about that, young lady."

"So, I wanted to ask you about the new ELA teacher, Gwen Townsend."

"Great lady. A fantastic teacher too. She came with one heckuva résumé."

"She doesn't have much control over her classroom. I had to reprimand her for the unruly behavior of her students."

"Really?"

"Yes. The students were throwing paper at each other. They were yelling and screaming. I think she might be a problem."

"Huh. I'm surprised. I figured she'd be a shining star."

"I'm not impressed with her."

"I guess I could talk to her."

"No, don't worry about it. I'm on it. I am her evaluator."

"Don't be too rough on her."

Janet tilted her head. "Of course not."

CHAPTER 9

Gwen and the Gossip

Gwen stood in her empty classroom, fiddling with the HDMI cable on her document camera, the picture still blue on the projector. She turned off the device, then turned it back on. That usually worked when she ran into technical difficulties. She waited for a moment. Still a blue screen. She went back to her desk, grabbed a few almonds, and took a swig of kombucha to wash it down. A portly woman breezed through her open door.

"Hi," she said, approaching. "I'm Rachel Kreider. I'm the gifted teacher, and I'm also the union president. I wanted to introduce myself." Rachel thrust her hand out to Gwen.

Gwen smiled and shook Rachel's hand. "I'm Gwen Townsend. It's nice to meet you."

Rachel's brown hair was cut to shoulder length, her bangs short and straight across her forehead. She wore a short-sleeve sweater and high-waisted khakis. She looked like a mom circa 1987.

"Are you planning to join the union?" Rachel asked. "I can get you the paperwork. It's supereasy."

"Thank you, but I'm not interested in joining. I'm on a really tight budget."

"It's not very expensive but definitely worth it."

"I'll think about it."

Rachel forced a smile. "So, how's your first day been? Got any nixie boys?"

"*Nixie?*"

Rachel giggled. "You know. Little troublemakers. It's always the boys."

"So far the students have been very well behaved. Maybe too well behaved."

"Oh, that's not possible."

"Everything's so structured for them. It can stifle creativity."

"You give them an inch, they take a mile."

"Sometimes, but sometimes they need freedom and the responsibility that goes with it."

Rachel narrowed her small eyes for a split second. "So, I heard you used to teach in Philly."

Gwen nodded but didn't elaborate.

"Why did you leave? You get tired of all those nixie boys?" She giggled again. "I'm sure they're a handful down there." Rachel lowered her tone to a whisper. "You know? Most of them don't even have fathers at home."

Gwen exhaled. "Having two engaged parents is a challenge everywhere."

"Oh, don't I know it. Is that why you left?"

A knock came from Gwen's open door. Gwen and Rachel turned to the man walking toward them.

"Gwen?"

"You must be Greg," Gwen said, extending her hand to the man.

Greg looked young despite his scruffy beard. He was thin but had a paunch. His arms were pasty, without muscle definition. Occupational hazard of a sedentary tech guy.

"Yepper. I got your ticket about the document camera," Greg said, shaking her hand. His other hand held his phone.

Gwen said to Rachel, "Will you excuse me for a minute?"

"It's gonna take a while. You might wanna come back," Greg said to Rachel.

Rachel scowled at Greg, then smiled at Gwen. "I'll see you later. It was so nice to meet you."

"It was nice to meet you too, Rachel," Gwen replied.

Rachel waved and grinned on her way out.

"You can thank me now," Greg said, looking Gwen over with his eyes and holding his phone out front as if he were taking her picture.

Gwen furrowed her brow. *Did he just take my picture? That can't be right. He wasn't even looking at his phone.*

"Rachel's the biggest gossip here. She'll come into your room, waste your time, and then spread everything you tell her."

Gwen nodded. "Okay, … thanks for the heads-up."

Greg glanced at Gwen's desktop with her containers of carrots, almonds, and cheese. "You have sixth period lunch?"

"Seventh period. This is my planning period, but I was starving."

"I'm seventh period too." He stared at her, his pupils dilated. "You, um, … uh, … wanna have lunch tomorrow?"

Gwen forced a smile that didn't reach her eyes. "That's really nice of you to offer, but I normally eat at my desk and work through lunch."

Greg stepped back as if he'd been slapped. He adjusted his wire-rim glasses. "Let's look at that document camera." He spoke in a monotone, his kind affectations off in an instant. Greg walked toward the document camera, Gwen behind him.

"I keep getting a blue screen," Gwen said.

Greg ignored her comment and powered on the camera and the projector. He tapped on the remote. The screen read Input, then HDMI. Her lesson appeared.

"It's working," Gwen said, grinning. "Thank you so much."

He set down the remote and narrowed his eyes at Gwen. "You have to have it on the right input. You could've figured that out with a five-minute Google search. I'm not here to fix every little problem for you. My time is valuable."

"I'm sorry. At my old school we didn't have document cameras or much technology at all."

"Google is your friend." He exited her classroom.

CHAPTER 10

Caleb's Fine

Students hurried to the lunchroom, a cacophony of raucous voices. The quicker they got their lunch, the more time they had to socialize with their friends. Caleb wasn't sure where he'd sit. He didn't have many friends. It had always been him and Madison, but she'd moved over the summer. There was Jamar, but he was in B lunch. Caleb trudged down the hallway, purposely slow, preferring to wait in line than sit by himself.

Caleb glanced around, scouting out a seat. Metal and laminate tables were arranged in perfect rows and columns, like cemetery plots. He *should* sit with the football players, but Shane and Lance were there. The last thing Caleb needed was to be bullied in front of the entire lunchroom. He knew a few other kids but not well enough to sit with them. *What if they rejected me? How would that look?* He hoped the line moved slowly enough that he wouldn't have time to think about socializing. Nobody would care if he sat by himself for five minutes just to eat.

Caleb was nearly last in line. The line twisted around the ropes like a popular ride at Disney World. He pushed his tray and Styrofoam plate along the metal counter. Cheese pizza, tater tots, and creamed corn. The food groups: yellow and brown. The cashier swiped his free-and-reduced lunch card, and he stepped to the lunchroom with his tray in hand. He found a corner table that was mostly uninhabited. He ate quickly, but the bell rang before he was finished. The lunchroom emptied as he continued to eat, finishing the last of his tater tots. He tossed the remnants of his lunch in the trash and stacked his tray with the others. He had to pee, so he hurried from the lunchroom toward the bathroom.

The tardy bell rang, the hallway empty now. Caleb turned into the bathroom, but Aaron Fuller blocked the doorway. Aaron was a sophomore—like Caleb, but taller and more athletic—and a total hellion, much like his older brother, Drew. Also like his brother, Aaron was an excellent linebacker. Last year, everyone on the freshman team had been afraid of him. Everyone thought he'd start varsity alongside Drew, but Aaron hadn't come out for football as a sophomore.

Aaron lifted his chin. "What the fuck you think you're doin'?"

"I have to take a piss," Caleb replied, trying to sound tough.

"Go to another bathroom, bitch."

"Who is it?" Drew called out from inside the bathroom.

"Shit, I don't remember," Aaron replied. "Little fucker. Plays football."

"Caleb Miles," Caleb said.

"Caleb Miles," Aaron repeated for his brother.

"Let him in," Drew said.

Aaron stepped aside, and Caleb walked into the bathroom. Shane, Lance, and Drew stood by the sinks. The best football players in the school. All seniors. Shane heated the end of the pipe with a Bic lighter and inhaled a vapor. He grinned and handed the pipe and lighter to Lance.

"You want a hit, little man?" Shane asked.

Drew and Lance laughed. Lance took a hit.

"Don't be a punk-ass bitch," Drew said.

"I just have to take a piss," Caleb said, his voice higher than normal, almost pleading.

"Go on then," Lance said.

Caleb stepped up to the urinal, unzipped his jeans, and pulled his penis through the hole in his boxer shorts. The seniors surrounded him, and he couldn't pee, not a drop.

"I thought you had to take a piss," Lance said.

"Leave me alone," Caleb said, his penis in hand.

"Look at that little thing. Have you even hit puberty yet?"

Shane snapped a picture with his camera phone.

"Hey." Caleb shoved his penis back into his pants and zipped up. He reached for Shane's phone.

Shane held up his phone, out of reach of the much smaller boy. "You better back the fuck up."

Caleb stepped back. "Come on. That's not cool. Erase it." He sounded desperate.

Shane put his phone in his pocket. "You don't like people lookin' at your dick, do you?"

"No, I don't."

"Then why were you lookin' at mine, you little faggot?"

"I wasn't. I swear."

"That's some bullshit," Lance said.

"I'm sorry. I didn't mean to," Caleb said.

"It's cool," Shane said with a crooked smile.

"Can you please erase the picture?"

Shane shrugged. "Relax. It's just a dick pic."

"I want you to erase it," Caleb said, his arms crossed over his chest.

"I don't give a fuck what you want." Shane lifted his chin toward the exit. "Get the fuck outta my face."

Caleb exhaled, hung his head, and left the bathroom without a word. He trudged to another bathroom to finish his business. Afterward, he went to Mr. Phelps's world history class eight minutes late. He was happy it was Mr. Phelps. He had had Mr. Phelps last year for American history. He never yelled at anyone. Lewis Phelps didn't say anything to Caleb as he took a seat. Mr. Phelps simply nodded, placed a syllabus on Caleb's desktop, and continued his instructions.

* * *

After class, as Caleb started for the door, Mr. Phelps asked, "Caleb, can you hang back for a minute?"

Caleb stopped, blew out a breath, turned around, and approached Mr. Phelps. Caleb looked down on Mr. Phelps, and Caleb was only five foot six.

Mr. Phelps waited for the last student to exit, then he asked, "You all right?"

"I'm sorry about being late," Caleb replied.

"It's okay. You didn't miss much. You do look a little stressed. Anything I can do to help?"

Caleb shook his head, a lump in his throat. "I'm fine."

CHAPTER 11

Rick and Sugar's Addicting

Posters of male and female athletes hung from the walls, along with the new food pyramid. The students and their desks were aligned in perfect rows and columns. Rick stood at the head of his health class. The students were sleepy—droopy eyes and heads propped within their hands. An hour after their corn-syrup-filled-lunches, they were crashing.

"Everyone stand up," Rick said.

The class groaned and stood. Many students leaned on their desks.

"Stop leaning on your desks," Rick said. "You guys are like wet noodles. Do you know why you're so tired?"

A disheveled boy said, "Because we stayed up too late last night."

"Were you guys this tired a few hours ago?"

"No," Ashlee Miles said from the front row.

"Then what happened between now and two hours ago?" Rick asked.

"We ate that crappy lunch. Well, some of us did anyway. I don't eat that junk." Ashlee smiled at Rick, fingering the gold locket around her neck.

"That's good." Rick nodded at Ashlee, then addressed the class. "Much of what you guys eat for lunch is loaded with sugar, and that sugar acts just like a drug. It's highly addictive. When you have too much sugar, you have that sugar high, then you crash. That's why you're all so sleepy. Starting tomorrow, your homework is to keep a food journal. Buy yourself a notebook tonight, and, every time you eat something, I want you to record what you ate and when you ate it. At the end of the week, we'll take a personal health survey. The next week, we're gonna continue with the food journal, but we're gonna do our best to eat as healthy as possible. At the end of that week, we'll take another survey. Then we'll analyze the data. Got it?"

The disheveled boy raised his hand.

"Yes, Craig."

"I don't understand," the boy said. "What's eating healthy? People say stuff's healthy. Then they say it's not."

"That's a great point but don't worry about that right now. We'll get into the specifics of healthy eating. For now, eat like you normally do and record it in your journal."

The bell rang, and the students grabbed their purses and book bags.

"Don't forget your journals tomorrow," Rick said as they exited his classroom.

Ashlee Miles tapped on her cell phone as the room emptied. She had olive skin, brown eyes, and dark wavy hair, much like a shampoo commercial. She was taller and prettier than her mother, Heather, and she looked nothing like Caleb. They had different dads.

Rick approached her. "Ashlee, you know you can't have that in class."

She shoved her phone in her little purse and grinned. "Sorry, Mr. Barnett. I thought class was over."

"It is, but I don't allow cell phones in my classroom. Your cell phone can be very addicting. It's good to take a break from it."

"I think the food journal is a good idea. I already eat pretty healthy though."

"Sometimes we don't realize what we're eating. Writing it down can be very eye-opening."

"Do you eat healthy, Mr. Barnett?"

"I try, but it's a struggle."

She looked him up and down. "It doesn't look like it's a struggle."

Rick was stone-faced. "You should head to class. You're gonna be late."

"I guess I better mind that bell." Ashlee sauntered for the door, her hips rocking back and forth. She turned at the threshold and waved. "Bye, Rick." She giggled. "Sorry. I mean, Mr. Barnett."

CHAPTER 12

Janet and Silent Snowballs

She thinks she can do whatever she wants. We'll see about that. Janet's heels click-clacked on the linoleum as she marched to Gwen's classroom. *They never expect me twice in one day. She's the type of teacher who needs to know her place.* As she neared Gwen's classroom, she thought she'd made a mistake. It was dead silent. *Maybe she doesn't have a class last period.*

Janet pushed into Gwen's classroom. Another group of students were playing snowball fight. They threw paper balls at each other with wide smiles and bright eyes, but they were quiet, not a word or even a sound, apart from the occasional sneaker squeak.

Gwen glanced at Janet but continued to throw "snowballs" as if Janet were invisible. Janet stood with her arms crossed over her ample chest, scowling. Eventually, Gwen held up her hand, like a stop sign, the students stopping immediately, all of them still—except for their chests moving up and down, their breathing elevated, their smiles still plastered. Gwen then completed her icebreaker lesson, not addressing Janet until the dismissal bell.

Once the last student exited the classroom, Janet approached Gwen, who was standing near her desk.

Gwen smiled at Janet and said, "Twice in one day. I feel special."

Janet deadpanned, her expression serious as cancer, "It's not a good thing, Ms. Townsend. My criticism this morning was very serious, yet you didn't seem to take it seriously. It's my job to make sure that you comply with the high standards of this school."

"Well, I certainly learned something from this."

"And what *exactly* did you learn?"

"I learned that, as much as the students like the snowball-fight icebreaker, they like silent-snowball fight even better."

CHAPTER 13

Gwen and Buster

Gwen shut her laptop and placed it in her computer bag. Lewis Phelps knocked on the open door. "You headed out?"

Gwen sighed and forced a smile toward Lewis. "I think I've had enough for today."

"Looks like we're the last ones again."

She walked toward him, her mouth turned down.

"Tough first day?" he asked.

Gwen turned off her light and locked her classroom. "The kids were great."

Lewis chuckled. "Not the adults?"

"You could say that."

They walked down the hallway toward the parking lot.

"Lemme guess. Janet?" he asked.

"She gave me a hard time because my class was making too much noise. We were doing the snowball-fight icebreaker."

"That's a good one."

"I like it because I have the kids do a lot group work, and it's important that they know and like each other."

Lewis nodded. "Makes sense."

"I understand the reprimand. I wasn't upset about that but just the way she talked to me."

"Like she's above you?"

"Exactly. Like I need to know my place."

Lewis opened the door for Gwen. She stepped outside, followed by Lewis. They walked across the asphalt toward the parking lot. "Janet had it out for me my first year."

"What happened?" Gwen asked.

"She gave me a hard time about my lesson plans, picking apart anything that she considered out of the ordinary. She gave me a bad evaluation, which I fought and won. Then she just stopped. I don't know why. Maybe she moved on to easier targets. We haven't said a single word to each other in five years."

"I just want to do my job. I don't need this."

"I hear you. I sympathize. I do. Just ignore her and do your job. You'll be fine. In the meantime, be careful who you vent to." Lewis motioned back to the school. "Those walls have ears."

The parking lot was empty except for two vehicles. One car was parked close to the school, the other in the back of the lot.

Gwen stopped next to an old Volkswagen Jetta, parked near the school. "Thanks, Lewis."

"No problem." Lewis glanced at Gwen's car. "I like the TDIs. Nobody wants to buy them after the debacle, but they're still good cars."

Gwen opened the door with her key fob. "It was cheap, and it gets good gas mileage."

"Fifty-five miles per gallon on the highway, 236 pound-feet of torque, and a motor that'll run forever."

"You know more about my car than I do."

"I'm a bit of a gearhead."

"Are you parked way over there?" Gwen asked, motioning to the back of the lot.

"Too many kids with driver's licenses around here. I like to keep my car out of harm's way." Lewis paused for a moment. "I'll see you tomorrow."

"See you tomorrow, Lewis."

Gwen drove past farms and the grocery store toward the tiny town of West Lake. The town was a cluster of aging row homes with rusted metal roofs and mom-and-pop businesses. Main Street was only a few hundred yards long. Gwen stopped at the only red light in town.

Lewis's black sedan pulled up alongside her, in the left turning lane. His car had bulging fenders, a wing attached to the trunk, and a throaty exhaust. He beeped his horn and nearly peeled out as the light turned green. His car made a *whoosh* noise, almost like an airplane, as Lewis sped away from town. Gwen turned right and drove the short distance to the town's only apartment complex.

The apartments had been converted from old row homes, with four units per building or two units per building, depending on how many bedrooms you wanted. Gwen climbed the metal steps to her one-bedroom apartment.

Inside, she flipped on the overhead light. Boxes still sat in the living room next to the couch. The jingle of Buster's tag followed her into the kitchen. Buster meowed and did a figure eight around her calves. Gwen set her computer bag, keys, and purse on the kitchen table.

"Hey, sweetheart," Gwen said to the black cat, bending down and petting her head.

Buster purred and rubbed her head against Gwen's hand.

"You hungry?" She grabbed a can of cat food and fed Buster. Gwen didn't have the energy to cook, so she mixed up a can of tuna with peas, mayo, pickles, and the remnants of a bag of lettuce. She ate at the kitchen table for two, while Buster ate from her bowl on the floor. The wooden table was the first piece of furniture she and Brian had purchased together. From Value City Furniture. Back when they were broke the first time.

She thought about the finality of her marriage. *Maybe Brian's right. Maybe it is time to move on. Twenty-two years is a long time. He has it much worse than I do, and yet he's still trying to do the right thing for me.* She wondered if Brian mailed the divorce papers. *Of course he did. That's the thing about Brian. If he says he'll do something, he does it.* She pushed away her dinner. A tear slipped down her cheek.

CHAPTER 14

Caleb and Perspective

Ashlee's Jeep was gone, but the Pontiac was parked under the carport. *You know what Pontiac stands for? Poor old nigger thinks it's a Cadillac.* That's what one of his mother's redneck boyfriends had said, but she'd been proud of her car. She'd bought it used eight years ago. The salesman had called it previously owned. They'd had a station wagon with wood paneling prior to that. The Pontiac was her red sports car, complete with a spoiler and a V6. It was the last of the Grand Ams. The end of an era of shitty American-made cars. Now, eight years later, the paint was peeling, the wheels scratched from rubbing concrete curbs, and the interior was a mobile trash can, housing empty Starbucks cups and bottles of vitamin water.

Caleb walked along the car to the side door of the house. He smelled faintly of BO from football practice. He still stayed clear of the showers at school. It was quiet inside the double-wide trailer. He stepped to the kitchen and opened the refrigerator. Nothing but a few expired condiments and wine coolers. He checked the pantry. Stale cereal, a big can of fruit cocktail, a can of creamed corn, and coffee filters. They still had some pasta but no more Ragu. His stomach rumbled.

He stepped down the hall and knocked on his mother's bedroom door. "Mom, it's me."

"What do you want?" Heather said, her voice strained.

His mother had been in a funk since Saturday, staying in her room, watching television night and day. She hadn't even gone to the gym.

"We need to go to the grocery store," Caleb said through the door.

"Ask your sister to take you."

"She's not here."

"Make yourself some spaghetti."

"We don't have any Ragu left."

"Just use margarine."

"Whatever."

Caleb walked back to the kitchen, put pasta and water into a pot and set the electric burner on high. He grabbed some clean clothes, went to the bathroom and showered as his dinner cooked. He dressed and brushed his hair in the mirror. His straight brown hair was long in the front and covered his ears. He wore it swept to the side, like a certain pop star that he had a crush on, although he'd never admit that. Caleb had a cute face, clear skin, and bright green eyes. That wasn't the problem. The problem was that he looked so young. People often thought he was a middle-schooler.

He returned to the kitchen with damp hair. He checked the pasta by throwing a piece against the wall. It stuck, so he turned off the burner. He strained the water through a colander and put his pasta in a bowl. The margarine was expired by four months, but he used it anyway. He opened the fruit cocktail and poured half the can into another bowl. He took his meal, along with a glass of water, to his bedroom. Caleb sat on his bed, looking at his phone as he ate. He sent a text.

Caleb: Hey

Madison: Hey yourself

Caleb: How was your first day of school

Madison: Actually pretty great. I met some nice girls. Love my classes. How about u

Caleb: Sucked as usual. I wish I could've moved with you. I hate it here

Madison: Wherever u go there u are

Caleb: Huh?

Madison: Something my therapist told me. I hate to say it but she was right

Caleb: Right about what

Madison: I thought I hated West Lake too but it's a perspective thing. It doesn't matter where u go ur problems follow u

Caleb scowled at his phone.

Caleb: U hated it here then u moved and now u love Cali

Madison: I got help over the summer. Everyone should go to therapy. So enlightening. Know thyself! U should go. Seriously

Caleb: With what money?

Madison: Talk to the school counselor

Caleb: Mrs Baumgartner is an idiot

Madison: If u keep doing the same things you'll keep getting the same results. Thinking that u won't is the definition of insanity

Caleb: Easy for u to say ur not stuck in this shithole

Madison: No it's not. I worked at getting better

Caleb shook his head and tossed his phone to the foot of the bed. *I liked you better before.*

CHAPTER 15

Rick's Summer Fling

Rick's phone buzzed as he parked in his driveway. He blew out a breath and exited his truck. Again, his phone buzzed in his pocket. He stopped at his front door; an envelope was taped to it. He looked around, expecting her to be watching. The sun was low on the horizon, coating everything and everyone in an orange glow. Grasshoppers flew and hopped, hanging on to the last bits of summer bliss.

He snatched the envelope from his door, entered his brick rambler, and walked to the kitchen. He set his keys on the counter and removed his WL Wolf Pack hat. He took a deep breath and opened the envelope. It was a messy handwritten note, pen strokes jagged, as if the pen were a conduit for her anger. It wasn't signed, but he knew who wrote it.

Rick,
Who the fuck you think you are? Your nobody. A fucking high school football coach. A loser. You will never do better than me. This is the biggest mistake of your life.

I will not go away. You will not get away with this!!!!!!!!!!

Fuck you, asshole

Rick tossed the letter in the trash and checked his text messages. While he was at practice, he'd gotten eighteen new texts.

Heather: Need to talk to u
Heather: Call me
Heather: Where r u
Heather: I need u
Heather: Don't do this to me
Heather: I still love u I know u still love me
Heather: We can make it work
Heather: Don't do this it's a mistake
Heather: I can make u happy
Heather: Why r u afraid to b with me
Heather: R u a coward
Heather: Where r u
Heather: Talk to me please
Heather: Don't ignore me
Heather: U will regret this. I'm the best thing ever happened to u
Heather: Guys at gym r always asking me out. I don't need ur bullshit
Heather: U think u can throw me away
Heather: I will make ur life a living hell

Rick tapped her number.

"Hello," Heather said.

"I'm gonna tell you this once," Rick said. "You are not welcome at my home. Don't text me or call me again. Do you understand me?"

"You called *me*. I should call the police and file a PFA. Then I'll tell your principal."

"You're insane."

"You're not gonna tell me what I can and can't do. Fuck you, you fuckin' asshole, loser, piece of shit—

Rick disconnected the call and blocked her number.

CHAPTER 16

Janet and Rachel

Red and white streamers dangled overhead as Janet walked down the empty hall. Rachel Kreider, the president of the teachers' union and also the teacher for the gifted students, rounded the corner up ahead, coming from the opposite direction. She was dressed and ready for football Friday—mom jeans and a red-and-white WL football sweatshirt. Teachers were permitted casual dress on Fridays, provided they wore school-spirit attire. The chubby woman stopped and waited, then turned and accompanied Janet toward the main office.

"I spoke with Gwen again," Rachel said, walking in lockstep with Janet.

"Anything interesting?" Janet asked.

"No. She asked me to leave her classroom. Said she had work to do. Can you believe the nerve of that woman? What a snob."

"Something's been bothering me about her ever since I met her. She looks familiar to me, but I can't place her."

"Maybe you saw her at a conference?"

Janet shook her head. "I haven't been to a conference in years."

"Maybe you should call her last school."

"I did and all her references. They all had nothing but nice things to say about her. What's weird is, she hasn't worked in four years. I asked her old principal about it, and he said she needed time off to deal with a family tragedy, but I think he's full of shit."

"That is weird."

They arrived at the main office, passed the reception desk, and entered Janet's back office. Rachel shut the door behind her and sat across from Janet at the desk.

"Well, I'll keep digging," Rachel said.

Janet nodded. "We'll find something. Everyone has something to hide."

"I noticed that she's gotten rather chummy with Lewis."

"He's another one I'd like to get rid of."

"Such a know-it-all."

"He's constantly undermining the administration. Principal Pruitt could've fired him a long time ago for insubordination, but you know Pruitt."

"He never wants to rock the boat."

"Sometimes the boat needs to be rocked."

"Yes, it does."

Janet pursed her lips, waiting for Rachel to justify her existence in her office. "I should get back to work." Janet's eyes flicked to the door.

"I do have something else I wanted to tell you. It's about Shane and Coach Barnett."

Janet leaned toward Rachel, her elbows on her desk.

Rachel had a hint of a smirk, relishing her temporary position of power. "One of the gals in my stitch-and-bitch group is good friends with Coach Schneider's wife. She said that Coach Barnett likes that Jamar Burris kid. You know. The black boy?"

"Of course Rick likes him. He's the JV quarterback."

"But Coach Schneider thinks that Coach Barnett might bench Shane if he doesn't play well."

Janet frowned. "Shane'll be great. He won't let some sophomore take his position. And Rick won't bench a senior, especially one as good as my son. Just the other day I was talking with Rick about scholarship opportunities for Shane."

CHAPTER 17

Gwen and the Personal Narrative

Gwen stood in front of her class, holding a double-sided piece of paper, reading from the typewritten text.

"'Just lose ten more pounds. Have smaller thighs. Your butt is too big. You'd be so pretty if you just lost some weight.' These messages run through my head like a bad song on repeat. Why haven't the messages gone away? I've learned to eat healthy, to exercise. I'm a healthy weight. I should have this obsession licked, but *fat girl* scars run deep.

"'Buffalo butt. Bubbles. If you were the leader of a gang, they would call it the chub gang.' That last one's my 'favorite.'"

Gwen heard a few stifled giggles from the back of the class. She glanced up from her paper, and the laughter ceased. She continued.

"This is what I heard from the ages of ten to eighteen. These utterances came from my sister, my mother, classmates, and even strangers. Every incident inflicted emotional scarring to the point that I felt physical pain.

"One incident in particular comes to mind. It was my senior year of high school. I had just turned seventeen, and I was ten pounds lighter than the year before. I was feeling a bit better about myself. The first semester went by quickly. Teachers and classes were fine, friends were decent, and the football team had just won the division championship. Things were looking up, or so I thought.

"A few weeks after Christmas break, my best friend Amy and I sat in the lunchroom. I talked and she ate. I never ate lunch in high school. Not once. Two tables over, Mr. Football himself, Jim Davidson, razzed Donald, who was one of my neighbors and a kid who I had gone to school with since elementary school.

"'He looks like a weasel,' Jim said in reference to Donald. 'Seriously, look at him. The teeth and that big-ass nose. And look how close together his eyes are.'

More laughter from the back of the room. Gwen glanced up from her paper. Shane and Lance, wearing their football jerseys, stifled their laughter with fists over their mouths. Gwen went back to the story.

"Donald stood with his head down and tears in his eyes.

"'Shut up, Jim,' I said, barely above a whisper.

"Jim glared at me. 'Did you say something, fat ass?'"

Again, Shane and Lance chuckled. Gwen paused but didn't reprimand them, then continued.

"I spoke up, louder and clearer this time. 'I said, shut up.'

"Amy was shocked, her eyes wide open in response to my outburst. Donald used my distraction to walk away. Jim stood from his table and approached me, most of the cafeteria watching the fireworks.

"'What the hell's *your* problem, Buffalo Butt?' he said."

This time when Shane and Lance laughed, one of the girls in the front row turned to them and said, "Stop laughing. It's not funny."

Another girl said, "You guys are so immature."

Again, Gwen did nothing, waited for the disturbance to pass, and continued.

"I glared right back. 'You're my problem. I'm tired of you picking on everyone. How would you like it if someone picked on you?'

"Jim grinned and said, 'There's nothing to pick on me about.'

"'You're a loser.'

"He laughed. 'Loser? I'm the best football player in this school. I'm popular, and I can get any girl I want.'

"I stood from the table. 'Did you get a football scholarship?'

"He didn't respond.

"'You're a good football player for this little school, but, at a bigger school, you'd be just another guy. You didn't get a football scholarship because you're not good enough.'

"The lunch crowd laughed and heckled. Jim looked around, worry etched across his brows. He knew he was losing the crowd.

"'And what kind of grades do you get?' I asked, twisting the knife.

"Again, he didn't respond.

"I snapped my fingers. 'Oh, that's right. You're barely passing. Not exactly college material, huh? In nine months, I'm going to college. I'll get a good job. I'm exercising regularly, and I'll continue to lose weight, but you'll still be a loser.'

"The crowd hooted and hollered, saying things like, 'She got you,' and 'Loser,' and 'Burn.' Even his best friend laughed at him.

"For the first time, I walked out of that cafeteria with my head held high.

"After school, Jim accosted me at my locker. 'I need to talk to you,' he said.

"'Why do you even bother with me?' I replied.

"'Why did you get so mad? I was only kidding.'

"'Did you like it when everyone laughed at you?'

"He shook his head.

"'That's how I feel every time someone makes a snide comment about my weight. And I'm not the only one. Other people are tired of the teasing too.'

"'Like who? I'm friends with everyone,' Jim said.

"'No, you're not,' I said. 'Do you think Jenny likes it when you call her fish face? What about Bridget? Do you think she likes to be called whitey? Or Donald? Do you really think he likes to be compared to a weasel? To be honest, everyone's sick of you.'

"Four years later, I ran into Jim at a party. I had recently graduated from college, ready to begin my first year of teaching. I was healthy, happy, and twenty pounds lighter. I spotted Jim, but I acted like I didn't see him. He looked to be about thirty pounds heavier, and I had heard that he had failed out of college.

"He approached me. 'Could I speak to you outside? Alone?'

"I frowned. 'I guess.'

"We stepped outside, in the parking lot. It was warm and humid, the moon nearly full.

"He took a deep breath. 'I, uh, just wanted to tell you that I'm sorry for all the stupid stuff I said to you in high school. And I wanted to thank you for what you said.'

"I raised my eyebrows.

"'When you stood up to me, it was a wake-up call. You made me a better person, and, uh, … I wanted to thank you. So, thank you.'

"Jim had grown as a person. He was no longer that arrogant bully. He was an empathetic young man who had regrets. I forgave him, and I let go of my 'Fat Girl Scars.'"

Gwen's class applauded. She blotted her eyes with a balled-up tissue. It had been the fourth time she'd read the story today, but it still got to her.

"That's an example of a personal narrative," Gwen said. "We all have unique experiences. So dig deep, be brave, and write about something meaningful to you." She pointed to the due date on her whiteboard. "I'm giving you two weeks to complete your personal narratives. Does anyone have any questions?"

Lance Osborn raised his hand from the back of the class.

"Yes, Lance," Gwen said, pointing at the handsome senior.

"Is that really true, you being fat?" Lance asked.

"Don't ask that," said a girl from the front row.

"You're so rude," another girl said.

"It's okay," Gwen said. "I *was* overweight as a kid, but that didn't mean that I deserved the taunts and the bullying."

"Maybe they were trying to encourage you to lose weight, like a coach," Lance said.

"What position do you play in football?" Gwen asked, glancing at his red-and-white Wolf Pack jersey.

"Wide receiver. It's the guy who catches passes."

Gwen smiled. "I know what a wide receiver is. What if you dropped the winning touchdown pass—"

"He better not drop the winning touchdown pass," said Shane, wearing his number twelve jersey and sitting at the desk next to Lance.

The class laughed.

Gwen continued. "What if, after the game, the game where you dropped that winning touchdown pass, I said, 'Lance, you can't even catch a cold. You should quit because you're the worst wide receiver who's ever played the game of football.'"

"Damn, Ms. Townsend, that's cold," Lance said.

Gwen nodded. "Yes, it's cold and cruel. If someone said that to you, do you think it would be easier or harder to catch that next touchdown pass?"

Lance frowned but conceded. "Harder."

Gwen surveyed her class. They hung on her every word. "We all have things we'd like to improve about ourselves, but, if we have others bullying us and making us feel bad about ourselves, it becomes infinitely harder to do something about it because our self-esteem is so battered. Kids who are bullied are often neglected and abused at home, and, because of the abuse, they often lack self-esteem. This lack of confidence is like a bully magnet. So, not only do these battered souls deal with abuse at home but they also deal with it at school and will likely deal with it as an adult with an abusive boss or spouse."

"That's messed up," Jamar Burris said from the front row.

Caleb Miles, sitting next to Jamar, stared at his desktop.

"You're right, Jamar. It's a heartbreaking truth," Gwen said. "Bullying is something I absolutely despise. I challenge each and every one of you to be a hero and to stand up to bullies whenever and wherever you see them."

CHAPTER 18

Caleb and the Picture

Caleb walked through the crowded hallway from Ms. Townsend's classroom toward his locker. His head was tilted down, making eye contact only with the floor. He almost ran into two beautiful senior girls. He stopped and glanced at them.

"I'm sorry," Caleb said, then attempted to walk around them.

They moved with him, still blocking his way. "Why did you send us that dick pic?" the brunette asked with her arms crossed over her chest.

"Yeah, little pervert," the blonde said.

Caleb looked up, his brows furrowed. "I don't know what you're talking about."

A crowd formed around the trio, Shane and Lance front and center.

The brunette shoved her phone in his face. "That's your little dick, isn't it?"

Kids from the crowd laughed, craning their necks to see the picture.

"Look how small it is," Shane said, eliciting more laughter.

Caleb examined the picture of himself in front of the urinal, his penis in clear view. "I didn't take that picture."

"But you sent it to us with that disgusting message," the blonde said.

"What message?"

The brunette read from her phone. *"Hey, baby."* She put her finger in her mouth as if she were gagging. *"When I see you in school, I want you so bad. You're all I think about. I want you to suck my cock, and I wanna blow my load all over your face. Text me back so we can make it happen. XOXO. Caleb Miles."*

The crowd hooted and hollered.

Caleb turned beet red.

"Dude, that's fucked-up," Lance said.

A girl from the crowd said, "Eww."

Another said, "That's gross."

Caleb said, "But I didn't—"

The brunette slapped him across the face.

Caleb held his hand to his cheek, stunned.

"Don't text me. Don't even look at me," the brunette said, her finger in Caleb's face.

"Me either," the blonde added.

Shane and Lance fist-bumped.

CHAPTER 19

Rick and the Big Eye in the Sky

The football players filtered into Rick's classroom for films. They were groggy, staggering, a few wearing pajama pants, and some with ice packs for various bumps and bruises from the night before. Many of the players carried brown bags from McDonald's, doughnuts from Sheetz, and oversize energy drinks. Nobody spoke as the kids took their seats; communication was limited to nods, grunts, and gestures.

Rick moved from his desk and stood at the head of the classroom. He stroked his stubbly beard, waiting for the last of the stragglers to find a seat. Quite a few kids had to sit on the floor. Two boys argued over floor space.

"Shut up," Rick said, the argument ceasing, the room now at full attention. "There's no shame in losing. That team will probably be the 5A state champs this year. They're a much bigger school than we are. That's by far the toughest opponent we'll see all year. I'm not upset that we lost. I'm upset at *how* we lost." Rick paused, scanning the young faces.

"I stayed up until two watching the film, and I learned a few things about this team and about certain individuals. The big eye in the sky doesn't lie. If you played your heart out, the film showed that. If you played like a coward, if you laid down without a fight, the film showed that too. I scheduled this game as our first game of the season on purpose. I wanted to see what you're made of. I wanted to see who I can count on and who's gonna fold under pressure. There were some bright spots." Rick looked at Drew Fuller, his middle linebacker. "How much do you weigh, Drew?"

"About 180," Drew replied.

"You played much bigger than that. Drew was all over the field from the opening whistle to the final whistle. He didn't care that we were down by four touchdowns. He didn't care that the game was out of reach." Rick looked at Jamar Burris. "And Jamar's never played in a varsity game before. He gave us a spark in the fourth quarter. It was obvious to me that he was playing for the sheer joy of it."

"Yeah, because he was playing against the second string," Shane said.

Rick glared at his quarterback, sitting up front with his big breakfast and big soda. Shane still wore his pajama pants but had the time to put his diamond studs in both of his earlobes. "Think so, huh?" Rick said.

"Yeah." Shane took a drink of his soda.

"How do you think you played?"

"I did my best. It's hard to make throws when you're on your back the whole game. They gotta block." Shane glanced at a few of the offensive linemen. "I can't do it all by myself."

Rick nodded to his quarterback. "The offensive line play was porous. You guys looked scared and tired. You guys are better than that. We're gonna step it up in practice. You guys are gonna be in better shape. That's the last time you're gonna get manhandled like that. One way or another, you won't play like that again."

Rick narrowed his eyes at Shane. "It's *my* job as the head coach to figure out where we can improve. To figure out who's getting the job done and who needs to step it up. It's your job to lead, to inspire these guys to block for you." Rick stepped closer to Shane. "*Inspiring* quarterbacks take the blame for losses and give credit to others for wins.

Inspiring quarterbacks encourage their teammates. You understand what I'm trying to tell you?"

Shane dipped his head and nodded.

CHAPTER 20

Janet and the Watchdog

Janet sat at her desk, thinking about Shane and last Friday's football game. The first game of the season. It had been on her mind all weekend, and it still bothered her this Tuesday morning. Their opponent, the Lions, had been a much bigger school, but West Lake rarely lost, and Shane hadn't played well. She thought about what Rachel had said. *Did Rick really think Jamar Burris was better than Shane? It was only one game. Rick wouldn't bench Shane after one game. Would he?*

Her desktop phone rang, waking her to reality. She picked up the receiver. "This is Principal Wilcox."

"Hello, um, Principal Wilcox. This is Greg Ebersole. I have kind of an emergency. I need to talk to you in private about something I found on the servers."

Janet sighed. "You don't need to preface it, Greg. Just tell me."

"Bob Schneider visited some questionable sites on his school computer."

"What do you mean by *questionable*?"

"Porn."

Janet paused, thinking about the thirtysomething coach. Bob Schneider was Rick's offensive coordinator and probably much more in control of Shane's success or failure than even Rick. "Could you come to my office immediately?"

"I can do that."

"Do you have any printouts or evidence of his ... activities?"

"Yes."

"Bring everything here."

"Okay."

Janet hung up the receiver and waited, again the wheels turning in her mind. *Bob's transgression might be the perfect bargaining chip.* A few minutes later, Greg Ebersole knocked on her door.

"Come in," Janet said.

Greg stepped into her office, shut the door behind him, and loped toward her with a folder in hand. He forced a smile, his mouth closed. "Principal Wilcox."

"Sit down, Greg."

Greg sat in one of the chairs in front of her desk. He was skinny and fat at the same time. His limbs and shoulders were thin and delicate, but he had a little belly pressing on his fitted button-down shirt, like he had too much gas. He handed the folder to Janet.

Janet leafed through the papers. Bob Schneider had been quite active on adult sites. Apparently, he had a thing for cheerleaders. *How cliché.* A thought occurred to her. *That really is a lot of activity. Did Bob just start doing this, or has he been doing this for a long time? The server automatically flags questionable activity, but it's sensitive, so it flags legitimate activity too. Greg is supposed to be monitoring this every week.* She looked up from the folder and narrowed her eyes at Greg.

He looked down for a moment, then back to Janet.

Janet shut the folder and set it on her desktop, doing this without breaking eye contact with Greg. "Something is very odd about the volume of activity."

Greg pushed his wire frames up the bridge of his nose. "I don't know what you mean."

"I think you do."

His pale face flushed scarlet.

"Bob Schneider's been working here for eight years, and he's never been flagged for this kind of activity before. So I'm supposed to believe that he's never made any of these searches until now, or is it more likely that you've been neglectful in your duties?"

"I have been checking flagged activity. It's a lot of data though. It's possible that I missed it in the past."

Janet frowned and opened the folder. She scanned the top page. "You missed DirtyCheerleader.com? How about BarelyLegalCheer-leaders.com?"

Greg swallowed, his Adam's apple bobbing up and down. "This is the first time I've seen this."

"Now that I believe. I think the reason you missed this is because you haven't been doing your job. It would be very easy to go back and check the old data."

"That data's deleted at the first of every month."

Janet nodded. "Convenient."

"I probably did skim the data too fast."

Janet took a deep cleansing breath. "Cut the bullshit, Greg. You were lazy. You and I both know it. But I'm willing to forgive and forget."

Greg's slight shoulders slumped in relaxation. "Thank you."

"I do expect you to keep your mouth shut about this. If this gets out, I *will* hold you personally responsible."

Greg nodded. "What's gonna happen to Bob?"

"I don't know yet. That's for the school's lawyers and Principal Pruitt to decide."

* * *

Later that day, Bob Schneider entered her office, wearing a black polo and khakis, his lanyard and ID badge around his thick neck. The big man looked apprehensive.

"You wanted to see me?" he asked.

Janet sat behind her desk. "Shut the door."

He shut the door behind him.

"Have a seat."

Coach Schneider sat across from Janet.

"The tech guys went through the server, checking for inappropriate activity," Janet said. "Do I need to tell you what they found from your computer's IP address?"

Big Bob squirmed in his seat, his face beet red beneath his beard.

"Looking at pornography on your school computer is a fireable offense."

"Please, Principal Wilcox. I have a new baby at home. My wife doesn't work. I'm really sorry. It'll never happen again."

"I'd like to help you, but, if I give you a second chance, and you do something worse, then I'm on the hook because I didn't take action."

Bob leaned forward, on the edge of his seat. "Please. I promise it'll never happen again. I'll do anything." His eyes filled with tears.

Janet tapped her index finger on the desk. She shook her head. "I shouldn't, but I'll overlook your ... indiscretion."

"Thank you so much." He wiped his eyes discreetly with the shoulders of his polo shirt.

"My mercy comes with strings." Janet pursed her lips. "I may need you to do something for me."

"Anything."

"I'll let you know."

Bob Schneider went back to his classroom. Janet scanned her personal texts on her phone. A message from Rachel caught her eye.

Rachel: There's a new Facebook page called West Lake Watchdog. You have to see this! **LINK.**

Janet clicked the link, taking her to the Facebook page. The header of the page was a picture of the high school. The profile picture for the "West Lake Watchdog" was the paw print school logo. There were three posts. The first two had no likes, comments, or shares.

West Lake Watchdog
August 31 at 10:07 PM
Coach Rick Barnett is NOT a good guy. Youse don't know him like I do. If you want to know the truth ask his ex-wife. He is a cheat and a liar.

West Lake Watchdog
September 1 at 11:33 PM
The school board needs to go. Bunch of corrupt old men.

West Lake Watchdog
September 3 at 11:14 PM
The West Lake Wolf Pack lost on Friday because of Coach Barnett. Bad plays. Bad coaching. BAD COACH. WORSE PERSON. **#FireBarnett**
5 Likes 1 Share
Roger Elkins I agree. We have the best kids in triple A. Why play a 5A school? So stupid. They had like twice as many kids as we do. We could have been undefeated. Anyone could coach this team and win. Hopefully Barnett doesn't screw it up. This team should win a state title. **#FireBarnett** 2 Likes

Whoever this is, they're starting to get some support. Janet replied to Rachel's text.

Janet: Any idea who's behind the page?

Rachel responded immediately.

Rachel: I'll give you a hint. We went to school with her older sister Breanna.
Janet: Ha! I know who it is. How did you find out?
Rachel: I'm still friends with Breanna. I'm not supposed to tell anyone, so please keep it a secret.
Janet: Of course.

CHAPTER 21

Gwen, the New Girl

Three cars were left in the parking lot. Gwen's Jetta, Lewis's souped-up Mitsubishi, and a pickup truck. Gwen yawned and turned back from her classroom window and her view of the school parking lot. *I need some caffeine.* She grabbed her mug, honey, and a teabag, and walked to the teacher's room.

Inside, she was surprised to find an attractive man sitting at one of the round tables. "Oh, hi," she said.

The man stood from the table and his food—a Subway sub and a bottled water. He swallowed and said, "Hello. I'm Rick Barnett." He held out his hand.

Gwen moved closer, set her mug with teabag and honey on his table, and shook his hand. "Gwen Townsend. I teach ELA."

"You're the new girl."

She frowned. "I'm thirty-two years old."

"Sorry. That's what people have been calling you, but I don't think it's meant as an insult. Supposedly, there's this TV show called *The New Girl.* I guess you look like the actress, and, of course, you are new. I've never seen the show, so I couldn't tell you one way or another."

"I'm not sure how I feel about people talking about me behind my back."

"If gossiping was a sport, we'd win the state championship every year."

She laughed. "I'd like to stay out of it."

"So would I. Apparently, there's a Facebook page dedicated to destroying me."

"Really?"

He nodded. "Yep. I refuse to look at it. This type of nonsense happens after we lose a game. I coach varsity football."

"I have quite a few of your football players in my creative writing class," Gwen said.

"If they give you any problems, let me know. We have a conduct policy. And, if they're falling behind, also let me know. I'll make sure they get their work in."

"I will. Thanks. Do you have a tough game this Friday?"

"The Cumberland Vikings. They're tough. We'll have our work cut out for us."

"Well, good luck."

"Thanks." He glanced over her head, at the clock on the wall. "What are you doing here so late?"

"Research for a lesson. What about you?"

"Practice went long today, and I still have some planning to do for my health class. If I go home, ESPN and my couch are too much to resist. I'm working on a health survey that the kids'll fill out in conjunction with a food journal."

"That's a great idea. These kids eat so much junk."

Rick blew out a breath. "Thanks, but I don't know if they'll listen. Every year we have more and more obese kids."

"Some listen. At least that's what I tell myself."

"You're an optimist."

"At my own peril." She picked up her mug and honey from the table. "I should make my tea and get back to work."

He smiled. "It was really nice to meet you, New Girl."

She smiled right back.

CHAPTER 22

Caleb and the Goal Line Stand

Stadium lights illuminated the field. No open seat remained in the bleachers, many people standing along the chain-link fence. Caleb stood on the sideline, his uniform spotless. No chance of getting into this game, not that he wanted to play. He'd probably screw up. The score was much too close for even the second string, much less a third-string loser like Caleb. The scoreboard read twenty-seven to twenty-one, the West Lake Wolf Pack on top. On third and five, Shane tried to draw the Vikings' defense offside with a hard count, hoping for an easy first down and an end to the game. But the Vikings were disciplined. Coach Barnett stood next to a referee, watching the play clock tick down. As soon as it hit one, Coach Barnett called a time-out. He turned to Coach Schneider, the offensive coordinator, and said, "Run the zone read."

Coach Schneider nodded and trotted out to the huddle during the time-out break. The game clock now read 1:08, and the Vikings only had one time-out. The Wolf Pack needed a first down, and they could kneel themselves to victory. If they didn't get the first down, they could punt it, hopefully pinning the Vikings deep, making their offense go the length of the field to win. They were on the fifty, and they had an excellent punter, so that was a good possibility. Still, the best-case scenario would be to get the first down and to end the game right here, right now.

Coach Schneider jogged back to the sideline.

"What's the play?" Coach Barnett said to Schneider.

"Shane wanted to throw the smash route."

"I told you to run it."

"They're gonna pack the box to stuff the run," Schneider said. "The pass'll be wide open."

"It's too risky."

"I told Shane to throw the hitch for the first down, and, if it's not there, to tuck it and run."

Coach Barnett shook his head.

The crowd noise increased as Shane took the snap and dropped back to pass. The hitch was open, but Shane threw the deep-corner route to his favorite target. Lance was double-covered, and the Vikings' safety stepped in front, snagged the interception, and streaked down the field.

"Goddammit," Coach Barnett said, watching in vain as the safety sprinted toward the go ahead score.

Shane gave up on the play, not making any effort to catch the defender, but Lance chased the safety down the sideline, tackling him at the five-yard line, just shy of a touchdown. The Vikings now had a first and goal at the five-yard line with fifty-seven seconds left on the clock.

"What the hell were you thinkin'?" Coach Schneider said to Shane as he walked off the field. "I told you to throw the hitch. It was wide open."

Shane ignored his coach and sat on the bench, alone.

"Defense, goal-line package," Coach Barnett called out. The defensive players hustled out to the field, putting on their helmets as they did so.

The middle linebacker, Drew Fuller, stopped in front of Coach Barnett. "Gotta play, Coach?"

Coach Barnett put his hand on Drew's shoulder. "Goal line house zero. We need this stop."

Drew nodded. "I got you, Coach." He hustled onto the field.

Predictably, the Vikings ran the ball on first down, but Barnett had gambled, sending all eleven defenders on the blitz, and they stuffed the run for a three-yard loss. Barnett signaled another play to Drew. On second down, the Vikings' quarterback threw a fade route to the back of the end zone, but it was well covered and knocked away by the Wolf Pack defender—incomplete. The clock stopped on the incompletion.

On third and eight, the Vikings' quarterback threw a swing pass. The Wolf Pack outside linebacker was pinned inside, leaving the Vikings' running back wide open. He caught the pass and sprinted for the pylon. Drew Fuller dashed from his middle linebacker position, racing the running back to the end zone. At the one-yard line, Drew crushed the running back, the hit echoing through the stadium, stopping him just shy of the goal line.

With twenty-one seconds left on the clock, the Vikings burned their final time-out. Coach Barnett trotted out and talked to his defense during the time-out.

When he returned to the sideline, Coach Schneider asked, "What's the call?"

"Goal line, submarine, zero," Coach Barnett replied.

Lance waved his arms up and down on the sideline, encouraging the crowd to cheer louder. The crowd was at a fever pitch as the Vikings' offense broke the huddle. On the snap of the ball, the Wolf Pack defensive line dove at the legs of the offensive line, upending them and creating a pile. The Vikings' quarterback handed the ball to the running back, who sprinted up the middle toward the pile of players. He leaped over the pile, but Drew had the running back in his sights and had leaped over the pile in perfect synchronicity. They collided in midair, the running back going sideways and falling like a ton of bricks, just shy of the end zone. No touchdown.

The Wolf Pack defense and sideline celebrated. The fans cheered, the noise deafening.

CHAPTER 23

Rick and That Drink

The celebration had dissipated along with the crowd. Rick helped load the sideline gear onto the back of the Gator utility vehicle. With the Gator loaded with water coolers, the equipment manager drove toward the shed. Rick looked up at the scoreboard and smiled to himself, thinking about the gutsiest goal line stand he'd ever seen.

Vice Principal Janet Wilcox approached from the bleachers with a wide smile. She wore jeans and a tight Wolf Pack Football T-shirt. She clutched what was left of her youth with a death grip, the metaphorical feminine wall fast approaching.

"I can't take these close games," she said as she approached. "You're going to give me a heart attack."

"The Vikings are always tough. Hopefully they won't all be like this, but a win's a win."

"Well, the boys played great." She smiled wide. "You want to get that drink? Celebrate? I'm buying."

Rick forced a smile. "I still have three hours of film study tonight, then films with the team tomorrow morning."

Her mouth turned down for a split second. Then she smiled back and said, "Next time then."

Rick nodded. *How about never?*

"I was wondering why you threw the ball on third and five at the

71

end? I don't know that much about football, but I do know that was a questionable call. It put Shane in a really bad position."

Rick clenched his jaw and paused for a moment. "We make a lot of mistakes, and we do our best to learn from them, but it's never about one bad play or one bad call."

CHAPTER 24

Janet and the Facebook Friend

Don Pruitt sat at his desk, reading *Field & Stream*. Janet knocked on his open door. He set down the magazine and smiled at Janet, his beady blue eyes shrinking to mere slits. "Morning, Janet," he said.

Janet approached his desk, returning his smile. "Are you and Nancy going to the game tonight? It's at home again."

"We're looking forward to it. I tell you what. That game last week against the Vikings was something else. What about you?"

"I'll definitely be there. I don't want to miss a single minute of Shane's senior season."

"He's got one heckuva cannon for an arm. You must be proud."

"I am. Thanks, Don. I'll stop by and sit with you two, if that's okay?"

"That'd be great. Nance would love that."

"I'll see you tonight." Janet turned and started for the doorway.

"Janet," Pruitt called out.

She turned back at the threshold.

"What do Billy Graham and the Lancaster Indian football team have in common?"

Janet shrugged. "I don't know."

"They can both make a stadium of people say, 'Oh, Jesus.'" He chuckled, slapping his knee.

Janet forced a smile, then walked to her office. She shut her door, sat behind her desk, and sent a text.

Janet: I need to talk to you. Come to my office as soon as possible
Rachel: Be there in five

Rachel's knock came in three minutes.

"Come in," Janet said.

Rachel entered the office and shut the door behind her. She sat across from Janet at her desk, wearing little football earrings and a WL Wolf Pack sweatshirt.

"What do you need?" Rachel asked, her full attention on Janet.

"I think it may be time to do something about Don."

"I agree. I'm so tired of the old boys' club around here."

Janet nodded and sighed. "I really like Don as a person, but, for all intents and purposes, he's already retired. As you know, he does less than nothing. I worry that crucial things are falling through the cracks. It's not a good situation for the kids *or* the community."

"Do you think he should be fired?"

"Of course not. He just needs to retire. He has enough years, but he's hanging on to milk as much money from the district as possible. Maybe our Facebook friend can get that information out to the community."

Rachel grinned, her thin lips spreading across her chubby face. "I'm sure she can."

"With public support and a majority school board in favor of his retirement, I think he'd do the right thing. Unfortunately, we don't have a majority on the school board yet. As you know, the five mainstays are part of the old boys' club, but Daub and Pastor Goode are up for reelection this fall. If we could find a way to unseat one of them, we'd have the majority."

"It'll be darn difficult. They've been on the board forever."

Janet nodded. "Maybe you could do a little digging in the

community to find out anything that might be helpful."

"I'll ask around."

"Good."

"Who's gonna run against them? Are you backing someone?"

"Officially, I'm not backing anyone."

"Unofficially?"

"I haven't decided yet."

CHAPTER 25

Gwen and the Invisible Wish

Gwen stood in front of her class, the whiteboard behind her with various examples of dialogue punctuation.

"Does anyone have any more questions about punctuating dialogue?" Gwen asked. "This is very important for your short stories."

The class hung by a thread, with mouths open, heads propped up with hands, and eyes glazed over.

"All right, lovelies. Stand up. You guys are falling asleep," Gwen said.

The class groaned and rose from their seats.

"Everyone shake your arms." Gwen shook her arms with her students. "Now shake your right leg. Now your left." Smiles appeared, and a few students laughed. "Now spin around like a ballerina." Gwen and many of the girls held their hands gracefully over their heads and spun in a circle.

Many boys frowned with their arms crossed over their chests.

"I'm not doin' that," Drew Fuller said from the back.

"I thought you were an athlete," Gwen said, smiling, looking at his number forty-four jersey. "Maybe one of the girls should play linebacker tonight."

The class laughed, including Drew, who did a perfect pirouette. Much of the class clapped for him. Shane called him a "Homo" under his breath. Gwen heard the comment but ignored it, as Drew wasn't bothered in the least; she didn't want to give it extra life.

"All right, are we awake now?"

"Yes," the class said in unison.

"You can sit down."

The class slumped into their seats.

"Now that we've had a refresher on dialogue punctuation, let's talk about the content. Does anyone know what makes good dialogue?"

Nobody raised their hand.

"Anyone?" She looked at Caleb.

He sat in the front row, wearing an old T-shirt and shorts, an outfit Gwen was sure she'd seen him wear earlier this week. His bright green eyes were partially hidden by his mop of straight hair swept to the side.

"Come on, guys," Gwen said. "We learned all about dialogue the first week of school."

Jamar raised his hand.

"Jamar," Gwen said, pointing to the athletic young man wearing a number two jersey.

"You have to take out the boring parts," he said.

"That's good, Jamar." Gwen wrote Jamar's point on the whiteboard and turned back to the class. "Sometimes we might include some boring bits as setup, but we definitely want to edit out as much as we can. Anything else? Come on, guys. Just blurt it out. No need to raise your hand."

"It has to sound real but not too real," Caleb said.

Gwen smiled at Caleb. "You're exactly right. Can you tell me why?"

"Because, if it was really real, it would be a bunch of grunts and nods and boring stuff."

"Excellent, Caleb. Much of human communication is nonverbal, and a book of grunts and head nods would be pretty boring." Gwen added Caleb's point to the board, then addressed the class. "Anything else?"

The class was silent for a beat.

"Good dialogue should fit the characterization of the characters," Caleb said.

"Absolutely. Can you be more specific?" Gwen asked.

Caleb flipped his hair from his eyes. "Well, if a character goes to church, and he never swears, then he might say *gosh darn* or something like that if he got mad. If a character is really smart, maybe he might use more complicated words. I think you have to figure out who the characters are. Then what they say has to reflect that."

Gwen grinned from ear to ear. "Fantastic, Caleb."

Shane coughed into his fist and said, "Faggot."

Shane, Drew, and Lance laughed, along with a handful of other boys.

Caleb turned in his seat, his face scarlet. "Shut up, douchebags."

"What are you gonna do about it, bitch?" Shane replied.

"That's enough," Gwen said, glaring at the boys in back.

They quieted. Shane slouched in his seat with a smirk, his diamond earrings glistening in the fluorescent light.

"I'd like to talk to you in the hallway, Shane," Gwen said.

"What? Why?" Shane replied, not moving a muscle.

"You know why. Bring your stuff."

Shane pointed at Caleb and said, "He's the one who called us douchebags."

"In the hallway, *now.*"

The class gasped and whispered among themselves.

"Whatever," Shane said, standing from his desk.

Gwen addressed the class. "Everyone, take out your novels and read for the time being."

Gwen stood by her open door. Shane strutted past. She stepped into the hallway, shutting her classroom door behind her. Shane stood with his backpack looped over one shoulder, looking down on Gwen with one side of his mouth raised in contempt.

"There are two things I despise," Gwen said. "Bullying and lying. I won't have bullying in my classroom, and I don't give breaks to liars. Why do you feel the need to pick on Caleb?"

"I didn't do nothin'," Shane replied. "Why isn't he in trouble for callin' me a douchebag?"

"He didn't start it. You did. And he's a tenth grader who's half your size. Do you really think it's cool for the captain of the football team to pick on someone half his size?"

Shane was stone-faced. "I didn't do nothin'."

"You're not leaving me with any options, Shane. If I write you up, you won't play tonight."

He shrugged. "You must not've heard right. I said, 'Farmer,' 'cause he walks through the cornfields. I didn't mean it bad. This is bullshit. He's the one who should be in trouble."

Gwen walked across the hall and knocked on Lewis Phelps's classroom door. She knew he was without students that period. Lewis opened his door.

"Can you watch my classroom for a few minutes?" Gwen asked. "They're just reading."

"Sure."

"Thank you, Mr. Phelps."

"Let's go," Gwen said to Shane.

Gwen led Shane to the main office.

"Sit down," Gwen said, pointing to the waiting area across from the reception desk.

Shane slumped into one of the plastic and metal chairs.

Gwen turned her attention to the reception desk and Principal Pruitt's elderly secretary, Grace Moyer. "Hi, Mrs. Moyer."

She cocked her head. "It's Ms. Townsend, right?"

"Yes, ma'am. I have a discipline issue for Principal Pruitt."

Mrs. Moyer glanced at Shane, who was tapping on his phone. "Principal Pruitt's gone for the day, but Vice Principal Wilcox's here."

Gwen frowned. "Isn't that a conflict of interest?"

Mrs. Moyer shrugged. "Would you like to see her or not?"

"Yes."

Mrs. Moyer called Janet's office. "Ms. Townsend's here. She has a discipline problem for you." She listened for a beat. "Okay, I'll send her back." She hung up the phone and looked to Gwen. "You can go back now."

"Thank you," Gwen replied.

Gwen walked down the hallway, passing the counselor's and Pruitt's offices. She knocked on Janet's door.

"Come in," Janet said.

Gwen entered Janet's office and approached her desk. The vice principal was in her mid-forties, voluptuous, with fake blond hair, and stylish glasses.

"I'm sorry to bother you, but I have a disciplinary issue," Gwen said.

"Sit down," Janet said, motioning to one of the chairs in front of her desk.

Gwen sat and crossed her legs. "I hate to put you in this position, but with Principal Pruitt gone for the day ..."

"What's the problem, Gwen?"

"It's Shane. He called another student a ... faggot, threatened the student, then lied about what he did."

Janet sighed and shook her head. "Where is he now?"

"He's in the office waiting area."

"Are you planning to write him up?"

"I'm sorry but yes. I don't tolerate bullying in my classroom. I know it means he can't play in the game tonight."

Janet pursed her lips. "Well, you must have a class to get back to. Send Shane back to my office. I'll take care of it."

"Do you want me to give the write-up to Mrs. Moyer?"

"No, please put it in my mailbox. Grace can be quite the gossip. It wouldn't be fair for Shane to have his mistake spread among the staff. Do you understand?"

"Of course. Thank you, Principal Wilcox."

Gwen sent Shane to see his mother. Gwen filled out the discipline report, put it in Wilcox's mailbox, and returned to class. Shortly after she thanked Lewis for watching her class, the bell rang.

"Don't forget to turn in your personal narratives, if you haven't already done so," Gwen said to her class as they readied their backpacks and purses. A handful of students added personal narratives to the stack on Gwen's desk. As Caleb passed her desk, she said, "Caleb, may I speak with you for a moment?"

Once the kids were gone, Gwen turned her attention to Caleb. "I'm sorry about what happened in class. Are you okay?"

Caleb shrugged. "I'm fine."

"You sure? You want to talk about it?"

He frowned. "I'd rather not. Can I go?"

"Of course, honey. I'm here if you need to talk."

He nodded and left her classroom.

Gwen sat at her desk, leafing through the stack of essays, especially interested in one bright student. She had been looking forward to her free period, the chance to rest her aching feet and to read their essays. Caleb's personal narrative was entitled The Invisible Wish.

Here's my big fat disclaimer. You may not wanna read this because it's stupid bullshit. I don't even wanna write it. I'd rather be invisible.

I *wish* I was invisible. I wish I could breeze through my day, unfettered and unmolested. I don't want attention, but somehow I seem to attract it just by being me. I'm not nothing. I'm less than nothing because, if I was nothing, I'd be invisible. I wish I could be so lucky to be nothing, to be invisible. That would be a huge step up.

I think the problem originated with me. It's nobody's fault but my own. It's about who I am deep inside. I do my best to hide, but somehow they know, somehow they can see me. I don't have the strength to own who I am, to tell them all to go fuck themselves. I wish I did, but that's not who I am. Maybe one day—if I ever get out of here.

My former best friend made it out. She moved to California. She hated it here more than me. People called her a dyke and a carpet muncher, even though she was straight. It was nice to have someone who hated this place as much as me. As they say, "Misery loves company." But my former best friend's no longer a whiny loser like me. She's in therapy. She's working on herself. Whatever the hell that means. Now she's just like everyone else. I liked her better when she was miserable.

My mother's a whore. I try not to be judgmental, but, in my limited experience, I think she qualifies. I've lost count of how many boyfriends she's had. Always some douchebag from the gym. Here's a fun fact. My mom goes to the gym nearly every day. I'm pretty sure she can bench more than me. I think she spends more time at the gym than she does at work. She's a part-time receptionist. Very part-time. We mostly live off my sister's child support payments. I worry about what's gonna happen when she turns eighteen. I hope I'm long gone by then, but she's older than me, so I probably won't be, unless I do something about it.

My sister and I don't have the same father. My father died in a motorcycle accident, or at least that's what I was told. Supposedly happened before I was born. He must've known what a loser I'd be. I picture him on his Harley, speeding away from me and my crazy mother. Maybe he was run over by a dump truck, obliterated into a million pieces. That wouldn't be a bad way to go. I bet that would be an instant death. You wouldn't feel a thing.

I tried to fit in, but it's never worked. I'm on the football team, if you can believe that. I weigh 115 pounds. I have no business playing football, but I liked it when I was younger. I was never good, but I made some friends. Like everything else in my life, it's gotten less and less fun over the years. I'm a third-string wide receiver with questionable hands.

When I was younger, I could catch everything. I scored five touchdowns on the freshman team. Now I get so nervous. I know when I drop a pass, someone's gonna make fun of me. And they should. So I concentrate real hard, and inevitably I drop the pass. But when it doesn't matter, when nobody's watching, I catch everything.

I'm like that Looney Tunes frog. You know? The one that starts singing and dancing like, "Hello, my baby. Hello, my darling." Then someone looks at him, and he sits there like a frog and says, "Ribbit." That's me. If I wasn't such a loser, well, I wouldn't be such a loser, and my life wouldn't suck big hairy balls.

In most stories, the calamities increase in frequency and intensity until the climax. You taught us that, Ms. Townsend. I think my life's like that. It's an easily discernable pattern. That's it in a nutshell. Oh, shit, I haven't really completed the assignment, have I? You wanted us to describe an event that meant something to us. To make the reader feel what we felt. Here goes.

Naked and seminaked boys surround me. They laugh and joke, comfortable showing their muscular chests and big dicks. I work the combination lock and open my locker. I remove my T-shirt. I have a skinny upper body. "Put the bird back in the cage." One of my mother's boyfriends told me that once. I wasn't sure what it meant, but I used my context clues, and I figured it out.

Context clues. See? I'm listening, Ms. Townsend.

Sorry. Back to the story. I glance to my right, then to my left. The Big Man on Campus stands in front of his locker, wearing nothing but a cocky grin. My eyes sweep over his tall, athletic body. For a moment, I look at his penis, and, if I'm really honest, I want to. In that same moment, when I sneak that peek, the BMOC sees me looking. After that, my life is never the same.

Caleb's personal narrative goes on to detail a locker-room shaming for looking at a teammate's penis. The main antagonists of his story are the BMOC and the SIC, Second in Command. Caleb didn't name any names. Gwen was particularly concerned about the final paragraph of his essay.

If it wasn't for Flash Gordon, maybe they would've beat me up or worse. I don't know, but now I walk around afraid every waking minute, just waiting for something bad to happen, for my climax to come to fruition. Maybe I should do it myself. Maybe I should do it on my own terms. Then nobody can ever hurt me again.

Gwen was partly disturbed by the content and partly impressed with Caleb's skill as a writer. She scrawled an A+ at the top of the paper, mostly because that's what he deserved, but partly so the counselor understood that she wasn't upset with Caleb. Gwen took the essay to the main office. Mrs. Moyer pecked away at a computer on the reception desk.

"Back for more?" Mrs. Moyer said with a smirk.

"Is the counselor in?" Gwen asked.

"Mrs. Baumgartner's out sick." Mrs. Moyer cocked her head. "She tends to get sick on Fridays."

Gwen sighed. "May I speak with Principal Wilcox again?"

Mrs. Moyer picked up the phone. "Glutton for punishment, huh?"

After she was allowed entry, Gwen was back in Janet's office, sitting across from her at the desk.

"You've had an eventful afternoon," Janet said.

"That's an understatement," Gwen replied. "I just read a personal narrative from Caleb Miles. He did a fantastic job, but I think he needs to talk a counselor. He may be at risk for suicide."

Janet perked up, her eyes widening.

Gwen handed the essay to Janet. "I'm sorry to drop this in your lap on a Friday afternoon."

Janet took Caleb's essay. "It's quite all right. It's not your fault that Principal Pruitt and Mrs. Baumgartner are both out." She glanced at the handwritten essay. "I'll take care of it."

"In the essay, Caleb talks about being bullied in the locker room. I'm pretty sure he's talking about the football team, and it might be related to what happened in my classroom. You might want to talk to Rick Barnett—"

"I've been in this school district for twenty years. I'm sure I can figure out who to talk to."

"Of course. Please let me know if there's anything I can do to help."

"I'll let you know."

CHAPTER 26

Caleb and Zolpidem

Bass pumped from the speakers—gangster rap. Boys bobbed to the beat as they put on their football uniforms. Jamar sat across from Caleb, eyes closed, leaning against his locker, his head bobbing to a different drummer. Ironically, the only black kid on the team didn't like rap. Jamar preferred R & B, jazz, and synthpop that sounded like refurbished and updated eighties' beats. Caleb glanced at the clock on the wall—5:35. They still had twenty-five minutes before warm-ups.

Caleb, already dressed and ready for his evening on the sideline, sat on the bench in front of his locker. He grabbed his phone and headphones and played his favorite playlist. He tucked his phone into his football pants, leaned against his locker, and shut his eyes. The rap music was drowned out by The 1975. Caleb didn't like rap either, preferring alternative rock. With his eyes shut and Matty Healy crooning in his ears, he floated away.

He awoke with a start, disoriented, something touching his face. Someone stood over him, standing on the bench, legs wide and squatting like a sumo wrestler, his hairy ass-crack close enough to smell, and his scrotum touching Caleb's nose. Caleb ducked his head and stood, getting out from under the guy. Shane still stood, naked from the waist down, standing on the bench, grinning from ear to ear. A half-dozen guys surrounded Caleb, laughing, jumping up and down, hysterical—Lance and Drew and a few other seniors. Caleb couldn't hear them, instead only hearing Matty Healy singing about somebody else.

Caleb pushed through the crowd toward the bathroom. They laughed and blocked his escape. Caleb struggled, his cleats sliding on the concrete, but finally making it through the gauntlet. He slipped and fell as he hustled to the bathroom, the crowd having one last laugh at his expense. Caleb stood, his headphones off-kilter, and scrambled into the bathroom. Jamar turned from the sink, his head still bobbing to his beats, and smiled. Caleb ignored him and went into the last stall, locking the door. The toilet seat was up, the water hazy yellow, and the rim stained with yellow splotches. Caleb kicked the lever, flushing the toilet.

Jamar's calves appeared beneath the stall door. Caleb removed his headphones.

"You all right?" Jamar asked.

"I'm fine." Caleb paused for a moment, thinking of a way to make him go away. "I just have to … take a dump."

Jamar walked away.

Coach Schneider shouted into the locker room, "Five minutes."

Caleb stood in the back corner of that stall, listening and watching for approaching legs. Nobody came for him. Caleb thought about Shane and how he could do whatever he wanted and not get into trouble. *He was sent to the principal. He shouldn't even be playing tonight. Of course, his mom's not gonna do shit. I should've known better to talk back. That's why it happened.*

Coach Schneider shouted, "Turn that shit off." The rap music was vanquished. "One minute. Let's go."

The rap-free quiet was unsettling. Now Caleb heard the *click-clack* of cleats on concrete, the smacking of plastic pads, and voices dissipating as players left the locker room and queued outside for the short walk to the stadium. Eventually everyone was gone, onto the grass, doing their warm-up routine.

Caleb stepped from the stall, his headphones around his neck, faint music emanating from the ear muffs. He stepped gingerly, expecting a coach or a player to reprimand him, but the locker room was empty. He went to his locker, took off his football uniform and pads, and dressed in his jeans and sweatshirt.

He left the locker room, the afternoon sun orange and low on the horizon. Caleb cut through the parking lot and walked along the roadside past the stadium. The stadium lights were already on; the loud speaker blared classic rock. His former teammates readied themselves for the game. Caleb crossed the highway and cut through the cornfield, the stalks tall but browning, the feed corn drying in place. Once concealed by the corn, he broke down, sobbing as he walked. *I wish I was invisible. I wish I was gone. I wish I was fucking dead. I might as well be. I don't think anyone would give a shit. And why would they? I'm nothing. Less than nothing.*

He made it home to his trailer, the sun now replaced by a clear starry night. *Madison would probably say how beautiful it is out. She gets some fucking therapy and what? Now she's got it all figured out? What the fuck does she know? She doesn't know me anymore. Nobody does.*

Caleb went inside, not needing his key. They didn't lock the door. Why bother? Wasn't anything to steal. He went to the bathroom, peed, washed his hands, and leaned on the sink, looking in the mirror. His green eyes were red-rimmed, the tip of his nose also red. He shook his head at himself. *I'd be better off dead.* He went to his bedroom, sat on his bed, and thumb-typed on his phone *the best way to kill yourself.*

A gun's out. They were one of the few families who didn't at least have a hunting rifle. He had a pellet gun. It looked like a real gun, but it didn't shoot like one. It would just hurt real bad. Jumping off a bridge or a tall building was out. It was a long way to the nearest tall bridge or building. It wasn't a great idea anyway. A lot of people supposedly survived that with major injuries. *Fuck that. What about slitting my wrists?* The article called it exsanguination. *Hell, no. I don't have the balls for that.* Sleeping pills were a possibility though.

Caleb went back to the bathroom and opened the mirror to the medicine chest, his phone in his pocket. A bottle of Ambien was on the top shelf. Actually, it read Zolpidem, but he knew it was Ambien because his mother had told him what it was and to stay away from it, that she needed it to sleep. She didn't have a prescription. She probably got it from one of her ex-boyfriends. He opened the tinted plastic bottle. It was mostly empty, a handful of white pills on the bottom.

How many does it take to do the job? He grabbed his phone from his pocket and thumb-typed *dosage for Ambien suicide*. He sat on the toilet and scrolled through various articles, but he couldn't find anything specific. He shoved his phone back in his pocket. *I could just take 'em all. But what if it doesn't work, and Heather wants to know what happened to her pills? What if I get really sick?* Caleb took a deep breath. *I have to do something.* He rummaged through the cabinet, looking through all the pill bottles. He found some aspirin that looked a little like Ambien. They were also white and round but a bit smaller. *Heather would never notice anyway, and, if she did, she'd probably think her old boyfriend got ripped off by some shady drug dealer.*

Caleb took the remaining seven Ambiens and placed them on the sink next to the faucet, careful not to drop them down the drain. He added seven aspirin to the bottle and placed it back on the top shelf. He went to the kitchen, grabbed a glass of water, and returned to the bathroom. His heart pounded in his chest. A lump formed in his throat. Tears welled in his eyes. He thought about what had happened in the locker room. He thought about Madison and his mom. He thought about himself. *I hate myself. I fucking hate myself.* He grabbed the pills, shoved all seven in his mouth at one time, and washed them down with the water.

For a moment, he panicked, hacking, trying to throw up the pills. He put his finger down his throat, but he couldn't do it. He couldn't puke. He thought about calling 9-1-1. Then he thought, *I can't keep doing the same thing and expect a different result. Isn't that what Madison said?*

Caleb went back to his room, shut the door, took off his jeans, and crawled under his covers. He wondered what it would be like. Half an hour later, he drifted off into the black.

CHAPTER 27

Rick and She's Trouble

"I'm starting Jamar next week," Rick said, sitting in the coach's locker room after the game.

Coach Bob Schneider sat across from him, on the bench in front of his locker, wearing khaki shorts and a collared shirt, embroidered with WL Wolf Pack on the breast.

"We won the game," Bob said, stroking his beard.

"Lancaster's terrible," Rick replied. "We should've put up sixty against those guys. With quarterback play like that, we won't win the big games."

Bob shook his head. "You know how I feel about it. Like I said before, it'll divide the team. You really think Lance is gonna be happy catching passes from Jamar? Shane's his best friend."

"Shane overthrew Lance twice tonight. Would've been two easy touchdowns. And he holds on to the ball too long."

Bob blew out a breath. "You're the boss."

"I'll let Shane and Jamar know after films tomorrow." Rick stood from the bench. "I'm beat. You ready to get outta here?"

Bob stood, grabbing his duffel bag. "Yeah."

Rick locked the coach's room and peeked into the player's locker room. It was empty except for the dirt clods that littered the floor. Rick and Bob went outside and walked together to the parking lot.

The lot was empty except for Rick's truck, Bob's SUV, and a Jeep. A female form leaned against Rick's truck. As they approached, Ashlee Miles flipped her dark hair and smiled wide. Bob looked at Rick with raised eyebrows. Rick shrugged in response.

"I'll see you tomorrow," Bob said, heading for his vehicle.

"Bright and early," Rick called out.

Rick approached his truck. Ashlee stood next to his driver's side door, her phone in hand. She wore bright red lipstick, skintight jeans, and a North Face fleece. Bob drove away, leaving them alone.

"Hey, Rick," she said with a giggle. "I mean, Mr. Barnett."

"Ashlee," Rick said, nodding. "You need something?"

"A ride. I locked my keys in my Jeep. I have a spare at home."

"Why don't you call your mother? She can bring your keys. I can wait here for a few minutes if you don't wanna be by yourself."

"She's not home. Probably out with some douchebag."

Rick rubbed his stubbly beard, relieved that Heather had moved on.

"My house is on your way," Ashlee said, her hands on her hips.

"You know where I live?" Rick asked.

"Your wife used to teach me piano. Don't you remember?"

Rick blew out a breath. "All right." Rick unlocked the cab, opened his door, and sat behind the wheel. He placed his phone in the cupholder.

Ashlee skipped around the truck and climbed in through the passenger door. Rick started the engine and drove toward Ashlee's house. He knew where it was but pretended he didn't.

"Tell me where to go," Rick said.

Ashlee skooched closer to Rick on the bench seat, close enough to smell her fruity perfume.

Rick glanced at her, dangerously close. "Where do I turn?"

"Not this left but the next one." Ashlee picked up Rick's phone from the cupholder. "This your phone?"

"Yes." Rick looked at Ashlee tapping on his phone. "Can you put that back please?"

"I'm just putting my number in it." She tapped a few more times and put his phone back in the cupholder. *Her* phone chimed with a musical ring tone. Rick had no idea who the artist was. She silenced the ring. "Now you have my number, and I have yours."

Rick turned left, onto a country road, with farms on both sides. "There's no reason for you to call me or for me to call you."

"You never know."

"When's the next turn?" Rick asked, knowing her neighborhood was quickly approaching on his right.

"Keep going straight."

Rick slowed his truck as the turn neared. "Isn't that your neighborhood?"

"You *do* know where I live." She giggled. "Have you been watching me?"

Rick shook his head and turned into the neighborhood of trailers and old ramblers.

"I'll tell you where I live, but I bet you know," Ashlee said, grinning.

Rick stopped the truck. "You can walk from here."

She flicked her tongue off the roof of her mouth. "Oh, come on. I'm just joking. *So serious.* Take the second left."

Rick drove and turned at the second left.

"You can drop me off up here," Ashlee said, pointing at a dark and deserted playground.

Rick stopped at the playground. "You sure?"

She turned to him and put her hand on his leg.

Rick immediately opened his door and stepped from the truck. "Go home, Ashlee."

She slid over and exited from the same door as Rick. "So touchy." As she stepped past him, she mouthed a kiss. "Bye, *Rick.*"

CHAPTER 28

Janet and Trust But Verify

Janet sat at her kitchen table, having her morning coffee, her laptop open in front of her, and her phone face up. Shane was at films after last night's big win against the Lancaster Indians. She perused the West Lake Watchdog Facebook page.

West Lake Watchdog
September 16 at 6:34 PM
I'm tired of Principal Pruitt making all that money and not doing nothing. I heard he ain't done nothing for ten years. He needs to retire. He can retire now but he don't want to because he gets more money if he waits. Always about money. Hes trying to steal taxpayer money. We work to dam hard for what we got. **#RetirePruitt**
7 Likes 2 Shares
Janine Thompson He makes like 140K. It's ridiculous. The property taxes go up every year. This is why. People around here aren't rich. Something has to change. **#RetirePruitt** 4 Likes
Rose Hendricks I totally agree, **Janine Thompson**. These people are out of control. They're going to bankrupt the district. What the heck is the school board doing about it? Nothing like usual. They are all in it together. 2 Likes

West Lake Watchdog

September 16 at 11:57 PM

The football team needs a better coach. Rick Barnett is a loser. They barely beet Lancaster and there BAD. I heard they should a won by like 50 points. **#FireBarnett**

10 Likes 3 Shares

Roger Elkins More like 100 points. The play calling is so bad. He almost lost the Cumberland game with that stupid pass at the end that got intercepted. Everyone knows you have to run it to get time off the clock. SO STUPID. He's lucky the defense stepped up. That's the kids and their talent. Barnett is getting in the way. The team has a ton of talent but Barnett is gonna blow it. He will probably lose the first round of the playoffs. They need to make a change. **#FireBarnett**

6 Likes

Will Gilroy Damn right Roger. 1 Like

Janet picked up her cell phone and tapped her Cliff Osborn contact. He answered on the fourth ring.

"Good morning, Janet," Cliff said. "To what do I owe the pleasure?"

"The community's pretty upset at Don. They want him to retire."

Cliff sighed. "It's Saturday, Janet. Don't you take a day off?"

"They want him gone now," Janet replied, ignoring his question.

"They'll have to wait."

"Have you seen this new Facebook page, the West Lake Watch-dog?" Janet asked.

"I'm not on Facebook."

"Well, everyone else is. Lots of people want him gone. They know he doesn't do anything, that he's just sticking around to pad his retirement. They're also saying that the school board's not doing anything about it."

"I wonder where they're getting their information?"

"It's not me. I have no idea who's behind the page. It's common knowledge that Don's lazy. Teachers and kids see him reading magazines during school hours. People aren't dumb."

"Well, they can bitch all they want. The board still has a majority in favor of Pruitt. You gotta get Pastor Goode or Daub's seat in November."

"You could help me with that. I know you have dirt."

"I might, but we've been through this, and you weren't interested in my offer."

Janet exhaled. "Don't you care about the school? The kids? They deserve better."

"It's not that simple. You're a big girl. You know that. How would it look if the president of the school board got caught spreading gossip about another board member?"

"Nobody would find out."

"These things have a way of coming out," he said. "I'd have to trust you."

"You can trust me, Cliff. Our boys are best friends."

"Ronald Reagan said, 'Trust but verify.' I gotta verify."

"And how will you do that? By fucking me in some seedy hotel?"

The line was silent.

"Cliff?"

"I'm gonna get back to my Saturday." He disconnected the call.

Janet set down her phone, thinking about how far she'd have to go to win. She heard the roar of an engine approaching, followed by the screech of tires. Janet went to the window and parted the blinds. It was Shane. *Why is he back so early?* Janet walked toward the front door, her slippers snapping with each step. Shane entered and slammed the door behind him. His face was red. His eyes were puffy, as if he'd been crying.

"What's wrong?" Janet asked.

"Fuckin' Coach Barnett benched me!"

CHAPTER 29

Gwen and Letting Go

"Brian? Are you there?" Gwen asked, sitting at her kitchen table, her cell phone to her ear.

"I'm here," Brian said. "What are you doing, Gwen? We talked about this."

"I know. I just wanted to talk to you."

"You need a clean break."

"Don't tell me what I need."

"I need a clean break then."

"I don't believe that."

"I filed the papers. Ira thinks the divorce should go through by Christmas."

Gwen frowned. "What a great present. I can't wait."

Brian ignored her sarcasm. "I've had this recurring dream for the past few weeks. I finally get out of prison, and I visit you. You're remarried, with two kids in college, and I'm happy for you."

She pursed her lips. "I'm not interested in dating, much less marrying someone."

"You're hanging on to us. You're not open to anyone else. That's the problem. ... I'm taking you off my approved list. I can't keep doing this."

Tears welled in Gwen's eyes. "You don't even want to talk to me?"

"That's not the point." Brian exhaled. "I wish like hell I could go back in time and protect you like I should've. I should've been there."

"It wasn't your fault."

"I couldn't undo what had already been done."

"Nobody could." She wiped her eyes with the side of her index finger.

"What if we got into a car crash, and you were wedged in the car, and it was gonna blow up?"

"What are you talking about?"

"Listen to me for a minute. We're in this car crash, and gasoline's spilling all around us, and the car's gonna blow up, but you're wedged in the car, and you can't get out. I try and try to get you out, but you won't budge. If I stay, I'll die when the car blows up. Would you want me to stay and die with you?"

"I know where you're going with this."

"Answer the question."

Gwen closed her eyes for a moment. "No. I'd want you to live."

"I want you to live, Gwen."

CHAPTER 30

Caleb and the Hangover

Sunlight streamed through Caleb's bedroom window. His eyes fluttered. He moved his tongue, his mouth bone-dry. His head pounded; his stomach lurched. Caleb removed the comforter from his body and struggled out of bed. He nearly fell, the room spinning. He staggered to the bathroom, his stomach hot, his gag reflex twitching. Caleb dropped to his knees in front of the bowl and vomited, his throat burning from the bile. He spit in the toilet, thinking it was over, but another wave washed over him, his stomach convulsing, and the hot sick splashing into the water. Caleb slumped to the tile, laying on his side, breathless, a cold sweat on his skin.

I can't even fucking kill myself.

A few minutes later, he washed out his mouth and brushed his teeth. His head still pounded, and his muscles ached, even though he hadn't even stepped on the football field last night. His only exercise had been the walk home from the locker room. Caleb leaned on the sink and looked at his pale face in the mirror. *I need to get a gun.*

Caleb shuffled down the hall to the kitchen. Beyond the kitchen, Ashlee sat on the couch in the living room, alternately watching reality TV and thumb-scrolling on her phone. Caleb grabbed a plastic cup from the cupboard—a leftover from a McDonald's promotion—and filled it with water. He took a tentative swig, then another.

Ashlee looked up from her phone. "What the hell happened to you?"

"I'm sick," Caleb replied.

"Stay away from me."

"Who said I wanna go anywhere near you?"

"Just stay away from me, germ boy."

"Whatever."

Heather's Grand Am parked under the carport, the raspy exhaust from the hole in the muffler announcing her presence. Their mother pushed inside, her hair caked in hairspray, one side still springy, the other side matted and disheveled. She wore a short skirt, bare legs, and high heels.

"Walk of *shame*," Ashlee said with a cackle.

Heather glared at her daughter. "I really don't wanna hear your shit right now, Ashlee." Bleary-eyed Heather walked past, ignoring Caleb, and headed for her bedroom.

Ashlee returned her attention to Caleb. "Have you seen this Facebook page?" Ashlee motioned to her phone with her eyes. "The West Lake Watchdog?"

"No."

Heather reappeared from the hall.

"It's so funny," Ashlee said. "Someone fucking *hates* your coach."

"So?" Caleb said.

"What are you talking about?" Heather asked, sounding more interested than angry.

"The West Lake Watchdog," Ashlee replied. "It's a Facebook page that's always talking shit about Coach Barnett."

Heather stood up straight. "Well, it's good somebody's puttin' that asshole in his place."

"I thought you liked Coach Barnett?" Caleb asked.

"I heard some pretty bad things about him."

"Like what?" Ashlee asked, her eyes narrowed at Heather.

"Like some of the things on that Facebook page."

Ashlee leaned back on the couch and stretched her arms over her head. "I don't know. Seems kinda like bullshit."

Heather glowered at her daughter. "He's a liar and a loser."

Ashlee dropped her arms and grinned, a twinkle in her eyes.

CHAPTER 31

Rick and the Crush

Rick slowed the video, examining the blocking scheme of their upcoming opponent. He sat in his home office, his eyes glued to his laptop, charting tendencies and looking for weaknesses to exploit. He had already found plenty. Their wide receivers only sprinted when it was a passing play, barely blocking on running plays. The receivers would make great run/pass reads for the Wolf Pack secondary. Their center dipped his head right before the snap. That tell would give the Wolf Pack defensive line a split-second advantage.

His phone buzzed. He glanced at the time on his computer—*8:31 p.m.* Rick blew out a breath, knowing that a Saturday night text likely meant that Heather had found a new phone to harass him with, or one of his players was in trouble. He checked the text.

Ashlee: I know a secret about u. ☺

Rick rubbed his temples and went back to the game film. His phone buzzed again.

Ashlee: I talked to my mom about u. Wanna know what she said?

A minute later, his phone buzzed again.

Ashlee: She said u r a liar and a loser. She HATES u. I think she's the WL Watchdog. What did u do to her? U were fing her weren't you? Then u broke up with her, didn't u? Hahahaha

Rick ran his hand over his face. Another buzz came from his phone.

Ashlee: The younger hotter version ☺

Attached to the text was a picture of Ashlee standing in front of a mirror, nude, her cell phone in hand, her long dark hair snaking around her breasts. Rick deleted the picture and blocked Ashlee's number.

CHAPTER 32

Janet and Second String

Janet sat in her office, scrolling through Rick's background check. Apart from his divorce, there was nothing. The bell rang. She left her office for Rick's classroom. It was his planning period.

She knocked on his door, opened it, and entered without invitation. Rick looked up from his laptop as Janet approached his desk.

"What can I do for you, Janet?" Rick asked, still sitting at his desk.

Janet stood in front of him. "We need to talk about Shane."

"What about?"

"Why did you bench my son?"

"Because Jamar's a better quarterback. I think he gives us a better chance to win."

"Shane's done everything you've asked of him. He doesn't deserve this. This is his senior year. Jamar's only a sophomore."

Rick took a deep breath. "I don't play favorites. The best kids play, period."

"What if Shane agrees to stay after practice and do extra work?"

"He can do that if he wants. It'll help his chances, but I doubt it'll be enough. Jamar's gonna get his chance. If he fails or gets injured, Shane'll get another shot, but, at this point, it's Jamar's job to lose."

Janet paused for a moment, poker-faced. "I'm a very powerful ally."

"I hope we can stay professional, but I won't compromise on this."

She glowered at Rick. "I'm a more powerful enemy."

Rick nodded, unblinking. "Do what you have to do."

Janet turned on her heels and marched back to her office. *Who the fuck does he think he is?*

Sitting at her desk, she picked up the desktop phone and called Coach Bob Schneider's classroom.

"I need you to come to my office," Janet said.

"I have a class," Bob replied.

"I don't care. Find someone to cover for you." Janet slammed down the receiver.

A few minutes later, Bob knocked on her office door.

"Come in," Janet said.

Bob Schneider entered her office, his head tilted down, like a whipped puppy. His button-down shirt was tucked in, accentuating his gut.

"Shut the door," Janet said. "Sit down."

Bob shut the door and sat across from her at the desk.

"Why is my son being benched after a *convincing* win?"

"It's not my fault," he said. "I told Rick it was a bad idea."

"It *is* a bad idea," Janet said.

"If it were up to me, Shane would start."

"You *will* find a way to make sure my son starts this Friday."

He held out his thick hands. "It's really not my call. There's nothin' I can do about it."

Janet pursed her lips. "Well, there's nothing I can do about your job then. Watching pornography on your school computer is grounds for immediate dismissal."

His eyes widened, and his face reddened under his bushy beard. "Maybe I can talk some sense to Rick."

"That's the spirit."

CHAPTER 33

Gwen and the Big Dumb Football Coach

Gwen sat at her desk, correcting personal narratives, and adding smileys and notes of encouragement. Many of the boys had written about their exploits on the football field, baseball diamond, or basketball court. Jamar had written about being the only black kid on the football team. Aaron Fuller had written about his older brother Drew. Apparently, Drew had looked out for his kid brother more than their mother. Many of the girls had written about body image and family issues. Ashlee had written an especially moving essay about her absent father. The Miles's siblings certainly had talent. Caleb had written the best personal narrative in her sixth-period creative writing class, and Ashlee's essay was head and shoulders above everyone in her second-period class.

Rick Barnett poked his head into her classroom. "I'm going to Subway to grab dinner. You wanna go?"

Gwen glanced at the stack of personal narratives on her desk. "No, but thanks. I do need to talk to you though, if you have a few minutes."

Rick approached her desk, wearing khakis and a button-down shirt. "Sure. What's up?"

"I heard you guys won on Friday. Congratulations."

"We didn't play very well."

"I'm sure it wasn't easy without your quarterback."

Rick furrowed his brows. "What are you talking about?"

"I wrote up Shane last Friday for bullying. I know he was ineligible—"

"Shane wasn't ineligible. Nobody told me that he was written up."

"I talked to Janet about it, and I put the form in her box."

Rick shook his head. "That doesn't surprise me."

"What?"

"Janet buried it. She's been enabling Shane for as long as I can remember."

"I'll go to Pruitt tomorrow then. I'm sorry, but you may be without a quarterback this week."

"I wouldn't bother."

"Why not?"

"Because Pruitt's soft on crime. And Shane won't be playing this week anyway."

Gwen raised her eyebrows.

"I benched him. Jamar's starting this week, and, if he plays like I think he will, Shane'll never see the field again."

"Wow. Does Janet know?"

"She talked to me this morning. Tried to talk me into not making the change. She told me that she's a powerful enemy."

"I've heard that. I'd be careful if I were you."

"I can handle Janet. I won't let a parent influence who plays and who doesn't. I don't care who they are. Sports are one of the last great meritocracies in this country."

"I still think something needs to be done about Shane. I think there might've been a hazing incident in the football locker room with Caleb Miles."

"Where did you hear that?"

Gwen gestured to the stack of essays on her desk. "From Caleb's personal narrative. He didn't name names, but I'm pretty sure Shane was involved and maybe Lance Osborn."

Rick blew out a breath. "Makes sense. Caleb quit on Friday. I'm embarrassed to say that I didn't even notice until Jamar told me today. Apparently, Caleb was in the locker room before the game but didn't come out for warm-ups. He just left. And he wasn't at practice today."

"Or school. The office told me that his mom called and said he was sick."

"I'd like to know all the details, but I'm running on fumes. You mind if I go grab my dinner real quick? Then we can talk about it."

"Of course."

"You gonna be here for another thirty minutes?"

Gwen gestured to the stack of essays on her desk. "At least another hour."

"You sure you don't want something from Subway? I deliver."

"You wouldn't mind?"

"Write down your order. If you don't, I can guarantee I'll get it wrong."

Gwen wrote her order on a sticky note—six-inch sub, apples, NO chips, wheat bread, turkey, provolone, lettuce, tomato, banana peppers, little bit of mayo.

Rick glanced at the note. "No drink?"

"I have water." Gwen pointed to the water bottle on her desk.

Rick smiled, his teeth white and straight. "No cookie?"

"I'm trying to be good."

"That's no fun."

Rick left, and Gwen continued to work, her stomach rumbling at the thought of food. Rick returned about twenty minutes later with two plastic bags and a drink.

He set her sub on her desk. "I bought an extra cookie if you want one."

"Trying to fatten me up?"

"You look like you've had a long day."

Gwen frowned. "I look that bad, huh?"

"No, sorry. That's not what I meant."

"It's fine. How much do I owe you?" Gwen reached for her purse.

"My treat."

"That's really nice of you. Thank you," Gwen said, extracting her sub from the tubelike plastic bag.

"You're welcome." Rick moved a student desk near Gwen and sat down.

They ate their sandwiches, Gwen devouring her sub, not realizing how hungry she was.

"I'd like to read the essay that Caleb wrote," Rick asked between bites.

Gwen wiped her mouth with a napkin. "I don't have it. Janet does, but I can tell you the gist of what happened."

Rick nodded, his mouth full.

"It happened in the locker room. Caleb didn't use any names except for his own, but he talked about being bullied for looking at someone's private parts. The bullying was very aggressive and homophobic. They called him a faggot. Someone grabbed Caleb and forced him to look at a boy's crotch. I think Caleb may be gay. I think he's struggling with his sexual preference."

"This town isn't exactly open-minded about homosexuality. Unfortunately, I doubt my football team is either."

Gwen stared at Rick, her head cocked. "I'm surprised you'd say that. I expected excuses for homophobia."

"Why? Because I'm a big dumb football coach?"

"No, of course not. I'm sorry. I—"

"I'm joking. It takes a lot more than that to offend me. Any other details from the incident?" Rick took a big bite of his sandwich.

"Caleb mentioned five or six kids laughing and heckling. Again, no names. Caleb wrote that Flash Gordon intervened and stopped the bullying. Do you know who Flash Gordon might be?"

Rick swallowed a bit of his sandwich and wiped his mouth with a napkin. "Probably Jamar. He's lightning fast, and I think he and Caleb are friends. Did he have nicknames for any of the bullies?"

"The boy he looked at, he called Big Man on Campus. The boy who forced him to look, he called Second in Command."

"If I had to guess, I'd say that's Shane and Lance."

"What are you going to do?"

"I'll talk to Caleb and the other kids. Try to get to the bottom of this." Rick paused for a moment. "You think Caleb could be making it up?"

"Anything's possible, but I think he's telling the truth."

"That's what I'm afraid of. If Shane and Lance are the ringleaders, this could get ugly. We already know what Shane's mother's like, and Lance's dad is the president of the school board. This could get real political."

CHAPTER 34

Caleb and Self-Hatred

Caleb's stomach churned as Ms. Townsend handed out their corrected personal narratives. He worried that he'd gone too far, that he'd shared too much of himself. *She'll probably make me go to Mrs. Baumgartner.* Ms. Townsend placed the essays facedown as she walked up and down the rows.

"I was so impressed with your personal narratives," Ms. Townsend said. "Everyone did such an outstanding job improving their first drafts with their revisions and the line edits. I was really touched by your writing. I laughed. I cried. I rooted for the protagonists, and I rooted against the antagonists in your life stories. Just fantastic." Ms. Townsend finished returning the essays, except for Caleb's. Instead, she bent toward him, situated at the desk in the front corner, and whispered, "Caleb, honey, will you stay after class? I need to talk to you."

The bell rang. Everyone collected their belongings and headed for the exit. On the way out, students compared their grades. Lance made fun of Shane's C+, calling him a dumbass, Shane pushing him playfully in response, reminding him of his own C+. Aaron Fuller bragged about his A.

"Check this out, bro," Aaron said, showing his essay to his older brother, Drew.

Caleb expected Drew to make fun of Aaron, but Drew simply said, "Nice job, bro."

As the classroom emptied, Caleb trudged toward Ms. Townsend. She stood in front of her desk, wearing a flowing dress and a white cardigan, her brown hair in a loose ponytail.

"Are you feeling better? I heard you were sick," Ms. Townsend said.

Caleb looked away for a moment. "Yeah, I'm fine."

"I wanted to talk to you about your personal narrative."

Caleb blushed.

"I gave you an A+. It was the best paper out of all my classes. I was very impressed. You have a real talent for writing."

Caleb nodded, his head tilted down. "Thanks."

"I'm sorry I didn't return it today. Principal Wilcox still has it."

Caleb felt like throwing up.

"I had to report it. I'm worried about you. The incident in the locker room must've been awfully traumatic. Are you okay?"

"It never happened. I was writing fiction." Caleb looked up. "I know we were supposed to write something real, but my life's boring, so I made it up."

Ms. Townsend nodded. "Well, you fooled me. It sounded very real."

"It wasn't."

"Are you sure?"

Caleb crossed his arms over his chest. "I would know if it was real or not."

"The character in the story was suicidal. Do you ever have any suicidal thoughts?"

He frowned. "No. And the character wasn't suicidal. He's just angry."

"Are you angry?"

Caleb shrugged. *I never should've written that stupid essay.* "I don't have anything to be angry about. Can I go?"

"Did Principal Wilcox talk to you?"

"No."

"What about Mrs. Baumgartner?"

Shit. I really hope I don't have to talk to the counselor. "I talked to her this morning."

"That's good. If you ever need to talk, I'm here."

* * *

Caleb flipped off his light, thinking about how he wished taking his life would be that easy. *If I could turn off my life like a light switch, I would've done it a long time ago.* He lay in his bed, the comforter wrapped around him like a cocoon. He shut his eyes, thinking about Shane … naked. Caleb was aroused. He blinked, tears slipping down his face. *They're right. You are a fucking faggot. Just fucking do it.* Caleb grabbed his phone from his bedside table. He took off one of his socks and put it over his erection. He stroked his penis, watching two men have oral, then anal sex on his phone. In that order. The other way grossed him out. The pleasure ended with his orgasm, quickly replaced by shame. He tossed the soiled sock in his dirty clothes pile, making sure to cover it with a shirt. Not that anyone would see it because Caleb did his own laundry.

He thought about Madison as he climbed back into bed. *Does she know? Does she suspect? She's always acting like it's no big deal. Like she's so liberal and open-minded. But she's not the one who feels this way. It's easy for her to act like it's perfectly normal.*

Madison had tried to kiss him once, but Caleb had pulled away and said, "I don't wanna ruin our friendship." *What a bunch of bullshit.* Madison had stormed from his room, but she'd gotten over it, and they went back to being friends, but they'd never talked about it.

He'd needed her now more than ever, but she wasn't even returning his texts. She'd been MIA through the weekend and into Monday. Caleb grabbed his phone from the bedside table and tapped Madison.

She picked up on the fifth ring. "I'm sorry I haven't returned your texts," Madison said in lieu of a greeting.

"Where have you been?" Caleb asked, laying on his back.

"I'm sorry. I just got my texts like five minutes ago. My friend Tanner and I decided to go on a technology fast. It was so eye-opening. I didn't realize how much technology's frying my brain. You really oughta try it. We could do it together, if you want."

"Who's Tanner?"

"He's my friend." She paused for a moment. "I actually think he might be my boyfriend. We kissed, and we've been hanging out a lot. We haven't, like, labeled it yet though. I'm so excited. I think you'd really like him."

Caleb sighed. "He sounds cool."

"You'd really like him."

"You said that."

"Well, you would."

An awkward silence followed.

"Your texts said you needed to talk," Madison said. "What's going on?"

"I can't take this place anymore."

"Did you talk to the counselor—"

"I don't wanna talk to the counselor. I wanna talk to you."

"Okay. I'm listening."

"It's really bad here. Like way worse than before."

"What happened?"

"It just fucking sucks. You know how it is. People are so fucking stupid around here. I wish a fucking nuclear blast would hit this place and destroy everyone and everything in it."

"You don't mean that."

"I do. One hundred percent, I do."

"If you put negativity out into the world, that's what you'll get back—"

"I really don't wanna hear your New Age California hippy bullshit."

"I'm trying to be kind to you, Caleb. You're not making it easy."

"By not responding to my texts for four days? Or even telling me that you're on some sort of fucking phone fast?"

"I said I was sorry. It's a struggle for me too, you know?"

"Sounds rough. You love your new friends, new school, new boyfriend. Everything got better for you when you left, but everything got worse for me, and nobody gives a fuck."

"That's not true. I do care, but I can't pretend to be miserable with you because you want someone to hate the world with you. I'm trying not to be that girl anymore."

"I liked you better before."

"Don't be an asshole."

"Tanner sounds like a *douchebag.*" Caleb disconnected the call and powered off his phone.

CHAPTER 35

Rick and the Saboteur

Rick knocked on Lewis Phelps's classroom door. Through the door window, he saw the diminutive teacher lecturing at the head of the class. Lewis turned toward the knock and waved Rick inside.

Rick stepped into the classroom. "I'm sorry to interrupt your class, Mr. Phelps. I need to talk to Caleb for a minute."

"By all means, Mr. Barnett." Lewis motioned to Caleb, sitting in the front row.

Caleb followed Rick into the empty hallway without a word, his face expressionless. They stood next to a wall of lockers.

"I'm disappointed that you quit football," Rick said.

"I'm surprised you even noticed."

"Everyone's an important part of the team."

Caleb smirked. "Really? How long would it take for you to talk to Drew or Lance if they didn't show up for a game? I doubt it would be five days after the fact."

"You're right, Caleb. I do pay more attention to the varsity guys. I'm sorry." Rick paused for a moment. "Why did you quit?"

"I don't like football anymore. It's not fun."

"Did something happen to you?"

Caleb shrugged. "No. I suck at football, and it's not fun to do things you suck at."

"I don't think that's true. You were one of our best receivers on the freshman team. If you'd get in the weight room, do the speed training, work on your routes and your hands, there's no reason you can't play by the time you're a senior."

Caleb flipped his brown hair from his eyes. "I don't wanna play anymore."

"Did something happen in the locker room?"

"No."

"Was anybody bullying you?"

Caleb looked away for a split second. "No."

"You sure?"

"Can I go back to class?"

* * *

The first-string offense practiced against the second-string defense. Shane sulked on the sideline as Jamar took the first-string reps at quarterback. Coach Bob Schneider gave the play to Jamar, who relayed it to the huddle.

In the huddle, Lance said, "You can't run it like that."

"That's what Coach said," Jamar replied.

"Run the goddamn play!" Coach Schneider said.

The offense ran the play. Jamar rolled to the right, but his protection went left. Jamar was swarmed by three defenders, who stopped before sacking him, obeying the rule not to hit the starting quarterback. Coach Schneider blew the whistle and stalked to Jamar.

"What the hell are you doing? That was 371 *L* Dump. Why the hell are you rollin' right? Don't you know your left from your right?"

"You said 371 *R*," Jamar replied.

"You think I don't know what I said?"

Jamar dipped his head. "No, sir."

"Then run it again."

Phil M. Williams

Rick walked over to Bob Schneider as the offense lined up. "You all right?"

Bob shook his head, his bearded face twisted in a frown. "He's not ready."

"Give him a chance. He'll get it."

"He doesn't even know his fuckin' left from his right. This is gonna be a disaster. We gotta put Shane back in."

Rick didn't reply, turning from Bob to the play. Jamar rolled left this time, set his feet, and fired a bomb, hitting Lance on the backside post. Touchdown.

CHAPTER 36

Janet Digs Dirt

"I did the best I could," Coach Bob Schneider said, sitting across from Janet.

Janet sat, her arms folded neatly on the desktop. "I don't care that you did *your best*. I care that my son's not starting tonight."

"I can fix this."

"By tonight?"

"I can call shitty plays for Jamar. Rick'll be forced to bench him. Jamar won't make it to halftime."

"And if that doesn't work?"

Bob shrugged his bulky shoulders. "I'll figure out somethin' else."

Janet pursed her lips. "I think we need to be a bit more proactive. The problem isn't Jamar. The problem is Rick."

Bob nodded in agreement. "Maybe you could fire him?"

I didn't think Bob had it in him. "We'd have to have cause. We can't go around firing people for no reason. He'd have to do something stupid"—Janet glared at Bob—"like looking at porn on his school computer."

Bob blushed.

"You know him pretty well, don't you?" Janet asked. "Are there any skeletons we can dig up?"

"I don't know. We don't really talk about much except football."

"You might want to think about it for a minute. Your career depends on it."

Bob stroked his bushy beard, the wheels turning in his head. "One thing happened that was weird."

"Go on."

"Last Friday, after the Lancaster game, Rick and I left the locker room together. It was late. Everyone was gone, except, when we got to the parkin' lot, Ashlee Miles was leanin' on Rick's truck. She was lookin' at him like they had somethin' goin' on."

Janet nodded. "Did she get into his truck with him?"

"Probably. I don't know. I didn't see. They were talkin' when I drove away."

CHAPTER 37

Gwen and Her Star Students

The bell rang; the students shuffled out. Gwen walked toward Caleb, hoping to have another chat, but he was gone in a flash. Jamar approached with a big grin, his thin mustache spread across his upper lip. He wore jeans and his white-and-red number two jersey. Jamar was slender, with well-defined muscles. His ears stuck out, accentuated by his short haircut. He had a strong chin, high cheekbones, and clear caramel-colored skin. A nice face to go along with smarts and athletic talent.

"I'm playing tonight," Jamar said.

"That's great," Gwen replied, matching his smile. "Not to change the subject on you, but I wanted to talk to you about your personal narrative."

"Okay."

Shane trudged past alone, glowering at Jamar. Lance and the Fuller brothers walked together, joking, oblivious to or ignoring Shane.

"Aaron," Gwen said to his back. "I need to talk to you for a moment."

Aaron turned with a frown. "What did *I* do?"

Lance and Drew laughed at Aaron and left the classroom.

"You're not in trouble," Gwen said as Aaron approached her and Jamar. "I'm glad I have you both here," she said, looking from Aaron to Jamar. "I was very impressed with your personal narratives. Both of you did a wonderful job."

Aaron blushed, his pale skin reddening.

"Thank you, Ms. Townsend," Jamar said.

"I don't even like writing," Aaron said.

Gwen smiled at Aaron. "I see you, Aaron Fuller. You're not fooling me. You don't write with that kind of passion and skill unless you love it."

He blushed again. "Can I go now?"

"Of course."

Aaron pivoted on his sneakers and left the classroom.

Gwen returned her attention to Jamar. "I hope you have a great game tonight."

"You should come and see for yourself," Jamar said.

"What time does it start?" Gwen asked.

"Seven. We're away, but it's Garden Grove. That's only like ten minutes away."

"I'll try to make it."

CHAPTER 38

Caleb and Doth Protest Too Much

The hallway was chaotic, kids boisterous and energized for the end of the school week. Caleb shoved his books into his locker. Planning took place all around him: car pools to Garden Grove, after-parties, beer runs by older siblings, and drug purchases. Drugs were easier to get than beer. You didn't need ID for your friendly neighborhood drug dealer. Caleb slammed shut his locker.

"Caleb, you got a minute?" Mr. Phelps asked.

Caleb turned to his history teacher and exhaled. "I have to go."

"Do you have to catch a bus?"

"I walk."

"It'll just be a few minutes."

Caleb followed Mr. Phelps into his classroom. Mr. Phelps shut the door behind them. He wore tight slacks and a sweater vest, his blond hair gelled to perfection.

Caleb stood with his arms crossed over his chest.

"You seemed distracted in class today," Mr. Phelps said. "Anything you wanna talk about?"

"I'm fine."

"It doesn't seem like you're fine. I'd like to help you, but I can't if I don't know what's going on."

"Nothing's going on. This school sucks. This place sucks. Not much *you* can do about that."

"Why does it suck?"

Caleb sighed, one side of his mouth raised in disgust. "The people here are stupid … total dumbasses. And not just the kids. The adults too. Everyone's so small-town. I'm sick of it." Caleb looked at the linoleum.

"I can understand that. I grew up here too. I went to this high school. I was bullied pretty bad."

Caleb looked up. "Why did you get bullied?"

"I'm five foot two and gay. I don't exactly fit in around here."

Caleb's eyes widened. "You're gay?"

"I am. I don't broadcast it, but I'm not ashamed either. If someone asks, I tell them the truth." Mr. Phelps paused for a moment, looking into Caleb's eyes. "There's nothing wrong with being gay."

Caleb broke eye contact with Mr. Phelps. "Yeah, whatever. I don't care if people are gay. Doesn't have anything to do with me."

"Are you sure about that?"

"Why would it?"

"Well, … if, um …"

Caleb scowled at his teacher. "You think I'm a faggot?"

Mr. Phelps shook his head, his voice calm. "Please don't use that word. There's nothing wrong with being gay, Caleb. Nothing at all. Even in this town, I have friends, a boyfriend, family. They all accept me for who I am."

"Good for you, Mr. Phelps."

"The first step is accepting who you are—"

"I know exactly who I am. I'm no faggot." Caleb turned on his sneakers and started for the door.

"Caleb, please. Talk to me."

Caleb opened the door and hurried down the empty hall. Once outside, he gazed up at the sun peeking through the clouds. A breeze rustled his hair. He cut through the parking lot toward the main road. Drew Fuller sold drugs—shielded by a Mustang and a pickup truck—to a group of dirt-ball kids with skateboards and patchy facial hair. Aaron Fuller kept watch during the transaction. Aaron didn't acknowledge Caleb as he walked by. Caleb was a nonentity, not worthy of concern. Nearly invisible.

Nearly.

CHAPTER 39

Rick and Garden Grove

It was third and eleven, West Lake down by a touchdown, less than a minute left in the half. Temps in the upper-fifties, clear skies, the stars twinkling overhead. A beautiful night for football at Garden Grove High School. Coach Bob Schneider talked to Jamar during the time-out, the two of them just out of earshot of the offensive huddle. Bob jogged from the field back to the sideline.

"What's the play?" Rick asked.

"PAP hitch seam delay," Bob replied.

"They're gonna be all over the hitch. They've been in cover two all night, and the seam runs right into the safeties."

"I told him to throw the seam if the safeties bite on the play action and to check down to the flare if they don't."

Rick nodded to Bob as play resumed on the field. Jamar barked out the cadence. The center snapped the ball through his legs to Jamar, who stood five yards back in the shotgun. Jamar faked the handoff to the running back, then threw a bullet to Lance on the hitch, but the cornerback stepped in front for the interception and sprinted down the sideline headed for the end zone. Jamar hustled after him, catching the Garden Grove defender at the three-yard line. Two plays later, Garden Grove scored as the play clock ticked down to zero. They now led West Lake by fourteen at the half.

Rick jogged with the team back to the visiting locker room. Bob stopped Rick before they entered. With the players inside, Bob made a plea.

"We're gonna lose this game if we stick with Jamar," Bob said. "We need to put Shane in."

Rick stroked his stubbly beard. "Lemme talk to Jamar. See where his head's at."

"I'll do it."

"No. I got it."

Rick walked into the locker room. Tile floors, powder-blue lockers, and his team sitting on benches, quiet, their heads down. Jamar had a towel over his head. Rick put a hand on his shoulder pad. Jamar looked up, his eyes red-rimmed.

"Let's step outside for a minute," Rick said.

Jamar followed Rick outside.

In their wake, one of the players said, "Put Shane in."

Rick and Jamar stood outside, in the moonlight, out of earshot of the locker room.

"You okay?" Rick asked.

Jamar shook his head, his jaw set tight.

"Why didn't you throw the flare on that last play? It was wide open."

"Because Coach Schneider told me to throw the hitch."

Rick furrowed his brows. "Are you sure you didn't mix up what he told you?"

"I'm pretty sure, but he's confusing. ... I don't know. I'm sorry, Coach. I know I'm messing up."

"What's confusing exactly?"

"He keeps giving me the wrong protection for the play, or he mixes up the routes. I've been changing it to try to fix it, but I don't know everything yet. And everything's happening so fast."

Rick nodded, his face blank.

"Are you gonna bench me?" Jamar asked.

Rick took off his WL Wolf Pack hat. "Garden Grove's a decent team, but we're more talented, and I've seen you run circles around our defense with a second-string line. No reason you can't run circles around these guys too. You're the best player on the field. You just haven't figured it out yet."

Jamar nodded.

"I want you to go back out in the second half and have some fun. Okay?"

"What about the plays?"

"Don't worry about that. I'll fix it. That's my job. I'll do my job, and you'll do yours. Deal?" Rick extended his hand to his quarterback.

Jamar shook his coach's hand, a smile developing. Rick rapped Jamar on the back, and they returned to the locker room. Coach Schneider was at the whiteboard, strategizing and drawing plays for Shane and Lance and the rest of the offense.

"Everybody, bring it in," Rick said, moving in front of the whiteboard.

"We're still workin'," Coach Schneider said.

"That'll have to wait, Coach."

Bob frowned but moved away from the whiteboard. The players settled on benches in front of Rick.

"We're not changing anything," Rick said.

The players looked surprised and worried but said nothing.

"We're gonna be fine," Rick continued. "We're only down by two scores. We're getting the ball, and the offense is gonna score. Then the defense is gonna get a three and out, and the offense is gonna score again, and we're right back in it. I want everyone to get a drink, stay off your feet, relax, and get your mind right."

After halftime, on the way back down to the field, Rick walked with Bob.

"I'm gonna call the plays in the second half," Rick said.

Bob's face reddened under his bushy beard. "Come on, Rick. You can't do that."

Rick stopped walking, letting the team continue ahead. They stood just outside the stadium, under the glow of the lights.

"We've been coaching together a long time," Rick said. "And I think you're an excellent coach, but something's not right tonight. I don't know where your head is, but this isn't all Jamar's fault."

"Rick—"

"Let me finish. I'm gonna call the rest of this game, and, provided you go back to coaching like the man I've known for the past eight years, you'll run the offense next week." Rick turned and walked into the stadium, leaving Bob standing by himself.

The second half went exactly like Rick had predicted. After the kickoff, Jamar ran the zone read to perfection, scoring on a sixty-six-yard run. The defense stuffed Garden Grove, forcing a punt. Then Jamar hit Lance on a fifty-two-yard bomb for the tying touchdown. After that, it turned into a blowout, with West Lake scoring three more unanswered touchdowns.

During the second half, the West Lake sideline was jovial, the visiting stands packed and cheering. Shane stood by himself on the sideline, watching his senior season go up in smoke as Jamar engineered touchdown after touchdown. Coach Schneider cheered and coached the offense between drives, but his slumped shoulders and downturned head told a different story.

After the game, the teams shook hands, then congregated at opposite end zones. The West Lake Wolf Pack took a knee near the goalpost. Rick stood in front of his team.

"I'm very proud of each and every one of you. We didn't play well in the first half, but you didn't get down on yourselves. You focused on your assignments, and you executed to perfection. That was the best half of football I've seen in quite some time. From here on out, I expect to see that level of precision for four quarters." Rick surveyed his team: helmets in hand, kneeling, hair matted and wet with sweat. "Tomorrow, films at 8:00 a.m. Do *not* be late. After films, we'll do conditioning and lift. If you're banged up, make sure you see the trainer for ice.

Oh, and don't do anything *stupid* tonight."

They laughed and cheered and meandered toward the bleachers to talk to their parents, friends, and girlfriends. Rick grabbed a drink before the equipment managers took the water jugs. His gaze swept across the visiting bleachers. Shane and Janet Wilcox talked out of earshot. Shane was red-faced, gesticulating with his hands. Janet's face was twisted in anger. Lance and Cliff Osborn were all smiles and back slaps. Jamar grinned from ear to ear as he recapped the game with his parents and Gwen Townsend.

Rick walked toward Jamar and his fan club—glancing at Gwen, looking her over, but trying not to be obvious. She dressed casually in jeans and a fleece. Even in casual attire, she was beautiful. Heart-shaped face, big blue eyes, perfect porcelain skin, and a button nose.

Rick waved to Gwen, then smiled at Jamar's parents. "I'm Rick Barnett."

They smiled back and shook hands, Jamar's father saying, "Gerald Burris and my wife, Enid." Jamar's parents were tall and thin and well-dressed—looking more like churchgoers than football fans.

"It's nice to meet you," Rick said. "Your son played a great game."

"That's very kind of you, Mr. Barnett," Enid said.

"Please, call me Rick."

Jamar smirked at Rick. "They're more impressed with my English grade. Ms. Townsend and my mom spent the whole game talking about school."

Gwen laughed. "The Burrises have their priorities straight."

Enid smiled at Gwen. "School comes first."

"Football is for fun. School is for life," Gerald said.

Rick nodded in agreement.

CHAPTER 40

Janet and Intel

"**I** don't wanna talk about it anymore," Shane said, pushing off the short chain-link fence that divided the bleachers from the football field.

"This isn't right," Janet said. "You're a senior."

"Stay out of it." Shane marched away, back to the locker room.

Janet took a deep breath. She glared at Rick and Gwen talking in the glow of the stadium lights. *She flipped her hair. Look at the way he's looking at her. They're fucking flirting.*

Most of the players were already in the locker room as Rick walked Gwen from the stadium toward the parking lot. Janet followed at a safe distance, careful not to be spotted. *No chance of that. They're fucking enamored.*

The parking lot was quiet and nearly empty. Most of the Garden Grove fans had left in the fourth quarter, when the game had turned into a rout. Gwen stood by her black VW, fiddling with her keys. Her straight brown hair was loose and flowing. *She thinks she's so fucking hot.* Janet ducked behind her BMW, half-a-dozen spaces behind them. Thankfully, her car was shielded by a Honda Accord. A few fans and students walked past, but they didn't notice Janet. Rick's and Gwen's voices carried across the parking lot.

"It was nice of you to come out and support us," Rick said.

"I have to admit, I'm not much of a football fan, but Jamar asked me to come," Gwen said. "He's such a nice kid. I couldn't say no."

"He's special. He has D-one talent, and he's only a tenth grader."

"I'm glad he did so well tonight."

"So am I. I didn't tell Jamar, but my ass was on the line. I'm sure Janet's plotting my demise. The last thing I wanted was to give her any ammunition."

"She was in the stands. I don't think she cheered at all, and she yelled, 'Put in Shane,' when Jamar threw the ball to the other team."

Rick cocked his head with a crooked smile. "You mean, the interception?"

"Yes, the interception."

"Janet's a piece of work. I feel bad for Shane. I can't imagine having a mother like that."

Janet, still eavesdropping, clenched her fists. *Who the hell does he think he is?*

"It explains her son's bad behavior," Gwen said.

Janet thought about getting into her car and running both of them over.

"This is true," Rick replied.

An awkward silence followed, Rick rubbing his stubble and Gwen playing with her keys.

"Would you like to get a drink with me?" Rick asked.

"Oh, … um ,… like, right now?" Gwen replied.

"There's a bar not too far from school. The Toad's Stool. They have food too. It's bar food, but, if you're hungry …"

"Um, okay, but I don't know where it is."

"I have to ride back with the team, but you could meet me at school. Then you could follow me."

Janet had a powerful urge to put them in their place. She thought about their cute little date to the Toad's Stool, wishing she could ruin it. … She smiled to herself, realizing that she could.

CHAPTER 41

Gwen and the Toad's Stool

The bar was dimly lit, with low ceilings, faux-wood paneled walls. Half-a-dozen old men sat at the bar, two couples at the tables, and a group of young adults at one of the booths along the wall. A thin fortysomething waitress approached, her mouth puckered from thousands of cigarettes.

"Booth or a table?" she asked Gwen and Rick.

"Booth," Gwen and Rick said in unison.

As they sat at the booth, the waitress said, "Youse jus' drinkin' or eatin' too?"

"I'd like to see a food menu," Gwen said.

"Me too," Rick added.

The waitress delivered a pair of menus and took their drink orders. Beer for Rick. Rum and Diet Coke for Gwen. With the waitress gone to retrieve their drinks, Gwen looked at Rick. His short brown hair was matted from the hat that sat on the table. She liked that he'd taken it off as soon as they'd stepped inside the bar. He looked tired, his eyes a little bloodshot, his stubbly beard getting a bit unruly. Despite this, he was handsome. Somewhere in between a pretty boy and a mountain man. The waitress brought their drinks and asked for their food orders.

"What kind of lettuce do you have?" Gwen asked.

The waitress furrowed her brow. "Just regular lettuce."

"Is it iceberg lettuce or mixed greens?"

"It's the crunchy kind."

"You don't happen to have kale or spinach, do you?"

Rick smiled at that.

"I don't think so. You want me to ask?" The waitress said this with no enthusiasm, signaling that she didn't want to ask, and it was likely futile anyway.

"No, it's okay. I'm, um, still not sure. You go ahead and order," Gwen said, gesturing to Rick.

"Cheeseburger and fries," Rick said to the waitress, handing her his menu.

The waitress smiled, looking him over. "A man who knows what he wants." She turned back to Gwen, one side of her mouth raised in disdain. "You decide yet?"

Gwen still looked over the menu. "Um, … uh, … I guess I'll have the grilled chicken salad, but can I get the dressing on the side? And no cheese. … Oh, and no croutons."

The waitress took Gwen's menu with a forced smile. "Comin' right up." She turned on her sneakers and headed for the kitchen.

"You're really particular about your lettuce," Rick said with a smirk.

"Iceberg lettuce has no nutrients. It's all water." Gwen had a crooked grin. "Even Subway has spinach."

Rick's expression turned serious. "Thank you for coming out. I haven't been out in a long time."

"Me either. I haven't had a drink in forever."

Then their conversation stalled.

"So, how do you like West Lake so far?" Rick asked.

"It's been different than what I'm used to, but it's been mostly good. Of course, I've only been here a month. My assessment is subject to change with time."

"Are you expecting trouble?"

"No, but Janet hasn't exactly been supportive. I worry about my evaluation."

"Talk to Lewis about that. He'll tell you how to handle it. Janet had it out for him the minute he stepped into the school."

"I don't understand her. Lewis is supernice. He works hard. The kids seem to like him."

"Lewis wouldn't do what Janet told him to do. He's very idealistic. He'll do what's best for the kids, even if it gets him into trouble. Janet doesn't know shit about instruction, but she wants to tell us how to teach, and we're supposed to respect her authority. Janet would've fired Lewis a long time ago if she could, but Lewis is a damn good teacher."

"Is Lewis, ... um ..."

"Gay?"

"Yes. I'm not trying to be rude. I was just wondering."

"He's out, but he doesn't broadcast it. I give him a lot of credit for staying here. This isn't the most open place on the planet."

"Well, I'm glad he's here."

Rick nodded.

"Did you ever talk to Caleb?" Gwen asked.

"I did. He denied being bullied. I also talked to Shane and Lance and a few other guys. They all denied that Caleb was being bullied."

"What about Jamar?"

"Jamar told me that an incident happened on the last day of football camp. Apparently, Shane and Lance accused Caleb of looking at Shane's penis. Jamar said some kids laughed, and Shane stood there naked, and Lance had his arm around Caleb. Jamar said he told Lance to let Caleb go, and he did. I asked Jamar if they hurt Caleb, and Jamar said he wasn't sure. He said it looked like they were just messing with him."

"That's almost identical to what Caleb wrote about," Gwen said, leaning forward on the table.

"I know, but what am I supposed to do about it? Caleb says nothing happened. Everyone except for Jamar says nothing happened. If I were to pursue something, Janet would twist this like a pretzel. Caleb would probably end up in trouble for sexually harassing Shane for staring at his penis. Then there's the embarrassment factor. I guarantee you Caleb just wants to forget about it."

Gwen sighed. "You're probably right."

Gwen and Rick talked and laughed, ate their food, and had another round of drinks. Rick picked up the tab despite Gwen's protests.

"You bought me Subway the other night," Gwen said.

"I invited you out. It's only fair that I pay," Rick replied.

Outside, in the gravel parking lot, Gwen felt a little woozy. They walked toward their vehicles, since they had driven in separate cars from the school. The sky was jam-packed with sparkly stars. They stopped in front of Gwen's Volkswagen.

"I think my drinks were a little heavy on the rum," Gwen said.

"Are you okay to drive?" Rick asked.

"I don't know. How long were we in there?"

Rick checked the clock on his phone. "It's 11:49. I think we got here around 10:40 or so."

"I should be fine. I only had two drinks."

"How much do you weigh?"

Gwen giggled. "That's not a polite question."

Rick smiled back. "For a blood-alcohol estimate."

"One thirty-five."

Rick tapped the voice command on his phone and said, "Blood alcohol calculator." He studied the screen. "Here's one." He tapped on his phone. "Female, 135 pounds, two drinks." Rick looked at Gwen. "Maybe I should put three, given how strong they were."

Gwen still felt a little woozy. "Good idea."

Rick went back to his phone. "Time passed in hours. We'll put half an hour. Now *calculate*. It says .117." Rick looked up from the screen. "You're officially drunk. I'll give you a ride home."

"Are *you* okay to drive?"

"I'm fine. I weigh 210, and I was only drinking beer."

"What about my car?"

"Do you have to go anywhere tomorrow morning?"

"No. I need to go to the grocery store, but that can wait."

"I have films in the morning, but I can come by around lunch and give you a ride back here."

Gwen hopped into Rick's truck and put on her seat belt.

"Where do you live?" Rick asked.

"Right in town," Gwen replied. "You know the apartments?"

"Glen View Apartments? The converted row homes?"

"Yes."

Rick drove Gwen away from the bar, toward town. A few minutes later, blue-and-red lights flashed in his rearview mirror. Rick glanced at his speedometer.

"I'm not speeding," he said as he pulled off the road and parked on the shoulder. Rick powered down his window and cut the engine. He leaned over Gwen, rifled through his glovebox, and removed his registration and insurance card. "This is bullshit."

"Good thing *I* wasn't driving," Gwen said.

"The cops around here raise extra money through excessive ticketing." Rick shook his head. "It's not like people here are rich. I know people who couldn't afford to pay and ended up in jail."

"Like debtor's prison?"

"Exactly."

The police officer sauntered to the open window with a lit flashlight. He shone the flashlight in the cab, snooping with his eyes. "License, registration, and insurance."

Rick handed the officer his documents.

"You know why I pulled you over?" the middle-aged cop said.

Rick blew out a breath. "No."

"Someone called and said you were drivin' erratically."

"Who? Nobody's on the road."

"You been drinkin' tonight?"

"I had two beers."

"How big were them beers?"

"They were bottles. Normal-size bottles."

"We'll see about that. Wait here." The cop went back to his cruiser with Rick's documents.

Rick looked at Gwen. "You all right?"

"I'm fine," Gwen replied. "Are *you* okay?"

Rick shook his head. "I don't like being harassed for no reason. It really gets under my skin."

"Just try to be calm."

The cop returned to Rick's open window. "Step out of the vehicle."

Rick opened the door and stepped out. He towered over the short and rotund cop. The officer held an electronic device with a tube attached.

"Blow into the tube for about four seconds. I'll tell ya when to go and when to stop." The cop held the device up to Rick's mouth. "Go on. Put your mouth on that hose and blow. I'll tell you when to stop."

Rick did as he was instructed, blowing into the hose, emptying his lungs.

"Stop," the cop said, removing the device from Rick's mouth, checking the digital readout. "Point zero three six. Looks like you're okay. Drive carefully now. You never know who's watchin'." The cop reached into his breast pocket and returned Rick's documents.

Rick took them without a word and returned to his truck.

"I'm assuming you passed?" Gwen asked.

Rick nodded, gripping the steering wheel, his knuckles white. "Before he returned my license and registration, he said, 'Drive carefully. You never know who's watching.'"

Gwen stared at his hands. "Are you okay?"

Rick let go of the steering wheel. "I'm fine. I can't stand people who abuse their power. This guy came out of nowhere. I wasn't speeding."

"The roads were empty too. I don't remember seeing any cars since we left the Toad's Stool."

"I wasn't weaving or anything either. Did he just wanna shake me down, see if I had any outstanding tickets?"

"Unless someone *did* call."

Rick's eyes widened. "*Janet.*"

"You think she called the police on us?"

"I wouldn't put it past her. Think about it. She was at the game. A game where her son sat on the bench and his replacement played great."

"But how would she know we went to the Toad's Stool together?"

Rick shook his head. "I don't know. Maybe she followed us there."

"You really think she'd do that?"

Rick deadpanned, "Yes."

Rick obeyed the traffic laws as he drove the rest of the way to Gwen's apartment. She pointed out her row house, and Rick parked in a visitor's space.

Gwen looked at Rick, her eyes unblinking. "Thank you for taking me home. You might've saved my job. I don't even wanna think about what would've happened if I was driving."

"You're welcome." Rick wanted to lean over the bench seat and kiss her, but she was too far away. "I'll walk you up."

"That's not necessary."

But Rick was already out of the truck. They walked up the metal steps to her one-bedroom apartment. They were quiet, both sensing what might happen. On the landing now, Gwen retrieved her keys from her purse. She lingered, fiddling with her keys.

"Thanks again, Rick," she said. "I had fun."

He leaned down and pressed his lips to hers. Gwen put her arms around his lower back and pulled him closer, her lips parting, their tongues touching. She felt woozy again, but this time it wasn't the booze. Rick stepped back. Gwen smiled and chewed on her lower lip. *He's blushing.*

"I'll see you tomorrow? For your car," he said.

Gwen nodded, blushing herself.

"Good night, Gwen." He turned and started down the steps. He stumbled and grabbed the railing.

Gwen giggled.

Rick looked back at Gwen, shaking his head with a smile. "I'd like to blame that on the beer, but you just saw me pass a breathalyzer."

CHAPTER 42

Caleb and Suicide Stats

Suicide wasn't so simple. Caleb lay on his bed, researching suicide, the only light coming from his phone. It was oddly comforting, like he was taking charge, solving his own problems. He knew from his prior research that committing suicide was problematic. But now he dug much deeper into the topic, and it was even more difficult and fraught with danger than he first thought. Not the danger that he'd kill himself but the danger that he'd try to kill himself, then instead make himself sick, brain-dead, or seriously injured.

In fact, for every successful suicide attempt, thirty-three failed. He was already zero for one with his weak-ass Ambien overdose. Actually, the odds were even worse for someone Caleb's age, somewhere between one hundred and two hundred to one. Old people were apparently pretty good at suicide, with successful attempts at a ratio of four to one. Grandpa was batting .250.

A post on Lostallhope.com listed the twenty-eight most lethal ways to kill yourself. It even listed the percentage of lethality, how long it takes to die expressed in minutes, and how much it will hurt on a scale of one to one hundred, with one hundred being the most painful. This was not looking good. A shotgun blast to the head was the most lethal, with a 99-percent success rate. *That's better than condoms.* But it wasn't instant. It took 1.7 minutes to die on average. *That must feel like an eternity.* Although the pain measurement registered only 5.5. *That's gotta hurt more than that.*

Number two was cyanide, with a similar success rate and time to death, but the pain number was fifty-two. *Ten times worse than a shotgun blast to the head. No thanks.* Hanging took like seven minutes with a 90-percent success rate. *No way I'm choking for that long.* Number twelve was setting yourself on fire. It took almost an hour to die. *An hour!* The pain was excruciating too—ninety-five out of one hundred. Jumping off a bridge took almost five minutes to die, with a 93-percent success rate.

You always see women in the movies, slicing their wrists in the bathtub, and some guy showing up and pulling the woman out of the bloodred water. But only 6 percent of people who slice their wrists are successful. And it takes forever—105 minutes—and hurts like hell, registering seventy-one out of one hundred on the pain meter.

Overdosing on illegal drugs was number twenty-one, with a 50-percent success rate, but it had the lowest pain rating. He could always try again if it didn't hurt too bad. *Ambien's a legal drug. Maybe I need an illegal drug. I don't weigh very much. I've never taken drugs before. Maybe it would be easy for me to overdose. I could just fall asleep. I'd have to figure out where to get 'em and what kind would work best. And how the hell am I gonna pay for 'em?*

Caleb put his phone on the bedside table. He rolled to his side and pulled his knees to his chest. He envisioned finding the perfect drug to overdose on or the right bridge to jump off or the correct way to blow his brains out. The bottom line was, the options each posed risks and obstacles he'd have to overcome. If he wanted to do it, which he did, he'd have to be creative and daring. He needed a foolproof, instantaneous, pain-free solution.

This was the problem that consumed him: the holy grail of suicide. He had to find it.

CHAPTER 43

Rick's Compromising Position

Rick hummed along with the country music crooner, a smile plastered on his face. He slowed his truck, the turn to his neighborhood approaching. Headlights shone in his rearview window. As he turned, he glanced through the passenger window, and caught a glimpse of a sedan. *Is that … ?* It was dark, no streetlights here, so he couldn't be sure, but the car looked like a blue BMW. The same car that Janet drove.

He eased off the gas, thinking about turning around and following *her*. Rick shook his head. *I'm being paranoid.* As he put his foot on the gas pedal, his mind drifted back to Gwen and that kiss. He cranked the country tune and grinned. Rick parked in his driveway and bounded to his front door and into his house, still humming that tune. He tossed his keys on the kitchen counter and went to his bedroom. Normally he was exhausted by Friday night, but he felt energized. He undressed and hopped in the shower. With the *whoosh* of the water shielding the truth, his humming turned into unabashed awful singing.

A door shut. Rick stopped singing. *Was that a car door? Or was that my front door? Shit. Did I lock my door?* He mentally retraced his steps into his house. *Did I turn the dead bolt?* He couldn't remember. He had tried to keep his door locked after Heather's uninvited visit, but it wasn't a habit yet, and he often forgot.

"Rick?" a female called out.

Rick's eyes widened. He shut off the water and exited the shower. He wrapped a towel around his waist, not bothering to dry off. He stepped into his bedroom. Ashlee Miles lay on his bed, her boots on the floor, her long dark hair spread out on his pillow. Thankfully, she still wore her jeans and fleece.

Rick held on to his towel, his face taut, water dripping on the floor.

Ashlee sat up, grinning. "Wow, look at you. If you evened out that farmer tan, you'd be perfect.

"You've got three seconds to get out of my house, or I'm calling the police."

She giggled. "What are you gonna tell them? That you invited me into your house, then took off all your clothes in front of me?"

"You broke into my house uninvited. You know that."

She pursed her lips. "The door was unlocked."

Rick thought about what might happen if he called the police. An underaged girl in his house. An *unstable* underaged girl. One who had his cell phone number and probably her DNA in his truck. *All that hair. She probably left at least one behind.* "You need to leave, *now.*"

"I've had a crush on you since I was little. Did you know that?"

"Ashlee, please—"

"I hated the piano, but I kept coming because sometimes I saw you. I used to get so jealous when you'd kiss Lindsey. She was so beautiful, and I was just this little pudgy girl." Ashlee smiled wide. "Look at me now." She cocked her head, striking a little pose.

"I'm serious about calling the police." Rick's voice was unsure.

"I don't think you are." Ashlee wagged her head. "I still can't believe you fucked my mother. *Gross.* She's in good shape and all, but she's kind of like a little man. All those muscles." Ashlee twisted her mouth in disgust. "Her face isn't near as pretty as mine either."

"I'm sorry that I had a relationship with your mother. It was a mistake."

"I knew it! Well, I didn't really know, but I suspected." She grinned. "I know now."

Rick pinched the bridge of his nose. "If you leave now, we can forget about this. Nobody has to get into trouble."

"Don't you think I'm pretty?" She pouted with those luscious lips.

"You are a pretty *girl*—"

"Then why did you block me?" Ashlee asked. "Didn't you like the picture I sent you?"

"I blocked you because you're a child. There's *nothing* between us."

She winced as if she'd been slapped. "A child? I'm more of a woman than my mother, yet you *fucked* her."

"Ashlee, stop this right now. I want you to leave." He pointed to his bedroom doorway.

"You gave me a ride and your phone number. I see how you look at me. I know what you're thinking."

Rick clenched his jaw. "You're delusional. You have two choices. You can walk out of here, and we can forget all about this, or I'll drag you out myself."

"You are so *hot* when you're angry."

"What's it gonna be?"

"You could have me." She bit the corner of her lower lip. "It'll be our little secret."

Rick moved to the bedside. "Get up."

"We can do it standing up."

Rick grabbed her under her armpit and pulled her from his bed. She fell to the floor.

She giggled again, sitting on the floor now. "So forceful."

"Get up. It's time to go."

Ashlee took off her fleece, revealing a tight T-shirt, displaying her ample cleavage. Rick blew out a breath and stepped closer, reaching to grab her. As he did so, she opened the overlap of his towel, catching a glimpse of his penis.

"Goddammit, Ashlee. Stop it," Rick said, hoisting her to her feet.

"Nice package," she said, smiling, still in Rick's grasp.

Rick grabbed her upper arm and pulled her from the room.

"*Ow*, stop it," she said, her face twisted into a scowl. "Let go. I'll walk myself."

Rick released her arm.

She walked down the hall as if she were window shopping, looking at the framed photos that decorated the hallway. Mostly pictures of his mother and football photos from his playing and coaching days. She stopped in front of a cluster of photos from college.

"Let's go," Rick said. "I'm not messing around."

She plucked a photo from the wall. Rick, a freshman in college, shirtless with two of his buddies after practice. "Can I keep this?"

"Put it back."

She ran toward the door, laughing.

Rick didn't chase her. He knew that was what she wanted. She stood in the foyer, the frame now on the floor, the photo nowhere to be found.

"Gimme the picture," Rick said.

She pursed her lips. "It's in a safe place. You can come and get it, if you want."

Rick grabbed her arm and pulled her to the front door.

"*Ow*, you're hurting me," she said.

When he opened the door, he had to reach around Ashlee, almost like an embrace. She took advantage of this, planting a kiss on his lips.

CHAPTER 44

Janet, the Photographer

Janet had been careful, following far behind, cutting her lights where possible, not worrying about losing him, given the nonexistent traffic. She'd followed Rick from Garden Grove to school, then to the Toad's Stool, then to Gwen's after that fat fuck cop let Rick go. That had really pissed her off. She'd slammed her palms on her steering wheel and screamed, "Motherfucker!" Then Gwen and Rick had had that syrupy-sweet kiss. Janet had imagined their heads exploding, like a watermelon at a rifle range. Not that she'd ever seen a watermelon at a rifle range or even been to a rifle range. She was antigun.

On the way to Rick's house, she'd gotten a little too close. Janet hadn't realized how slow he was driving. He might've seen her car as he'd turned into his neighborhood, but so what? Other blue BMWs were on the road. Janet had driven past, then turned around, before entering Rick's neighborhood. She'd parked down the street from his house, her lights off, with a decent view of his driveway.

Janet had hoped to find out if he was seeing someone other than Gwen. If so, Janet would take pictures and ruin their cute little relationship. It wasn't uncommon for attractive men to have respectable dates followed by a booty call. Janet had fiddled with her iPhone, reducing the exposure levels to help with the possible nighttime picture.

Janet had surfed her phone while she waited. She'd clicked the

Facebook notification from the West Lake Watchdog. She had to admit. She loved the West Lake Watchdog. Janet had read the post, bashing Rick's play calling in the first half of the Garden Grove game. The author had speculated that Rick didn't make the calls in the second half and was, once again, benefitting from the team's great talent, and the kids were being held back by poor coaching.

Janet had heard the rumble of an engine. She'd looked up from her phone to see a white Jeep park in Rick's driveway. Janet knew of only one white Jeep. It had been the talk of the town when Ashlee Miles's rich daddy had bought it for her.

Janet had felt a wave of euphoria and excitement. She'd exited her car and hurried to his house, hiding behind a tree with a good view of the front door. She had hoped for a picture of the girl's arrival, but Ashlee had already gone inside. Thankfully, the porch and garage lights had been on. Janet was no stranger to the difficulties of nighttime photography. When she had suspected her second husband was cheating, she had contacted a private investigator, but they were too expensive, so she'd had to DIY the investigation.

She'd followed her second husband to his whore's house. Janet had gotten great shots then but had learned the hard way about nighttime photography. None of the pictures had shown up, so she'd had to do it again. The second time had been much better. She'd learned that you had to have some light and you had to lower the exposure on the camera or the light you did have would turn the picture into a big white blurry mess.

But this time she had been ready and waiting. In fact, she had been poised for the shot, because she had heard Ashlee cry out. She had said something like, "*Ow*, you're hurting me."

When the door opened, Janet started shooting. Janet's eyes widened at Rick in his towel, and Ashlee planting a kiss on his lips. Rick pushed Ashlee onto the stoop and slammed the door in her face. Janet continued to take pictures. Ashlee stood, shoeless, wearing a tight T-shirt and jeans.

"Hey, I need my boots and my fleece," Ashlee said, banging on the door. She took a step back, her hands on her curvy hips. She pounded on the door again and said, "Oh, Rick, you felt so good." Then she said it louder, nearly shouting. "Oh, Rick, you gave it to me so good."

"Shut up," Rick said, from the other side of the front door. "I'll get your stuff."

Janet thought about switching to video, but she'd never tried to video at night. She worried it wouldn't come out, so she stayed silent, mostly shielded by the tree, but poised to shoot again when Rick showed his face. But he didn't. Rick simply opened the door just enough to toss a pair of boots and a fleece onto the stoop.

Janet watched Ashlee put on her boots and drive away in her Jeep. Janet crept back to her car and scrolled through the photos. A wide grin spread across her face. *Gotcha!*

CHAPTER 45

Gwen and a Change of Scenery

Leaves rustled overhead. To their left, ducks bobbed in the lake, dunking their heads and letting the water roll down their backs. Gravel crunched under their feet as Gwen and Rick walked on the trail. They were dressed for the occasion in jeans, hiking boots, and sweatshirts. Rick wore his worn WL Football hat.

"Look at the turtles," Gwen said, pointing and smiling at the four turtles sunbathing on a floating log.

Rick smiled at Gwen. "I used to come here all the time, but I haven't been in years."

"Why not?"

Rick shrugged. "Who am I gonna ask? Bob? I doubt he's up for a romantic hike."

Gwen raised her eyebrows. "Is that what this is?"

Rick turned beet red. "You know what I mean. I'm not even sure I'd invite him over to watch football at this point. He's been acting really strange. I had to call the plays in the second half of Garden Grove. He's been different ever since I benched Shane."

"Maybe he really likes Shane?"

"As far as I know, he doesn't have a close relationship with Shane. Unless ..." Rick stopped in his tracks.

Gwen stopped, facing him. "Unless what?"

Rick pinched the bridge of his nose. "Unless Janet has something to do with it."

"Like what?"

"I don't know. Maybe I'm being paranoid, but, after I left your apartment on Friday, I swear I thought I saw her blue BMW."

"Do you really think she'd stalk you because you benched her son?"

"I wouldn't put it past her."

"So, you think she's putting pressure on Bob somehow?"

"Maybe. I don't know. Bob's under a lot of stress. He has a new baby at home. I know he worries a lot about money."

"You may want to talk to him about it."

"Yeah." Rick nodded. "It may come to that, but I can't imagine he'd admit it."

They turned and restarted their hike, walking side by side. A blue jay chirped on a low-hanging branch. Rick's hand barely brushed against Gwen's as their arms gently swayed.

"Thank you," he said.

"For what?" she asked.

Rick took Gwen's hand, gently in his, not breaking stride. "It's been the best weekend I've had in a long time."

Gwen smiled, the corners of her mouth turning up for a second. "Me too."

They crossed a wooden footbridge, the creek underneath flowing into the lake, a bit of white water created by the submerged rocks. Gwen and Rick stopped in the middle of the bridge, leaning on the railing and taking in the view.

"This is my favorite spot," Rick said.

"I can see why." Gwen took in the scene: the green leaves overhanging the creek, the flowing water, the expanse of blue lake in the backdrop, the sounds of squirrels scurrying on the forest floor, and the quacks and honks from the waterfowl. "It must've been wonderful to grow up around all this natural beauty."

"It's not all creeks and ducks and turtles. We also have meth, poverty, and small-town politics."

"I don't know that suburbia's any better. I grew up with cookie-cutter houses, strip malls, and fast-food restaurants. Probably why I was overweight as a kid. I could've used a little more time outdoors."

Rick turned to her with a furrowed brow. "You were overweight?"

She nodded. "Sad but true. I know I'm a healthy weight now, but I still see that fat girl in the mirror."

"I see a woman who's beautiful, inside and out."

Gwen looked down, her face hot.

"Sorry. I didn't mean to …"

She looked back to Rick. "Don't apologize. It's sweet of you to say. Of course, I'm the one who needs to believe it." She took a deep breath and stood up straight, still gazing at the creek flowing into the lake. "What about you? What was it like being Mr. Football?"

"I was hardly Mr. Football."

Gwen had a crooked smile. "That's not what I heard."

Rick smiled back. "I see you're fitting right into rural life. Gossiping with the townies."

Gwen bumped her hip to his. "I wasn't gossiping. … Well, maybe a little. Lewis told me that you were like a football God around here."

"Lewis is exaggerating. I guess I was decent for around here. Everybody thought I'd be the first kid to get a D-one scholarship, but there wasn't much interest. I got a partial scholarship to Wingate College in Charlotte. It's a Division II school. Even at D-two, I wasn't prepared for the competition. I was used to being the big fish in a small pond. I did win the starting job my junior year, and I had a decent season, but I tore my rotator cuff in the first game of my senior year. That was it." Rick snapped his fingers. "Just like that, it was over. I never threw a football again." He blew out a heavy breath and leaned forward, his hands on the railing. "After I finished my degree, I came back home, my tail between my legs."

She put her hand on top of his. "You played football at a very high level. You finished your degree, and, from all my *gossiping*, I heard you're a really great teacher and coach."

"I suppose that depends on who you talk to." Rick forced a smile. "It all worked out in the end. The high school PE teacher was retiring, and I got the job. It was for the best anyway. My mom got sick, and I was here to be with her when she died."

"I'm sorry. ... I didn't know about your mom."

"It was years ago but thanks."

"Are you an only child?"

"Yes and no. My parents divorced when I was five. My father remarried, had a couple kids, but they were never really in my life. For the most part, it was just me and my mom. She never married after my father left." He paused for a moment. "What about you? Are your parents in Philly?"

Gwen frowned for an instant. "They live in King of Prussia."

"Any brothers or sisters?"

"One sister." She was blank-faced.

"You don't seem too enthusiastic about your family. Is that why you're here?"

Gwen shook her head. "I guess I needed a change of scenery."

Rick nodded.

After an awkward silence, Rick pushed off the railing and stood up straight. He held out his hand to Gwen. "You ready?"

She placed her hand in his, flashed a brief smile, and they continued on their hike.

CHAPTER 46

Caleb and Ice

It wasn't hard to find Aaron Fuller on Instagram. Drew Fuller, his brother and the team's best defensive player, was followed on Instagram by most of the football team, and Aaron also followed his big brother. Caleb figured the Fuller brothers probably conducted business via DM on Snapchat, given that messages were deleted after they're viewed by both parties. The only problem was, Caleb didn't know Drew or Aaron's Snapchat username. Fortunately, Aaron used the same Snapchat username that he used on Instagram. So Caleb sent Aaron a DM.

CalebMiles245: This is Caleb Miles. We played FB together freshman year. I need some stuff from Drew.

Caleb wasn't sure what to call drugs, but he knew it would probably piss off the Fuller brothers if Caleb mentioned "drugs" online, so he went with "stuff." He wasn't sure when or if he'd get a response. *Did drug dealers work on Sunday?* A response came a few minutes later.

AaronDowntoClown: You a narc?
CalebMiles245: ??? No. Just need stuff
AaronDowntoClown: You got money?

Caleb had eight dollars and some change.

CalebMiles245: Some
AaronDowntoClown: Come to my house at 7 tonight. Knock on back door. Know where it is?
CalebMiles245: No
AaronDowntoClown: 230 Riverside Drive West Lake
CalebMiles245: I'll be there
AaronDowntoClown: You better not be wasting my fucking time
CalebMiles245: I won't

Caleb sat on his bed, the afternoon sun shining through his bedroom window. He set his phone on the bedside table. He heard Ashlee shut her bedroom door, followed by her footsteps down the hall. He heard her exit their double-wide trailer, then the roar of her Jeep. The trailer was quiet now. Caleb stood, stepped to his bedroom door, opened it, and peered down the hall. His mother's door was shut. She was at the gym. Caleb walked down the hall and entered Ashlee's room, shutting her door behind him.

The walls were painted lavender. The king-size canopy bed, with the thick purple comforter, dominated the room. Her dresser and vanity were made of real wood. Not that pressboard shit he had. He looked through her drawers, under her bed, in her closet, but he didn't find any money. He opened her jewelry box. It was filled with gold and silver necklaces, bracelets, and gemstone earrings. Caleb had never seen Ashlee wear this jewelry. Caleb had no idea how much the jewelry was worth, but her dad had bought it for her, so it must be worth something. He took a gold necklace near the bottom of the box. *Hopefully she won't notice that it's gone.*

Caleb went back to his room with the necklace in the front pocket of his jeans. Riverside Drive wasn't that far away. Caleb figured he could walk there in fifteen minutes. He checked the time on his phone—5:37. Caleb went to the living room and turned on his PlayStation. He had bought the PlayStation 2 a few years ago off a guy on Craigslist. Paid twenty bucks for a twelve-year-old console, but the guy hadn't used it in a long time, so it still worked. He even threw in the games. Caleb played Grand Theft Auto. He stole cars, assaulted and murdered innocent bystanders, ran from the cops, and drove wildly through the mean streets of Vice City.

An hour later, Caleb left his trailer with eight bucks and a gold necklace. The sun was orange and low on the horizon. His stomach twisted in knots as he pounded the pavement. By the time he reached Riverside Drive, he began to sweat, the smell of fear emanating from his pores. It wasn't that hot, but he felt warm and nauseated.

Caleb continued on Riverside, finally stopping in front of house number 230, a rusted single-wide trailer. It looked like a shipping container with windows. Caleb checked the time on his phone—6:57. He walked around back, the smell of dog shit intensifying. A pit bull barked and jumped on the chain-link fence. Caleb flinched, stepping back. Drew Fuller lay on a bench, pushing a mountain of weight off his chest, seemingly impervious to the barking and growling. On his last repetition, he was red-faced, veins popping, as he slammed the barbell on the rack. Drew sat up, shirtless, the blood draining from his face, his chest and shoulders covered with tattoos. He glared at Caleb or maybe the dog and stood. He was average height, but he had a commanding presence and a bodybuilder's physique.

"Shut the fuck up," he shouted, as he walked across the spotty lawn.

The dog stopped barking and turned to Drew.

"Go lay down," Drew said. The dog loped toward the patio and Drew's outdoor gym. Drew approached Caleb with narrowed eyes, his upper body swollen with blood. "Caleb fuckin' Miles."

Caleb nodded, keeping his distance.

"Aaron told me that you were lookin' for some gay porn."

Caleb opened his mouth but nothing came out.

Drew smiled and opened the gate. "I'm just fuckin' with you. Watch your step. Fuckin' land mines everywhere."

Caleb followed Drew across the lawn, if you could call it that. It looked like a war zone. Land mines of dog shit in various stages of decay. Holes of various sizes. Patches of compacted dirt and super-green weeds, supercharged by urea. They stepped onto the brick patio, moving past the weights. Drew stopped at the back door and turned to Caleb.

"Gimme the money," Drew said.

Caleb furrowed his brows. "How much?"

"Depends on what you want."

"I need something that'll really mess me up. Like the stuff you gotta be careful not to, like, overdose."

A crooked grin spread across Drew's face. "You for real?"

"Yeah, I, uh, wanna get really fucked-up."

"Let's see how much you got."

Caleb retrieved the money from his pocket and handed it to Drew. He flipped through the bills and scowled at Caleb.

"You think this is the fuckin' Dollar Store?" Drew shook his head, still holding Caleb's money. "Get the fuck outta my face."

Caleb reached into his pocket and removed the gold necklace. "I got this." He held up the necklace.

"This shit real?" Drew asked, snatching the necklace.

"I got it off my sister, Ashlee. Her dad bought it for her."

"Didn't her dad buy her that sweet-ass whip?"

"Yeah. The Jeep."

Drew nodded. "On the real, she's fuckin' fine."

"She's a bitch."

"Ain't that the truth. They're all bitches. I'd still fuck the shit out of her. She still fuckin' college-boy Ryan?"

"I think they broke up."

"I heard that shit, but you never know with these hoes. Can't never make up their fuckin' minds. Let's do our business inside." Drew turned, opened the door, and stepped inside.

Caleb followed. The trailer was a wreck. Dirty dishes filled the sink and overflowed on the kitchen counter. Junk mail was strewn about the coffee table in the living room. The dingy couch had stuffing spilling from the armrests. It smelled like body odor, smoke, and skunk.

Drew shouted down the hallway. "Aaron, get your ass out here."

Aaron appeared, walking down the hall from a back bedroom. He wore jeans and a white tank top. A pit bull with bared teeth was tattooed on his upper arm. It was red and irritated around the edges, the tatt obviously brand-new.

"Get your boy a small bag of ice," Drew said to Aaron.

Aaron furrowed his brows. "You sure?"

"He wants to get fucked-up." Drew went back outside to his workout.

Aaron turned his attention to Caleb. "Follow me."

They moved down the hall to the bedrooms. One door was locked with a padlock. Aaron's bedroom was surprisingly neat and well-appointed. He had a MacBook and an iPhone on his desk. One wall had an entertainment center with an ultra-HD television and a PS4 game console.

"Wait here," Aaron said, going to the locked bedroom. He opened the lock with a key and entered the room. He returned with a small plastic baggie of bluish rocks. Aaron handed it to Caleb. "You wanna get fucked-up? This'll fuck you up."

Caleb looked at the little crystalline rocks. "Do you swallow them?"

Aaron laughed. "Are you fucking with me?"

Caleb remembered Shane and Lance and Drew smoking from a pipe in the school bathroom. "You smoke it?"

"What the fuck else you gonna do with it? I'm assuming you ain't got a pipe?"

"No."

Aaron went back to the other room and returned with a Bic lighter and a small glass pipe, open on one end, a small bowl at the other. The bowl end was blackened.

"Is this crystal meth?" Caleb asked, holding up the baggie.

"You said you wanted to get fucked-up. Crystal meth'll definitely fuck you up."

"Can it kill you?"

"If you take too much, but I'll show you how much to take." Aaron took two small rocks and deposited them into the pipe. "Hold the pipe like this," Aaron said, holding the pipe horizontally. "Take it."

Caleb took the pipe, holding it like Aaron instructed.

"Now heat up the rocks with the lighter and inhale that shit." Aaron handed the lighter to Caleb. "Put your mouth on the pipe."

Caleb lit the glass bowl, his mouth on the pipe, his heart pounding in his chest. *I'm doing meth!* Smoke moved from the bowl down the pipe and into Caleb's mouth and lungs. It tasted bitter. Caleb coughed, smoke spilling from his mouth and nostrils.

Aaron laughed again.

Caleb's heart pounded harder; he felt energized, a rush of euphoria washing over him.

"Feels good, don't it?" Aaron said.

It did. For the first time in a long time, Caleb felt good.

CHAPTER 47

Rick and Blackmail

Shortly after the bell rang, while his health students filtered out, his classroom phone rang.

Rick picked up the phone attached to the wall. "Rick Barnett," he said.

"Mr. Barnett, this is Principal Wilcox—"

"What do you want, Janet?"

"That's Principal Wilcox—"

"I don't care. I know who you are, *Janet*."

"You need to come to my office immediately."

"I'm busy."

"This is your planning period."

"Yeah, I'm busy planning."

"If you value your job, I expect to see you within the next five minutes." She hung up.

Rick sighed and hung up the phone. He locked his empty classroom and waded through the students as they went to their lockers and switched classes. Rick walked into the main office, waved to Mrs. Moyer as he passed the front desk, and headed for Janet's back office. Rick knocked on the open door. Janet looked up from her laptop as if she hadn't been expecting him.

"Shut the door," Janet said.

Rick shut the door and sat across from her at her desk. "What do you want?"

Janet pursed her lips and shut her laptop. She wore a black dress with a plunging neckline, exposing cleavage that would be unacceptable for a student. Her blond bangs hung over her forehead, covering her wrinkles.

"What do you think I want?" she asked.

"I don't have time for games, Janet. I'm busy."

"I'm not happy that you benched my son without cause. He's a senior, and he deserves to be treated with respect. I'm willing to forgive the transgression of last Friday, but I want you to start Shane for the rest of this football season."

Rick clenched his jaw, gripping the armrests. "And if I don't?"

Janet pushed a manila folder across the desk. "I'll expose you."

Rick opened the folder. An eight-by-eleven photograph was inside of Rick standing in his doorway, wearing nothing but a towel, and Ashlee clearly kissing him on the mouth.

"This is bullshit." Rick shut the folder and slapped it back on Janet's desktop. "I didn't do anything. She broke into my house. I was in the shower. I kicked her out. I didn't kiss her. She kissed me. And, if you took that picture, you'd know that, because I pushed her away."

"I can't say where I got the picture, but they didn't mention anything about the kiss being unwanted. For heaven's sake, you're naked with a student in the middle of the night. It doesn't look good. I have to say, I'm extremely disappointed." She smirked for a split second.

Rick shook his head, scowling. *She's enjoying this.* "You took the picture, didn't you? I thought I saw your car following me after the game on Friday. You called the police, told them I was drinking and driving. Didn't you? All this because I benched your son. You really are a piece of shit, you know that?"

Janet cackled. "But you're the piece of shit who's having an affair with a student, and everybody in this town will know what you did, including Gwen Townsend." She paused, adjusting her glasses. "Just put Shane back in. Is it really worth your career? Your reputation? Your freedom? You could go to jail."

Rick stood from his seat and glared at his boss. "This is corrupt, even for you. I won't be blackmailed. You can take your threats and shove 'em up your ass."

CHAPTER 48

Janet and Holier Than Thou

All he had to do was one simple thing. So fucking holier than thou. A knock came from Janet's door.

"Come in," Janet said.

Rachel stepped inside, shut the door behind her, and sat across from Janet at her desk. "I came as quick as I could. What in the world is going on?"

"I need you to get a message to our Facebook friend."

"What's the message?"

"It's about Rick Barnett. He's having an affair with a student."

"Oh, my word." Rachel's eyes were wide.

She was the same age as Janet, forty-five. They'd been classmates, but they weren't friends growing up. Janet was popular and pretty; Rachel was not. Janet probably had made fun of Rachel in school, not that Janet remembered. Rachel had been too insignificant to register. Now, a friendship with her had its benefits. The plump mom with the haircut and style, circa 1985, was an effective disseminator of gossip.

Janet continued. "He was seen at his front door, wearing nothing but a towel, kissing a scantily clad student. He's a sexual predator and has no business teaching students. He belongs behind bars."

CHAPTER 49

Gwen and Influence

Gwen knocked on the open door of the technology office. Greg Ebersole sat behind his desk, tapping on his cell phone and sipping a soda. He waved her in.

The technology office was a square room with long tables against the walls. Atop the tables, electronic equipment was charging, waiting for repair, or waiting to be loaned out.

Gwen approached Greg's metal desk. "I just came by to pick up that document camera."

Greg put up a finger, signaling for Gwen to wait. He continued to tap on his phone for a minute, while Gwen waited in silence. He adjusted his glasses and looked her over. "It's there, on the cart." He gestured toward the wall behind her.

"Thank you."

Gwen turned on her heels and walked to the cart. She felt his eyes crawling over her backside. She thought about her pencil skirt and bare legs. She glanced over her shoulder, and he stared with a smirk on his face, his phone pointed at her. She turned the cart and pushed toward the exit.

"You need to sign it out," Greg said.

Gwen stopped in her tracks and walked back to his desk, leaving the cart near the exit.

"Your legs are really white," Greg said. "I thought I was pale."

Gwen frowned.

He chuckled. "I'm just joking." He placed a form and a pen on the edge of his desk.

She leaned over and filled out the form. She glanced up, and he was looking down her blouse. Gwen stood abruptly, handing him the form. He took it with a crooked grin, his scruffy beard spreading across his face, hiding his weak chin underneath.

"You think you can figure this thing out on your own this time?" he asked.

"Don't worry. I won't ask you for help," she replied.

"Finally figured out the Input button, huh?"

"I have to go."

* * *

The bell rang, ending Gwen's creative writing class. The students packed their backpacks, grabbed their purses, and filed out. Caleb was the first to exit. Gwen suspected he was avoiding Shane and Lance.

"Don't forget to read," Gwen said. "Remember. If you want to be a good writer, you have to be a reader first."

Shane, Lance, Drew, and Aaron approached Gwen on the way out the door.

"Ms. Townsend, um, Lance doesn't know how to read," Shane said with a grin.

Drew and Aaron laughed.

"Shut the fuck up," Lance replied.

Drew and Aaron glanced at each other and stopped laughing.

"Language," Gwen said. "Go to class."

The boys filtered out, Lance and Shane walking out separately. Jamar put his backpack over his shoulders.

"Jamar, may I speak to you for a moment?" Gwen asked.

He approached with a broad smile, his retainer showing. "What's up, Ms. Townsend?"

"Are you friends with Caleb?"

"Yeah, we're friends, but we don't really hang out or anything. We hung out a little last year, but mostly he hung out with this girl Madison, but she moved."

"Why don't you hang out anymore?"

Jamar shrugged. "I don't know. I guess we're both busy. And now, with him not playing football, I don't see him much."

Gwen nodded. "I think he could really use a friend. And I think you could really help him by spending a little time with him."

Jamar pursed his lips. "I know what you're saying, Ms. Townsend, but Caleb's been kinda in his own world."

"Caleb's had it rough. I think you know that. You're very popular, Jamar. For better or worse, being the star quarterback in this school gives you a lot of influence. You could use that popularity for good."

CHAPTER 50

Caleb and GTA

Ashlee was at her friend's house, and Caleb's mother worked as a receptionist until six on Mondays. Well, the Mondays that she felt like going to work. She often needed to rest on those days, recovering from her busy, fun-filled weekends.

Caleb had taken advantage of the empty house, smoking meth as soon as he got home from school, then playing video games. For a few hours, the meth made him feel euphoric and dangerous and confident, providing a much-needed respite from his life. Caleb had thought he'd use it to overdose, but it worked better as an escape.

He sat on the couch, playing Grand Theft Auto. Caleb mimicked the sounds of car crashes and people being beaten as he wreaked havoc on Vice City. A knock came from the front door. Caleb paused the game, looking around, as if he'd heard incorrectly. Another knock sounded. Caleb went to the door. It was Jamar.

Caleb opened the door with wide eyes and a wide smile. He spoke faster than normal, almost manic. "Jamar, what's up? Come on in. What are you doing?" Caleb motioned him inside.

"You all right?" Jamar asked, stepping into the trailer.

"I'm great, man. You wanna play some GTA? I'm fucking killing it. Come on."

Jamar followed Caleb to the couch, sitting closer than Caleb expected.

"You wanna play?" Caleb held out the controller for Jamar. "I know this shit is old, but it's still badass."

"Nah, I'm good," Jamar replied. "I'll just watch you."

Caleb unpaused the game and continued his mayhem. Caleb gave the play by play, complete with sound effects, as he continued to commit crimes on the screen. "I stole a fucking tank. Can you believe that shit? You can literally run over everything, and they can't do shit."

"Really? You can get a tank?"

"I got one in my garage. I'll show you." In the game, Caleb drove an eighties Lamborghini to a garage. He parked it, got out, and hopped into the tank. Caleb proceeded to drive through the streets, running over people and destroying police cars. "Badass, huh? They can't do shit."

"Damn, that is badass."

"You sure you don't wanna try?"

"Yeah, I'll try."

Caleb paused the game and handed the controller to Jamar. "Don't lose my tank."

Jamar rumbled through the streets in the tank, picking up where Caleb had left off. He had a grin on his face, his mouth partially open, his eyes wide and trancelike on the screen. Caleb stared at his guest and smiled to himself, happy that he was happy. *His skin's so … beautiful. Like caramel.* Caleb's eyes roamed unabashed. Jamar's arms were lean and wiry, every muscle visible as he worked the controller. Caleb wanted to trace his fingers along Jamar's veins. His gaze returned to Jamar's face and those full lips, that thin black mustache. The perfect mix of man and boy. *He's not like the others.* Caleb sucked in Jamar's scent, his musky deodorant.

Jamar made it back to the garage with the tank, the military swarming just outside. "That tank is crazy." He handed the controller to Caleb, their hands touching in the exchange, the electricity charged between them. In that moment, that perfect moment, Caleb leaned in and pressed his lips to Jamar's.

Jamar nearly jumped from the couch, standing abruptly. "What the hell are you doing?"

"I'm sorry. I thought …" Caleb stood from the couch.

"I'm not like that." Jamar shook his head, his eyes glancing at Caleb's crotch. He took a step back, grimacing. "This is so messed up. Stay away from me." Jamar ran for the door, almost as fast as he ran for touchdowns.

Caleb looked down at his sweatpants, his erection creating a visible tent.

CHAPTER 51

Rick Takes a Hit

Rick should've known better. Shane had begged Rick to play free safety on the second-string defense. They were short a free safety due to injury, so Rick agreed. When the first-string offense began scrimmaging the second-string defense, Shane was at free safety, looking across the line at Jamar.

"You ain't shit," Shane said, as Jamar called out the cadence.

Jamar caught the snap and fired a rocket down the seam to the tight end. Shane was a split second late, touchdown.

On the next play, Shane taunted again. "Punk-ass bitch. You're lucky I can't hit you."

Jamar smiled at Shane as he called out the cadence. He caught the snap, checked his read on the defensive end, handed the football to the running back, and ran around the end, carrying out his fake. Shane sprinted from his free safety spot, ignoring the running back, with a full head of steam toward Jamar. Shane dipped his shoulder and nudged Jamar as he sprinted past. Jamar was unfazed.

"I woulda killed you," Shane said to Jamar as they passed each other on the way back to their huddles.

"You're too damn slow," Jamar replied with a crooked grin.

The next play was a sprint out pass, with Jamar rolling to his right and throwing a strike to Lance. This time, as soon as Jamar threw the ball, Shane slammed his shoulder into Jamar's back, knocking him to the ground. A few of the offensive linemen took offense.

"What the hell are you doin', Shane?" asked one of the linemen.

"Stay off the quarterback," Rick said to Shane.

"Yeah, stay off the quarterback," another lineman echoed.

Jamar popped up, turned to Shane, and glared. "It's like that?"

Shane laughed. "You need to learn how to take a hit."

Rick thought about pulling Shane, but Jamar seemed fine, and it was good for the team to see what Jamar was made of. It was good for the offensive linemen to protect and rally around their new sophomore quarterback. In retrospect, Rick was wrong.

On the following play, Coach Schneider called a quick toss. Rick was relieved when Jamar pitched the ball to the running back, knowing his quarterback was out of the play, but Jamar sprinted around the end. Shane loped toward the play, not interested in taking on their powerful running back and happy to let someone else make the play.

But Jamar had other ideas. Shane didn't see Jamar before it was too late. Shane was upright, unprotected, not expecting any action, but Jamar was like a rocket, his shoulders low and square, as he blasted into Shane's sternum. There was a *crack* of pads meeting, and Shane lay flat on his back, like he'd been run over by a freight train.

The team went crazy, laughing and jeering at the crushing block. Jamar stood over Shane, looking down on him. Shane staggered to his feet, face mask to face mask now.

"Maybe *you* need to learn how to take a hit," Jamar said.

"Fuck you, faggot," Shane replied, pushing Jamar.

Jamar tackled Shane to the ground. The boys wrestled on the ground, trading punches to the stomach. Rick and Coach Schneider pulled them apart.

"That's enough. Break it up," Rick said. "You two, twenty laps around the field."

Jamar and Shane looked at Rick with wide eyes.

"Go on. Get your asses moving. You got so much damn energy for fighting, it should be easy."

* * *

After practice, Rick walked across the parking lot to his truck. His mind inevitably focused on the meeting he'd had with Janet yesterday. He'd been on pins and needles, wondering what she had up her sleeve. His cell phone buzzed in his pocket. Inside his truck, he checked his phone. The text was from an unknown number.

717-555-9862: You belong in prison, you scumbag. **LINK**

His heart pounded, and his stomach twisted into knots as he clicked the link, leading him to the Facebook page, the West Lake Watchdog.

West Lake Watchdog
September 27 at 11:14 AM
I heard from people at the high school that Coach Barnett is having sex with a student. What a piece of shit! He was seen at his house butt naked kissing a female student. Rick is a perv. He should be in prison. **#FireBarnett** 11 Likes 4 Shares
Will Gilroy I'm not surprised. Bad coach. Worse person. **#FireBarnett** 5 Likes
Breanna Franks It's like Jerry Sandusky all over again. 4 Likes
Roger Elkins Damn right, Will and Breanna. He needs to go. NOW. **#FireBarnett** 2 Likes

Rick was relieved not to see a picture with the post. He sent a DM to the West Lake Watchdog.

Rick Barnett: Heather, I know you're running this page. What you posted is slander. I can sue you. If you don't take it down, I will.

Rick placed his phone in his cupholder, started his truck, and drove toward home. *Are people really gonna believe some stupid Facebook page?* He parked in his driveway and grabbed his phone from the cupholder. He made sure to lock his front door as he stepped inside. He showered and watched film of their upcoming opponent, but he was distracted, constantly glancing at his phone, waiting for a response from the West Lake Watchdog. *Maybe I should go to Heather's house. No. Ashlee might be there. It could go really bad.* His phone buzzed. He swiped right and checked his messages.

West Lake Watchdog: My source told me u can't sue if its true. They have a picture. As soon as I get the picture I'm gonna post it then ur life is over. Sucks to be u.

CHAPTER 52

Janet and Bending Wills

I bet he's a bit more receptive now. Janet strutted down the empty hallway, smiling to herself, thinking of the Facebook post and the growing demand to fire Barnett. She entered his classroom without knocking. Rick sat behind his desk and his laptop, but otherwise his classroom was empty during his planning period. She figured she'd try the element of surprise by showing up unannounced.

Rick stood from his desk and pointed to the door. "Get out of my classroom."

"That's not for you to decide," Janet replied as she sidled up to his desk. He looked tired. Bloodshot eyes with dark circles. *I bet he didn't sleep at all last night.* "You ready to make this go away?"

He glowered at Janet. "The truth'll come out. It always does."

"You're right about that, and I have the perfect *picture* of truth."

"Nobody gives a shit about those idiots on Facebook."

"We'll see. I heard that Jamar attacked Shane at practice yesterday. Fighting is an automatic suspension, and that means Jamar can't play this week."

"Jamar didn't start anything. They were both fighting."

"That's not what I heard from Coach Schneider and a number of players."

"Kids get in scuffles at practice all the time. That's football. It's not

174

a big deal. Nobody got hurt."

"Sounds like you can't control your team. If you won't write up Jamar, I'll do it myself. And then I'll make sure that picture falls into the right hands." Janet started to walk away.

"Wait."

Janet turned back to Rick with one side of her mouth raised in contempt.

Rick took a cleansing breath. "If I start Shane, will you let this bull-shit with Ashlee Miles go?"

"That's all I'm asking."

"What about the Facebook post?"

"If Shane starts, I'm sure it would all go away."

"Fine, but I want that shit off Facebook now."

"You'll have to deliver first." She turned on her heels and sauntered back to her office, a smile tugging on the corners of her mouth.

Janet shut her office door and sat behind her desk. She tapped the Cliff icon on her cell phone and leaned back, her phone to her ear.

"Janet. To what do I owe the pleasure?" Cliff said.

"Did you change your mind about helping me with Pastor Goode or Daub?"

"Did you change your mind about meeting me?"

Janet paused, the wheels turning in her mind. "How good is the information?"

Cliff chuckled. "Good enough to make a hooker blush."

"Do you have information on both of them?"

"You only need one seat."

"I'll take that as a no. I bet Pastor Goode's the one with the dirt."

Cliff chuckled again. "You let me know if you wanna find out. I have to go. I got business to attend—"

"I'll meet you. When and where?"

"Well then. How about this Saturday night around nine? Days Inn in Hershey."

"That's fine. I'll see you then."

"I can't wait. It'll be—"

Janet disconnected the call, not interested in being sold on the affair. She exhaled and closed her eyes, imagining what she'll have to do.

CHAPTER 53

Gwen's Divided Class

The desks were shoved against opposite walls, creating a dance-floor-size space in the middle of Gwen's classroom.

"Everyone for Trump move to the right," Gwen said. "Everyone for Hillary to the left, and everyone who's undecided stand in the middle."

Most of the boys along with half of the girls stood on the right. The other half of the girls and Jamar moved to the left. Caleb stood in the middle.

"Okay," Gwen said. "This is definitely a pro-Trump class." Gwen looked at the crowd of kids on the right. "Lance, can you tell us why you're a Trump supporter?"

"Because he tells it like it is," Lance replied. "Obama didn't care about us. That's why we don't have any jobs. Trump's gonna bring back jobs. He cares about people in towns like ours."

One girl from the Hillary camp switched sides.

"Very persuasive," Gwen said. "Does anybody else from the Trump side have anything to add?"

Aaron Fuller raised his hand.

"Go ahead, Aaron," Gwen said.

"Lance is right. Trump cares about us. I know for sure that Hillary doesn't. She called us deplorable and racist. That's bullshit."

"Language."

"Sorry. … We're not racist just because we're white and Republican. Democrats act like we're stupid rednecks who wanna bring back slavery. I never cared about political stuff before, but I do now after she said all that crap. *She* should be in prison."

Two more girls moved from the left to the right, leaving only five girls and Jamar on the left, with Caleb still in the middle.

"Excellent, Aaron. That's an example of an effective emotional appeal. Remember our lesson on propaganda and influence? Emotional appeals are far more effective than facts and figures." Gwen walked from the right to the left. "Who wants to speak up for Hillary?"

A chubby blonde raised her hand.

"Jessica. Go ahead."

"Trump doesn't have any experience," Jessica said. "He's this idiot on television. He's not qualified. But Hillary's been the first lady, and she was a senator, and she's the Secretary of State."

One girl moved back to the left.

"Very persuasive, Jessica. Excellent." Gwen addressed the class. "Jessica's argument is an example of an appeal to authority. The bottom line is, people will support others simply based on their authority. In many cases, this makes sense. If your doctor tells you to do something for your health, you'll be more likely to listen to them, versus a friend without medical training. One thing to always remember though. Just because someone has authority, doesn't mean you should automatically listen to them." Gwen turned back to the left. "Anybody else in the Hillary camp?"

Jamar raised his hand.

"Go ahead, Jamar."

"Trump made fun of handicapped people. That's messed up. And he was talking trash about John McCain. He's a Republican too. McCain was a pilot in Vietnam, and he was shot down and captured and spent a long time in a terrible prison. And Trump made some dumb comment about how he likes soldiers who weren't captured. Trump was never a soldier. He's a disgrace to this country."

Two girls moved from the right to the left.

Jamar continued. "And don't get me started on the racism. Trump's making it okay to be racist. You can't tell me this town isn't racist. I've seen it many times, and I think it's getting worse with Trump running his big fat mouth."

"Black people are always playin' the victim," Shane said from the right.

Jamar shook his head. "*That*, right there, is racist. What if I said, *White people are always playing the victim*?"

"I wouldn't care because I know it's not true."

"I've heard you use the N-word."

Shane shrugged. "So? It's just a word. We have freedom of speech in this country. Again, playin' the victim. I wouldn't care if someone called me white trash."

"You *are* white trash."

Gwen shook her head. "No name-calling, Jamar. Let's be respectful."

"Sorry, Ms. Townsend," Jamar replied.

"You should be sayin' sorry to me," Shane said.

Jamar glared across the room at Shane. "I'm sorry I'm so much better than you at football that I ruined your senior year."

The class laughed and hooted and hollered.

"Quiet. That's enough," Gwen said.

Shane was unfazed as they quieted, a smirk on his face. "If you're so much better than me, why am I startin' this Friday?"

Jamar furrowed his brows. "That's not true."

"Why do you think we've been splittin' first-string reps?"

"Let's stay on topic," Gwen interjected.

Gwen moved near Caleb in the middle of the room. "Caleb, can you tell us why you're still undecided?"

Caleb flipped his hair from his eyes and shrugged.

Gwen smiled. "Come on, Caleb. You're a free thinker. Otherwise you wouldn't be here all by yourself. I think we'd all benefit from your wisdom."

Shane laughed.

Gwen glared at Shane until he stopped laughing, then returned her attention to Caleb.

"Nothing ever changes," Caleb said, barely above a whisper.

"Could you repeat that, a little louder?" Gwen asked.

Caleb cleared his throat. "Nothing ever changes. Republicans think things'll get better if they get their guy elected, and Democrats think the same thing, but nothing ever changes. It doesn't matter if it's a Democrat or a Republican president. You can bet nothing's gonna change. It's like they make us mad at each other so we won't be mad at them. Maybe we'd be better off not supporting anyone."

Three boys and three girls moved to the middle.

"Fantastic, Caleb. Very persuasive."

"What about you, Ms. Townsend?" Lance asked. "Who are you gonna vote for?"

"I don't like politics," Gwen replied.

"You're not gonna vote?"

"Probably not."

"But, if you were, who would you vote for?"

Gwen was saved by the bell. "Put all the desks back please." The kids arranged their desks into place, grabbed their bags, and headed for the exit. Gwen approached Jamar. "I need to speak with you for a minute." They stood in front of Gwen's desk as the other students filed out. As soon as they were alone, Gwen asked Jamar, "How's Caleb doing?"

Jamar looked away for a moment. "He's fine."

"Did you talk to him?"

"Yeah."

"What did he say?"

"Not much." He looked away again.

Gwen nodded. "Did something happen?"

"I tried to be his friend, Ms. Townsend. I really did, but I don't think it's gonna work."

"Why not?"

Jamar shrugged. "He's just different. We don't have anything in common."

Gwen furrowed her brows. "How is he different?"

"I don't know." Jamar pursed his lips. "Can I go now?"

"Of course. Thank you for trying."

CHAPTER 54

Caleb's Got a Gun

Caleb paced in his bedroom, his cell phone in hand. He tapped his Madison contact. It rang once, then went straight to voice mail. He'd already sent five unrequited texts. She was screening him out.

"Hi, this is Madison. I'm not available. Leave a message, and I'll call you back … maybe." *Beep.*

"Hey, Madison," Caleb said. "I'm, uh, really sorry about all the shit I said. I know I need to be happy for you, and I'll try. I promise. Just, um, please call me back." Caleb disconnected the call and set his phone on his dresser.

His thoughts drifted to his big problem. *How do I end this thing quickly and with as little pain as possible?* Overdosing on meth hadn't worked. He got so fucked-up from just smoking a little, and it kind of made him feel better, at least while he was high. He was afraid to smoke too much. *I'd probably just get really sick. Who knows? Maybe I'd get brain damage and have to live the rest of my life as a retard. It has to be a gun.*

Caleb opened his closet and removed his gun case. *Pellet* gun case. He opened the case and removed the pellet gun that looked exactly like a Berretta 9 mm. It didn't even have one of those orange tips. For as long as he could remember, he'd wanted a real gun, like a rifle to go

182

shooting and hunting, like everyone else did. At least everyone with a fucking father.

His mother had finally acquiesced last year, but the gun had come with a ton of strings. First, she wouldn't buy him a real gun. Second, if he broke anything with it, she'd take it away. Third, it had to count for his birthday *and* Christmas. And she'd been serious. He hadn't gotten a thing last Christmas. He had had a sour face as Ashlee enjoyed her loot, and Heather had let him have it.

"You fuckin' ungrateful little bastard. Just like your fuckin' father." Usually, when she mentioned his father, she said about how tragic it was, how they'd been in love, how he was handsome and smart and going places. She never disparaged him. Her obvious hatred had made Caleb think that his father was still alive. Maybe he hadn't died in a motorcycle accident. Maybe he was just a white-trash loser piece of shit. *Like father, like son.*

Caleb put the gun to his temple and pulled the trigger. Nothing happened of course. It wasn't even loaded with pellets. He wondered if it was better to shoot yourself in the temple or in the mouth or in the chest. Caleb set his gun on his dresser and went to his phone. He typed, *What's the best way to shoot yourself,* into the Google search bar. Caleb read an article that recommended not shooting yourself in the chest because you might flinch, and the bullet could ricochet off your ribs. Under the chin was also bad because of flinching.

Apparently, the temple was the most popular place to shoot your-self, followed by the mouth. Either of those were efficient. He did need to get the right bullets though. Full-metal-jacket bullets should be avoided as they don't expand on impact. He needed hollow-point bullets. Technically, he only needed one hollow-point bullet. That was the new plan. A real gun and one hollow-point bullet. He messaged Aaron.

CalebMiles245: I need something else. I have more gold

183

Aaron responded almost immediately. Caleb's friendly neighborhood drug dealer was a better friend than Madison.

AaronDowntoClown: I'm home tonight. Come on over. Knock on front door
CalebMiles245: B there in 20

Caleb's trailer was quiet, as it usually was on a Friday evening. His mother was at the gym, but she'd be back soon to shower and to put on some tight-ass dress to go out in. Ashlee was already gone. Out with friends. They were probably eating somewhere in Myerstown on the way to the game against the Raiders. Caleb went into Ashlee's room and took half of the jewelry from her box. He thought she might notice, but it would be too late. But, then again, maybe she wouldn't. She rarely wore anything from her jewelry box. The stuff she mostly wore was on her.

Caleb walked to the Fullers' trailer. It was only a mile and a half away as the crow flies. The sun was low on the horizon. It was breezy, a little nip in the air. He wore his jacket for the first time since spring. Caleb knocked on the front door of the rusted trailer. The front door felt flimsy, like he could kick it in. Caleb was thankful not to have to go around back. That pit bull scared him, and he didn't like the idea of navigating the shit-filled backyard with the sun going down. Aaron opened the door.

"Caleb, what up? Come in." Aaron stepped aside, holding the door open.

Caleb stepped inside.

"Come on back."

Caleb followed Aaron to his back bedroom. "You're not going to the game tonight?"

"Nah, I don't feel like it," Aaron replied with his back turned.

"You were one badass linebacker last year. How come you're not playing football anymore?"

Aaron opened his bedroom door and said, "Gotta make that paper."
Inside Aaron's bedroom, Halo 5 was paused on the big screen.

Aaron turned to Caleb. "Need more ice? We just got a new shipment. Some good shit too."

Caleb deadpanned, "I need a gun."

CHAPTER 55

Rick Lies

"I'm starting Shane tonight," Rick had said an hour ago.

"What did I do wrong?" Jamar had asked, his eyes brimming with tears.

"I think Shane gives us the best chance to win."

Jamar had nodded and walked back into the locker room. That had made it that much more difficult. If he'd freaked out or called Rick an asshole, it would've been easier. But he hadn't. Even worse than that, now Jamar stood on the sideline with his teammates, cheering on the defense as they forced the Raiders to punt on their first drive.

After the punt, Shane and the offense trotted out to the field for the first drive. Coach Schneider called a rocket screen to Lance. It was an easy throw. Great for padding Shane's stats. Shane caught the snap from the center and threw the screen pass to Lance, who broke a tackle and gained twenty-two yards before being tackled by the safety. Rick glanced to his right and left. His players cheered. *Jamar* cheered. Rick had never felt so low. A wave of shame washed over him. Rick called a time-out.

Coach Schneider looked at Rick with his hands held out. "What are you doing?"

"What I should've done an hour ago," Rick replied, jogging out to the offensive huddle. He stopped short of the huddle, in the middle of the field, and called for Shane to come over. The quarterback jogged away from the huddle.

"What's up, Coach?" Shane asked.

"I'm sorry, Shane. I made a terrible mistake. I hope you'll forgive me for what I'm about to do. This isn't your fault. It's mine."

Shane's eyes were wide.

"I'm taking you out of this game, and I'm putting in Jamar."

Shane's face twisted in disgust. "This is fuckin' bullshit."

"I'm sorry, son."

"I'm not your son." Shane stepped closer, every bit as tall as Rick. "Fuck you." He turned and walked to the sideline.

"Jamar," Rick called out, motioning with one arm. Jamar put on his helmet and jogged onto the field, stopping in front of Rick. "I lied to you, Jamar. I'm sorry. I can't tell you why I started Shane, but I can tell you that it had nothing to do with your skill as a quarterback."

Jamar nodded and paused for a moment. "You got a play?"

"Run the zone read."

The next play, Jamar ran forty-eight yards for a touchdown.

CHAPTER 56

Janet and Hershey Kisses

Cars drove on Chocolate Avenue, the road lit by streetlights that looked like Hershey kisses. Janet shut the curtains of their third-floor hotel room and turned to Cliff.

"He totally humiliated my son," Janet said.

"I have to say, I've never seen anything like that," Cliff replied, unbuttoning his shirt. "A quarterback benched after one play. It was a good play too." Cliff shook his head as he removed his button-down shirt, revealing a white T-shirt underneath. The T-shirt rode up, a bit of his pale gut hanging over his belt.

Janet clenched her jaw. "I want him gone, immediately."

Cliff sighed. "You sure know how to kill the mood."

Janet stepped closer, wearing her little black dress that was two sizes too small. In heels, she looked down on the stocky man. It's not that he was short. In fact, he was average height, but Janet was six two in her six-inch heels. She pressed her lips to his, opening her mouth and swirling her tongue around. He placed his large hands on her ass and squeezed. Abruptly, Janet disengaged and stepped back, biting the lower corner of her lip.

"He has to go," Janet said.

"I don't disagree," Cliff replied. "The school district won't have a choice with that picture. I'd prefer to let him resign though. It'll be a serious black mark for the district if the press gets wind of this."

Janet glowered at Cliff. "He's having sex with a child."

"She is sixteen."

"Exactly."

"Girl looks about twenty-five. I'm sure he's not the only teacher who thought about her with bad intentions." Cliff chuckled to himself.

"This isn't funny, Cliff. I'm dead serious. I want him gone by Monday afternoon."

Cliff showed his palms. "All right. We can go to Pruitt's house tomorrow and show him the picture."

"I don't think I should be there, what with all this mess with Shane. Pruitt might think I have a grudge."

"You do."

Janet frowned. "The picture has to come from you."

"I don't have anything to do with that picture."

"Neither do I. Just tell him that you were sent the picture anonymously."

"Where did you get it?"

"An anonymous source."

"I don't believe that for a second."

"You have to protect the reputation of the school district, and I have to protect the students."

Cliff had a crooked grin. "Is that what this is about? Protecting students?"

Janet crossed her arms over her chest. "Absolutely."

"All right, I'll talk to Pruitt tomorrow. We can suspend him, but we can't fire him without an investigation and a private hearing. I'm guessing he'll resign and make it easy."

Janet nodded and dropped her arms. "I'll make sure we have a sub for him on Monday."

Cliff stared at her deep line of cleavage. "That dress is something else."

"You like it?"

"I'd like it better if you took it off."

"What about our agreement?"

"I wasn't born yesterday. Besides, I have a feeling you'll be more *motivated* if I tell you after."

"I'm a woman of my word."

"Then take off that dress."

"You first."

He kicked off his shiny dress shoes and undid his belt. He dropped his slacks to the carpet and stepped out of his pants, now standing in silk boxers, a white T-shirt, and black socks.

"Your turn," Cliff said.

Janet shook her head, smiling coy. "You wanna know what I have under my dress?"

He nodded.

"Nothing." She pursed her lips.

Cliff smiled wide and strutted toward Janet, but she stepped back and held her arms out in front of her, blocking him.

"You're not finished," she said, glancing at his underwear and T-shirt. "I'd like to see the merchandise before I buy."

He laughed. "You are a wild one." Cliff took off his shirt. He had a pale beer gut and a farmer's tan on his neck and lower arms, but he wasn't totally devoid of masculinity, with stocky shoulders, chest muscles, and thick calves. "What do you think?"

"Not bad," Janet replied. And she meant it. He wasn't a terrible-looking guy for a fifty-year-old. His brown hair was thinning; the skin around his eyes was puffy, and he had deep forehead wrinkles to go along with a double chin, but he did have a charming bit of confidence, a decent smile, and he wasn't overly hairy. She'd never fuck him under normal circumstances. She was forty-five, so it's not like he was out of her age group, but she preferred younger men who were in better shape. "Let's see that cock of yours."

His eyes widened, and he slid his boxers down his legs. He stroked his penis, causing it to grow in his hand.

Janet put her hand to her chest, staring at his circumcised penis, and low-hanging scrotum. "Wow, that's impressive." It wasn't anything special, but there was always power to be gained from complimenting a man's penis. Janet reached behind her neck and untied her dress. She held on to the straps, the fabric of the dress still partially covering her breasts. She stared into Cliff's unblinking eyes as she dropped the straps, freeing her breasts, her dress clinging to her hips.

"No," he said, grinning. "*That's* impressive." He stepped closer, his hands outstretched for the grope, but Janet blocked him again.

"I'm not done."

He stopped in his tracks, his penis semierect now. Janet lifted her dress, revealing her lack of panties as she pulled her little black dress over her head. He was all over her the second that dress landed on the carpet—his tongue in her mouth, his hands on her breasts, rough, then between her legs. His mouth clamped on her nipple, then to her neck. Still standing, he grabbed his penis and rubbed the head against her vagina, pushing, panting, but not having the angle to enter. Janet wriggled from his grasp and stepped back.

"What's wrong?" Cliff was flushed, his penis still in his hand.

Janet adjusted her glasses like a sexy librarian. "I have a treat for you." She grabbed her purse and removed a blindfold. "Do you trust me, Cliff?"

"Is that a trick question?"

"Let me take care of you. Turn around."

He cocked his head for a moment, then turned his back to Janet. She slapped his ass, Cliff chuckling in response. Janet covered his eyes with the blindfold and tied it behind his head, tight.

"No peeking," she said, leading him by the hand to the king-size bed. She pulled the comforter and the top sheet from the bed. "Lay down. On your back."

He did as he was told, feeling for the bed with his hands before climbing on and laying on his back. Janet walked back to the desk.

"Where are you going?" he asked, sitting up, moving the blindfold, and peeking at Janet.

Janet frowned. "You're ruining it. No peeking. I'm getting a condom, if you *must* know."

He replaced the blindfold and lay back. "Sorry."

"Just relax," she said, grabbing a condom and her phone from her purse. She snapped a few pictures of Cliff, spread-eagled on the bed, the sound effects on her phone turned off so he wouldn't hear the *click*s. She replaced her phone in her purse and stepped back to the bed, setting the condom on the bedside table. She climbed into bed, next to him, his hands immediately groping her, but she removed them.

"Naughty boy. No touching," she said.

He put his hands down, and she kissed him. Soft on the lips. Then his neck. His nipples. She moved down his body with her mouth, kissing everywhere but where he really wanted. He bucked and moaned, trying to get her to do it, but she continued to tease, his penis pulsing in anticipation. Finally, she kissed it. Once. Very chaste. He lifted his pelvis, encouraging more. But she moved back up his body with her mouth, now kissing his more forcefully, then moving back down with more urgency. This time she lingered on his inner thighs, his pelvis, her hair brushing across his penis as she worked her magic. He groaned, his breathing labored. She ran her middle finger along the shaft, her fingertip barely touching.

It went like this for fifteen minutes, Janet teasing, giving him a little more touch, a little more of her tongue, then straddling him and rubbing her vagina against his penis. She thought he was gonna blow when she straddled him. Unfortunately, he was holding out. She took the head into her mouth, and he thrust upward, but Janet pulled back, slapping his hip playfully.

"Be a good boy, or you'll go to bed without dessert," she said.

She leaned over, barely taking him into her mouth again, her knees between his. This time he didn't move. Without warning, she took him entirely, her mouth at full suction, nearly gagging. His penis spasmed, and she tried to pull back, eager to avoid the happy ending, but he held her head in place as he climaxed. Janet breathed out of her nose, waiting for it to end. When it did, she left the bed without a word, headed for the bathroom. At the sink, she spat and washed out her mouth several times. She put on a hotel robe and returned to the bed, grabbing his boxers and T-shirt from the floor on the way.

"Damn, Janet," he said with a wide grin. "You are something special. Sorry about the end. I got a little out of control."

Janet tossed his boxers and T-shirt to him. "Get dressed and tell me what you know about Pastor Goode and Daub."

"You don't waste any time, do you?" His eyes flicked to the unused condom. "I just need a little break, and we can still use that condom. I can make you feel real good."

Janet sat on the edge of the bed, her torso turned to Cliff. "I need you to live up to your side of this agreement."

He put on his boxers and T-shirt, and sat up in bed, leaning against the headboard. "You wanna order in some food?"

"It's Pastor Goode, isn't it?"

"You are like a pit bull with a bone. I tell you what. I'd hate to be on your bad side."

Janet glared at Cliff.

Cliff showed his palms. "All right, all right. I was just being friendly."

"By holding my head down so you could come in my mouth? You're lucky I didn't bite it off."

Cliff smirked. "I said I was sorry. I was in the throes of passion. I wasn't thinking straight. It'll never happen again."

"That's for sure." Janet crossed her arms over her chest.

"Don't be like that. I thought we were friends?" He paused for a moment, but Janet didn't fill the silence. "You're right. It's Pastor Goode. Daub's a regular Boy Scout, but Pastor Goode's a different story." Cliff took a deep breath. "This'll knock your socks off. Sixteen years ago, Pastor Goode had an affair with a young parishioner. Very young. Eighteen years old. He paid the woman fifty grand from the collection plate so she'd keep quiet."

Janet uncrossed her arms. "How do you know this?"

"I was friendly with the church secretary. She heard them arguing, and she did the books, put two and two together."

"Think she'll talk?"

"Probably not, considering she died two years ago."

"Is there any other proof?"

Cliff smiled wide. "A child."

CHAPTER 57

Gwen and Secrets

Gwen's eyes fluttered, the ceiling coming into view. She was disoriented, staring at the ceiling fan, knowing that she didn't have one in her bedroom. Then it all came back to her. Rick, grilling steak for dinner, not wanting to go out. They'd watched a movie on his couch, falling asleep before the credits. Rick had carried her to his bed, Gwen acting asleep as he tucked her in and kissed her softly on the lips. He had whispered something like, "I hope this isn't the end." She must've heard him wrong. Maybe he was referring to the movie. Maybe he said, "We missed the end." A big part of her had wished that he would make a move, but she hadn't been with a man in three years. Not since Brian. She wasn't sure if she was ready to begin again.

Rick had been sweet last night but distracted. In fact, he'd been distracted all week, melancholy even. He'd said he was worried about the Myerstown Raiders, but Lewis had said that they weren't very good. And they weren't. They'd beaten the Raiders forty-two to six.

Then there had been that snafu with Shane and Jamar. He had started Shane, but he had been so happy with Jamar. *Why would he start Shane, then pull him after one play?* Everyone in the stands had been shocked. Janet had left the stadium in a huff. And, even after the game had been won, Rick had still been distracted, so it couldn't have been about the Raiders.

Gwen had expected Rick to invite her over after the game, but he had said he was tired. He did ask her to come over the next night, but he still seemed preoccupied. She knew he wasn't telling her something important, but they'd only been on a few dates. He wasn't obligated to spill all his secrets at this point. It was only fair. She had secrets of her own that she wasn't telling him. She sighed. *I have to at least tell him that I'm still married.*

She removed the covers, still wearing her jeans and blouse from the night before. The room was relatively dark, the clouds dimming the sun. She stood and checked herself in the mirror attached to Rick's dresser. Her straight brown hair was disheveled, her eye makeup smudged. She went to the attached bathroom, washed her face, and used his hairbrush to make herself a bit more presentable. She found a brand-new toothbrush under the sink and brushed her teeth. She tiptoed into the living room. He slept on the couch, his stocking feet uncovered, a flannel blanket on top but not large enough to fully cover the big man. She kissed him on the cheek, his stubble rough on her lips, but he didn't stir.

Gwen went to the kitchen and poked around the refrigerator. She removed eggs, bacon, butter, bread, and orange juice. She found plates and pans and glasses in the cabinets. Gwen hummed as she poured a glass of orange juice.

"Good morning," Rick said.

Gwen jumped and yelped, startled. She turned around. "You scared me."

Rick stood by the fridge, dark circles around his eyes, wearing a T-shirt and sweatpants. He filled out his shirt nicely, his body bulging in the right places. "Sorry. I heard you in the kitchen." He paused for a moment. "Did you sleep okay?"

"Yes. Thank you for giving up your bed. You didn't have to. I could've slept on the couch."

"You don't want any part of that couch. Trust me." He bent his torso left and right, his back cracking.

"You could've slept next to me. I trust you not to …"

"Take advantage?"

"This is all very new for me. It's been a long time since I dated."

Rick nodded. "I understand. No pressure is coming from me. I enjoy being around you. We can take it slow."

"Thank you." Gwen paused. "I—"

"There's something I have to tell you."

"That's exactly what I was about to say to you."

"You first."

Gwen nodded, her face resigned. "I really do like you, Rick, but …" She took a deep breath.

Rick smirked. "What? Are you married?"

Gwen looked away, her face hot.

"That was just a bad joke. Are you actually *married*?" Rick asked.

Gwen looked back to Rick. "Technically, yes."

Rick winced as if he'd been punched in the gut.

"I've already signed the divorce papers. It should be final by Christmas."

Rick sat at the small kitchen table, slumping into a chair. "Do you still love him? Sorry. That's none of my business. Of course you do. He's your husband."

Gwen sat at the table next to Rick. She took his hand. "I do love my husband, but we've been separated for three years, and we're not getting back together. I need to move on. Slowly and cautiously but I do need to move on. I'm sorry I didn't tell you sooner."

Rick nodded again. "What happened between you two?"

Gwen swallowed hard. "Our lives went in different directions."

Rick was quiet, his eyes vacant.

Gwen's stomach tumbled with the feeling that something was really wrong in Rick's life, even beyond her marriage revelation. She almost didn't want to know. "What did you want to tell me?"

Rick blinked, his eyes alert again. "I don't know how to tell you this." He ran his hand over his face. He looked tired. "To be honest, I'm terrified. Nobody's said anything to me about it, but I'm sure people at school have seen it. I wanted to tell you when it happened, but this between us is so new, and I didn't want this to ruin everything before we even got started. And I thought I was gonna make it go away, but, when the time came for me to do what I was supposed to do, I couldn't do it."

"I don't understand. I'm not following."

"You know that Facebook page I was telling you about, the West Lake Watchdog? The one that's always criticizing me?"

"Yes."

"They posted something really bad about me."

"I don't care about what some stupid Facebook page says. I'm not even on Facebook."

"I had a relationship with Heather Miles."

Gwen retracted her hand from his. "Caleb Miles's mother?"

Rick nodded. "Unfortunately. It was stupid. I never should've gotten involved with her. I've never been involved with a player's mother before. I ended it about six weeks ago, and the Facebook page started shortly after that."

"You think Heather Miles is running the page?"

"Along with Janet."

"Janet?"

"Yeah, I think what Heather posted came from Janet. She's black-mailing me because she wants me to start Shane—"

"Blackmailing you? With what?"

Rick rubbed his temples for a moment. "She has a picture of me."

"Doing what?"

"This is gonna sound crazy, but I'm telling you the truth. I swear."

Gwen crossed her arms over her chest.

"Ashlee Miles broke into my house while I was in the shower. I told her to leave, but she wouldn't, so I had to remove her. When I opened the door, she kissed me, and I'm pretty sure Janet was there, and she took a picture."

"Of you kissing Ashlee?" Gwen's voice went up an octave.

Rick looked away for a moment. "Yeah."

"Were you naked?"

"I had on a towel."

Gwen stood from the table. "So, let me get this straight. Ashlee broke into your house?"

"Yes."

"How did she do that?"

"The door was unlocked."

"And you just happened to be in the shower?"

"Yes. I know it sounds bad."

Gwen shook her head. "It's beyond bad. And they have a picture of you kissing her in your towel."

"She kissed me."

"I can't believe this. I'm so *stupid*." She glanced around the kitchen. "Where's my purse?"

"Gwen, I'm telling the truth—"

"Where's my purse!"

"On the coffee table."

Gwen went to the living room and grabbed her purse from the coffee table, Rick on her heels.

"This is what Janet wants," Rick said. "She wants to ruin me."

"Did you make up all that stuff about seeing her car that night after the Toad's Stool?"

"No, she was following us. That was the night she took the picture. She must've followed me home from your house."

"And Ashlee Miles just happened to show up?"

"Yes."

"Or did you call her because I didn't put out?"

"I was so happy with our date. I didn't even think sleeping together was an option—"

"Save it for your lawyer." Gwen left Rick's house, slamming the door behind her.

CHAPTER 58

Caleb Ditches

It was overcast and cool, the wind whipping through the drying corn, the brown stalks crackling. Caleb lit the end of his pipe and sucked the meth into his lungs. Shortly thereafter, hidden in the middle of that cornfield, his heart beat rapidly, ecstasy coursing through his veins. The meth made him feel strong, like he could do anything. He opened his backpack and glanced inside. His gun was right where he'd packed it. Caleb shouldered his backpack and continued toward school.

He thought about the look on their faces. The fear. It was time for them to be afraid of him for once. It was time for the world to know what they did.

As he approached the school, beat-up cars and trucks drove too fast into the parking lot. Yellow buses lined the front entrance. Kids, zombie-eyed from the weekend, barely awake, with backpacks strapped to their backs, trudged into school. Girls, gossiping in packs, walked inside like they owned the place. Big boys walked slowly, hogging the sidewalk, causing the smaller and the less cool to walk around.

But they all went inside, as if they didn't have a choice, as if it wasn't even a consideration. *Sheep. Fucking sheep. That's what I've done my whole life.* Caleb stopped in his tracks, the realization smacking him across the face.

I have a choice.

Fuck these people. Fuck this place. My life is gonna end up in the same place regardless. I might as well do whatever the fuck I want. Caleb turned on his sneakers and walked back home. Fortunately, his mother wasn't there. She didn't come home last night, which wasn't out of the ordinary. *She's probably with some dickwad who she met at the gym.*

He lay on his bed, too wired from the meth to go back to sleep. He thought about how he'd ditched school. He had felt powerful making his own decision. In that moment, he was more powerful than every kid in school. He had had the courage to do what he wanted. He thought about what he had to do. His Holy Grail. *Soon.*

CHAPTER 59

Rick and That God-Awful Picture

On Monday morning, Rick walked into the locker room for his first-period PE class. He was on time but barely. He hadn't slept well, then slept through his alarm. He had felt nauseated on his way to school, wondering how he'd be treated by his coworkers. By Janet? Principal Pruitt? A middle-aged man stood in the locker room with a clipboard, the roll call attached. Kids were already changing quietly. They were always subdued in the morning.

"Can I help you?" Rick asked the man.

"I'm the substitute," the man replied.

Did they think I wasn't coming? "Are you sure you're in the right place?"

"Pretty sure. Are you Mr. Barnett?"

"Yeah."

"Principal Pruitt told me to send you to his office if you showed up."

"Why wouldn't he call me?" Rick asked more to himself than the sub.

The man shrugged.

Rick left the locker room, remembering that, after Gwen left, he'd turned off his phone and vowed not to open his laptop. He thought, if he ignored everything, it might go away. Rick hurried to the office.

"Good morning, Grace," Rick said as he entered the main office.

The old secretary looked up from her laptop and looked back down without a word, one side of her mouth raised in disgust.

Rick walked to Pruitt's office and knocked on his door.

"Come in," Principal Pruitt said.

Rick stepped inside.

"Close the door. Sit down." Pruitt motioned to the chairs in front of his desk.

Rick shut the door and sat across from Pruitt, his heart pounding in his chest. "Why do I have a sub? I was a little late, but I made it before the bell."

Principal Pruitt wagged his head. "It's not about that, Rick. You might wanna get your union rep in here."

"I'm not in the union."

Pruitt removed the upside-down picture from his in-box and turned it over. It was the same picture that Janet had showed him. Rick, wearing nothing but a towel, kissing Ashlee at his front door. It looked like a good-bye kiss after an intimate affair.

"I can explain," Rick said. "Janet's blackmailing me. She's pissed that I benched Shane. She followed me after the Garden Grove game. The Friday before last. I went out for drinks with Gwen Townsend, and Janet followed us to the Toad's Stool."

"Did Gwen see her following you?"

Rick shook his head. "No, but I know it was her. I was pulled over by a cop on suspicion of a drinking and driving—"

"I don't need to hear this," Pruitt said, putting his hand up like a stop sign.

"I wasn't drinking and driving. I only had two beers. I passed the breathalyzer. You can probably call the police. They might tell you that Janet was the one who called them. She was trying to get me in trouble. I dropped off Gwen at her house, and, when I went home, I saw Janet's car."

"Where was her car?"

"She passed by right when I turned into my neighborhood."

"Are you certain it was her? Did you see her?"

"I saw a blue BMW."

"But you didn't see her."

"No."

Pruitt frowned. "Go on. Explain how you ended up in this god-awful picture."

"I went home, and I took a shower, and Ashlee Miles broke into my house while I was in the shower. I left the front door unlocked, but I didn't invite her."

Pruitt nodded, his beady eyes narrowed. "Go on."

"I asked her to leave. Told her that I was gonna call the cops if she didn't. Then she threatened me. Said she'd tell the cops that I invited her in and that I took off all my clothes in front of her. I was pissed, and I was in a no-win situation, so I grabbed her by the arm and dragged her from my room. She got the message and walked on her own to the front door. I had to reach around her to open the door, and, when I did, she kissed me. That's when Janet took the picture. But a split second afterward, I pushed Ashlee away and slammed the door in her face."

Principal Pruitt sat silent for a moment, his jaw taut.

Rick tried to fill the silence. "I'm telling the truth, Don. There has to be pictures of me pushing her away. I swear on my mother's grave."

"Don't do that," Pruitt said, shaking his head. "There are no pictures of you pushing the girl away."

"Janet destroyed them then—"

"Stop. I'm a nice guy. You know that, but I didn't fall off the turnip truck yesterday. First of all, Janet didn't give me the picture. Second, do you really expect me to believe that Janet was waiting out front of your house to take some picture of you kissing Ashlee in a towel? What are the chances that she just happened to be there? I think it's more likely you've been doing this for quite some time, and you finally got caught."

"Don, I swear—"

"Shut up, Rick. You've put this school district in one heckuva bad position. People are talking about it on Facebook. You're lucky they haven't posted the picture." Pruitt paused for a beat. "I can't guarantee that Ashlee's parents won't press charges. You could end up in prison."

Rick hung his head and rubbed his temples. "What am I supposed to do?"

"That's for you to decide, but, as of now, you're suspended, pending the investigation. I suggest you get a lawyer."

Rick swallowed the lump in his throat. "What happens next?"

"We'll investigate. We have a tentative hearing scheduled for next Tuesday the eleventh. I suggest you be there with your lawyer. It'll be there that we decide whether or not to initiate termination proceedings." Principal Pruitt leaned forward, his elbows on his desk, glaring at Rick. "If we find evidence of a crime in our investigation, we'll have to hand that information over to the police."

"Even if I did kiss her, technically that's not a crime."

Pruitt shook his head. "That's the *only* reason the police aren't here right now. If we find evidence that you had sexual relations with that girl, you better believe your job'll be the least of your worries."

"Did you talk to Ashlee? She has issues, but I can't imagine she'd lie about this."

"We'll talk to her and her parents. In the meantime, don't be stupid, Rick. Stay away from the girl. During your suspension, you are not allowed contact with any students or to be on campus for any reason whatsoever. That includes extracurricular activities. I better not see you anywhere near the football team. Coach Schneider will take over as interim head coach. Any questions?"

Rick shook his head, his eyes cast down.

Principal Pruitt stood from his chair and motioned to the door. He wore a sweater with a leaf pattern in a band across his chest. Very festive. His face told a different story. This debacle had already taken its toll. His beady eyes were bloodshot, and his ruddy face was especially blotchy. The stocky principal escorted Rick like an expelled student, neither man saying a word. Thankfully, classes were in session, so the halls were empty.

Rick glanced into Gwen's door window as they walked past her classroom. The sight of her standing and smiling at her students, as if nothing had happened, as if Rick had meant nothing, was the straw that almost broke his back. He hadn't cried since his mother had died, but he almost lost it, right then, right there.

In the parking lot, Rick opened the door to his truck. He turned to Principal Pruitt. "I didn't do this."

Pruitt crossed his arms over his barrel chest. "It sure looks like you did."

CHAPTER 60

Janet and Bob's Lucky Day

Janet waltzed into Bob Schneider's classroom. It was a somber affair, the desks orderly, the walls mostly barren. Bob stood by his desk. He shoved his keys into his pocket and shut his laptop.

He glanced at Janet as she approached. Barely making eye contact, he said, "I'm headed to lunch."

Janet slithered within touching distance. "Lunch can wait." *You could stand to skip a few meals.*

His voice quivered. "Please, Principal Wilcox. I tried. I really did. I'm not even calling the plays anymore. I have a baby. My wife stays home. If I lose my job, we're screwed." His eyes brimmed with tears. He hung his head.

Janet smiled wide. "Then this is your lucky day."

He looked up tentatively, like a soldier peering out of a foxhole.

"I think congratulations are in order."

Bob glanced side to side, shifty-like, waiting for the other shoe to drop.

"You haven't heard?"

"Heard what?"

"Rick's been suspended. You're the new head football coach. Congratulations."

He smiled small, still waiting for the strings. "Why was he suspended?"

"That's confidential, but I will tell you that it's serious, and I don't think he's coming back. It's your team now. Pruitt wanted to interview for the job, but I told him that you were the brains behind the operation."

"Thank you."

"I believe in you, Bob. If anyone can lead the team through this transition, it's you."

Bob nodded.

"Big game this week."

Bob nodded again.

"I do worry that this turmoil with Rick will be a distraction for the team. There's not much we can do about that. That's baked into the cake. I do think you can limit *other* distractions, like the so-called quarterback controversy."

"You don't have to worry about—"

"*Who* do you plan to start at quarterback?"

"Shane."

CHAPTER 61

Gwen's a Mandatory Reporter

Gwen slumped into her chair, exhausted from putting on a happy face all morning for her students, even though she still reeled from Rick's confession. It was her lunch period, but she wasn't hungry. She thought about going to Principal Pruitt. By law, she was a mandatory reporter of child abuse.

Maybe Rick's innocent. Maybe it happened exactly like he said it did. It's obvious from Ashlee's personal narrative that she has some serious daddy issues. Rick's a good-looking guy. It's not shocking that Ashlee might find him attractive. But what are the chances that she'd break into his house, and he'd just happen to be in the shower, and someone just happened to be outside his house in the middle of the night, waiting to get a picture?

Maybe someone hired a private investigator, and they were waiting to get the shot. But why? Maybe Rick's done it before. Maybe someone wants to expose him. A former student who he abused? Or a parent? Or maybe it is Janet because Rick benched Shane? Does it matter why he's being targeted? It matters whether or not he did it. He's so gentle, and he seems to care about his students. But that's not uncommon. These predators know how to present themselves. I have to tell Pruitt.

Gwen stood from her desk and left her classroom, headed for the office. The hallway was empty, students now at lunch or in class. Rachel

Kreider exited the faculty bathroom, straightening her sweater.

"Oh, hi," Rachel said as Gwen approached. "Just the person I needed to talk to."

Gwen stopped in front of Rachel, in the middle of the hallway. "Hi, Rachel. Can it wait?"

Rachel ignored Gwen's question. "I wanted to tell you that I'm *really* sorry about what happened to your boyfriend. You must be devastated."

Gwen furrowed her brows. "I don't know what you're talking about. I don't have a boyfriend."

"I heard you were dating Rick Barnett."

"We're not dating."

Rachel pursed her lips. "Well, I never know what people call it these days. I've been married forever, thank God. I can't imagine being single."

"I have to go—"

"I just wanted you to know that nobody thinks you did anything wrong."

"What are you talking about?"

"This mess with Rick having an affair with a student. He was suspended today. I heard they even have a picture. I used to think he was a nice man, but he's disgusting. I heard he's done it before too. My heart just breaks for these girls. Anyway, everyone knows you two are together, but nobody blames you. Well, some people think that you knew, but I don't think that's true—"

"I have to go." Gwen turned on her heels, leaving Rachel in midsentence.

Gwen hurried back to her classroom, locking her door and sitting at her desk. *How does Rachel know all this stuff? Do people think I knew? I guess technically I did. Too late to say something now.* She had an urge to call her lawyer. The one who had helped her in Philly. But she couldn't afford him. She also had an urge to call Rick and to scream at him for getting her wrapped up in this mess.

She turned on her cell phone. She had a new text. It was from a number she didn't recognize.

717-555-2863: I thought you might want to know who you're getting involved with.

A picture was attached. It was the picture Rick had described to her. Rick was at the front door, bare-chested, wearing a towel like a kilt, clearly kissing Ashlee on the lips. Gwen studied the image. It looked like they were embracing, but Rick didn't have both his hands on her. One of his hands was on the doorknob and the other looked to be just under her chest. *Maybe he used that hand to push her away. Maybe he pushed her away because he saw the person taking their picture.*

Gwen studied Rick's face, trying to find the truth in his expression. It was hard to tell, the picture was taken from an angle, so she didn't see Ashlee's or Rick's faces straight-on. One thing Gwen did notice was that his hair looked darker than usual and was matted to his head. It looked *wet.*

If they were having an affair, why would he get out of the shower without drying his hair? He has short hair, it would probably dry really quick with a towel. It looks like he got out of the shower without drying off at all, which is consistent with his story. And why would someone send me this picture? Maybe Janet is trying to ruin him. She does have access to my cell phone number. But so does everyone else at school. My number's on the phone tree for snow days.

Gwen tossed her phone on her desktop. *Maybe I'm just seeing what I want to see. He is kissing her. She is at his house. He is half-naked, with a student in the middle of the night. We only went out on a few dates. I don't really know him.*

CHAPTER 62

Caleb and Stupid White Trash

Caleb lay on his bed, scrolling through his Instagram feed. A bunch of people were talking about Coach Barnett. He was suspended for having an affair with a student. *That's gotta be bullshit.* There was a link. Caleb clicked the link, taking him to the Facebook page entitled the West Lake Watchdog. He remembered his sister, Ashlee, talking about this page a few weeks ago. The page that bashed Coach Barnett. He read the most recent post, which was from last Tuesday. The comments were posted sometime between last Tuesday and today.

West Lake Watchdog
September 27 at 11:14 AM
I heard from people at the high school that Coach Barnett is having sex with a student. What a piece of shit! He was seen at his house butt naked kissing a female student. Rick is a perv. He should be in prison. **#FireBarnett** 22 Likes 9 Shares
Will Gilroy I'm not surprised. Bad coach. Worse person. **#FireBarnett** 8 Likes
Breanna Franks It's like Jerry Sandusky all over again. 7 Likes
Roger Elkins Damn right, Will and Breanna. He needs to go. NOW. **#FireBarnett** 4 Likes

Trina Grisham I'm so sick of this school district. These people are disgusting. 2 Likes

Caleb clicked on the About tab. It read, *I'm a concerned parent and a West Lake resident on a mission to drain the swamp. I'm tired of all the crap. It has to end!* Caleb clicked back to the Home page. There was a new post.

West Lake Watchdog
October 3 at 8:37 PM
Coach Barnett now banned from school and football team for having sex with a student. I knew he is creepy perv. Coach Sneider is new coach. Everyone needs to support him. Coach Sneider is a good man. **#FireBarnett**

Caleb checked the clock on his phone: 8:39 p.m., Monday, October 3, 2016. *Someone just posted.* Caleb set his phone on the bedside table and went to the bathroom. He peed, washed his hands, and looked for his cup. His mouth was so cottony dry. The cup was gone. He went to the kitchen for a cup of water. His mother sat at the kitchen table on her laptop. She was typing. She never typed unless it was a text. She mostly clicked around on her computer. Caleb grabbed a plastic cup and filled it with water from the sink. He took a drink and looked at his mother. A connection clicked in his mind. He thought about the conversation he'd had with Ashlee about the West Lake Watchdog. *Heather was interested in our conversation. She was happy that the page was bashing Coach Barnett, but that doesn't make sense. She always liked Coach Barnett. Last year she helped with team meals and fund-raisers, but now she hates him?* Caleb inched closer to his mother, trying to get a look at her screen.

She shut her laptop. "What do you want?"

Caleb narrowed his eyes. "How come you don't help with team meals anymore?"

She frowned. "Because you ain't on the team. I did that for you, not me."

"But you quit helping before I quit the team, and you never helped with the freshmen last year. You helped with the varsity, and I wasn't even on varsity."

"I was tryin' to get in good with the coach for when you went on varsity. I wish I woulda known you were a quitter. Big waste of my time."

"And why do you hate Coach Barnett? You used to like him. Did something happen between you two?"

She looked away for a moment, her face flashing scarlet. "I don't like him because he's a piece of shit. You know that he's suspended for havin' sex with a student?"

"Are you the West Lake Watchdog?"

She was speechless for a beat. "No, ... but it's good what they're doin'."

"You *are* the West Lake Watchdog, aren't you?"

"What I do is none of your business."

"You just posted about Coach Schneider being the new coach, didn't you?"

"I'm not talkin' to you."

"You know, you could get sued. You can't post gossip like that. There are laws."

"It ain't against the law if it's true, but it don't matter to me. I ain't the one."

"Whatever, *Heather.*"

"Don't you call me that." She glowered at Caleb.

"Whoever's writing those posts sounds stupid."

"Shut up." Heather stood from the kitchen table and pointed toward the hall. "Go to your room."

"You can tell that they're stupid white trash."

Heather marched within striking distance and slapped Caleb across the face. "Who the hell do you think you are?"

Caleb touched his cheek and looked at his mother with one side of his mouth raised in disdain. "If you're not the West Lake Watchdog, then why are you so mad?"

CHAPTER 63

Rick and Any Body Fitness

After his ejection from campus, Rick wasn't sure what to do. He didn't bother looking for a lawyer. His divorce and his mother's medical bills had wiped out his savings. He had spent the rest of Monday and much of Tuesday holed up in his house, surfing the internet, trying to glean free lawyer advice. By Tuesday evening, he had an idea. It was a Hail Mary, but what did he have to lose?

Rick drove his truck to Heather Miles's double-wide trailer. Ashlee Miles's white Jeep was parked along the curb, but the carport was empty, Heather's Pontiac Grand Am conspicuously absent. Rick didn't linger, driving past the Miles household, exiting their neighborhood. He drove across town to Any Body Fitness, scouring the parking lot, and finding Heather's red Grand Am. The parking lot was packed, but Rick found a space a few rows back from her car. He backed his truck into the space, so he had a good view of her car.

He didn't have a membership to Any Body Fitness. He didn't like their lackadaisical attitude toward working out. He'd heard from Heather about the pizza Fridays, their lack of free weights, and the meathead alarm, which was a strobe light that they flashed anytime someone acted like a meathead, which they defined as someone who grunted, clanged weights, and carried a gallon jug of water.

By their standards, Rick was a meathead. He suspected the alarm and the lack of free weights was an ingenious way to rid their gym of the bodybuilder types who spent three hours a day at the gym, hogging the machines and the floor space. That place preferred the overweight accountant with a New Year's Resolution that he'd likely break by March, never to come back again. But he'd keep the membership because it was only twenty dollars a month, and he was sure that he'd go back, and to cancel the membership would be proof of his failure.

Rick much preferred to work out at school.

Rick suspected Heather went to Any Body Fitness because it was the most popular gym in town. For her, it was the place to show off her stuff and to collect young strapping boyfriends. *Speak of the devil.* Heather and one of her young strapping boyfriends exited the gym, all smiles. It was cool, in the low-fifties, but Heather wore yoga pants and a tiny tank top, showing off her veiny arms and shapely calves. Her beau looked like he'd stepped out of an Under Armour commercial. They stopped in front of a black SUV. He leaned toward her and kissed her under the glow of the streetlight. It wasn't a peck. It was a full-on openmouthed tongue twister, with his hands on her ass. *It looks like she's moved on. Then why try to ruin me?*

Under Armour guy gave her a smile and a smack on the ass as she turned on her sneakers and headed for her Pontiac Grand Am. Rick exited his truck, now on a collision course with Heather. Under Armour guy gunned his engine, exiting the parking lot. Heather pushed the button on her key fob, the Pontiac flashing lights in return. She opened the driver's side door.

"Heather," Rick said, standing ten feet away.

She turned around, eyes narrowed. "Are you followin' me?"

"I need to talk to you for a minute. Please."

"*Now* you wanna talk to me?" Her hands were on her hips. "I thought you never wanted to talk to me again."

"I didn't think you'd try to ruin my life."

"I didn't think you liked to have sex with little girls."

A woman walking past with a gym bag cast a sideways scowl at Rick.

He moved closer, within striking distance. "You know that's not true."

"I thought I knew you, but obviously I don't."

"I swear to God I've never had a sexual relationship with a student. Never."

Heather cackled. "That's what they all say. You wouldn't be suspended if you ain't done nothin'."

"I'm not asking you to believe me. But can you please remove all that crap until after the investigation? You're convicting me without a trial or even an investigation."

"I don't know what you're talkin' about. I ain't got nothin' to do with that Facebook page."

"Come on, Heather, I know it's you and Janet Wilcox."

"Janet Wilcox? The principal?"

"Don't play dumb."

"I don't know that bitch."

Rick ran his hand over his face. "Please, Heather. I'm begging you to cut me a break."

A smirk formed on her thin lips.

Rick thought, *She's enjoying this.*

"You deserve everything that's comin' to you." Heather climbed into her car and drove away, nearly hitting Rick with her sideview mirror.

Rick watched her taillights dwindle in the distance, along with his hope of redemption. *I'm fucked. Totally fucked.*

CHAPTER 64

Janet and #FirePruitt

Janet sat behind her desk, smiling to herself, reading the latest installment of the West Lake Watchdog.

West Lake Watchdog
October 4 at 11:14 PM
I heard Principal Pruitt wants to let Rick Barnett resign. He is a child molestor! He should already be fired. Pruitt is part of good ole boys. I heard he tried to cover it up. Pruitt and Barnett need to go! **#FireBarnett #FirePruitt** 32 Likes 14 Shares
Sadie Ollinger I agree. Principal Pruitt don't do nothing. My grandson said he reads magazines and looks on the internet all day. 17 Likes
Ellen Schneider When will this district start thinking about the kids first? **#FireBarnett** 24 Likes
Will Gilroy Probably never, **Ellen Schneider**, but calling these creeps out is a step in the right direction. They think there untouchable, but there not. Tell your husband good luck this Friday. Were pulling for him. **#FireBarnett #FirePruitt** 11 Likes
Caleb Miles This page is full of the biggest bunch of white-trash losers ever assembled on the internet.
Roger Elkins This is grown up business, Caleb. I'd stay out of it if I were you. I know about what you did in the locker room. Don't

219

worry. I won't tell. Stay out of it for your own good. 7 Likes

Breanna Franks If caring about school and our community is white trash I guess we r white trash. Don't matter to me **#WhiteTrashPride** 9 Likes

Trina Grisham I'm so tired of all this bullcrap. Barnett and Pruitt should go to prison. 7 Likes

Janet wondered when she should drop the bombshell about Pastor Goode. *Not too soon. Don't confuse the white-trash mob. Let them focus on Barnett and Pruitt first.* Janet frowned, thinking about a potential snag. *She might be a problem. She's kept that secret for sixteen years. I doubt it's out of loyalty to Pastor Goode. It must be vanity. She must not want the town to know she fucked that crypt keeper. Or maybe she's still getting money from Goode. I doubt it's about protecting her kid. When the time's right, I may have to sell it to her myself.*

CHAPTER 65

Gwen and the Confidant

Her phone went straight to voice mail and a generic greeting. After the beep, Gwen said, "Hi, Mrs. Miles. This is Gwen Townsend. Hopefully this is your number. I wanted to talk to you about Caleb. Could you please call me back at your earliest convenience? Please call me anytime. My cell phone number is 215-555-8991." Gwen disconnected the call and set her phone on her desktop.

She stood from her desk and walked across the hall to Lewis Phelps's classroom. The school was quiet. The students had been dismissed hours ago. Gwen knocked on Lewis's open door. He looked up from his laptop and motioned for her to come in. Gwen shut the door and approached his desk.

Lewis forced a smile. "You okay?

Gwen shrugged and slumped into the chair next to Lewis's desk. "I can't remember the last time I was okay." She sighed. "I thought he was one of the good ones."

Despite the end of another long day, Lewis looked sharp and fresh with his gelled blond hair and tailored button-down. "It may be a big misunderstanding. We shouldn't convict him based on a rumor. You know how everybody gossips around here."

"I think it might be true. I'm not trying to be a gossip, but something happened, and I have to tell somebody, and you're the only one

I trust to keep it a secret."

Lewis rolled his chair a bit closer to Gwen. He nodded. "Okay."

"You know the rumor about there being a picture of Rick kissing a student?"

"Unfortunately. But I'm sure it's bullshit."

Gwen shook her head. "Somebody sent it to me."

Lewis's eyes widened.

"In the picture, Rick's at his front door, wearing only a towel, kissing Ashlee Miles."

Lewis winced. "I'm shocked. I've known Rick for a long time, and I've never seen him act inappropriately with a female student. And they *do* flirt with him. You should've seen it when he was younger. It was really bad, but he was always professional."

She nodded. "I was shocked too."

"Did you talk to him? Maybe there's an explanation."

"I talked to him on Sunday. He gave me an explanation, but it's really difficult to believe. He thinks Janet orchestrated the whole thing as payback for playing Jamar over Shane."

"Really? How?"

"I guess I'm getting ahead of myself. I should start from the beginning. Do you remember the Garden Grove game? The Friday before last?"

"That was Jamar's first start."

"It was. After the game, Rick and I went out for drinks and food at the Toad's Stool."

"I heard."

Gwen sighed.

"The rumor mill," Lewis replied, with a little shrug.

"It wasn't a secret, although, if I'm honest, given everything that's happened since then, I kind of wish nobody knew about us. I know that sounds really selfish."

"I understand."

"Anyway, we'd driven separately to the bar, so Rick offered to drive me home, since we both had been drinking, and I was worse off than him. Then he got pulled over, and he was given a sobriety test. He passed the breathalyzer, but Rick thought that Janet had followed us and had called the police."

"Did you see Janet?"

"At the game, in the stands, but not afterward. Rick said he saw Janet's car after he dropped me off from the bar. Then he went home and showered, and he claimed that Ashlee broke into his house. Well, she didn't actually break in. Rick said he left the door unlocked. Then Ashlee came into his bedroom. Rick heard her, got out of the shower, put on a towel, and had to forcibly remove her from his house."

"Why didn't he just call the police?"

"I think he was worried about how it looked. An underaged girl in his bedroom, him not having any clothes on. He was worried that Ashlee would lie to the police."

"What about the kiss?"

"Rick said that, when he opened the front door to push her out, he had to reach around her, and, when he did, she kissed him. He thinks that's when Janet took the picture. But it doesn't make sense. I mean, what are the chances that someone would be waiting for that shot at that perfect time? He claimed that he pushed Ashlee away immediately, so Janet, or whoever took the picture, only had a second or so to get the shot."

"Unless Rick's lying."

Gwen blew out a breath. "Right. Unless Rick's lying. What do you think? You know Rick better than me."

Lewis shrugged again. "We're work friends, but we don't spend time together outside of school. He's always busy with football, and, for a long time, he was taking care of his mom."

"But you know this town. Do you think Janet would blackmail him just so her son can play high school football?"

"I wouldn't put anything past her."

"What about his house being unlocked? Is that normal?"

"I don't know if that's normal for him, but a lot of people leave their houses unlocked around here."

"What about Ashlee? That's a bold move for a sixteen-year-old. Do you think she'd go into Rick's house unannounced and try to seduce him?"

Lewis took a deep breath. "It does sound unlikely, even for her, but I will tell you that Ashlee has some problems. She's extremely intelligent, but something is off about her. This is straight-up gossip, so take it with a grain of salt, but supposedly one of her mother's boyfriends sexually abused her when she was younger."

"How old was she?" Gwen leaned forward in her chair, toward Lewis.

"I think eleven or twelve."

"If that *is* true, that would explain her bold behavior. Maybe she did initiate it, but Rick went along with it. Does Mrs. Baumgartner know about her past?"

"I'm sure she does. Ashlee's spent quite a few hours in her office."

"I just tried calling Ashlee's mother, not about Ashlee but about Caleb. He hasn't been to my class all week."

"I don't think he's been at school. He hasn't been to my class either. Did you talk to his mother?"

Gwen shook her head. "No."

Lewis leaned back in his chair. "Lemme guess. Straight to voice mail?"

"How'd you know?"

"I called her for the same reason. She's not exactly an involved parent. I wouldn't expect a return call. Just to give you an example of the type of mother she is, a few years ago I saw her in her car in the grocery store parking lot, tapping on her phone, while Caleb was inside doing all the shopping. As far as I can tell, Caleb and Ashlee have mostly raised themselves."

"That's awful. I think Caleb might be depressed, and who knows what this mess is doing to Ashlee."

"Well, the school's gonna investigate what happened with Rick. I'm sure they'll get Ashlee the help she needs, but I think Caleb's falling through the cracks. I think he's having some issues with his sexual preference. I think he might be gay and doesn't wanna face it." Lewis paused for a moment and leaned toward Gwen. "I know what he's going through. Fourteen years ago, I was Caleb. I tried talking to him, but he doesn't wanna hear from me."

"He won't say much to me either. I even tried getting Jamar to talk to him."

"How'd that go?"

"Jamar said that they're different."

Lewis sighed. "That sounds about right."

"What are we supposed to do?" Gwen held out her hands.

"We can't be their parents."

CHAPTER 66

Caleb, the Liberal Faggot

A loud knock came at his bedroom door. Caleb awoke from his slumber, the room now dark. He had been high all day but had crashed a few hours ago.

"Unlock this door," his mother said.

Caleb stirred.

"I said, *Unlock this door*," his mother shouted.

Caleb staggered to his door, bleary-eyed. "Hold on." He opened his door. Heather Miles stood with her arms crossed over her chest, wearing a tight shirt and yoga pants. Showing off her assets. All those hours in the gym on display.

"I got a message from school," she said.

"So?" Caleb replied.

"So, you haven't been at school all week." His mother glared at him. "Did you go to work today?"

"What I do is none of your business."

"What I do is none of your business either."

"As long as you live in *my* house, what you do *is* my business."

"What do you care?"

"You've missed three days in a row. If you miss another, I have to produce a doctor's note, or I'll get fined."

Caleb smirked. "That makes sense. You only give a shit because it might affect you."

She dropped her arms. "You know what? I *don't* care. I'll just call the police. You can ruin your life. You're not punishin' me. Just another West Lake loser. Ain't nothin' special about that."

"What about you? You drive a Pontiac Grand Am and live in a *fucking* trailer."

Heather glowered at Caleb. "You ungrateful little piece of shit. How do you think I ended up like this? You and your sister have ruined my life. No good man wants a woman who already has children. If I didn't have you two leeches, I'd probably be livin' in a big house, watchin' some Mexican cut my lawn."

Caleb shook his head. "That's racist."

"You think you're some kind of liberal faggot now?"

Caleb gritted his teeth, his face hot with shame.

Heather pointed at her son. "You're goin' to school tomorrow."

CHAPTER 67

Rick and Disrespect

It was the end of an ugly road game. West Lake was winning fourteen to zero, but it should've been fifty to zero. Rick sat in the home team stands, wearing a knit cap, blending into the Tamaqua Valley crowd. Tamaqua Valley High School was a small soccer school with a traditionally bad football team. Drew Fuller and the defense had been stellar that night, but the offense wasn't clicking. They could've just taken a knee and walked away with the win, but Shane needed his stats. So, on first and ten, with less than a minute left in the game, Shane threw a deep pass to Lance, who was wide open on a post pattern. The boo birds in the stands squawked at the meaningless touchdown pass. Shane shook his fist and high-fived Lance.

Jamar stood on the sideline, holding his helmet, his uniform clean. He'd dutifully cheered the entire game, but he hadn't cheered that last touchdown.

After the game, the teams lined up on the fifty-yard line and slapped hands. The Tamaqua Valley coach was red-faced as he met Coach Schneider in the middle of the field. They shook hands, but the Tamaqua Valley coach didn't let go, instead giving Coach Schneider an earful before releasing him.

CHAPTER 68

Janet and Complications

Janet stretched out on her king-size bed, like a snow angel, sunlight brightening her curtains. She grabbed her phone and her glasses from the bedside table and checked the time—*8:27.* She smiled, thinking about Shane's big win last night. She checked her text messages and email. Nothing interesting. She navigated to the West Lake Watchdog on Facebook. Nothing new. She slipped from her bed and padded into her bathroom.

She leaned against the sink, glaring at her reflection in the mirror. She'd slept almost nine hours, but her frown lines looked deep, her face blotchy. She needed an appointment at the tanning bed. She lifted her blond bangs, her face twisting in disgust at her forehead furrows. She brushed her teeth, peed, and put on a pair of West Lake Football sweats. She went to the kitchen and turned on the coffeepot. While she waited, she sat at the kitchen table, tapping on her phone.

A squeaky door opened and shut upstairs. *What's Shane doing here? Shouldn't he be at films?* With the open floor plan, she had a good view of the stairs. Whispering carried downstairs, followed by tiptoeing teenagers. Shane led Ashlee Miles down the steps, holding her hand, his finger to his lips. *Shit. This better be a fling. We do not need to be connected to that white-trash family, especially when people find out about Ashlee and Rick.* Janet stood from the kitchen table and met them at the bottom of the stairs.

Ashlee's long dark hair was disheveled. She wore jeans and a long-sleeved shirt, partly covered by a Patagonia vest. Her makeup had worn off, but her face was radiant. Once upon a time Janet could stay up all night, fucking the hottest guy in school, and still look radiant in the morning, never shameful on her walk home. Now she got nine hours of sleep and still looked like a fucking hobgoblin without makeup.

"Good morning, you two," Janet said, with a smile.

Ashlee's eyes were wide, a tight smile on her face.

"Hey, Mom," Shane said, with a little smirk. The cat that ate the canary. "You know Ashlee Miles from school."

"Of course," Janet said. "It's nice to see you, Ashlee."

Ashlee gave a quick wave. "Hi, Principal Wilcox."

"Please call me Janet."

Ashlee nodded.

"Are you guys hungry? I was about to make breakfast."

Ashlee glanced back at Shane, then said, "I really need to get home."

Shane walked Ashlee outside. Janet parted the blinds and watched them make out, Shane pushing her against her Jeep, kissing open-mouthed, their hands all over each other. A few minutes later, Shane returned. Janet waited for him in the foyer. *He fucked her. It's written all over his face. That self-satisfied smirk.*

"We need to talk," Janet said.

"About what?" Shane asked, playing coy.

"About you and Ashlee Miles."

Shane sucked in his lower lip, trying to fend off the smile that tugged at the corners of his mouth. "She's a nice girl."

Janet shook her head. "Did you wear a condom?"

Shane blushed. "I know what I'm doin'."

"I hope so, because she's been around the block a few times."

Shane crossed his arms over his chest. "She's not like that."

"How do you know?"

"I'm not talkin' about this with you. I'm goin' back to bed." Shane walked past his mother toward the stairs.

Janet followed. "I'm not finished talking to you."

Shane shrugged but didn't stop walking.

Janet followed him up the stairs, talking at him, nagging him like a pest. "Aren't you supposed to be in films?"

He stopped at the open doorway to his room and turned to Janet, leaning on the frame. "I texted Coach Schneider and told him I was sick."

Janet crossed her arms over her chest. "Do you think that's smart? I bet Jamar Burris is there."

"So what? They're not gonna bench me for missin' films. Especially with Barnett gone. I can pretty much do whatever I want now. You know that touchdown I threw to Lance at the end of the game last night?"

"What about it?"

"I was supposed to take a knee, but I knew it would be wide open. After the game, I thought Schneider would be pissed, but you know what he said to me?" Shane paused for a beat. "He said, 'Good game, Shane.'"

"Well, maybe he saw that your play worked."

"Maybe he's afraid of *you*."

Janet dropped her arms, her brows furrowed. "What are you talking about?"

"Come on, Mom. Don't bullshit me. I heard Coach Schneider does whatever you say."

"That's not true. Who told you that?"

"Drew Fuller's been sayin' that the only reason I'm startin' over Jamar is because of you."

Janet frowned. "That's ridiculous."

Shane lifted one shoulder in a half-shrug. "Is it? Coach Barnett thought Jamar was better, but then he gets suspended, and now I'm startin' again."

"Coach Schneider is a better judge of talent, and Coach Barnett had an affair with a student."

Shane pursed his lips, looking down at his mother, diamond studs glistening in his earlobes. "Is that even true?"

"I've seen pictures."

"Of Coach Barnett?"

"Yes."

"With a student?"

"Yes."

"What's he doing?"

"Kissing her … and he's naked."

Shane shook his head. "He's goin' to jail, huh?"

"He might." She paused for an instant, reflecting on her handiwork. "At the very least, he'll never teach or coach again."

"Who's the girl?"

Janet broke eye contact for a moment. "I can't say."

Shane smiled that perfect smile. "Come on. Who is it? I won't tell."

Janet paused again, the wheels turning in her mind. *If I don't tell him now, he'll be more involved with Ashlee when this thing breaks.*

"Come on. Who is it?"

Janet looked him in the eyes and said, "Ashlee Miles."

Shane recoiled as if Janet had punched him in the face. "That's not true."

"I'm sorry, Shane. I wish it wasn't."

"Bullshit." He turned and marched into his bedroom, swiping his keys off the dresser. He pushed past Janet and hurried down the stairs.

"Where are you going?"

He didn't look back as he said, "To talk to Ashlee."

CHAPTER 69

Gwen and Grocery-Store Gossip

Gwen parked her cart in the produce aisle. She collected kale, carrots, bell peppers, tomatoes, apples, sweet potatoes, and strawberries. As she placed apples into a plastic bag, she saw Enid Burris pushing a shopping cart her way, with Jamar walking alongside. They were dressed in their Sunday best.

Gwen twisted a tie around her apples and approached the Burrises. "Hi, Mrs. Burris. Jamar."

Mrs. Burris smiled. "Gwen, it's so nice to see you. Please, call me Enid."

"Hi, Ms. Townsend." Jamar's head was tilted down, his voice barely above a whisper.

"You two look so nice," Gwen said, referring to Jamar's suit and Enid's dress.

"Thank you, Gwen. We just came from church. I needed to pick up a few things for the week."

Jamar was nonplussed by the compliment.

"My cupboards are literally bare," Gwen said.

Enid motioned to Jamar. "This one's eating me out of house and home." She poked Jamar in the stomach and giggled. "I don't know where he puts it."

Gwen laughed. "I wish I had his metabolism."

Jamar remained stoic.

Enid frowned at her son and pushed the cart toward him. "Go pick out some salad vegetables and some fruit for breakfast."

Jamar pushed the cart toward the lettuces, leaving Gwen and Enid alone.

"Is he okay?" Gwen asked.

"Oh, he's been in a funk since Friday. He didn't play. I told him that his studies were more important, but I think that was the last thing he wanted to hear. He thinks that Coach Schneider's cheating him somehow. I don't know how that's possible."

Gwen nodded, her mouth turned down.

"Jamar misses Coach Barnett."

Gwen glanced across the produce section at Jamar moving with the speed of an octogenarian, shuffling with slumped shoulders. Gwen returned her attention to his mother.

Enid lowered her voice to a whisper, "I heard he's been suspended for having an affair with a student."

Gwen exhaled heavily. "That's the rumor."

"Is it true?"

"I don't know."

"I sure hope it's not."

"Me too."

The Burrises went back to their shopping. Gwen skipped a few middle aisles, landing in the canned goods section. She grabbed canned tuna fish, pickles, and organic mayonnaise.

Jamar appeared in the aisle. He grabbed a jar of olives and walked toward Gwen. He looked up and down the aisle, but it was just the two of them. "I have to ask you something."

"What is it, honey?" Gwen replied.

"Did he do what they're saying?"

"I don't know."

Jamar's face was taut, jaw clenched, eyes unblinking. "I think it's all a lie. Coach Barnett was my teacher in health last year, and the class was filled with a bunch of pretty girls, but he never acted weird or anything. I don't think he's like that. I think Coach Schneider lied or something to get his job. Can you help him?"

Gwen shook her head, her eyes glassy. "I'm sorry, Jamar. There's nothing I can do."

CHAPTER 70

Caleb and Popping Bubbles

Standing near the edge of the cornfield, shielded by trees, Caleb lit the bowl end of his pipe. He sucked in the vapor from the meth, his body percolating with energy. It wasn't like the first time, but it still felt pretty damn good. He tossed his pipe to the ground. He didn't need it any longer. Today was the day. His Holy Grail. He opened his backpack and checked to make sure it was there. Of course it was. Right where he'd put it.

He'd been bringing it to school, kind of like a trial run. He'd been going to school since his mother had freaked out about him missing three days last week. It's not that he was afraid of her, but he *was* afraid that she'd call the police on him for truancy. That would ruin everything. He zipped up his backpack, slung it over his shoulder, and walked into the cornfield, or what was left of it. The combine-denuded field looked brown and barren, with short stubby cornstalks. The field no longer provided any protection, but he didn't need it. Not anymore.

He continued, walking along the roadside now, the school in the distance, his breath creating a cloud of condensation. Caleb approached West Lake High School. Buses queued along the front entrance. Kids drove their beat-up cars and trucks recklessly through the parking lot, without a care in the world. Groups of girls talked and laughed, oblivious. Groups of guys were more subdued, looking like they had just rolled out of bed.

Everyone had one thing in common. They lived in a bubble of extended infantilism, childish responsibilities, and guaranteed safety and security, their needs being met by their parents and the state.

That bubble was about to be pricked.

CHAPTER 71

Rick and the Deal

Rick shook hands with the three men, which felt forced, like shaking hands with his executioners. Rick sat on one side of the shiny table, alone. Principal Pruitt, Superintendent Matthews, and Solicitor Burks sat on the other side. If this was a physical fight, Rick liked his odds against the three middle-aged men. But this fight was about the law, and Rick's mind was no match for three men who knew the law far better than him.

"Is everyone ready to begin?" Solicitor Burks said, sitting front and center and directly across the table from Rick.

Head nods and muted affirmations came from the men.

"We won't beat around the bush," Solicitor Burks said. "We've conducted our investigation, and we've found ample evidence to suggest that you've had an affair with Ashlee Miles." Harry Burks looked like an egg, round and fat around the middle, capped by a bald dome.

"You said, 'evidence to suggest.' Does that mean there's no evidence to convict?" Rick asked.

"This isn't a trial, Mr. Barnett. If we had enough evidence for a trial, you would've been arrested. Having said that, we do have enough evidence to terminate your employment with the West Lake School District, effective immediately, without recourse."

"What does that mean? *Without recourse?*"

Harry Burks had a small smirk, his hands folded neatly on the tabletop. "That means, we are comfortable terminating your employment, and we are very confident that we would win any wrongful termination suit that you might bring forth."

"I'd like to see the evidence."

The men looked at each other.

"You said, you have enough evidence to fire me," Rick said. "I'd like to see the evidence."

Solicitor Burks opened a fat manila folder and slid the image of Rick kissing Ashlee Miles across the table.

Rick glanced at the image, unsurprised. "She broke into my house while I was in the shower. I was escorting her out. When I opened the door, she kissed me."

"That may be," Burks said, "but I doubt a jury would believe that."

"But, even if I did kiss her, that's not against the law."

Solicitor Burks nodded, his neck fat jiggling. "You're right. This picture isn't enough for a criminal charge, but you are clearly violating the code of conduct for the West Lake School District as outlined in the employee handbook that you signed." He opened the manila folder again and removed a highlighted and photocopied passage from the employee handbook.

Rick read over the passage about fraternization with students. He was clearly in violation, if they took the picture at face value. Rick looked to Principal Pruitt. "You know me, Don. I'm telling the truth."

"Don't embarrass yourself, Rick," Pruitt replied.

"This picture isn't the only evidence we have," Burks said. "We also have an eyewitness who places you and Ashlee Miles, together, late at night after a football game. The eyewitness said that she leaned against your truck, approached you as a girlfriend would, and that you drove away with her in your truck, which is also a violation of the code of conduct."

Rick shook his head. "Bob Schneider tell you that?"

Burks didn't reply.

"I don't know why she was waiting for me. She's fixated on me. She needs help."

Solicitor Burks raised one side of his mouth in contempt. "It doesn't matter if she's fixated. Having an affair with the young lady is clearly not helping her. In fact, it's criminal."

Rick glared across the table. "I *didn't* have an affair with Ashlee Miles." He turned to Pruitt again. "Did you talk to Ashlee? She might have issues, but she won't lie about this."

Principal Pruitt looked to the solicitor.

"We did speak with Ashlee Miles," Solicitor Burks said. "She denied the affair."

"Then why are you doing this to me?" Rick asked, his hands held out like a beggar.

"She said she didn't break into your house. She said you invited her over. Our investigator inspected the doors and windows at your home, and nothing appeared broken. There were no teeth marks from pry bars or any other tools used for breaking and entering."

"I left the door unlocked."

"That's convenient. But she also said *you* kissed her, not the other way around. If push comes to shove, she will testify in court."

"She's lying."

"The picture says otherwise."

Rick rubbed his temples, then looked at the men on the other side of the table. "If you're just gonna fire me, why am I here?"

"The West Lake School District is prepared to give you a satisfactory evaluation," Solicitor Burks said, "provided you resign immediately and obey the terms of the nondisclosure agreement." Burks slid a piece of paper across the table, with a pen. "This deal is more than fair. I suggest you take it while you can."

Rick turned to Principal Pruitt, still looking for a lifeline. "Don, please. You know I didn't do this."

Pruitt clenched his fists, his ruddy complexion flashing red. "You disgust me. You should thank your lucky stars that you're not going to prison. I suggest you take this deal and get yourself some psychiatric help."

Rick read the terms of the contract, the heavy pen in hand. A cell phone rang, and Rick instinctively reached for his, but it wasn't his phone. Pruitt answered his phone and stepped from the room.

Immediately afterward, Superintendent Matthews's phone buzzed. The old man checked his text, his face going white as a ghost. Matthews turned to Solicitor Burks and said, "This is an emergency. I have to go." Dr. Matthews hurried from the room.

Rick and Solicitor Burks were left alone.

"Can I take this home and read it over?" Rick asked.

"By all means," Burks said. "The offer's good for a week. After that, we will terminate without recourse."

Rick nodded and headed for the exit, the papers in hand. He hurried out to the parking lot, hoping to catch Pruitt. Maybe he could reason with him. The man had known him since he was a student at West Lake. In the parking lot, Pruitt and Matthews drove away with urgency. Rick gazed down the highway, watching them speed through a late yellow light, eliciting a few honks. *What the hell's going on?* Rick's stomach lurched. *They're driving toward school.*

CHAPTER 72

Janet Never Lets a Good Crisis Go to Waste

The phone rang on Janet's desktop again. The third time in the past minute.

Janet frowned at Rachel and disconnected the phone line, silencing the ring. "I'm tired of doing everything around here. This is what happens to me when Pruitt takes off like he does."

"He needs to just retire already," Rachel replied.

Janet sighed. "Where was I?"

"You said that you told Shane that Ashlee is the one who had an affair with Rick."

Janet shook her head. "I thought my son had some sense, but, after I told him what that little whore was up to, he went over to her house. I'm sure she spun her web around him because he hasn't spoken to me since Saturday."

"Oh, my word. That's awful. What did she say to him?"

Janet scowled at Rachel. "Like I said, he won't talk to me, but, if I had to guess, she probably said the same thing to Shane that she said to Pruitt."

Rachel leaned forward in her seat, desperate for the juicy gossip.

"She told Pruitt that she wasn't having an affair with Rick. She did say that Rick came on to her and kissed her. I personally think it's bullshit. We both know he was having sex with the girl. He may not go to jail, but he's never coming back here."

"Good riddance. Does Heather know?"

"She was there."

"She hasn't posted anything on Facebook."

"I doubt she will. Ashlee would have a shit fit."

Despite the closed door and the location of Janet's back office, she heard shouting. "Do you hear that?"

Rachel narrowed her eyes, listening. "It sounds like kids yelling in the hall."

Janet blew out a breath and stood from her desk. "*Again*, I have to do everything."

They exited Janet's office. The main office was empty, but the halls looked like the Running of the Bulls. Students shouted and ran for the exits, as if their lives depended on it. Janet hurried from the main office into the hall, Rachel hot on her heels.

"What in the world?" Rachel said.

Janet stomped her foot. "Stop running!"

A few kids slowed, but most ignored her, still headed for the exits. A teacher ran toward them in bare feet, her heels in hand. "Principal Wilcox," the teacher said, nearly out of breath, "Caleb Miles has a gun."

"A gun? Where is he?"

"He's barricaded himself in Gwen Townsend's classroom." The teacher paused to catch her breath. "I think Gwen and her students are in there too—"

"Shane's in there!"

"Oh, my word," Rachel said with her hand over her mouth.

"Nobody knows what to do," the teacher continued. "Some teachers barricaded their classrooms, and others told the kids to run."

Janet glanced to the exits, her heartbeat rapid. A big part of her wanted to run, but she thought about the opportunity. *Think. What do they need to do?* "Everyone needs to evacuate. Tell everyone to assemble in the stands at the football field."

The teacher stood there, her eyes wide open.

"Now!"

The teacher ran for the exits, shouting at the kids to go to the football field.

"I should go too." Rachel touched Janet on the forearm. "I'm sure Shane'll be fine."

Janet glowered at Rachel.

Rachel removed her hand as if she'd been burned.

"Call the police," Janet said.

"I'll call outside." Rachel hustled for the exit.

Janet tried to block out the chaos, planning her next move. *Never let a good crisis go to waste. If I handle this correctly, I can be the hero while Pruitt's out. This might be enough to get rid of him.* She thought about how she could best be a hero without putting herself in harm's way. *Caleb's barricaded in. I doubt he'll come out and start shooting. If I'm the last one out, I'll be the principal who refused to leave until all the kids got out, and, if I stay near the front doors, I can remain safe. If I hear shots, I can still easily run outside. I'm not surprised that little creep became a school shooter. Someone should've seen that coming.* Janet thought of Shane holed up in that classroom. *Shane had bullied Caleb. That can't get out. This whole thing might be about Shane. Caleb might shoot him.* Her mind flashed to Caleb's essay. Her stomach tumbled. She almost vomited, bile climbing her esophagus. *It's in my desk!*

Janet ran back to her office.

CHAPTER 73

Gwen's Held Hostage

A pile of desks barricaded Gwen's classroom door. The blinds were closed. Gwen and her students crowded together on the shag carpet in the classroom library. During her creative writing class, Caleb had stood, pointing a handgun at Gwen, then waving it at the class. They'd been forced to barricade the door, to shut the blinds, and to move the beanbag chairs to create more room on the carpet. Gwen had seen multiple students texting, their thumbs rapidly tapping. Caleb had probably seen it too, but he didn't seem to care.

He stood over them now, pacing, his gun sweeping over them from time to time, creating a collective gasp each time. One girl cried softly. Gwen heard a cacophony of voices in the hallway and the sound of sneakers slapping the linoleum as students ran past the door.

Caleb spoke more to himself than his captive audience. "This school is so *fucking* shallow. This town is so *fucking* small-minded. I'm so *sick* of it."

"You're right, Caleb," Gwen said. "You're absolutely right. We can work it out."

Caleb shook his head and glared at Gwen. "No, we can't."

"That's not true. I can fix this for you."

"Come on, Caleb. You're making a big mistake," Jamar said.

"It's too late," Caleb replied. "I've already passed the point of no return."

CHAPTER 74

Caleb and the Truth

"It's *not* too late," Ms. Townsend said.

"You can let us go," Aaron Fuller said. "We won't say shit."

"We won't," Drew Fuller added.

"They're right," Jamar said. "We won't say anything."

Two girls embraced, consoling each other. The hallway noise dissipated.

Shane whispered with another girl, looking at his phone.

"What are you doing?" Caleb said, pointing his handgun at Shane.

Shane looked up from his phone. "Nothing."

"Bullshit."

"The police are coming."

Ms. Townsend gave Shane a look. "Be quiet, Shane."

"You think I don't know that?" Caleb said, waving his gun over the crowd. "I saw you guys texting for help. You guys think you're so fucking cool. You guys think you're better than me, don't you?"

"We don't think that," Jamar said.

"You're the brightest student I've ever had," Ms. Townsend said. "I'm begging you not to throw it away."

Caleb flipped his hair from his face. "Everybody's so *fucking* fake." He paused for a beat. "I'm no better. I'm just as fake as everyone else, but at least I have an excuse. I can't be real. If I am, some asshole like

Shane'll fuck with me." Caleb gestured with his gun toward Shane. "Right, Shane?"

Shane looked away.

"Come on. Tell everyone what you did to me."

Shane remained silent.

"What did you do?" a girl asked.

"Tell 'em, Shane," Caleb said.

Shane was stone-faced and still silent.

Caleb paced in front of his captives for a moment. His gaze settled on Shane again. "How are *you* fake?"

Shane lifted his chin. "I'm not."

Caleb laughed, almost maniacal. "That's bullshit, and you know it. You act like you're so tough, but you'd be on the bench if it wasn't for your mother. Jamar's better than you, and you and everyone else knows it."

Shane clenched his jaw. "That's bullshit."

"The truth hurts, doesn't it?"

Shane shook his head, silently seething.

"You're right, Caleb," Ms. Townsend said. "We're all fake in our own way, but we don't have to be. We can change. We can be more accepting, more authentic. Is that what you want? To be accepted for who you are?"

"It's too late for that. You and I both know there's no acceptance anymore. I doubt the police or anyone else will be accepting at this point."

"It's not too late. If you let everyone go, the police will understand. I'll make them understand. If you let everyone go, I'll stay with you and make sure that nobody hurts you."

Caleb looked at Gwen Townsend. "I might be willing to let everyone go."

A palpable wave of relief washed over the students.

"That's great, Caleb," Ms. Townsend said.

"I have two conditions," Caleb said. "The first condition is Shane stays."

"I'll stay," Gwen repeated. "I'll be a much better hostage than Shane."

"If he does what I say, I won't hurt him."

"Please, Caleb—"

"No! The first condition is, Shane stays. The second condition is, Shane tells the truth about *everything*." Caleb glowered at Shane. "Let's hear it. Tell us how your mommy fixed it so you'd start over Jamar. Tell everyone what you did to me in the locker room before the Lancaster game. Tell them about that picture of me in the bathroom, and the text you sent those girls."

"I don't know what you're talkin' about," Shane said, not making eye contact.

"Well, I guess nobody's going anywhere."

The class murmured among themselves, clearly displeased by Shane's silence.

"Dude, just tell him the truth," Drew Fuller said.

"Shut the fuck up, Drew," Shane replied.

"I'm gonna beat your fuckin' ass—"

"Guys, stop," Ms. Townsend said.

"I don't give a fuck who your mother is," Drew added.

Ms. Townsend gave Drew an exasperated look, and Drew showed his palms in surrender.

"This says a lot about you, Shane," Caleb said. "You have the chance to tell the truth and be the big hero, but you're too selfish. Maybe you need your mommy here."

Aaron and Drew Fuller stifled grins at that last comment. Shane looked away, his face flashing red.

Caleb addressed the group. "Raise your hand if you think Shane should tell the truth, so you guys can leave."

Hands were raised, tentative at first, until every hand was in the air, except Shane's and Ms. Townsend's. After a beat, Ms. Townsend raised her hand.

Caleb smiled. "This is your last chance, Shane. Are you a hero or a coward?"

"Tell him the truth," Jamar said.

"Just tell him," a girl said.

Shane looked around at his classmates. "This is bullshit. It doesn't matter what I say."

Caleb pointed his handgun at Shane. "You're a coward who doesn't deserve to live."

Shane ducked his head, and the surrounding classmates scooted away from him.

Ms. Townsend stood and stepped into the line of fire. "Don't, Caleb. Please."

The classroom phone rang.

CHAPTER 75

Rick and Chaos

Police cars zoomed past, their lights flashing. Rick followed the police in his pickup. A news van followed Rick. As he approached the high school, he observed students and teachers running from the main entrance toward the football stadium. Police cars littered the scene, parking sideways in front of every exit, officers leaning over their hoods, wearing bulletproof vests, with rifles and shotguns trained on the doors. A fire truck and three ambulances idled nearby, ready for action.

Rick parked in the teacher's lot and ran toward the scene.

CHAPTER 76

Janet, the Hero

Janet had finally found Caleb's essay, buried in her bottom drawer. But she wasn't running down the hall with *that* essay. When she thought about her fingerprints on the original, she made a copy of that essay. Then she shredded the original. Thankfully, she had a shredder and a small copier in her office. Security cameras covered the shared copiers to discourage personal use.

She didn't have gloves, so she had pulled the sleeve of her sweater down over her hand, creating a makeshift glove to hold the copied essay. Now she ran down the hallway, toward Gwen's classroom, running against the current of kids.

Lewis stood guard in front of Gwen's classroom. "Go to the football field," Lewis said to the kids as they ran past.

Janet approached Lewis, the essay held discreetly at her side. "I need you to go to the football field too and get a head count."

Lewis said, "You should go. Print the attendance list for today and take that to the football field. I'll make sure everyone gets out."

"My son's in there!" Janet's eyes flicked to Gwen's classroom door.

"I can help. Caleb and I have a relationship."

"I don't care. Go. Now!"

Lewis stepped away from the door and herded students on his way out. Janet looked into the window. The door was bombarded by

251

desks stacked three high. Her view was obscured by the desks, but she caught a glimpse of Shane and his classmates sitting in the back of the room. Janet breathed a sigh of relief. *He's okay.*

Shane sat by himself, like he had a communicable disease. His classmates clustered together, at least five feet away, creating a ring of empty carpet around him. Janet doubted anyone would notice a single piece of paper under the barricade of desks. She turned around and waited in front of Gwen's classroom until a group of kids passed.

As they shielded her from view of the security camera, Janet bent down and slid the essay under the door. With her mission accomplished, Janet ran from Gwen's classroom to the main entrance.

Janet kept her word, sort of. She wasn't about to stand in front of a door with a gunman on the other side, but she did stand near the exit, safely away from the scene, instructing students to go to the football stadium. A few minutes later, the school was dead silent, and Janet exited a hero, the educator who risked her life for her students.

CHAPTER 77

Gwen and the Negotiation

The classroom phone rang again. The first time, Gwen had offered to answer it, but Caleb had told her to sit down. Thankfully, he hadn't shot Shane.

"Someone has to answer that," Gwen said, looking up at Caleb.

"No," Caleb said.

"I'll answer it," Aaron Fuller said.

"No."

"That ringing is annoying as fuck," Drew Fuller said.

The phone stopped ringing.

"It's probably the police," a girl said.

"I know who it is," Caleb replied.

"Let me talk to them for you," Gwen said. "I can get you out of this."

The phone rang again.

Caleb looked at Gwen, the handgun pointed to the floor. He motioned with his chin toward the phone. "Go ahead."

Gwen stood and hurried to the phone attached to the wall. She picked up the receiver and put it to her ear. "Hello, this is Gwen Townsend."

Caleb moved closer to Gwen, now standing in between her and his hostages. Everyone watched Gwen, hoping to glean some information about their fate.

"Gwen, I'm Trooper Dexter Trombley with the state police. Is anyone injured?"

"No, everyone's fine," Gwen replied.

"How many students are in there?"

"Twenty-five—"

"How many cops are outside?" Caleb said to Gwen.

"He wants to know how many police officers are outside?" Gwen said into the phone.

"We've had word that Caleb Miles is the gunman," Trombley said. "Just say yes if that's correct."

"Yes—"

"How many cops?" Caleb said.

"How many police officers?" Gwen asked again.

"I don't know exactly," Trombley said. "Tell him a lot of officers are here and that he has our full attention, and we don't want anyone to get hurt, including him."

Gwen turned to Caleb. "He said a lot of police officers are here, and they don't want anyone to get hurt, including you."

Caleb nodded, the wheels turning in his mind. The hostages looked at each other with renewed hope.

"Ask him if he's willing to release the kids," Trombley said.

"He wants to know if you'll release your classmates," Gwen said. "I'll stay here with you. I won't leave you, and I won't let anything happen to you. I promise."

Caleb's shoulders slumped, his head hung for a moment, as if he was resigned to his fate. He turned to his hostages. "Go."

The students looked at him but didn't move.

Caleb motioned with his gun. "Get the fuck out!"

"He's letting everyone go," Gwen said.

"That's great news. Please tell him I said thank you."

"He said, thank you," Gwen said to Caleb.

"Hang up the phone," Caleb replied.

"He wants me to hang up now," she said before hanging up.

The students unbarricaded the door and ran from Gwen's classroom, leaving the door wide open. Shane was the first from the room, pushing his way through the group of students.

"Do you want me to shut that?" Gwen asked, gesturing to the open door.

Caleb shook his head and sat at a student desk, his handgun resting on the desktop. He put his head in his hands and sobbed. Gwen thought about grabbing the gun, but there was no way she'd use it, and she wanted his trust, so she approached and put her arm around the boy. Caleb leaned into Gwen, and she bent down and hugged him with both arms. His body shook with his sobs.

"It'll be okay," Gwen said, rubbing the boy's back. "We'll fix this."

A minute later, Caleb sat up straight, breaking Gwen's embrace. He sniffled, wiped his face with the sleeve of his hoodie, and said, "I'm sorry, Ms. Townsend." Caleb stood from the desk, grabbed his gun, and backed away from Gwen.

"Don't apologize," Gwen said, stepping toward him, her hands held out. "I know people have hurt you. I know your home life is difficult. I care about you, Caleb. I don't want anything bad to happen to you."

Caleb took another step back and pointed his gun at Gwen. "Too late."

CHAPTER 78

Caleb and His Holy Grail

The classroom phone rang again. Caleb had seen enough movies to know what was next. Either he came out, or the cops came in. But this would be on his terms.

"It's time to go," Caleb said, pointing his gun at Ms. Townsend. "I'm gonna hold my gun to your back, and we're gonna walk out together, but I don't want you to be afraid. I promise I won't shoot you."

Ms. Townsend nodded, tears slipping from the corners of her blue eyes. "I know you won't." She looked to the phone still ringing. "I'd like to tell them that we're coming out and that you're not violent."

Caleb shook his head and stepped behind Ms. Townsend, poking her in the back with his gun. "Let's go."

"I think this would be much safer for you if you left the gun here."

"No. Let's go." He prodded her in the back again.

The halls were empty and dead silent. It was eerie, the only sound their footsteps on the linoleum. They made it to the end of the hall, which opened to the main entrance on their right and the main office to the left. Through the windows on the entrance doors, Caleb saw the army of police officers shielded by their cars and pointing rifles.

Ms. Townsend stopped. "Caleb, please put down the gun."

He took a deep breath and prodded Ms. Townsend forward with the barrel of his gun. "Open the door."

She opened the door, and they walked outside, Ms. Townsend in front and Caleb behind her, his gun touching her lower back. The air was crisp and cool, but the sun warmed his black hoodie. Ms. Townsend's long dress swayed gently in the breeze. A helicopter hovered overhead. Behind the wall of police, reporters and cameramen jockeyed for position.

She put her hands in the air. "Don't shoot," she shouted. "Please don't shoot."

Caleb felt her shaking, her fear reverberating through her body into the barrel of his handgun. He bent into an athletic stance and shoved her with his left hand, using his legs for power. She fell easily, her wedge heels and her shakiness providing a poor base. Caleb raised his gun and ran toward the police.

He only took a few steps before his body was riddled with bullet holes.

CHAPTER 79

Rick's Banished

A flurry of gunshots came from the school. Kids screamed and ducked in their seats on the stadium bleachers. Rick looked toward the school, a lump in his throat. He thought about Gwen and her class, hoping she and her students were okay, knowing that at least one person was likely dead. *Caleb Miles.* Rick thought about the hazing rumors. *I didn't protect him.*

"Stay calm everyone," Lewis said, from a bleacher near Rick.

"Mr. Barnett?" a girl said, handing him a clipboard.

Rick blinked, his mind returning to the task at hand. He took the clipboard from the girl. "Thank you." Rick glanced over the names, making sure they were legible. He moved to the next row.

"Everyone, print your name on this sheet. Please print legibly. When your parents come to pick you up, they'll have to sign you out." Rick handed the clipboard and paper to the first student in the row. As the kids printed their names and passed the clipboard, Rick surveyed the bleachers. They were filled with students, talking with each other, texting and thumb-swiping on their phones. Lewis and a few other teachers also collected names and provided emotional support.

Mrs. Moyer and Mrs. Baumgartner sat near the front corner of the bleachers, tapping on laptops. They'd signed in remotely to the school's database, checking attendance to cross-reference with the names added to the clipboards being circulated. The school had to account for each and every student and staff member. Earlier, Rick had heard them say that Ashlee Miles was absent.

Principal Pruitt approached the bleachers, his eyes locked on Rick. *Shit. Here we go.* The chubby principal didn't bother climbing the bleacher steps. He simply stood at the bottom and called out, "Mr. Barnett. I need to speak with you."

Rick addressed the first kid on the row. "When the clipboard comes back, start it down the next row."

The boy nodded. "Okay, Mr. Barnett."

Rick walked down the bleacher steps.

Principal Pruitt stood, red-faced. "Where are you parked?"

"Teacher's lot."

"Let's take a walk."

Rick nodded, and they walked away from the bleachers, cutting across the practice fields, toward the teacher's parking lot.

Once they were away from the scene, Pruitt said, "What the heck do you think you're doing? Don't you think I have enough to deal with?" Pruitt gestured to the school and the police and media presence.

"What happened? Is everyone okay?" Rick asked.

"Caleb Miles held Gwen and her class hostage."

"I heard. Was anybody hurt?"

"Just Caleb." Principal Pruitt shook his head, his beady eyes brimming with tears. "The police shot him in front of the school."

"I'm sorry, Don."

Pruitt shook his head. "You can't be here, Rick. You know that. What the heck's wrong with you? I should be dealing with this mess, not escorting you to your car."

"This school is all I know. These kids are the only family I have left."

"You should've thought of that before ..."

"I'm being setup."

Pruitt sighed. "Did you sign the papers?"

"Not yet. Burks said I have a week to make a decision."

"If you really care about these kids, sign the papers and move on. The last thing this school needs is more bad press."

CHAPTER 80

Janet Does Damage Control

Janet sat in an interview room at the Swatara Township Police Department. Sitting across from her, at the square table, was Detective Lee Strickland. The detective was middle-aged, short and thin, his cheap suit a bit big. He was clean shaven, his dark hair feathered and parted in the middle. *Nineteen eighty-five called. They want their detective back.*

Detective Strickland slid Caleb's essay encased in plastic across the table. "Do you recognize this paper?"

Janet looked over the essay, giving a good show. "I've never seen this before."

The detective nodded. "The paper indicates that Caleb was suicidal. Gwen Townsend said she gave it to you and talked to you about it."

"I've never seen this before."

"Why do you think she'd lie?"

Janet shrugged. "Maybe she's mistaken. Maybe she went to see the counselor, Mrs. Baumgartner."

"Ms. Townsend mentioned that the counselor was out that day."

"What day?"

"Friday, September 16th. We've already verified that Mrs. Baumgartner was in fact out that day."

"Well, Gwen Townsend didn't give me this paper. If she had, I would've been on the phone with Caleb's mother that day. I did talk to Gwen about Caleb on that day, if my memory serves me correct."

"What did you talk about?"

"There was an issue in her class between my son, Shane, and Caleb."

The detective nodded. "What was the issue?"

"It was a misunderstanding over some name-calling. You know how teenagers are." She forced a brief smile.

The detective narrowed his eyes at Janet. "Ms. Townsend claims that Shane bullied Caleb, called him a faggot, and she went to you for disciplinary action."

Janet frowned and shook her head. "That's not what happened. Yes, she did bring Shane to me for discipline. Normally, this would've gone to Principal Pruitt, but he was out that day."

The detective nodded, nonplussed.

"Apparently, Shane called him Farmer Caleb or something like that, but that was after Caleb called Shane and a number of other boys *douchebags*."

"Do you think Shane was lying to you?"

"Maybe, but, even if he did call Caleb a faggot, and I didn't find any evidence that he did, it was after Caleb called Shane and several other students douchebags. I suppose I could've given both of them detention, but, if I gave detention to every kid who called another kid a name, nearly the entire school would be in detention."

"So, it was a nonissue?"

"As far as the school's concerned. Don't get me wrong. I punished Shane at home, but I hold him to a higher standard because he's my son."

The detective put his elbows on the table and leaned forward. "We heard from numerous students that Caleb claimed that Shane did something to him in the locker room. Coincidentally, his essay portrayed an incident of bullying in the locker room. Do you think Shane bullied Caleb in the locker room?

"I highly doubt it."

The detective paused for a moment. "We think Shane did, in fact, bully Caleb."

Janet's eyes widened. "Shane's not a bully. If something did happen between them, I'm sure they're both at fault."

The detective stared at Janet for a beat.

"Is he in trouble?" she asked.

"We haven't found anything criminal … *yet*."

Her stomach tumbled over the word *yet*. "Do you think Shane did something criminal?"

"I don't know. We're still investigating."

"My son's not perfect, but he's not a criminal. He's never been in any trouble before."

Detective Strickland didn't respond, creating an uncomfortable silence.

"One thing bothers me about this." Janet pointed to Caleb's essay still sitting on the desk in front of her. "Why would Ms. Townsend give Caleb an A+ if she was so worried about him? Why would she even grade it at all?"

"Ms. Townsend said that she didn't want you or the counselor to think she was mad at Caleb for what he wrote. She also said the writing was excellent."

Janet skimmed over the essay, giving the detective another show. "It's filled with expletives. It's definitely not an A+ paper."

"Why do you think Gwen Townsend would say that she talked to you about this paper if she never did?"

Janet took a deep breath. "Ms. Townsend's new to our school this year, and I've already had to reprimand her on several occasions."

"What did she do?"

"She has poor classroom management. To be honest, her students are out of control. She's shown that she'll allow bad behavior in her classroom, so it's not a stretch to believe that she'd be perfectly fine with an essay of this nature. She probably thought Caleb was simply expressing himself, and she didn't think he was suicidal. After what happened, she probably wanted to cover her backside."

The detective nodded. "We found the essay on the floor, near Gwen's classroom door. How do you think it got there?"

"Gwen or Caleb must've put it there."

"We think Caleb left it for us to find because he wanted the world to know what he went through. We think it was his suicide note. The paper he left on the floor wasn't the original though."

"Caleb photocopied it?"

"We don't think so. We think Ms. Townsend made a copy and kept the original. We think she gave the photocopied paper back to Caleb. We think Ms. Townsend did go to Mrs. Baumgartner on September 16th, but she was out that day. We think Ms. Townsend was concerned about Caleb, but, for some reason, she didn't follow up."

"Did you find the original?"

"Not yet."

"What Gwen did, her negligence, is that criminal?"

"I doubt we'll press criminal charges, unless we find new evidence, but Ms. Townsend might be sued in civil court, and I imagine the school might want to take action, but you'd know more about her employment situation than I would."

Janet nodded.

"Well, that's it for now. Is there anything you wanted to add?"

"I know my son. He's a good boy."

The detective nodded and stood from his chair.

Janet stood as well.

The detective removed a business card from his wallet and handed it to Janet. "If you think of anything, call me anytime, day or night."

"I will."

Janet left the police station with mixed feelings. She felt like a weight had been lifted in regard to Gwen and Caleb's essay, but Janet was worried about Shane. The sun peeked through the dark clouds, tempering the chill in the air, as if God had adjusted the thermostat just for her. Classes had been canceled for the rest of the week, so she drove home. Of course, the football game would proceed as usual on Friday. On the way home, she thought about the situation and how best to play it. *I'm not finished yet. Caleb's death might just be the catalyst I've been waiting for. Maybe I can get rid of Rick, Gwen, and Pruitt. I do need to get in front of this thing with Shane.*

As she pulled into her driveway, her cell phone rang. She put her BMW in Park, removed her phone from her purse, glanced at the screen, and swiped right. "Hello, Rachel."

"I have some really bad news," Rachel said, her voice high and panicked.

Janet frowned, used to Rachel's overreactions. "What is it?"

"People are saying that Shane bullied Caleb, and that's why Caleb did what he did."

Janet clenched her jaw. "Who said that?"

"It's on the West Lake Watchdog page."

"Heather said that?"

"No, she posted a memorial for Caleb, asking for donations for his funeral, and Drew Fuller posted something about it in the comments."

Janet sighed, grabbed her purse, and stepped from her car. She slammed the door shut. "You said, 'people.' Drew Fuller is *one* person." Janet walked to her front door.

"If he's saying it, probably other people are too."

"You don't know that for a fact, do you?" Janet unlocked her front door and stepped inside.

"Well, no."

"Then don't *fucking* say it. Do you understand me?"

Rachel paused for a beat. "I'm sorry, Janet. I didn't mean to offend you."

Janet stepped into her kitchen, depositing her purse on the counter. "You didn't offend me, but I can't have you spreading lies about my son—"

"I would never say anything about Shane. I'm really sorry. I didn't mean it like that."

Janet took a deep breath. "Keep your facts straight from now on."

"I will."

Janet sat at the kitchen table and opened her laptop. "We have one person, Drew Fuller, who's lying about Shane."

"That's right."

"Hold on. I'm going to the page now." Janet set down her phone and navigated to the West Lake Watchdog Facebook page.

West Lake Watchdog

October 11 at 11:34 PM

RIP Caleb Miles May 14, 2001–October 11, 2016

Caleb Miles was killed today. He was so gentle. Never hurt nobody. He didn't even have a gun. It was a PELLET GUN. The cops didn't have to kill him. And that damn school! That school drove him to it. His mother don't even have enough money for a funeral. Please donate on the Go Fund Me Page for funeral expenses. **Https.GoFundMe-CalebMiles.com** 78 Likes 22 Shares

Trina Grisham That's awful. I feel so bad for his mother. Losing a child is the worst pain anyone can endure. You should find out what that school did to him. How many kids have to be hurt before that school changes? I donated. 26 Likes

Sadie Ollinger I donated too. My heart goes out to the Miles family. 19 Likes

Will Gilroy This school is corrupt. These people are corrupt. ALL OF THEM. THEY NEED TO GO. **#FireBarnett #FirePruitt #FireEverybody** 23 Likes

Drew Fuller It's not the schools fault. Caleb was mad at Shane Wilcox

Roger Elkins You don't know what we know about the school. I think it's great that a young person is speaking there mind, but this is not the time. 9 Likes

Drew Fuller You don't know shit. I was in that classroom, dick. Caleb said it himself.

Breanna Franks Why was he mad at Shane?

266

Drew Fuller Because Shane put his balls in Calebs face

Janet winced at that last comment. *Fucking Drew Fuller. That white-trash degenerate.* She picked up her cell phone from the table. "Rachel?"

"I'm still here," Rachel replied.

"I need to call you back." Janet disconnected the call. She sat at her kitchen table, thinking through her options, thinking about the cause and effects of different actions. Fifteen minutes later, Janet grabbed her purse from the counter and sat back at the table. She fished Detective Strickland's card from her purse and called his cell phone.

"Detective Strickland," he said.

"Hello, Detective, this is Janet Wilcox. We spoke a few hours ago."

"Of course. What can I do for you?"

"I just spoke with one of my teachers, and he has some important information for you."

"Does he wanna come in and talk?"

"He does."

"What's his name and number?"

"He's a little nervous. I told him that I talked to you, and it went well, and you gave me your card, so he asked me if I would set up a meeting with you."

"Okay. When do you think he can come in?"

"Are you available tomorrow? I think it's important that he talks to you sooner rather than later. What he has to say is very important in my opinion."

"I can make time. Hang on a minute." After a moment Strickland said, "How about eleven?"

"That'll be fine."

"What's his name?"

"Bob Schneider."

"What's he planning to talk about? I'd like to be prepared."

"They're his words, not mine, so I'd rather not misquote him, but

I will say it has to do with bullying that Caleb Miles endured prior to his death."

"Okay. Thank you, Ms. Wilcox. I have Mr. Schneider on the schedule for eleven tomorrow."

"You're welcome, Detective."

Strickland disconnected the call.

Janet called Rachel back.

"Janet?" Rachel answered.

"I want you to get a message to Heather," Janet said. "Tell her to delete Drew Fuller's posts and ban him from the page. Tell her that Drew Fuller was the one who bullied Caleb, not Shane."

"Is that true?"

"Do you think I'd lie?"

"No, but Heather might want proof. I mean, her son just died."

"Do you have a pen and paper?"

"Hold on a sec." Rachel put her phone down for a minute. "I'm ready now."

"Tell Heather that Coach Schneider saw Drew standing over Caleb naked from the waist down. He thought they were just roughhousing, so he told them to knock it off. Also, after Caleb quit football, Coach Barnett told Coach Schneider that he felt guilty because he knew Caleb was being bullied by Drew Fuller, and he didn't do anything about it. He thought the bullying might toughen up Caleb, make him a better football player."

"Oh, my word. I'll call her and let her know."

"Call me back after you talk to her."

"Okay, bye."

Janet disconnected the call and tapped Bob Schneider from her contact list. After two rings, her call went to voice mail. She tried again, this time one ring and straight to voice mail. Janet pounded her table with the side of her fist, like a gavel. *He thinks he can avoid me?* She rose from her seat, grabbed her purse from the counter, and left the house. She drove to Bob Schneider's vinyl-sided rambler and parked behind his SUV.

The clouds converged to stifle that brief respite of sun. She stepped from her BMW, the wind whipping through her pantsuit. Janet marched to the front door and rang the doorbell.

A tiny pale woman with a baby on her hip answered the door. Janet had a vision of the Schneiders having sex. Big fat Bob crushing the poor woman while he pumped away, the Mrs. faking orgasms, too meek to ask for what she really wanted.

Janet smiled. "You must be Bob's wife. I'm Principal Wilcox." Janet extended her hand.

The woman forced a smile, moved the baby to her left hip, and shook Janet's hand limply. "I'm Ellen."

Janet turned her attention to the baby dressed in a tiny football jersey and pampers. "And who's this beautiful boy?"

Ellen forced another smile. "This is Liam."

"You must have your hands full."

Bob appeared at the door, wearing a West Lake Football sweatshirt and ratty jeans. His eyes darted between Ellen and Janet. "What's goin' on?"

"Hello, Bob," Janet said. "I'm sorry to bother you at home, but I need to talk to you about some logistics for the game on Friday. I tried to call, but you weren't answering. It's kind of important."

"I already worked everything out with the AD."

"There's been a new development. May we talk for a few minutes?"

"Come on in," Ellen said, stepping aside.

"I'd rather not impose," Janet said to Ellen. Then she addressed Bob. "We can talk in my car."

"I'll be right back," Bob said to his wife.

Ellen nodded and went back inside, clutching Liam tight to her chest.

They sat in Janet's BMW, Bob's side of the car bouncing a bit as he slumped into the leather seat. Bob didn't look good. His brown hair and beard were disheveled. His clothes looked dirty and stained. His body odor filled the interior of the car, wafting into Janet's nostrils.

"You can't come to my house," Bob said, trying to sound authoritative.

Janet cracked her window. "I can do whatever I want. Don't forget that."

Bob looked down, his face reddening.

"Why are you avoiding my calls?" Janet asked.

"I wasn't. My phone's not working."

Janet removed her phone from her purse, swiped right, and tapped Bob Schneider from her contacts. Bob's pocket chimed. He shut his eyes for a moment.

"Go on. Answer it," Janet said.

Bob removed his phone from his pocket, swiped right, and looked at Janet, dumbfounded.

"Answer it," Janet repeated, placing her phone to her ear. "Hello, Bob. Are you there? I can't hear you."

Bob put his phone to his ear and said, "Hello."

Janet smiled wide. "There you are. I'm glad your phone's working now." Janet disconnected the call, placed her phone in her purse, and glared at Bob. "When I call, you answer. Do you understand me?"

Bob nodded and shoved his phone into his pocket.

"I didn't hear you. Do you understand me?"

"Yeah."

"Good." Janet paused for a beat. "You're lucky I tracked you down, because *you* have a big problem."

He held out his palms. "Please, Janet, leave me alone."

"I'd love to, but I'm constantly cleaning up your messes."

"I don't understand."

"Drew Fuller sexually assaulted Caleb Miles in *your* locker room."

"I heard it was Shane. It was on the West Lake Watchdog."

Janet glowered at Bob. "That's a lie coming from Rick because he hates me and my son. Caleb Miles was sexually assaulted by Drew Fuller. Apparently, Drew put his scrotum in Caleb's face. To make matters worse, Rick knew that Caleb was being bullied but did nothing about it."

"That's on Rick then, not me."

"Rick's claiming that you knew about the bullying but did nothing about it. Not only that, he's claiming that you *saw* the bullying and didn't stop it."

"That's not true!"

"Relax, Bob. I know that, but let's be honest. The kids are still loyal to Rick. Did you know that he still talks to them? He has quite a few kids backing his story. I think this is his little bit of revenge."

"Jesus. What am I supposed to do?"

"I've already taken care of it. You just have to go to the police and tell them that you saw Drew standing over Caleb naked from the waist down. You thought they were just roughhousing, so you told them to knock it off. After Caleb quit football, Coach Barnett told you that he felt guilty because he knew Caleb was being bullied by Drew Fuller, and he didn't do anything about it. He thought the bullying might toughen him up."

Bob's shoulders slumped. "I can't lie. All they have to do is interview guys on the team."

"It's not lying. You didn't see Drew put his scrotum in Caleb's face, but you *did* see Drew standing over Caleb naked from the waist down. Who's to say you didn't see that? Everyone knows Drew Fuller's a degenerate. Who's to say Rick didn't tell you that he knew Caleb was being bullied, and he felt guilty because he didn't do anything? Rick's the only person who'll say differently, and his reputation isn't exactly credible. If it'll make you more comfortable, I'll go with you when you speak to the police tomorrow."

Bob's eyes widened. "Tomorrow? What are you talking about?"

"You really have to get ahead of these things. The police are like bloodhounds. As soon as they get a scent for a suspect, they won't stop until they get their man. Would you rather they have a scent for you or for Rick?"

"I didn't do anything wrong."

"That's not entirely true, is it? Does your wife know you watch porn at school? Do you think she'd stay with you if you lost your job because of it?"

Bob clenched his jaw, the vein in his forehead throbbing. "They'll wanna know when and where I talked to Rick. They're not stupid. They'll check to see if I'm lyin'."

"That's easy enough. Tell the police you don't remember the exact date, but it was at practice after Caleb had quit and before Rick was suspended. Who's to say you're lying? Maybe Rick did say something like that. It wouldn't surprise me."

Bob let out a heavy breath. "What time's the meetin' with the police?"

"It's at eleven."

Bob nodded.

"I'm glad we're on the same page."

Bob exited the BMW and turned back to Janet, his meat hook on the open door. "This is the last thing."

Janet smiled. "Give that baby of yours a hug and a kiss for me."

CHAPTER 81

Gwen and Detective Strickland

"Would you like to change your story?" Detective Strickland asked.

"No. I told you the truth already," Gwen replied, sitting across from the detective in an interview room.

"Mrs. Baumgartner said that she had no idea Caleb was suicidal."

"That may be true. I never talked to Mrs. Baumgartner. I talked to Janet Wilcox."

"Janet Wilcox said she never talked to you about Caleb Miles being suicidal, only about a verbal altercation between Caleb and her son, Shane."

Gwen clenched her fists. "She's twisting the truth. I *did* talk to her about the verbal altercation, but later in the day I gave her the essay, and we talked about Caleb being suicidal."

"Why didn't you follow up with Mrs. Baumgartner?"

"I should have. I asked Caleb if he'd talked to her, and he said he did. I thought he was telling the truth."

The detective lifted one side of his mouth in disdain. "And now you think Janet Wilcox is lying."

"Do I need a lawyer?"

"Did you do anything wrong?"

Gwen exhaled and glared at the detective. "Yes. I didn't follow

273

up with Mrs. Baumgartner, and I didn't stop you guys from killing Caleb."

The detective narrowed his eyes at Gwen. "Where's the original copy of Caleb's essay?"

"I told you this yesterday. I gave it to Janet Wilcox."

"Did you make a copy of the essay?"

"No."

"Then how did Caleb get a copy?"

"It wasn't from me. We've been through this."

The detective ignored her last statement. "Do you normally leave graded papers on the floor of your classroom?"

Gwen blew out a breath, exasperated. "No, I don't. I don't know how it got there."

"In the essay, Caleb references Flash Gordon. Do you know who that might be?"

"I think he's talking about Jamar Burris, but I'm not certain. Jamar was Caleb's friend."

The detective scribbled Jamar's name into his notepad. "You said that you thought that Shane Wilcox and Lance Osborn were the bullies Caleb referenced in his essay."

"I don't know that for certain, but, yes, that's what I think."

"What about Drew and Aaron Fuller? Could they be the bullies?"

"I guess it could be Drew, but Aaron doesn't play football. I really don't think it's Drew though. I know he's a little rough around the edges, but I think he has a good heart."

CHAPTER 82

Rick and the Funeral

"Thank you for coming in on such short notice," Detective Strickland said.

"Sure," Rick said, settling into a seat.

The detective stared across the table at Rick, silent.

Rick's heart thumped in his chest. *Is it hot in here?* He wondered if they would arrest him for Ashlee Miles. It had been a constant worry since he'd seen that picture. The silence stretched into discomfort. Rick felt compelled to fill the quiet. "What do you wanna talk to me about?"

Despite his middle-aged face, the detective looked small and childlike in his oversize suit, like he was playing detective dress-up. "Did you ever see Caleb Miles being bullied?"

Rick relaxed, thrilled that it wasn't a question about Ashlee. "Not that I can think of, not that he wasn't. He probably was bullied."

"What makes you think he was bullied?"

"I would imagine it's tough for a small boy on a football team."

The detective nodded as if he knew from experience. "Are you sure you've never seen Caleb being bullied?"

Rick shrugged. "I don't know. It's possible I have. Sometimes the kids talk trash and get into fights in practice. Not sure if that counts as bullying."

"So, you did see Caleb being bullied."

"Maybe. I don't remember."

"Did you do anything about it?"

"Like what?"

Strickland narrowed his eyes at Rick. "Did you stop the bullying? Did you reprimand the bully? Did you provide any counseling services? Did you refer Caleb to a counselor? Did you do anything at all, or did you just let it happen?"

Rick leaned back in his chair, as if he were dodging punches from the detective. "Look. I don't know what you're getting at, but, if I saw something bad enough, I dealt with it."

"Were fights and trash-talking a regular occurrence?"

"What do you mean by *regular*?"

"How often does trash-talking and fighting occur?"

"Every few weeks we might have a fight. And trash-talking? ... I don't know. I suppose that probably happens every day. It's not about bullying though. It's part of the game. It's competitive."

Detective Strickland nodded. "Then you *were* aware of Caleb being bullied."

"I don't remember a particular instance."

"But you said, 'He was probably bullied.'"

"Do I need a lawyer?"

"Did you do anything wrong?"

"No."

Strickland shrugged. "Then you have nothing to worry about."

"Am I in some sort of trouble?"

"Are you aware that Drew Fuller sexually assaulted Caleb Miles?"

"What are you talking about?"

"We have an eyewitness who says that, in the football locker room, Drew Fuller put his scrotum in Caleb Miles's face."

Rick's face twisted in disgust. "I don't know anything about that."

"I hope not, because, if you did, and you didn't do anything about it, you could be charged with negligent endangerment of a child or even child abuse neglect."

* * *

The interview had ended with Detective Strickland saying, "I'll let you know if I have any more questions." Rick drove home from the interview, an uneasy feeling deep in the pit of his stomach. *What have they found out about Ashlee Miles? But the only evidence is that picture. What if Janet finds someone to lie? Would she go that far? Isn't it enough to fire me? Does she want me to go to prison too?*

Rick made it home, went inside, and changed into his black suit. He checked the time, left his house, and drove to school. He knew he wasn't allowed on campus, and he had no intention of going inside, but he felt compelled to show up for Caleb. Rick parked his truck in the back of the school parking lot, near Gwen's black Jetta. He watched as students, parents, and teachers exited their cars and made their way to the school auditorium for the funeral reception. Three reporters with their cameramen stood at the entrance, hoping for interviews and sound bites.

Teachers and parents wore suits and dresses, but many students wore jeans and sneakers. The Burris family parked their sedan nearby. Jamar surveyed the parking lot as he stepped from the back seat. Unlike his classmates, he was dressed to the nines. He looked in Rick's direction, held his gaze for a moment, then said something to his parents. Mr. and Mrs. Burris followed the crowd into school, but Jamar approached Rick's truck. Jamar knocked on Rick's passenger window, and Rick powered it down.

"Hey, Coach," Jamar said.

"Jamar," Rick replied. "You all right?"

He lifted one shoulder. "Can I talk to you?"

Rick unlocked the door. "Come on in."

Jamar climbed onto the bench seat. The October sun warmed the cab. He pursed his lips. "I heard you're not coming back."

"It doesn't look good."

Jamar nodded, silent for a moment. He looked at the school through the windshield. "Are you going in?"

"No. Technically, I'm not even allowed in the parking lot."

Jamar looked at Rick and his dark suit. "Then why are you all dressed up?"

"I wanted to pay my respects."

"Are you going to the game tonight?"

"I'll have to sit on the East York side, but I'll be there."

"I think I should quit. I don't even know why we're playing after what happened to Caleb."

"Playing or not playing won't bring him back."

"I know."

"Do you like playing football?"

"I'm not playing anymore."

"You don't play in practice?"

"Yeah, but ..." Jamar shook his head. "It's not fair."

"What if I never would've started you this season? Would you've quit?"

Jamar frowned at Rick. "I guess not."

"Then why do you wanna quit now?"

"Because it's not fair. If I wasn't playing because Coach Schneider thought I wasn't good enough, I wouldn't care. I mean, I would care, but I would understand. Even if he was wrong. I'd just wait till next year. But I think he knows what he's doing, and he's doing it on purpose. How am I supposed to trust the man?"

"This world's full of weak, selfish, and dishonest people. You can complain about the unfairness of it all, and you're right. It is unfair. But are you gonna let another man's weakness run your life and determine your fate?"

"But he does control my fate."

"To a certain extent, but you control your reaction. Coach Schneider is making the wrong choice here, no doubt. You can quit and tell everyone how unfair it is, or you can go to practice every day and get better as a quarterback. You can work hard in the off-season and get even better. It's gut-check time. You can let all this bury you, or you can keep fighting."

"What about you? Are you still fighting?"

Rick rubbed the back of his neck. "I haven't decided."

Jamar took a deep breath and looked at the school through the windshield. "I guess I should go in." He opened the door and stepped from the truck.

"Hey, Jamar."

Jamar stood on the asphalt, facing Rick, his hand on the open door.

"Don't let small-minded people grind you down. You're gonna be great at whatever you decide to do with your life."

Jamar blinked, his brown eyes glistening. "What about you?"

"I had my time."

CHAPTER 83

Janet and the Funeral

Janet stood with Rachel in the back of the auditorium, away from the crowd.

"Oh, my word. I can't believe she came," Rachel said, watching Gwen join the line of people offering condolences to the Miles family.

"It's inappropriate," Janet said. "Heather might slap her."

"Heather wanted to *kill* her after I told her about the essay."

"I've already spoken with Pruitt and Cliff Osborn about Gwen's role with the essay. I think they're planning to fire her."

"Don't let the door hit you on the patootie on the way out." Rachel giggled.

"Did you tell Heather that Pruitt was out when it happened?"

"I did. She wasn't that upset about it though. She was already so mad at Gwen—and for good reason."

"I don't know why Pruitt was so high on Gwen. She's not a rigorous teacher. Her students might be having a great time, but I question whether they're learning anything. If, for some miracle, she's not fired, I'll be giving her an unsat."

Rachel nodded. "I didn't like her the first time I met her. She acts so high and mighty, like she's better than everyone."

"Well, she's about to be taken down a few pegs." Janet gestured to the receiving line.

Gwen neared the front of the line. Heather Miles glared at Gwen, her fists clenched. Gwen turned and hurried to a seat away from the scene. Janet and Rachel stifled their laughter.

Janet's cell phone chimed in her purse. She checked the number, recognized it as the newspaper reporter she had called, swiped right, and walked away from Rachel. "Hello, Phillip."

"Janet. I have some good news," Phillip said.

"Hold on a second." She stepped out of the auditorium and walked down the hall, headed for the main office. "Is the paper running the story?"

He chuckled. "Better than that. There's been a new development."

Janet walked back to her office. "What's the new development?"

"Are you sitting down?"

Janet sat behind her desk. "I am now."

"Gwen Townsend's married name is Walker."

"So?"

"She was married to Brian Walker."

"Okay?"

"You don't remember the Brian Walker case a few years ago? It was in Philly. It was all over the news."

Janet shot out of her seat. "Holy shit!"

CHAPTER 84

Gwen and the Funeral

Gwen sat in the audience of the half-filled auditorium, flanked by Lewis Phelps and the Burris family. The football team and most of the young people congregated near the back, the adults near the front. Shane and Lance were noticeably absent. Pictures of Caleb flashed across the projector screen, programmed in an endless loop, with instrumental music in the background. She'd seen the loop five times already. There were only a dozen pictures. His fifteen years had been reduced to twelve pictures, not even one per year. There were baby pictures, a school photo, and football pictures, with Caleb smiling, on one knee, a football in the crook of his arm. There was one selfie with a blue-haired girl who Gwen had never seen before.

Principal Pruitt stepped to the stage and stood behind the podium. The music was cut, but the pictures still scrolled. Pruitt waited for the audience to quiet. "Thank you for coming. I'd like to extend my deepest condolences to the Miles family." Pruitt nodded to the front row where Heather sat next to Ashlee, along with half-a-dozen adults who Gwen didn't recognize. "We're here today to pay our respects and to remember Caleb Miles. His life was taken far too soon. I hope we can be there for each other in this time of need. We have a few speakers who knew Caleb best. They'd like to share a few words." Pruitt stepped away from the podium.

Lewis Phelps stood from his seat and walked down the aisle toward the stage. It had been prearranged as to who would speak and in what order. Gwen had volunteered to speak, but Pruitt had said they already had enough speakers. Gwen was pretty sure that was a lie, especially after trying to offer her condolences to the family and Heather giving Gwen a look of pure hatred. It had nearly brought Gwen to her knees.

"I had Caleb for American history last year and world history this year," Lewis said, standing behind the podium. "He was extremely bright, thoughtful, and introspective." Lewis paused, swallowing hard. Gwen thought he might lose it, but Lewis regained his composure. "We had a project to design your own government, and students had to decide what type of government they wanted and to explain why. Some students chose a monarchy or a theocracy or a republic or a democracy. I had a few students who even made the case for a dictatorship. I've done this project for seven years now, and I've never had a student do what Caleb did. Caleb argued for anarchy or no government.

"I know what you're thinking. Caleb was rebelling, but it wasn't like that at all. He argued that all governments were inherently evil because they derived their revenue and power from force. He thought the only ethical way for people to arrange themselves was voluntarily. Not only did Caleb successfully argue for no government but he also provided ample criticism for every other type of government throughout history.

"I wanted Caleb to share his project with the class, but he refused. He didn't want to be singled out. He just wanted to fit in. But Caleb was different, and I mean that in the best possible way. He had a unique way of looking at the world. He was a special person, and this world is worse off without him." Lewis's voice caught on his final sentence. He stepped back from the podium, and the audience applauded.

Jamar gave a short speech about playing video games and football with Caleb. Heather Miles followed Jamar. She wore a little black dress and high heels. She held tight to the podium, her tan arms flexing in the fluorescent light. She read from a handwritten piece of paper, never lifting her eyes to the audience.

"Caleb Miles was my only son, my baby. I've been told that the worst pain anyone can feel is losin' a child. I'll never be whole again. A piece of me was taken on Tuesday, and I'll never be able to get it back. Caleb should still be alive, and he would be, but mistakes were made. Big mistakes. He had a pellet gun because I refused to buy my son a real gun, even though almost every kid in this town has a gun for huntin'. But the cops shot him anyway. That ain't right.

"This school ain't innocent either. They knew that Caleb was havin' problems. They knew he was thinkin' about killin' himself, but they didn't do nothin'. They knew he was bein' bullied, and they didn't do nothin'. I ain't got much. I ain't got a fancy house or a fancy car or a fancy degree, but I know what's right and what's wrong." For the first time, Heather looked up from her paper and glared at the audience. "What they did to my baby was wrong." Heather stomped from the podium, much of the audience applauding.

Gwen hurried from the auditorium, feeling nauseated. She went to the teacher's bathroom, opening it with her key. She dropped to her knees, her stomach lurching, hot vomit creeping up her esophagus. The tile was rock-hard and ice-cold on her knees. She leaned over the bowl and puked foamy scrambled eggs. She gagged and lurched again, bile mixing with the last of the eggs. Her breath was labored.

Gwen grabbed the sink and hoisted herself to her feet. She flushed the toilet and washed out her mouth. *Heather Miles thinks this was partly my fault. Maybe she's right. I should've checked with Mrs. Baumgartner.* Gwen went to her classroom and sat in her desk chair alone, afraid to face the funeral crowd or the reporters outside. On the way in, they had swarmed her, but a few teachers had blocked them. The reporters had been calling her day and night. She had turned off her phone in response.

A knock came to her door. Lewis appeared in the door window. Gwen stood and walked to the door, opening it, but not letting him in.

"Are you okay?" Lewis narrowed his eyes at her face. "You look pale."

"I'm fine," Gwen replied. "I'm just tired."

"You need anything?"

Gwen shook her head. "I'm fine."

"Did you wanna walk out with me?"

"I'm gonna stay here for a bit."

"Okay. Give me a call if you need anything."

Gwen nodded.

Lewis hugged Gwen, the gesture taking her by surprise, but she reciprocated, almost breaking down in tears.

He let go and stepped back. "Seriously, call me if you need anything," Lewis reiterated.

"I will."

Lewis left. Gwen shut the door, went back to her desk, and slumped in her seat. She sobbed so hard that she nearly hyperventilated, mucus running from her nose and mascara from her eyes. She cried until no tears were left. Then she wiped her face, grabbed her purse, and walked to the parking lot. It was mostly empty now, except for a handful of cars and trucks. Thankfully, the reporters were gone.

Gwen felt faint and empty, but she put one foot in front of the other, her head down as if it was too heavy to hold upright. That's why she didn't see him approaching. She stopped at her car and removed her keys from her purse. She looked up as his footsteps neared.

"Gwen?" Rick stood, wearing a dark suit, dark circles around his eyes. "I wanted to see how you're doing with ... everything."

"You shouldn't be here," Gwen replied.

"I know. I was worried about you. I can't imagine what you're going through."

She took a deep cleansing breath. "No, you can't. I have to go." She unlocked the door with her key fob.

"If you ever need to talk—"

"I'm sorry. I can't."

Gwen entered her car and drove from school to her row-house apartment. On the ride home, she was so distracted. Someone beeped at her for sitting at the green light. Then she'd driven past her apartment and had to turn around. Her mind had been on Caleb and Heather and the essay and Mrs. Baumgartner and Janet and the police. Maybe that was why the reporter and the camera crew seemed to appear out of nowhere, blocking the steps to her apartment.

"Gwen Walker, Gwen Walker," the reporter said, a pretty boy with his hair in perfect order. "Can you comment on allegations that you were aware that Caleb Miles was suicidal, yet you took no action to report it?"

Walker. Shit. They know. "No comment," Gwen said. "Can you move, please?"

The reporter didn't budge. "Do you think it's a coincidence that you're involved in another controversial school incident?"

Gwen pushed past.

The reporter followed her up the stairs, talking to her back. "Do you still maintain that Emory Jackson's guilty?"

Gwen's hands shook as she tried to unlock her door, dropping her keys on the steps.

"The story's running tonight," the reporter said. "Don't you wanna tell the world your side?"

Gwen finally opened the door, stepped inside, and slammed it in the reporter's face.

CHAPTER 85

Rick Goes to East York

The game clock ticked down. Nine seconds, eight, seven. Rick watched from the home team's bleachers. The East York Eagle fans were at a fever pitch, chanting, "Defense, defense, defense!" The chant was apropos. After nearly four full quarters of play, the game was still scoreless. But Shane and the West Lake offense were knocking on the door, deep in East York territory. A camera crew filmed the scene, eager for another angle on the Caleb Miles suicide. Would his former teammates, wearing CM stickers on the back of their helmets, emerge victorious?

Shane caught the snap and tossed a fade, high and deep in the corner of the end zone. It looked like he'd overthrown the pass, but Lance leaped and snagged the ball with his fingertips. His momentum on the way down nearly carried him out of bounds, but he managed to drag one foot inside the white line. Touchdown.

The East York stands went silent as Shane and Lance and the West Lake crowd celebrated. West Lake kicked the extra point with three seconds left on the clock. Not wanting to risk a touchdown on the return, the West Lake kicker squibbed the football. The pigskin skidded across the ground, bouncing this way and that way, making it difficult to set up blockers for a return. The East York returner scooped it up and tried to find a seam, but he was swallowed up by Drew Fuller and a host of West Lake defenders. Game over.

After the handshakes between the two teams, Rick still stood on the home bleachers, surveying the visiting WL sideline. He watched as Janet Wilcox approached Coach Bob Schneider. From this distance, Rick couldn't read facial expressions, and he definitely couldn't hear them, but their body language was clear. Janet was upset, and Bob was afraid.

CHAPTER 86

Janet and the Game after the Game

"You need to open up the offense, let Shane throw some more," Janet said with her hands on her hips. "He's not getting the stats he needs for a scholarship." She was bundled, wearing her puffy black jacket and red scarf.

Coach Bob Schneider removed batteries from the headsets, barely looking at Janet. "I'll do that."

The kids were already in the visiting locker room, the West Lake fans mostly gone, the assistant coaches giving these two a wide berth. They were essentially alone under the lights.

Janet slithered closer. "Look at me, Bob."

Bob looked up from the headsets. His face was ashen under his bushy beard. "What do you need now?" His voice was whiny.

"Nothing. I'm here to see what you need. Relax. You're in the clear. You did what you needed to do for your family."

"Is that what you're doin'?"

"Of course. Isn't that what everyone does?"

He glared, his face flashing red. "I lied to the police for you."

She smirked. "Not really. Everything you told them is possible. There's no way for them to prove you were lying."

"They told me that, if I saw the sexual assault and didn't do anything, I could be arrested."

"But you didn't see it. You didn't know what Drew was doing."

He exhaled, shaking his head. "I've paid my debt to you. We're finished."

She stepped closer, within kissing distance. "We're finished when I say we're finished."

CHAPTER 87

Gwen and NBC

Friday after the funeral, Gwen had been a zombie, barely functioning. She lay in bed all afternoon and night, tossing and turning, afraid to face the world. She awoke the next morning, startled as if she'd forgotten something. Then it all came back to her. *Caleb. The funeral. Heather. The reporter.* She went to the bathroom, peed, and brushed her teeth. She slipped on her flannel pajamas and padded to the kitchen, Buster meowing and following. Gwen poured a little milk into Buster's bowl and made herself some herbal tea with honey.

Gwen took her tea to the living room. At the living room window, she parted the curtains and peered outside to the parking lot. A news van was parked in a visitor space. This wasn't going away. She placed her tea on the coffee table, grabbed her laptop, and sat on the couch. She googled *Gwen Townsend-Walker* and winced at the results. She found tons of news articles, opinion pieces, and videos about her. She clicked on the first video.

NBC Nightly News host Kate Snow appeared, statuesque in her blue skirt suit. Her blond hair skimmed her shoulders. Her face was sucking inward and aging but still pretty, with high cheekbones, professional makeup, and a perfect nose that looked to be too perfect to be natural. Gwen appeared on the screen next to her, a school picture from Philly, and a caption that read Gwen Townsend-Walker under Fire.

Kate said, "Gwen Townsend-Walker, the English teacher who Caleb Miles held hostage along with her class, is under fire amid allegations of negligence. According to an anonymous source, Mrs. Townsend-Walker was in possession of an essay written by Caleb Miles entitled The Invisible Wish. This essay indicated he was suicidal nearly a month before he killed himself, but, by all accounts, Mrs. Townsend-Walker made no attempt to contact Caleb's mother, the school principal, the school counselor, or anyone else for that matter. In fact, she liked the essay so much that she gave Caleb Miles an A+ for his efforts."

The essay appeared on the screen, an excerpt highlighted and blown up. Kate Snow read the passage. "'I'm not nothing. I'm less than nothing, because, if I was nothing, I'd be invisible. I wish I could be so lucky to be nothing, to be invisible. That would be a huge step up.'"

Another passage appeared, which Snow read aloud too. "'I walk around afraid every waking minute, just waiting for something bad to happen, for my climax to come to fruition. Maybe I should do it myself. Maybe I should do it on my own terms. Then nobody can ever hurt me again.'"

The video cut back to Kate Snow. "NBC News correspondent Joan Didier spoke with West Lake High School counselor, Sophia Baumgartner, at her home in Lebanon, Pennsylvania."

They cut to a chubby middle-aged woman standing in her doorway. The pretty young reporter stood, holding her microphone. "Mrs. Baumgartner, did Mrs. Townsend-Walker ever come to you with concerns regarding Caleb Miles?"

"No, she did not," Mrs. Baumgartner said. "Suicide is a very serious issue facing young people. We have to be vigilant. We have to have good communication with everyone to prevent these tragedies. Unfortunately, Caleb's suffering was never communicated to me."

NBC showed Kate Snow standing next to an image of Gwen's soon-to-be-ex-husband, wearing his jailhouse jumpsuit, bound, and flanked by two sheriff's deputies. "Gwen Townsend-Walker is no stranger to controversy. In 2013, her husband, Brian Walker, was arrested and convicted for murdering a former—"

Gwen shut her laptop and hung her head, not wanting to relive the past. *It'll never end. Wherever I go, it'll follow me.* Her eyes filled with tears. She wiped them with her sleeve before they overflowed. She glanced at her phone on the coffee table. It had been off for days. *Will I be fired? Arrested?* She decided it would be better to hear that she was fired over the phone, than to go to work on Monday and be humiliated, so she turned on her phone.

She winced at the number of voice messages, texts, and missed calls. She went through the texts first. All sixty-seven of them. Most of them were from reporters wanting an interview or a comment, but a few were from people she knew. Rick and Lewis sent concerned texts.

Rick: Gwen, I wanted to see how you're holding up.
Rick: Please let me know if you need anything.
Lewis: I'm worried about you. Let me know if you're ok.

A few texts weren't so concerned. Most of these people didn't identify themselves.

717-555-7344: You should not be allowed near a child ever again. You are a disgrace to good teachers everywhere.
717-555-6521: I HOPE YOU ROT IN HELL BITCH.
717-555-9634: This is Heather Miles. I'm gonna sue the shit out of u
717-555-9634: If I ever see u I will beat yur fucking ass

Gwen's hands shook after reading the threats. She set down her phone, took a deep calming breath, and sipped her tea. She set the cup back on the coffee table, her hands steady now. She picked up her phone again. There was a text from Don Pruitt. They'd talked via his cell phone when he'd hired her this past summer, so his number was stored in her phone. Don was one of the main reasons she'd come to West Lake. He seemed so kind and welcoming. He knew about what had happened in Philly, but he had believed Gwen's story and was willing to go to bat for her if anyone questioned it.

Principal Pruitt: Gwen, call me as soon as you get this. It's an emergency.

Gwen tapped her Principal Pruitt contact on her cell phone, her heart pounding.

"Hello?" he answered.

"It's Gwen," she said, her voice shaky.

"Thank you for getting back to me." His voice sounded beaten and monotone.

"Of course."

He exhaled heavy. "I'm sorry to tell you this, but you're suspended pending an investigation into your actions regarding Caleb Miles."

"But—"

"If you need to get some things from your classroom, let me know, and I can meet you after school. Other than that, you are not to be on campus for any reason during the suspension."

"But I gave the essay to Janet, and I spoke to her about it. Did you talk to Grace? She saw me come to see Janet twice that day."

"We know," Pruitt replied. "You're on camera going into the main office to see Janet, but Grace said you went there for a discipline issue with Shane, but you never filed a report. Janet said you came back to apologize to her, that you thought you were heavy-handed with Shane. That's why you never filed the report."

"That's a lie!"

"I'm sorry, Gwen. I can't talk to you about this. I've already said too much."

"I should've followed up with Mrs. Baumgartner. I know that. I'm sorry, Don."

"I know this is a terrible situation, and I think you're being overly blamed for this tragedy, but the powers that be and the people want their pound of flesh."

"What'll happen to me?"

"It doesn't look good for you." He sighed. "To be honest, it doesn't look good for me either."

CHAPTER 88

Rick and the Breaking Point

Rick sat at his desk, reading the latest post by the West Lake Watchdog, aka Heather Miles.

West Lake Watchdog
October 15 at 11:27 AM
I told u the school screwed up and so did Barnett and Townsend and Pruitt. I heard Heather Miles is sueing. She's gonna get a lot a money and she should for what they put her thru. Everybody thought I was crazy but now its in the papers on the news. U can't deny it no more. Read this newspaper article! **LINK #FireBarnett #FirePruitt #FireTownsend** 83 Likes 26 Shares

Trina Grisham I'm glad she's suing. I hope Barnett and Pruitt and Townsend-Walker all go to prison too. I can't believe Barnett had sex with a student. 36 Likes

Roger Elkins That article is good. Everybody should read it. These people are lowlife scum. Especially Barnett. He should be strung up by his ball sack. **#FireBarnett #FirePruitt #FireTownsend** 29 Likes

Sadie Ollinger I can't believe Principal Pruitt hired her after her husband murdered that boy. Its ridiculus. 21 Likes

Ellen Schneider My heart goes out to Heather Miles. **#FireBarnett** 18 Likes

Will Gilroy They're going to be fired at least. Barnett and Townsend-Walker might be going to prison too. They were negligent, not to mention the statutory rape. **#FireBarnett #FirePruitt #FireTownsend** 27 Likes

Aaron Fuller Hey fucktards, you have no idea what you're talking about. Coach Barnett never saw Caleb being bullied and the article didn't say he had sex with a student. It said that an anonymous source said he had sex with a student and he was suspended until the investigation. What happened to innocent until proven guilty? Go ahead and delete my post because you can't deal with the truth. Fucking losers! 3 Likes

Breanna Franks How do you know? You weren't with Coach Barnett 24/7. Your the one who doesn't know what your talking about. 19 Likes

Rick clicked the link to the news article. It was from the *Lancaster Daily News*, written by Phillip Graves, and entitled West Lake Web of Lies. Rick closed his laptop. He'd already seen it. Phillip Graves was the first to break the story. If you could call it that. It was mostly lies and twisted truths, but the local paper ran with anonymous sources, exaggerations, and outright fabrications.

Then the national papers and news organizations snapped it up, many of the papers printing the story word for word. *Does anyone check sources anymore?* Phillip Graves cited Rick's suspension and the anonymous source that confirmed he'd had sex with a student. To add the cherry on top, Rick didn't protect Caleb from bullying. Principal Pruitt was thrown under the bus along with Rick. The article stated that Pruitt was often absent and wasn't at school when Caleb took Gwen's class hostage. They even had a picture of Don reading a hunting magazine at his desk. People in the community had a field day with that, posting in the article's comments, asking if that was what he did for his six-figure salary.

Gwen was hit just as hard. She was blamed for not reporting Caleb's essay to the counselor, and they dredged up her past, a past Rick hadn't heard about prior to the article. She had been evasive when he'd pried into her marriage, but he'd figured maybe her husband had been abusive or maybe an adulterer but a *murderer*? That, he hadn't seen coming. The quotes from the Jackson family had made his skin crawl. Rick hadn't known Gwen for that long, but he didn't believe what they were saying. Not for a second. He had tried texting and calling Gwen multiple times, but her phone was off, and he wasn't sure she wanted to talk to him anyway. Rick had left his phone on, just in case she called.

Over the past twenty-four hours, he'd probably received over one hundred calls, emails, and texts. Mostly from reporters looking for fodder, but some were crazies threatening Rick's life. Hence the loaded shotgun laying on his bed behind him. This thought spurred Rick to check the locks on his house again. Part of the reason he was in this mess was because he'd left his doors unlocked. A habit from childhood. His mother never bothered to the lock the doors, and neither had he, and nothing had ever happened to them. West Lake had always been so safe.

Rick took the shotgun with him. He checked the front door, the side door, the sliding glass door, the windows. Everything was locked, and the shades and curtains were drawn. He walked to the big bay window in front and parted the curtains, peering outside into the darkness. Two news vans were still outside. Strangely, that made him feel more comfortable, like he wasn't totally alone.

His phone chimed in his bedroom. He went back to his room, not in a hurry, figuring it was another crazy or some news outlet. Over the last thirteen years as a coach, he had given his cell phone number to every parent and player he'd had. He was regretting that now. Rick set the shotgun back on his bed and turned to his desk, glancing at the chiming phone. It was Pruitt. Rick grabbed the phone and swiped right.

"Don?" Rick said.

"Thanks for picking up," Principal Pruitt said, his voice monotone. "I wanted to let you know that Dr. Matthews and the school board have decided to rescind the resignation offer, instead opting to terminate your employment immediately. You'll receive a formal termination notice in the mail in a few days."

Rick sat on his bed, next to his shotgun. "That's it? No investigation? No hearing?"

"Given the latest developments, we feel it's the right thing to do for the school, the community, and the students."

Rick disconnected the call. He sat silent, slack-jawed, in shock. He knew things were bad, but he thought the truth would eventually come out. *Maybe not.* He picked up his shotgun and thought, *Maybe Caleb had the right idea.*

CHAPTER 89

Janet and Heather

West Lake High School was back in session on Monday. The blood on the concrete had been bleached. A few news vans still hovered for additional fodder, but the hysteria had died down. For the most part, it had been a normal school day. For Janet, it felt more like a rebirth. Rick Barnett had been fired over the weekend. Gwen Townsend-Walker had been suspended. Soon to be fired, no doubt. Pruitt was on his way out. Janet thought he might resign.

After school, Janet drove into a run-down neighborhood, smiling, thinking about her good fortune. She lowered her visor, blocking the afternoon sun. Janet parked her BMW in the driveway of the double-wide trailer. Thankfully, the media wasn't present. The grass was unruly. An old red Pontiac was under the carport. Ashlee's white Jeep was parked along the street. Mold grew on the trailer where it was shaded by the carport. Janet stepped to the front door and knocked.

Heather Miles opened the door, wearing yoga pants and a fleece, her face unnaturally tan. "What do you want?"

"I wanted to personally offer my condolences—"

"I don't need shit from you."

"I'm friends with Rachel Kreider," Janet said.

Heather cracked a tiny smile. "That's where she's been gettin' all that information."

"Can we talk for a minute? I tried to call first, but your phone goes straight to voice mail."

Heather narrowed her eyes, thinking for a moment. She stepped aside and said, "Come on in."

Janet stepped into the trailer. It felt cramped, the ceilings low compared to *her* home. Ashlee sat in the living room, watching television and tapping on her phone.

"I had to turn off my phone," Heather said. "Damn reporters been up my ass."

Ashlee stood from the couch and flipped off the television. She glared at Janet and disappeared into a back bedroom, a door slamming behind her. Heather didn't comment on her daughter's behavior.

Janet and Heather sat at a tiny table in a narrow kitchen, Janet brushing off her seat before putting her expensive skirt on it. The kitchen smelled a bit like garbage. The lid of the offending can was partly open, trash overflowing. Plastic cups and plates littered the sink and counter.

"What do you wanna talk about?" Heather said, leaning back, her arms crossed over her chest.

"I admire you," Janet replied.

Heather blinked, a smirk on her face. "For what?"

"I think you're a strong and brave woman. I think you represent a toughness and realness that's sorely needed in this school district."

Heather leaned forward, folding her hands on the table. "I didn't think nobody noticed what I been doin'."

"I've noticed. People are following you. You're a leader in this community now. People listen to you."

"Maybe some people. Every day I get more and more people on the Facebook page."

"I don't know if you heard. Rick Barnett's been fired, and Gwen Townsend was suspended."

"Rachel told me. Good riddance. I'm suin' both of 'em. Pruitt too, the school district, and the cops."

"You'll be a wealthy woman once this is over."

"It ain't about the money."

"Of course. You want to do what's right. You don't want what happened to Caleb to happen to another child."

"Damn right."

"As a female principal, I've been struggling against the old boys' club of this district for years. I'm the only female administrator. The school board is made up entirely of old white men. The corruption turns my stomach. Our first priority should be to the students of this community, but you and I know the district cares more about money and power than the kids."

Heather nodded along with Janet's diatribe. "Ain't that the truth."

"I'd like for you to be the first woman on the school board."

"How would I do that? I don't know nothin' about the school board."

"There's an election in November. It's not too late to add you to the ballot. I have plenty of people who would support you."

"What would I have to do?"

"You'd have to tell your story. The whole story."

Heather furrowed her brows. "What are you talkin' about?"

"One board member in particular is a total creep. His seat's up for reelection. Pastor Francis Goode."

Heather's eyes went wide, her mouth slack-jawed.

Janet leaned forward on the table, her hands held like a prayer. "I know what happened, Heather. I know what he did to you."

"I can't." Heather shook her head. "I don't wanna be airin' dirty laundry."

"You didn't do anything wrong. You were just a child. He took advantage."

Tears welled in Heather's eyes. "I can't."

"If you stand up and speak your truth, you're standing up for every girl and woman in this town. You're telling them that they can be more powerful than a man. You're telling them that they don't have to take bullshit from men. They don't have to break their backs, taking care of children, while the man in their life leaves them high and dry. You just have to tell the truth." Janet paused for a moment. "We need you to be the voice for all of us. We need you to be a hero, Heather. Will you do it?"

A smile spread across Heather's face, reaching her eyes.

CHAPTER 90

Gwen Has a Change of Heart

"This is my last message. I won't bother you anymore," Rick said through Gwen's voice mail. "I'm starting to feel like a stalker. I know this stuff about the essay is bullshit. It's textbook Janet. This is exactly what she'd do to cover her own ass. And I, um, I can't even begin to tell you how sorry I am for what you went through in Philly. I know it's none of my business, but I wanted you to know that I'm here if you need to talk. To be honest, I could use someone to talk to. I don't know if you heard, but they fired me." Rick exhaled, pausing for a moment. "I thought maybe we could commiserate and compare notes. No pressure. I know my credibility's not good. That's probably an understatement. Anyway, I'll leave you alone now. I'm sorry … about everything."

Gwen set her phone on the coffee table. That was Rick's last message. She'd listened to it at least ten times since Saturday night. His messages had been a comfort to her. Rick had said *that* would be his last message, and he'd been a man of his word. Forty-eight hours later, he hadn't contacted her again. He had sounded desperate, like a man groping for a lifeline. He also sounded like a man who was telling the truth. He reminded her of Brian. Honest to a fault. *Maybe Janet was waiting at Rick's house for that picture. I have no idea how that essay ended up in my classroom, but it was there.*

Gwen called Rick's cell phone. It went straight to voice mail. She disconnected the call. *He must've turned off his phone. He probably got tired of waiting for me to call.* She stood from her couch and walked to the window. Parting the curtains, she surveyed the parking lot. Despite the darkness, enough glow from the streetlights confirmed that the news van was gone. She grabbed her purse, put on her peacoat, and left her apartment. She drove to Rick's without incident.

Her stomach fluttered as she parked behind Rick's truck. The hairs on the back of her neck stood up. His house was pitch dark, the only one in the neighborhood without a single light shining. *Something's wrong.* Gwen stepped from her car and walked to the front door, her head on a swivel. The wind whistled through the large oak, the leaves rustling. Gwen knocked on the door, not hard. She waited, listening for movement. Nothing. She knocked again, harder. Still nothing. Another wind gust, more leaves rustling. She heard footsteps, outside footsteps trying to be quiet. Turning to the sound, she saw the silhouette of a man with a shotgun. She screamed.

The silhouette stepped closer. "Gwen?"

"Rick?"

She could see him now. "You scared me."

Rick wore all black and held a pump shotgun. "I'm sorry. I've been getting threats–"

"Threats?" Gwen put her hand to her chest.

"Yeah, I've had a few threatening calls and emails."

"Did you talk to the police?"

"I'm not exactly popular with the police these days. They're probably using fake accounts and anonymous cell phones anyway."

"But they could find the IP addresses."

"The entire town thinks I'm a pedophile. The cops don't give a shit what happens to me."

"I'm sorry," Gwen said.

Rick shrugged, acting like he didn't care, but the look on his face said the opposite. "What are you doing here?"

"I need a friend, and I thought maybe you needed one too."

"That's an understatement." He forced a smile. "Front door's locked, so we'll have to walk around back. I came from the back to surprise whoever was at the door."

"You certainly surprised me."

Rick led her around back and through the sliding glass door.

"I tried to call," Gwen said.

"I'm sorry. I know I said I'd leave my phone on, but I couldn't take it anymore with the crank calls and the reporters." Rick locked the door and put a broom handle into the tracks. He turned on the lights, illuminating the kitchen. "You want some tea? I still have that tea you left here."

"Tea would be great." Gwen sat at the kitchen table.

He set the shotgun on the counter, the barrel facing the wall. He put on the teakettle and joined her at the table.

"I've been thinking about your situation," Rick said.

"I've been thinking about yours too," Gwen replied.

"My situation's a done deal." He looked like death. Bloodshot eyes, dark circles, disheveled hair and beard.

"What if we got someone to talk?"

"*We?*" Rick asked with raised eyebrows.

"I'm sorry I didn't believe you."

Rick narrowed his eyes, studying Gwen for a moment. "Now you do? Just like that?"

"My situation's pretty unbelievable, but here I am, suspended for something I didn't do. I know it's selfish to get it only because it happened to me, but I guess that's where I am."

He nodded. "That's fair."

"Your voice mails were sweet."

"I hope you deleted them. I was rambling on and on." A smirk spread across his face. "Your voice mail's been my best friend over the past few days."

She smiled in return. "They're mine now. I'm keeping them."

"It's you and me against the world then?"

She lifted one shoulder. "I guess so." Gwen paused for a beat. "Seriously though, why can't we get someone to talk? Janet can't be doing this all by herself. What about Rachel Kreider?"

"She'd stop a bullet for Janet."

"What about Bob Schneider?"

"I think Janet has something on him. I doubt he'd talk."

"He might not incriminate himself, but he might give you some information that could help. If Janet has something on him, I'm sure he'd like to get out from under her."

Rick paused for a moment, stroking his beard. "That's a really good point. Maybe I'll go see him tomorrow. What do I have to lose, right?"

"If you want me to go with you …"

"Thanks, but he'd be more likely to talk without an audience."

She nodded.

"I, um, I'm really sorry about everything that happened in Philly. I didn't know."

She looked away for a beat, then back to Rick, her eyes glassy. "I didn't tell you."

"If you ever wanna—"

"I'd rather not talk about it, if that's okay?"

"We don't have to talk about it, … but I'm here."

"Thank you," she said, barely above a whisper.

"I've been thinking about the essay," he said, changing the subject. "I think Janet planted it in your classroom. She could've slid it under the door. She was the last one out of the school. She had plenty of time to do it."

Gwen nodded. "I think you're right. I just can't prove it."

"What about video? The school has cameras."

"Wouldn't the police be looking at that footage?"

"Probably, but they might not see it if they're not looking for it. Janet's not stupid. She knows where the cameras are, so I'm sure she probably did it in a way that would be hard to see. Did Detective

Strickland interview you?"

"Yes."

"You should send him an email, telling him that you think Janet slipped the essay under the door."

"That makes sense. It would be nice if we could get the footage."

"You could ask him?"

"I doubt they would just give me the video."

"Greg Ebersole might have the footage or at least access to it."

Gwen frowned at the mention of the school's tech guy.

"You don't like Greg?"

"I can't stand him. He creeps me out. He's always staring at me and making weird comments."

"You're not the only one. There've been complaints from quite a few female teachers. I coached him for a day when he was a tenth grader. He quit after the first day of two-a-days and never came out for football again. His mother was friends with mine. I think he still lives with his parents."

CHAPTER 91

Rick and the Truth'll Come Out

Rick waited, parked on a side street in a middle-class neighborhood of ramblers and colonials. The sun glowed orange and low on the horizon. He listened to a country music station, watching the community entrance, knowing that Bob would be home from practice soon.

Bob's SUV drove past, right on time. Rick started his truck and followed. As Bob parked in his driveway, Rick parked directly behind him and exited his truck. Bob stood next to his vehicle, his posture defensive.

"Hey, Bob," Rick said as he approached, his tone and expression neutral.

Bob's jaw tightened; his face reddened under his bushy beard. "I don't have anything to say to you."

Rick glared. "You have a lot to say about me behind my back."

"I'm not talkin' to you." Bob turned and marched toward the front door.

Rick followed, talking to his back. "What does she have on you?"

Bob didn't respond.

Rick said, "You're a liar, and you know it."

The front door opened, and Ellen appeared, their son on her hip. Her eyes flicked to Rick, then to her husband. "Why is *he* here?"

Bob, now standing on the stoop, turned to Rick. "He's just leavin'."

"I'm not going anywhere until you tell me the truth." Rick looked at Ellen. "Your husband's being blackmailed by Janet Wilcox."

Ellen's mouth hung open, her eyes like saucers.

"Go inside." Bob shut the door in his family's face. He turned back to Rick with clenched fists, his face flashing red. "If you don't get the fuck off my property, I'm gonna call the police."

Rick was unblinking and undeterred by the threat. "Eventually, the truth'll come out. If you think Janet'll protect you, you got another thing coming." Rick walked back to his truck, Bob still on the stoop, speechless.

CHAPTER 92

Janet and #VoteMiles

She used it. Janet sat at her desk, looking at her laptop, a shit-eating grin on her face. Heather had taken Janet's version of her story and copied it word for word. It was mostly true, but Janet did take some poetic license to make Heather more sympathetic. Janet didn't have to write it, but she was tired of Heather, aka the West Lake Watchdog, sounding like a total dumbass. This was an important post. It had to paint Heather as the victim but also as a strong woman ready to take charge of the school board.

West Lake Watchdog
October 18 at 9:55 PM
Sixteen years ago, Pastor Francis Goode took advantage of Heather Miles. At the time, Heather Miles was an eighteen-year-old single mother. She'd recently been left by her abusive fiancé, also the father of her daughter. Alone, scared, and vulnerable, Heather looked to God for guidance, and what she found was the devil. Pastor Goode was thirty-nine at the time, married, with five kids. He counseled Heather, manipulated her, made her feel like she needed him to survive.

When the "Goode" Pastor made his move, Heather was powerless to resist. Pastor Goode took advantage of Heather's pain, using his power and influence as a man of God to have sex with a teenage girl. Heather became pregnant, and Pastor Goode paid her to keep quiet, the money coming from the church collection plate. That child, Pastor Goode's son, was Caleb Miles.

Heather didn't want to take the money, but she had two children to think of. Heather raised her children on her own, struggling and scrapping against adversity, and, even after the tragic death of her son, she's still fighting for the children of this school district.

Heather Miles is running for School Board Director this November. I hope you'll vote for her because she's exactly what this district needs. No-nonsense toughness, honesty, and an understanding of the needs of children. A vote for Heather is a vote against the corruption and the political cronyism of this district.

To top it off, one of the seats up for reelection belongs to Pastor Francis Goode. Do not let this lying child predator back on our school board. Vote for Heather Miles! **#VoteMiles** 378 Likes 78 Shares

Sadie Ollinger Wow, she's so brave for sharing her story! **#VoteMiles** 91 Likes

Trina Grisham Goode needs to go to prison for stealing that money. What a creep! **#VoteMiles** 76 Likes

Will Gilroy I don't think he will go to prison. It's probably outside the statute of limitations. But he is a total piece of shit. **#VoteMiles** 57 Likes

Roger Elkins I've been saying it. These people are lowlife scum. This guy is as bad as Rick Barnett. **#VoteMiles** 53 Likes

Ellen Schneider Heather Miles is such a strong woman. We'd be lucky to have her on the school board. **#VoteMiles** 44 Likes

Glen Gentry I can't believe these people! We need to drain the WL swamp. Fire Goode, Barnett, Pruitt, Townsend, ALL OF THEM 34 Likes

Breanna Franks Drain the swamp! **#VoteMiles** 22 Likes

David Harrison Drain the WL Swamp! 15 Likes

Janet heard heavy footsteps, just outside her office. She stood from her desk, walked to her door, and opened it. She peered down the hallway toward Pruitt's office. Detective Strickland spoke to Principal Pruitt, flanked by two uniformed police officers. They said something about an arrest and Drew Fuller. Strickland nodded to Janet as he left the office with Pruitt and the uniformed officers in tow. Janet followed, keeping a polite distance.

She stood in the hallway, twenty-five yards away as Drew Fuller was taken from his classroom. Principal Pruitt was on the handheld radio.

Drew was indignant. "I didn't do nothin'."

Detective Strickland read him his rights. The head custodian approached the scene. They walked down the hall to Drew's locker. The custodian opened his locker with the master key. Detective Strickland searched inside, wearing latex gloves. The detective held up a plastic baggie filled with pills.

CHAPTER 93

Gwen and MGTOW

"I'm sorry that Bob didn't talk," Gwen said, looking at Rick as he drove.

Rick glanced her way, then back to the road. "I didn't think he'd talk, but it was worth a try. Hopefully, you can get this video footage."

"It might help both of us."

Rick nodded. "Janet's the catalyst for both of our predicaments." He turned onto a gravel road.

It was overcast, clouds pregnant with rain. Gravel crunched under their tires as they drove down the driveway. Rick parked his truck in front of the old stone farmhouse, behind another pickup and Greg's Nissan 350Z. Denuded corn and soy fields lay fallow in the background. A dilapidated barn stood to the right of the house.

Rick looked at Gwen and said, "You ready?"

"I think so."

"You sure you don't want me to go in there with you?"

"I do, but he'll be less likely to give me the video if you're there."

"I don't like you being alone with this guy."

"Neither do I, but what choice do we have at this point?"

"Be assertive. He's weak." Rick powered down his window so he could hear any signs of distress. "Yell for me if you run into any problems, and I'll be there in a flash."

Gwen nodded. "Wish me luck?"

"Good luck."

Gwen stepped from the truck and walked to the house, climbing the porch steps to the front door. She wore her peacoat and a knit cap. It wasn't cold enough for a knit cap yet, but she was worried that Greg's parents might recognize her. Gwen wasn't exactly popular with the locals at the moment. She knocked on the door. Half a minute later, a middle-aged woman appeared. Greg's mother, Gwen presumed. She wore a long dress that looked like it was from the set of *Little House on the Prairie*. She had curly salt-and-pepper hair and wore no makeup.

"Can I help you?" the woman said.

"I was looking for Greg Ebersole," Gwen replied.

"I think he's in his room. What's your name, young lady?"

Gwen swallowed and said, "Gwen."

The woman did a double take but didn't let on if she knew who Gwen was or not. "Lemme get 'im. You're welcome to come in."

"I'll wait here if that's okay," Gwen replied.

"Suit yourself."

The woman left and walked down the hall to the stairwell. She called out, "Gregory, honey, could you come down here?"

"I'm busy," Greg said, his tone terse.

"You have company."

"Who is it?"

"A young woman. Gwen."

He paused. "I'll be down in a minute."

The woman appeared at the door again. "He'll be down shortly. You sure you don't wanna come in?"

"I'm fine out here but thank you."

Greg appeared behind his mother. "Excuse me, Mom."

His mother stepped aside and retreated into the house. Greg stepped onto the porch with Gwen, shutting the door as he did so. He wore tight jeans and a flannel shirt. His beady eyes were magnified by

315

his glasses. His eyes crawled up and down Gwen's body, before settling on her face.

"What are you doing here?" he asked, a smirk on his lips.

Gwen forced a smile. "I need your help."

He raised his eyebrows. "You need my help? I'm surprised. At school, it doesn't seem like you wanna be in the same room with me."

"Come on, Greg. I'm desperate. I really need your help. Janet's framing me, and you could help me."

"I doubt that." He crossed his arms over his scrawny chest, as if protecting something.

Gwen ignored his dissension. "Do you have the video from the day of the shooting?"

"The police have it."

"You don't have a copy?"

"I might."

"Did you watch it?"

Greg shrugged. "Maybe."

"Does it show Janet sliding a piece of paper under my classroom door?"

"It might."

"I need it. It'll prove that I wasn't negligent. Please, Greg, my career's in jeopardy."

"What do I get?"

"What do you want?"

He stroked his scraggily beard and shrugged. "I don't know. What are you offering?"

Gwen frowned. "Let's not play games."

"You're the one who came to my house, asking me to risk my job, and for what? You don't even like me."

"I never said I didn't like you."

"I'm not stupid."

"What do you want, Greg?"

He pursed his lips. "You know what I want."

"I'm not a mind reader."

"Use your imagination." He smirked again, showing a little of his crooked teeth.

"You have a chance to be a good guy here. Maybe we could be friends."

Greg shook his head. "I tried being your friend. I invited you to happy hour, lunch at school, but you kept turning me down. Obviously, you never wanted to be my friend, but now you want something, so you're trying to use me."

"I'm sorry I turned you down. I wasn't trying to be mean. I was just busy."

"You're not too busy to hang out with a child molester." He lifted his chin to Rick's truck parked about thirty yards away. "But you can't hang out with a nice guy like me? This is why men aren't getting married or even having girlfriends. We don't need women using us, taking our money, then riding the cock carousel behind our backs."

Gwen took a step back. "What are you talking about?"

"I'm a MGTOW. Stands for *men going their own way*. I don't need a girlfriend or a wife or kids. I'm not gonna be some workhorse so some bitch can go shopping for makeup and clothes."

"I don't understand what this has to do with me."

"Because you women are all alike, trying to use your feminine skills to manipulate me. I know you're trying to use me."

Gwen blew out an exasperated breath. "I'm asking for your help. If you won't help me, fine." She turned to leave.

"I didn't say I wouldn't help you."

She turned back to Greg.

"I just said I know you're trying to use me. I'm okay with that, provided I get what I want in return."

"Spit it out, Greg, or I'm leaving."

"I want you for one night." He paused for a moment. "And you pay for the hotel."

"You know why you don't have a girlfriend?"

"Because I choose not to be played by some materialistic whore."

She placed her hands on her hips. "No, it's because you're not a nice person. You claim to be this nice guy, but you objectify women and think women owe you something. Maybe you should work on being a better, more successful person, instead of hiding behind some ideology because you're too afraid to admit that you're a loser."

He opened his mouth to reply but nothing came out.

Gwen turned on her sneakers and marched back to the truck.

CHAPTER 94

Rick and *What Are We Now?*

It was getting late. She'd changed into her flannel pajamas. *What does that mean? She is wearing pajamas in front of me, but they're flannel pajamas, not exactly meant to be sexy. But she's still so pretty. She could wear a burlap sack. What are we now?*

Rick took a swig from his beer bottle and placed it back on the coffee table. He flashed a small smile toward Gwen. She sat on the opposite side of her couch, sipping her wine, way out of his reach. He wanted to make a grand gesture. Sit next to her, hold her, kiss her. But he didn't know where they stood. *Maybe she's still not sure whether or not I'm innocent. How could she be? Maybe I'm only here because of our shared interests. Maybe because there's nobody else.*

"Rick?"

He broke from his trance, his gaze focusing on her big blue eyes and porcelain face that looked just as beautiful without makeup. "Yeah, sorry."

Gwen set her empty wineglass on the coffee table. "What were you thinking about?"

Buster hopped up on the couch.

"Oh, … nothing," Rick said. "I guess I'm just worried about Heather getting on the school board."

The cat kneaded the couch cushion and sat next to Gwen.

"I know. Judging from that Facebook post and the comments, I bet she'll win in a landslide," Gwen replied.

"Unfortunately, you're probably right. To make matters worse, Janet already has four board members who consistently vote which-ever way she wants. With Heather, she'll have the majority. And Dr. Matthews is gonna retire soon, which means she'll basically be choosing the next superintendent, which also means she'll be choosing the administration as well."

Gwen frowned. "She'll have total control then. She has the teacher's union with Rachel Kreider as the president."

"The union officers are Janet's cronies too."

"She'll have everything. The school board, the administration, the superintendent, the community. Nobody will be able to touch her."

"I think she might be positioning herself to be the next super-intendent."

"Really? Don't you have to be a principal for a while, or does vice principal count?"

"I think you have to be a principal for at least a year to be consid-ered. Vice principal doesn't count as far as I know, but I think she's gunning for Pruitt's job. Think about all the *hashtag fire Pruitt* stuff on Facebook."

"Shit, you're right," Gwen replied.

"If she gets rid of Pruitt, she'll slide into his job. Then she gets Heather on the school board, and, when Matthews retires in a couple years, the school board will pick Janet to replace him."

"It'll be unbearable for anyone who opposes her. Anyone good enough to get a job elsewhere will leave."

Rick nodded, his mouth turned down. "And who loses the most?"

"The kids of course."

"We gotta figure out a way to get the truth to people."

"Why can't we start our own Facebook page? They post all those lies. Why can't we post the truth?"

Rick smiled. "That's a great idea. We'll have to really think about what we wanna say."

"Could *we* get sued?"

Rick shrugged. "Do you have any money?"

Gwen laughed.

Rick laughed with her. "The silver lining of being broke."

Her laughter dissipated. "When do you want to work on it?"

Rick checked his watch—*10:24 p.m.* "It's getting late. Maybe we should pick this up tomorrow."

"Will you stay with me tonight?"

Rick raised his eyebrows.

She blushed fire-engine red. "Not together. I didn't sleep very well last night. I'm afraid to be here by myself. I feel like the whole town wants my head on a platter."

"I understand."

"Buster's not much of a watchdog." She petted the cat, Buster purring in response. "I know this is a big imposition. You can sleep in my bed. I'll take the couch."

Rick shook his head. "I'll take the couch."

CHAPTER 95

Janet and Cracks in the Facade

The score was tied, seven all. Another low-scoring affair. Another poorly called game by Bob Schneider. Shane had thrown two interceptions and no touchdowns. Lancaster Catholic had the ball on the West Lake thirty-yard line. It was still out of range for their kicker, so they had opted to use the last few seconds before overtime to throw a Hail Mary into the end zone, hoping one of their receivers might come down with the game-winning touchdown.

Janet watched from the visiting bleachers as the Lancaster Catholic quarterback launched a bomb. A crowd of defenders and receivers jockeyed for position, like basketball players going for a rebound. As the football fell from the sky, Lance Osborn stepped in front and leaped, snagging the ball from the cool air. Lance landed on his feet and took off down the sideline. The opposing quarterback had a shot at him, but Lance cut inside, leaving him grasping for air. Lance sprinted the rest of the way, untouched, doing a little high step for the last ten yards. He'd gone 103 yards on the interception return for the game-winning touchdown.

Like déjà vu, the West Lake football players and their fans celebrated the last-second victory. Well, except for one player and one fan. Janet stood with her face puckered, like she'd eaten a lemon, and Shane stood on the sideline, apart from his teammates, his head hanging.

After the handshakes and a short speech by Coach Schneider, the players dispersed to talk to their people near the visiting stands. Ashlee Miles argued with Shane, away from the rest of the team and their parents and girlfriends. Ashlee was red-faced, her finger jabbing toward Shane. Janet approached the pair.

"It was Drew," Shane said, his hands held out like a beggar. "That's why he got arrested."

"If you're lying—" Ashlee stopped midsentence as Janet arrived on the scene.

"Great game," Janet said.

"I'll talk to you later," Ashlee said, walking away, back toward the crowd.

"What's her problem?" Janet asked.

Shane frowned at his mother. "Stay out of it."

Janet forced a smile. "Well, congratulations. That was a big win."

"I threw two picks."

"Those were catchable passes. Your receivers screwed that up. It's not your fault. And those play calls? Bob Schneider's an idiot. He should let you call your own plays—"

"Shut up, Mom," Shane said, glowering at Janet.

Janet took a step back, her hand to her chest, as if she'd been punched.

Shane brushed past his mother on the way toward the locker room and the showers.

Janet composed herself and found Bob Schneider on the sideline, dumping water from the coolers.

"What are you doing to my son?" Janet said to Bob.

Bob grabbed another cooler and dumped the water, dangerously close to Janet. "I'm not doing anything to your son."

"These plays are terrible."

"I know. You told me to throw more, so I did, and Shane threw two picks, almost costing us the game." Bob slammed the empty cooler on the bench. "He's starting, but I have very little control over how well he plays."

Janet pointed at Bob. "I don't care what you have to do. Change the plays, give Shane some extra coaching, whatever it is, *do it*. I expect this to be fixed by next Friday."

Bob didn't react. He simply heaved another water cooler.

Janet turned on her boots and marched toward the parking lot. On the way, she passed Ashlee Miles, talking with the hero of the game, Lance Osborn. They were all smiles and googly eyes. Janet glared, but they were oblivious, lost in each other's gazes. In the parking lot, she found her blue BMW and gasped.

Someone had keyed her driver's side door with a four-letter word. CUNT.

CHAPTER 96

Gwen and Telling the Truth

They called their Facebook page the Truth about West Lake. Gwen sat at one end of her couch, typing on her laptop. Rick was on the other end, typing on his. Buster was between them, sleeping in a neat circle. They'd spent the better part of the last three days trying to find additional evidence to back up their stories, but they hadn't found much. Except for Lewis, their coworkers wouldn't talk to them; they didn't get the video from Greg, and the West Lake Watchdog continued to crank out propaganda. Ultimately, Gwen and Rick decided to tell the truth to the best of their ability. If people didn't believe them, so what? They already didn't believe them.

Gwen looked up from her laptop, watching Rick peck on his keyboard. He looked better, more rested. His color looked healthy; his eyes weren't dark-circled. She wondered what they were doing together. She wondered if he was for real. He had all the alpha-male markers. Tall and built. *Check.* Strong jawline. *Check.* Athletic. *Check.* Quiet confidence. *Check.* But he didn't always act like it. There was a gentleness in the way he spoke to her, the way he took the couch without looking for gratitude, the way he looked at her. Not like a predator after prey but someone who cared for her. He'd kept his distance, not making any attempt to touch her or kiss her or even flirt. *Maybe he's still hurt that I thought he had an affair with Ashlee Miles? Maybe he did? If he did, he should be on Broadway, because he's a great actor. There's just no way.*

"You okay over there?" Rick asked.

Gwen blinked, awakening from her daydream. "I'm pretty much done," she said, her gaze flicking to her laptop screen. "Do you want to hear it?"

"Yeah, let's hear it." Rick set his laptop on the coffee table.

"Here goes." She took a deep breath and told her story. The essay. Meeting with Janet and the subsequent lies. Her repeated unrequited attempts to contact Heather Miles. The day Caleb held her class hostage. Her speculation that Janet had a copy of the essay and shoved it under her door. Her thoughts on Caleb's motives and her admission that she should've followed up with Mrs. Baumgartner. The regret she'll carry for the rest of her life. Gwen looked up from her laptop.

Rick clapped. "That's really good."

Gwen frowned. "I don't know. I'm worried that everyone will hate me even more."

"Why? It's the truth."

"I'm not sure how popular it'll be to talk about Heather not calling teachers back about Caleb."

"We're not the only people who know what a horrendous mother she is."

Gwen sighed. "I guess I feel bad too. She just lost her son."

"That doesn't change what she did or didn't do. That woman's suing everyone for Caleb's death, but, the truth of the matter is, it's her fault more than anyone else's."

"What about Pastor Goode? He didn't have anything to do with Caleb, left him without a father."

Rick paused, the wheels turning in his mind. "That's a good point. Maybe he's more to blame than Heather. I don't know, but I do know it's not your fault. I think you blame yourself too much as it is."

"I do feel guilty, like I didn't do enough. I think his essay was a cry for help, and I didn't answer it."

"That's not true."

She lifted one shoulder. "Maybe." Gwen paused for a moment. "I'm surprised Heather isn't suing us."

"If we had any money, I'm sure she would."

Gwen smiled. "The silver lining of being broke, right?"

Rick smiled back. "Right."

Gwen's eyes flicked to her laptop, then back to Rick. "Should I go ahead and post it?"

"I would."

"I made some screenshots from my phone of the calls I made to Heather. Do you think I should post them too? I hate to give out her phone number like that. I'm probably violating confidentiality somehow since I pulled her number from school."

"I think we're beyond that, but you could blur part of the number."

"I guess I could do that." Gwen copied the letter and pasted it on their new Facebook page. "It's done. I just have to add the screenshots."

"How do you feel?"

"A little nervous but happy that I told the truth. How do we get people to go to our page and read it?"

Rick had a crooked grin. "I thought we could troll the West Lake Watchdog page. We could comment and put links to our page."

"They'll delete our comments."

"Probably, but I've noticed that Heather doesn't post in the morning. She sleeps in a lot. She's usually out late partying Saturday night, so tomorrow morning might be perfect. I think our posts would at least stay up for a few hours. Then, once a few people see it, it'll spread like wildfire."

"We can use the rumor mill to our advantage for once," Gwen said.

"Exactly."

"What about you? Are you ready for your post?"

"Just about. I could use your editing expertise."

Gwen set her laptop on the coffee table and sat next to Rick. She had to sit close not to disturb Buster. She felt a jolt of electricity as their thighs touched. "Let's see."

Rick handed her his laptop, seemingly unaffected by her proximity.

Gwen read through the document, making a few grammatical edits along the way but not too many. He wasn't a dumb jock. Rick told the whole story about Shane and Ashlee and Janet and the extortion attempt. He didn't mention Ashlee's or Shane's name, but everyone would know he was talking about Shane, given the circumstances. Ashlee would remain anonymous. Gwen handed the laptop back to Rick.

"It's very good," Gwen said. "Well written too. Janet'll be super-pissed."

"I don't like throwing Shane under the bus, but I don't feel like I have a choice here."

"I'm sure the kids already know he's only starting because of Janet."

"I'm sure they do. Shane's played terrible over the past few games."

The doorbell rang. They looked at each other, like deer in headlights.

"Are you expecting anyone?" Rick asked, whispering.

"No."

They crept to the door together, not wanting to alert whoever it was to their presence.

Gwen looked through the peephole and whispered, "It looks like a young man with a package."

The man knocked again.

"Should I open it?" Gwen asked.

"Might as well," Rick replied.

She opened the door.

The young man smiled. "Are you Gwen Townsend-Walker?"

"Yes."

He handed her a legal-size envelope. "You've been served." The young man looked up at Rick. "Rick Barnett?"

"Yeah."

"You've been served too." The young man handed Rick the other legal-size envelope. He smiled again. "Have a nice day."

Rick and Gwen frowned at each other.

Inside, they both opened their envelopes. They were being sued by Heather Miles and the Law Firm of Boyd and Yarborough.

"So much for silver linings," Gwen said.

CHAPTER 97

Rick and Pariahs

After being served, Rick and Gwen had talked about pooling their limited resources to hire a lawyer, but they needed more evidence to give themselves a fighting chance. They needed an investigative team to unravel Janet's conspiracies, but they weren't even sure they could afford a lawyer, much less a team of investigators. West Lake was a DIY town. People mostly mowed their own grass and painted their own houses and even did a little plumbing and electrical work. Like most of West Lake's rural poor, Rick and Gwen would have to DIY their own investigation.

They'd spent the rest of the afternoon putting the final touches on the Truth about West Lake Facebook page. Rick had done some more editing and posted his story. Gwen had added those screenshots, detailing her many unreturned phone calls to Heather Miles.

"Now we just need traffic," Gwen said, shutting her laptop.

"Hopefully Heather sleeps late tomorrow." Rick shut his laptop and set it on the coffee table. "Are you hungry?"

Gwen lifted one shoulder. "A little."

"I'm starving." He stood from the couch and stretched his arms over his head. "Do you wanna make dinner?"

"We can, but my cupboards are pretty bare. We ate the last of the eggs and bread at breakfast."

Rick walked into the kitchen. "I'll take a look." He checked the fridge and the cupboards and walked back to the living room. "There's not much. We should make a grocery run."

* * *

He felt newly married, pushing the cart, Gwen walking alongside, adding items as they went. Thankfully, the store was mostly empty, only a handful of customers shopping and minding their own business. An old guy wearing dirty jeans stared at them in the dairy aisle, but Rick figured he was looking at Gwen. She had that effect on men. Rick didn't blame the guy. Gwen grabbed eggs and cheese, adding the items to the cart.

"I think that's about it," she said.

Rick pushed the full cart toward the checkout, Gwen still walking alongside. He stopped, looking at the line of registers. Only one was open, and he recognized the cashier.

"What's wrong?" Gwen asked.

"The cashier. That's Breanna Franks," Rick said. "Heather's older sister."

"I've seen her name on Facebook."

"Yeah, she's been posting with the other crazies." He sighed. "Let's get this over with."

They approached the register, Rick parking the cart next to the conveyor belt. Breanna was thin, mid-forties, but she looked at least ten years older with deep wrinkles, yellow teeth, and the puckered mouth of a smoker. She stood, glaring at the couple, her arms crossed over her chest. Rick ignored her, simply piling the groceries on the conveyor belt counter. He intentionally blocked Gwen with the cart and his backside, not wanting her to be the object of Breanna's ire. He expected Breanna to start scanning and bagging, but she just stood there, glowering.

As Rick stacked the last item from the cart, their groceries now completely covering the counter, he looked at Breanna and asked, "Are you gonna scan the groceries?"

Breanna shook her head. "You two make me sick. You should be in prison. I can't believe you have the balls to come in here. You can put all this shit back in your cart and put it back where you got it, because I ain't checkin' you out. Maybe you should go to the WalMart in Lebanon with the rest of the scumbags."

Rick looked around, hoping for a manager, but saw nobody but the old man walking toward the line with a few items in a handheld plastic basket.

"You don't own this store," Rick said.

"You see anybody else in charge?" Breanna replied, one side of her mouth twisted in disdain.

"You're that piece of shit teacher from Philly," the old man said to Gwen, his eyes narrowed. "Why don't you go back where you came from?"

"Sir, I didn't do anything wrong," Gwen replied.

"Ain't what I heard, and that one's even worse." The old man pointed a craggy finger at Rick. "Havin' sex with young girls. If you touched my daughter, I'd shoot you dead. You better watch your back. Whole lot a folks want a piece of your hide."

Rick grabbed Gwen's hand. "Let's go." He pushed the empty cart through the line one-handed, his other still holding on to Gwen. Once through the narrow aisle, he pushed the cart aside.

"You gotta put this shit back," Breanna said.

"I don't work here." Rick looked around. "And I don't see anyone else working, so it must be *your* job." They left the store, still holding hands. Rick glanced at Gwen as they walked to his truck. Her face was flushed, her eyes glassy.

"You okay?" he asked.

She shook her head. "It's one thing to read stuff on Facebook. It's a different thing to live it in real life."

CHAPTER 98

Janet and the Eye of the Hurricane

Janet had been livid about the Facebook page. The Truth about West Lake. Rick's and Gwen's lame attempt to gain public support. Last Sunday, Rachel had sent her a text about the page. Between Janet, Rachel, Heather, and their many supporters, they were able to shut down the page with a barrage of complaints to Facebook. A few days later, it was back up again. They would've complained again, but the whole thing backfired on Rick and Gwen. The comments to their posts were overwhelmingly negative, ranging from accusations of dishonesty to wishes for their untimely demise.

Rick and Gwen were learning a truism that Janet knew well. Whoever's first to control the narrative has a huge advantage because, once adults make up their minds on a particular subject, they are very unlikely to change it, especially if their peers support that perspective.

Janet enjoyed visiting the Truth about West Lake and reading the hateful comments, which is exactly what she was doing now. Janet's phone buzzed with a text. She set her laptop on the bed and grabbed her cell phone from the bedside table.

Rachel: There's an article about Drew Fuller. **LINK**

Janet clicked the link. The article was from the *Lancaster Daily News*.

West Lake Bully Pleads Guilty
By: Phillip Graves
October 27, 2016

West Lake High School senior, Drew Fuller, 18, pled guilty to drug possession with the intent to sell and to sexual harassment, a charge that was reduced from sexual assault. Drew Fuller was sentenced to twenty-four months in prison. The sexual harassment charge and conviction involved a hazing incident against deceased former classmate, Caleb Miles.

District Attorney Blake Drummond said, "Along with the help of the Swatara Township Police Department, my office successfully negotiated a guilty plea for Drew Fuller's drug-dealing operation and the sexual assault of Caleb Miles. My office will continue to protect our young people against drugs and sexual assault."

Caleb's mother, Heather Miles, was less sanguine about the result. "He didn't hardly get nothing for what he did to my son. It was rape, if you ask me. It was way more than sexual harassment."

The front door slammed shut. Janet set down her phone and stood from her bed. She approached her bedroom door, her hand on the knob, standing and listening. Heavy feet climbed the stairs, followed by the slamming of another door. Shane's bedroom. Then there was a crash, followed by another, followed by another. Janet hurried from her room, headed for Shane's. Another crash. Janet opened his door and gasped. His room looked like it had been in a hurricane. Two fist holes were in the drywall. His desk was overturned. His laptop was on the ground, near the wall, smashed. Shane stood in the eye of the hurricane, breathing heavy, his face beet red, tears streaming down his face.

"*What* is going on in here?" Janet said.

Shane's breathing slowed. He sat on his bed and put his head in his hands, crying.

"*What* is your problem?" Janet moved closer to Shane.

"Go away." His voice was whiny.

"Not until you tell me why you're destroying my house."

He sniffled, sucking back mucus. "It's my room."

"This isn't a debate." Janet had her hands on her hips. "*What's* wrong?"

He looked up at his mother, his face red and blotchy and tear-streaked. He glowered as he pointed to his fingertips, counting the ways in which his life had gone off the rails. "I suck at football. Everybody's pissed that you made Coach Schneider start me. Kids have been saying that it's my fault that Caleb killed himself. Even Ashlee believes it. She broke up with me. It's fuckin' bullshit. It's not fair. Caleb was the one who looked at my dick."

Janet raised one side of her mouth in disgust. She *was* disgusted. *Where was his fucking pride?* "Stop feeling sorry for yourself."

Shane's eyes went wide.

"If you suck at football, fix it! Who gives a shit about a bunch of white-trash losers? They were never your friends. A year from now, you'll never see those kids again. You'll be in college. They'll be working at a fucking gas station or some shitty restaurant. And Ashlee? You should be thanking your lucky stars that you're rid of that toxic whore."

Shane still sat on his bed, his mouth wide open.

"Stop being a baby. Be a man for once." Janet looked around the room. "And clean this shit up." She slammed the door and left his room.

CHAPTER 99

Gwen and the Facebook Peanut Gallery

Gwen and Rick sat at her kitchen table, reading the comments on their Facebook posts.

Trina Grisham This is so sad. Its all lies. The VP and the counselor never saw the essay. Just admit you didn't do anything about Caleb. 22 Likes

Heather Miles Your a real piece of shit Rick. I hope you rot in hell. RICK BARNETT IS A LIAR!!!!!!!!!!!!!!!!!!!!!!!!!!!!!!! 15 Likes

Breanna Franks OMG these two retards were in my store. I told them to get the F out! 7 Likes

Will Gilroy They're desperate! What do you expect from a child killer and a child molester? 10 Likes

Sadie Ollinger These people disgust me. Townsend-Walker killed that boy as far as I'm concerned. Barnett has sex with young girls. 11 Likes

Ellen Schneider Rick came to my house threatening my husband. He is a total creep and a child molester. 15 Likes

Glen Gentry I'm sorry to hear that, **Ellen Schneider**. We are behind your husband. He's still undefeated! Barnett and Townsend-Walker both need to go to prison. 12 Likes

Aaron Fuller Coach Barnett and Ms. Townsend are telling the truth. That bitch Janet Wilcox is a liar. She lied about my brother. 2 Likes

Roger Elkins STFU Everybody knows you and your brother deal drugs. The cops found drugs in his locker. 17 Likes

"Should we delete these comments?" Gwen asked.

Rick shook his head. "I think, if we leave those comments, there'll be more traffic, and more traffic means a greater likelihood someone will come forward with evidence."

Gwen sighed. "I guess. It's just these people are so hateful."

"They're misinformed."

"And stupid."

"That too."

"Aaron Fuller stuck his neck out for us," Gwen said.

"Unfortunately, the Fuller family doesn't have a lot of credibility at the moment."

"I don't think Drew assaulted Caleb. Based on the essay, it had to be Shane."

"The police had to have *some* evidence to charge him with the assault," Rick replied.

"Maybe Janet got Bob to lie to the police, to take the heat off Shane."

"Then why did Drew plead guilty?"

"They had him on the drug charges already. Sexual harassment's a misdemeanor. He probably pled guilty to avoid trial. I doubt it even added much time to his sentence. I'm sure the cops were happy to close the case. Sexual assault charges are really hard to prove and prosecute." Gwen clenched her jaw and her fists.

Rick unfurled her fist and placed his hand in hers. "You okay?"

She nodded. "I'm fine. Sorry."

"Don't apologize."

She nodded again.

"What do you think about taking another run at Greg Ebersole?"

Gwen frowned in response.

"Based on what he said, he probably has the video footage. We could go together and talk to his parents. His mother was friends with mine. Maybe she'll make Greg help us."

CHAPTER 100

Rick and the Kerfuffle

Rick and Gwen had decided to go during the school day, while the tech guy, Greg Ebersole, was at work. Rick thought they'd be more likely to convince Greg's parents to help them without Greg interjecting. Rick had met Greg's mother a few times, but they certainly weren't close, and he'd never met Greg's father.

They drove down the gravel driveway to the Ebersole farmhouse. The maples that lined the driveway were in their fall glory, the leaves fire-engine red. They passed the dilapidated barn, and Rick parked his truck behind another Ford pickup, a bit more beat up than his own. A clothesline stretched across the front lawn, shirts and pants and dresses waving in the wind.

"You ready?" Rick asked, turning to Gwen.

She nodded. "Hopefully they're not as angry with us as the rest of this town."

"I guess we'll find out."

They stepped from the cab. It was gray, the cold breeze biting their ears. They walked side by side to the front door. Rick glanced at Gwen, then knocked. Mrs. Ebersole answered the door. The middle-aged woman looked sturdy, like she was built to work. She wore a bonnet on her head and a coat over her *Little House on the Prairie* dress. Like many in the area, the Ebersoles waited as long as they could to turn on the heat, often wearing coats and hats in the house to stay warm.

"Rick?" she said, her eyes narrowed in his direction.

"Yes, Mrs. Ebersole," Rick replied. "How are you?"

She pursed her lips. "Better than you, I imagine."

"May we talk to you for a minute? It's important."

"You were here the other day," Mrs. Ebersole said, staring at Gwen. "You're the other one who's part of this ... kerfuffle."

"Yes, ma'am," Gwen replied, her head bowed.

"Well, I don't want no part of it, and I don't want youse bringin' Greg into it neither."

"We're innocent," Rick said.

Mrs. Ebersole frowned. "We're all sinners."

"Please, just hear us out. You know me. My mother must've told you what type of person I am."

She sighed. "I know what you done for your mother, takin' care of her all those years. I was real sorry when she died."

"Thank you."

Mrs. Ebersole stepped onto the porch, placing her hands in her jacket pockets.

"Greg has video of the day of the shooting," Rick said. "We think it'll show Janet Wilcox planting an essay, proving that Gwen wasn't negligent in her duties as an educator. Please, we just wanna find the truth."

"Ain't that for the police?" Mrs. Ebersole asked.

"They won't release the video. At least not yet. But Gwen's suspended now. She might lose her job. Plus, we're both being sued by Heather Miles. The video would help with that too."

Mrs. Ebersole exhaled, her breath condensing in a cloud. "I can't say I blame her."

"She's misinformed," Rick said.

Mrs. Ebersole nodded, considering the situation. "What makes you think Greg has the video? The police would've taken it from the school."

"Greg told me that he has it—or at least a copy of it," Gwen interjected.

"Why would he do that if he wasn't gonna give it to you?"

"He said he'd give it to me if I spent the night with him in a hotel."

Mrs. Ebersole blanched and shook her head. "I'm sorry. He ain't right sometimes. It's that malarkey on the internet. Tellin' him not to get married. Not to have children. Don't make no sense to me."

"Will you please ask him to give us a copy of the video?" Gwen asked.

The front door opened, and Mr. Ebersole stepped onto the porch, wearing dirty overalls. His face was ruddy and wrinkled, his eyes like lasers. "What in the world's goin' on out here?"

Mrs. Ebersole turned to her husband. "Greg has a video that Rick and this young woman need."

"Our son ain't gettin' involved in this mess." He put his arm around his wife and guided her inside. He turned to Rick and Gwen, standing on the threshold, and said, "Go on, get. Get off my property." He slammed the front door.

Rick and Gwen trudged back to the truck, dejected. Inside the cab, Rick started the engine, and put the truck into Reverse, turning around.

As he put the transmission into Drive, Gwen said, "Hold on. I have an idea."

Rick put the truck into Park, the engine still running.

Gwen rifled through her purse, extracting a pen and a business card. "I think she knows her son's a creep. I think she wanted to help us."

"I agree, but Mr. Ebersole has her pretty well controlled."

"It may look like that, but I bet she does plenty behind his back."

"How do you know?" Rick asked.

"Just a feeling I get. My dad thinks he controls my mom, but my mom finds a way to do whatever she wants." Gwen crossed out the plumber on the business card.

"What are you doing?"

"I'm giving her a chance to contact us behind his back." Gwen wrote her name and number on the back of the card, with a little note that read, *Please call if you can help. We'll be discreet.*

"How are you gonna give it to her?"

Gwen had a crooked smile. "Watch." She opened the passenger door, ran over to the clothesline, and put the card into a dress pocket.

CHAPTER 101

Janet and Stop, Just Stop

The West Lake Wolf Pack football team was at home for the last game of the regular season. They were 8-1, a win guaranteeing a postseason berth. Janet sat in the stands with Rachel, sharing her blanket. They had been excited and talkative as the game began, but much less so after Shane threw his first interception. And even less so after the second. The Cornwall Crusaders were up 14–0. Shane and the West Lake offense drove deep into Cornwall territory, with a minute left in the half.

That's when it happened. Again. Shane forced the ball into double coverage, and the Cornwall defender intercepted the pass and nearly ran it back for a touchdown. Cornwall scored on a screen pass as the half ended, making the score 21–0.

"At least we get the ball in the second half," Rachel said, as they watched the band perform the halftime show.

Janet glared in response.

After halftime, West Lake received the kickoff, the returner downing it in the end zone for a touchback. Cornwall had an excellent kicker who could boot kickoffs into the end zone. Jamar and the offense trotted onto the field.

Janet's eyes were like saucers. "What the hell does Bob think he's doing?"

"Maybe Shane's hurt," Rachel said.

Shane stood on the sideline, apart from his teammates, his helmet on.

"He doesn't look hurt," Janet said, standing from her seat.

Jamar completed a twenty-yard pass to Lance, the West Lake crowd showing some life.

"Where are you going?" Rachel asked.

Janet didn't answer, simply stomped down the stadium steps. The home team crowd cheered again as Jamar broke loose for a long run. Janet opened the short gate that separated the crowd from the sideline. She marched passed the cheerleaders, who shook their pom-poms on the rubber track. Janet stepped onto the grass and the sideline. The crowd erupted once more as Jamar threw a touchdown pass to Lance. Janet pushed through the celebrating players, finding Coach Schneider, wearing a headset, all smiles after the touchdown.

"What the hell do you think you're doing?" Janet said.

Bob Schneider walked away from the players and assistant coaches, toward the empty benches. Janet followed. Out of the corner of his mouth, in a hushed tone, he said, "Are you crazy?"

Once they were alone, Janet said, "I want Shane back in, *now.*"

"Cliff Osborn told me at halftime to put Jamar in. He said that you'd understand. He was supposed to talk to you."

School Board President Cliff Osborn came their way, cutting across the track to the sideline. Bob and Janet both watched his advance, Bob's face showing hope, Janet's showing hatred.

Cliff approached, showing his palms. "We need this game to make the playoffs."

"I want Shane back in, *right now.*"

"Not gonna happen," Cliff replied. "Lance has a real chance at a scholarship but not if the season ends tonight. Shane has had more than enough chances. It's obvious to everyone that he's not getting the job done."

Janet moved into Cliff's personal space. She spoke in terse whispers.

"You have no right to get involved in—"

"Stop, Mom. Just stop," Shane said.

Janet turned to Shane. "This doesn't concern you."

"Of course it does."

"They cannot take you out. You're a senior."

"Seriously, just fuckin' stop." Shane sounded exasperated.

Bob and Cliff took the opportunity to walk away from the scene, leaving mother and son to battle it out.

"Do you have any *idea* what I've done for you?" Janet said.

"You've ruined my life." Shane tossed his helmet to the ground and walked toward the locker room.

Janet followed. "What do you think you're doing?"

"Get the *fuck* away from me."

Janet stopped in her tracks, her mouth open, in shock, watching her son walk away.

CHAPTER 102

Gwen and the Throwback

Gwen stood from the blanket, a pair of binoculars in hand, cheering the touchdown pass from Jamar to Lance Osborn. It was the third touchdown he'd thrown to Lance in the second half. Rick had also stood from the blanket, cheering in obscurity, also holding a pair of binoculars. They'd watched the game from the top of the hill, just off school grounds. It was the best place to watch the game if you weren't allowed on campus or were too broke to buy a ticket. Thankfully, only a handful of people were spread across the massive hill, probably too drunk to notice or to care about Gwen and Rick.

The score was now 21–20, Cornwall on top by one, pending the extra point, with thirty seconds left in the game. Coach Bob Schneider burned his final time-out and jogged onto the field.

"I'd go for two," Rick said.

"Why not just kick the extra point and win it in overtime?" Gwen asked.

"Our kicker makes about 70 percent of his extra points, but we make about 55 percent of our two-point conversions. That number is much higher with Jamar as quarterback because he's such a threat to run. Plus, in overtime, the kicker is much more important, and their kicker is clearly better than ours."

"You think that's what they'll do?"

"Probably. If I know Bob, he'll run the quarterback throwback."

"What's that?"

Rick grinned. "You'll see."

The kicker never came onto the field. West Lake lined up in a jumbo set, with three tight ends and two running backs. Cornwall took out two defensive backs, replacing them with two big linemen. On the snap of the football, Jamar pitched the ball to the deep back. The running back sprinted around the end. He wasn't going to make it, the Cornwall defenders swarming and clogging the running lanes. But the running back stopped, turned, and threw the ball across the field to Jamar, who was wide open. The running back was crushed as soon as he threw the football, disappearing in a heap of Cornwall defenders. Gwen held her breath, watching through her binoculars, as the ball hung in the air, Jamar sprinting underneath, the spiral dropping into his outstretched hands. The referee threw his arms up signaling the successful two points. The stadium erupted in pandemonium. The fans were on their feet, high-fiving each other. The Wolf Pack sideline celebrated. Rick hugged Gwen. She wondered if he might kiss her. He didn't.

With a one-point lead, and thirty seconds left, West Lake did have to kickoff and stop Cornwall from scoring, which they did, the game ending on a sack.

After the game, Gwen and Rick watched the sideline through their binoculars, hoping to see something that might help them. With Janet and Shane leaving in the third quarter, the sideline was drama free. Lance Osborn kissing Ashlee Miles was the only interesting development.

CHAPTER 103

Rick and Too Much to Drink

After the big win, they went back to Gwen's to celebrate with popcorn and wine for her and beer for him. Rick was a big guy, and he drank the occasional beer, but he hadn't eaten much that day, and he hadn't polished off a six-pack in less than two hours since he was in college. It felt good to be a little drunk, a little out of control. Rick placed the empty beer bottle on the coffee table and looked across the couch at Gwen and her wineglass and her flannel pajamas. Those big blue eyes. That perfect face. Rick scooted across the couch, now within touching distance.

"I'm so proud of Jamar," Gwen said.

Rick nodded but didn't reply audibly because he felt like now was the time. "You're so beautiful." His speech was slurred.

Gwen giggled. "Sounds like someone's a little drunk. I think it's time to go to sleep."

"I'm not drunk. I'm stating facts. You're beautiful. That's a fact." Rick put his big meat hooks on her waist and leaned in to kiss her, but she turned her head and placed one hand on his sternum, holding him at bay.

"Rick, you're drunk."

He pulled away abruptly, his hand accidentally smacking her wineglass, a splash of red wine ending up in Gwen's lap.

"Shit, I'm sorry," Rick said, recoiling farther.

Gwen set her wineglass on the coffee table. "It's fine." She stood from the couch. "I should go to bed."

Rick looked at her like a puppy dog begging to be invited.

"I'll see you in the morning," she said before walking into her bedroom and shutting the door behind her.

* * *

"Oh, my God!" Gwen said.

Rick sat upright on Gwen's couch, jolted from his slumber. He rubbed his eyes, his vision coming into focus.

"I'm sorry," Gwen said, sitting at the kitchen table in her pajamas. "I didn't mean to wake you."

"What is it?"

Gwen pointed to the laptop in front of her. "Lance Osborn commented on your post." She smiled wide. "You should read this."

Rick moved the covers off his body and stood from the couch. His mouth tasted terrible. He cringed, feeling a flash of embarrassment as he remembered what had happened. He staggered to the kitchen.

Gwen looked bright-eyed and bushy-tailed, her face radiant and flawless without makeup, and her hair in a loose ponytail. Rick slumped into the chair next to her.

"You feeling okay?" she asked.

"I'm fine."

She raised her eyebrows and giggled. "You don't look fine." Gwen stood from the table and stepped to the sink. "You need water."

"Thanks. I'm sorry about last night."

She sat next to him at the kitchen table, placing the water in front of him. "There's nothing to be sorry for. I had fun."

He nodded and took a huge gulp of water. Rick looked at the laptop. "What's going on?"

She moved the computer in front of him, leaning over him for a moment, close enough for Rick to smell her hair. A hint of vanilla and something else. *Flowers maybe?* Rick looked at the screen, his Facebook post followed by tons of terrible comments about how he was a child predator, a creep, and how he encouraged kids to bully Caleb to toughen him up.

"Scroll down a little," she said.

Rick scrolled down and found it.

Lance Osborn: You people are stupid. Coach Barnett never even saw Caleb being bullied. Neither did Coach Schneider. Nobody did but the football players. I saw someone put his balls right on Calebs face and it wasn't Drew Fuller like everyones been saying. Shane Wilcox did that.

CHAPTER 104

Janet Ups the Ante

Janet barreled into school on Monday morning. A few people said good morning, but she didn't acknowledge their existence. She'd had an awful weekend. Shane still wasn't talking to her and those fucking Osborns ... She was still fuming mad at Cliff Osborn's interference at the game. Then his piece-of-shit son had posted about Shane on that fucking Facebook page. It wasn't enough to take Shane's starting position. They also had to try to ruin his life. Then other fuckwad football players had backed up Lance's story with posts of their own.

Janet had called Cliff multiple times over the weekend, but he hadn't answered or returned her messages. She had thought about going over to his house but decided against it. She had been afraid she might punch him in the face. As much as she hated to admit it, she needed his support on the school board, and his seat wasn't up for two years. Once she was done with him though, she'd fucking bury him. So, she'd spent much of the weekend sending abuse reports to Facebook, flagging the posts about Shane, and telling her supporters to do the same. Unfortunately, Facebook wasn't very responsive on the weekend, so the posts were still up.

She shut her office door, went to her desk, and slumped into her chair. She powered on her laptop and checked the Facebook page. Nothing new about Shane. She called Cliff again from her cell phone.

Her call rang once, then went to voice mail. Her messages over the weekend had sounded urgent, but she hadn't made any threats. It was time to up the ante.

After the beep she said, "Good morning, Cliff. I hope you had a nice weekend. I was thinking about our little meeting in Hershey and those beautiful pictures I took. The ones with you on the bed, blindfolded and naked as the day you were born. I was wondering if you think I should send copies to your wife. I wasn't sure, so I thought I should ask you first. If I don't hear back from you, I'll assume you want me to send them. I'm sure your wife will be thrilled." Janet disconnected the call.

Five minutes later, Janet's cell phone rang. She swiped right, a wicked grin on her face. "Cliff."

"I haven't been avoiding you," Cliff said.

"Really?"

"The wife and I are in the Poconos. We're on our way back now. I'm in the men's bathroom of a goddamn Cracker Barrel."

"Did you see what your son posted on Facebook?"

He exhaled. "I heard about it."

"You need to tell him to get his story straight."

He was quiet for a beat. "I don't think you wanna go down this road. If the police talk to my son, which they might, he *will* tell the truth. Even if he backed Shane, too many other kids saw what happened. You're not gonna contain this."

"Then you leave me no choice but to send these pictures. They're quite compromising."

"I'm gonna level with you for a minute. I don't want my wife to see those pictures, no doubt about it, but, if I have to make my son lie to the police to keep those pictures from my wife, I won't do it. I'd rather deal with my wife than do that to my son. And here's the other thing. If you do that, the repercussions won't simply be me and my marriage. I'll come after you with every ounce of influence I have in this town. I'll make your life a living hell."

"You don't scare me."

"I'm not trying to. What should scare you is the fact that there's a locker room full of witnesses. If I were you, I'd concentrate on getting Shane a good lawyer, and I wouldn't burn your bridge with me. You're not the only one who knows how to play hardball."

Janet gritted her teeth, her mind groping for another card to play but never finding it. "Fine, but I won't be bullied."

"You're the one doing the bullying."

"What about Pruitt? He has to go."

"Pastor Goode's reputation is pretty well destroyed at this point. He may withdraw from the election. If you want Pruitt gone, you'll have a majority on the school board to do it, provided you still have *my* support."

"*Do* I still have your support?"

"If you ever threaten me again, our relationship is over. Do you understand me?"

Her entire body tensed. "Yes."

Cliff disconnected the call.

Janet picked up her empty coffee mug that read Kids First and whipped it across the room, the mug shattering against the wall.

CHAPTER 105

Gwen's Priorities

"This is getting bad," Rick said, sitting at the kitchen table.

Gwen turned from the stovetop, where she stirred the spaghetti noodles. "The posts about Shane?"

"Yeah, some of them are pretty brutal. I know this is good for us, but he's still a kid. Maybe we should delete them?"

Gwen turned down the burner, walked over to the table, and read over Rick's shoulder. There were a bunch of replies underneath Lance's comment about Shane being the one who had sexually assaulted Caleb.

Lance Osborn: You people are stupid. Coach Barnett never even saw Caleb being bullied. Neither did Coach Schneider. Nobody did but the football players. I saw someone put his balls right on Calebs face and it wasn't Drew Fuller like everyones been saying. Shane Wilcox did that. 47 Likes

Aaron Fuller: I knew my brother would never do that. Vice Principal Wilcox is a lying bitch and Shane is a fucking pussy. He had to have his mom get him a starting position. 22 Likes

Chris Shelton: I saw it 2 Shane did it 6 Likes

Angelo Lewin: That shit was so gay. Shane is a fag 8 Likes

Colton Weiss: Vice Principal Wilcox is biggest bitch ever. Everybody knows Shane did that shit 9 Likes

Eric Gorman: Jamar should have been starting all year. I heard Wilcox threatened Coach Barnett to start Shane. Remember that game when Shane started one play? Then Coach Barnett put Jamar back in right away. That's why he got fired. Then she did the same thing to Coach Schneider. 15 Likes

Jamar Burris: I wasn't in the locker room when that happened to Caleb, but everyone that was there says Shane did it, not Drew. I think Vice Principal Wilcox lied about Coach Barnett and Ms. Townsend. It's so messed up. 12 Likes

"This is bad," Gwen said, sitting in the chair next to Rick. "Do you think Shane's seen it?"

"I'm sure he has," Rick replied. "What do you think we should do?"

"I think we should screenshot everything, then delete the posts that are abusive to Shane. I'll send the screenshots to Detective Strickland. Maybe it'll help Drew Fuller."

"Almost all of them are abusive to Shane," Rick said. "If we delete everything, the kids will stop posting, which would be bad for us."

Gwen deadpanned, "We have to do what's right for our students first. Our needs are secondary."

CHAPTER 106

Rick and Shattered

Rumors had swirled during the week about Shane and whether or not he'd be arrested for sexually assaulting Caleb Miles, but that's all they'd been, rumors with no confirmation. Despite the controversies, everything stopped for football Friday. West Lake had home field advantage through the playoffs. They'd been 9-1, their only loss coming against a much bigger school and a 6A playoff team. Thankfully, through the postseason, West Lake would only be playing schools with similar class sizes.

Rick and Gwen sat on the hill, just off-campus, watching the first round of the playoffs. Jamar had been spectacular, running for three touchdowns and throwing three more. Halfway through the fourth quarter, content with a forty-two-point lead, Bob Schneider put in the second string.

The hill was a little more crowded than last week, but Rick and Gwen still mostly had their privacy. Initially, when they'd walked to their spot, a few townspeople had stared, but nobody had said anything. Now, with the game well in hand, people packed up their blankets and camping chairs, and headed for their cars. Gwen shivered and scooted closer to Rick, their thighs and arms touching.

"You cold?" Rick asked.

She wore a puffy jacket, gloves, and a knit cap, but they'd been sitting still for two hours, and the temperature had dropped into the thirties. "A little," Gwen replied.

"We can get going if you want."

"You don't mind?"

Rick shook his head. "I'm getting cold too."

He stood from the blanket with a groan and reached for Gwen. She took his hand, and Rick hoisted her to her feet. He grabbed the blanket, and they walked across the hill toward the roadside. Along the way, they passed a young man sitting by himself, wearing a dark jacket, his hood up.

Gwen stopped, looking up the hill toward the dark figure. She whispered to Rick. "I think that's Shane."

Rick glanced at the figure. "I think you're right."

"Should we say something?"

Rick retrieved his keys from his pocket and handed them to Gwen. "Why don't you get the truck warm. I'll go talk to him."

Gwen nodded and kissed Rick on the cheek. Rick was stunned for a moment, wanting to ask Gwen what the kiss was for, but she was already walking to the truck.

Rick hiked up the hill to Shane. "You mind if I sit down?"

"Free country unless you're in prison," Shane replied, his speech slurred.

Rick sat next to Shane on the cold hard ground. Shane held a bottle of something in a brown paper bag. The tip of his nose was red from the cold. His blue eyes were red-rimmed, probably *not* from the cold.

"You really think that's the best idea?" Rick asked, glancing at the booze bottle in Shane's hand.

"Doesn't make a fuckin' difference," Shane replied. "My life's over."

"You have your whole life ahead of you."

Shane wagged his head and tossed the booze bottle down the hill. Even drunk and from a sitting position, Shane had an arm. The bottle sailed through the air and shattered on the fence at the bottom of the hill. Beyond that fence was West Lake High School property. "I'm going to prison. Sexual assault." He shut his eyes. Rick thought he might pass out, but Shane opened them and said, "It was a fuckin' joke."

"What happened?" Rick asked.

"You know." He laughed, but he didn't sound happy. "Everybody knows." Shane collected mucus in his mouth and spat down the hill.

Rick looked at Shane, dubious. He hadn't even heard Shane was arrested. *There's no way the justice system works this fast.* "Were you arrested?"

"Not yet. My lawyer said they might soon. Cops have witnesses, ... lots of witnesses." Shane hung his head. "They used to be my friends."

"I'm sorry, Shane."

"Lawyer said I could get ten years."

Rick gasped. "Jesus. Ten years? That can't be right."

Shane raised his head. "If I go to trial. If I plead guilty, maybe a year and the registry, like a fuckin' rapist." Shane leaned over, turned his head and retched, vomiting in the grass. He spat, his breathing labored. "Fuck." He spat again and held his head in his hands. He began to cry, quiet at first, trying to contain it, then harder, his body racked with sobs.

Rick put his arm on the boy's back.

Shane didn't pull away.

"A year will go by in the blink of an eye," Rick said. "Keep your head down and your mouth shut, and you'll be fine. You're a tough kid, Shane. You'll get through this."

CHAPTER 107

Janet and the Election

"We have nineteen witnesses prepared to testify," District Attorney Blake Drummond said.

Shane sat in his seat with a deer-in-the-headlights look on his face. The plea deal sat on the table in front of him, unsigned. He was flanked by Janet and his attorney, Jacob Byers. His attorney was a bald man, compact and sturdy. He looked like he could've been a fullback twenty years ago.

DA Drummond sat across the polished table, his fat fingers steepled. Drummond looked like a cop-turned-lawyer, complete with an ill-fitting suit and a gray mustache.

Janet put her hand on top of Shane's. "It's a good deal."

Shane removed his hand from hers. "I can't go to prison." He pushed the plea deal and the pen away from him. "It was just a joke. I wasn't assaultin' him. This isn't fair."

"Stop talking, Shane," Byers said.

"Listen to Mr. Byers," Janet said.

"I can't do this." Shane put his face in his hands and cried.

Janet scowled at her son, embarrassed by his behavior.

"I thought we had a deal," DA Drummond said.

"We do," Byers replied. "Can I have five minutes alone with my client?"

Drummond stood from his chair. "I'll be back in five." He left the room.

As soon as the DA shut the door behind him, Janet leaned into Shane's personal and said, "Stop your crying."

Jacob Byers raised his hand to quiet Janet. "Shane. This isn't going away." Byers spoke softly, trying to be the good cop to Janet's bad. "A trial will take longer than the six months they're offering, and, if we lose, you could get ten years. This is a great deal. I know prison is scary, but it'll be over before you know it."

Shane sniffled and lifted his head from his hands. "It's not fair." He wiped his eyes with the side of his index finger. "You know how many kids grab drunk girls at parties? That's sexual assault. What I did, … it was just a joke." He trailed off into a whisper.

Janet glowered at her son. She wanted to punch him in the face. At every turn, she'd tried to help him, yet he continued to throw it all away.

"I know, Shane," Byers said. "If Caleb hadn't killed himself, we probably wouldn't be here, but he did. It's bad luck, no question. But we are where we are. You have to play the hand you're dealt."

"But wouldn't, like, a jury or whatever, see that it was just a joke?" Shane asked. "I could tell 'em what happened. They'd understand. I didn't mean nothin' by it. It was a mistake."

"Maybe, but it's a gamble."

Shane looked at his mother. "I think we can win."

Janet shook her head. "If you make this decision, there's no *we*."

"What are you talkin' about?"

"I won't waste any more money cleaning up your messes. If you want to fight this thing, you can pay for it yourself."

Shane's face reddened. "I don't have any money."

"That's what public defenders are for."

"You don't think I can win?"

Janet deadpanned, "I know you can't."

360

* * *

The school board meeting took place in the library. Two long tables were set up at the head of the room and covered with a red-and-white tablecloth, matching the school colors. The nine school board directors and the superintendent sat behind the table, with name plates in front of them. Plastic chairs were set up for the sparse audience. Janet took her customary seat in the back.

Today's newspaper was on her seat, turned to the article about Shane's guilty plea. Janet looked around the room, searching for the culprit, but nobody dared make eye contact with her. He'd signed yesterday, and he was already in the paper. *Perfect. Just fucking perfect.* Thankfully, Jacob Byers had convinced Shane to take the deal. A trial would've been a lot more press. Besides, it was the smart play. And, even if it wasn't, Janet didn't have the money for a trial. She barely had enough to pay Byers for negotiating the plea. They'd given Shane a week to get his affairs in order before he had to report to prison, but Janet had secretly wished they'd taken him right away. She'd grown tired of dealing with his entitled attitude. Janet tossed the newspaper in the trash can and returned to her seat. Fortunately, Shane's quiet little plea was overshadowed by the US presidential election.

Rachel sat next to Janet. They whispered back and forth, gossiping, while the school board talked about budgetary items and approved a kid's request to help the local food pantry by setting up a donation table at this Friday's football game.

"How's Shane?" Rachel asked, her face braced for bad news.

Janet scowled and shook her head. "I'd rather not talk about it."

Rachel nodded and changed the subject. "I'm still in shock over the election. I was so upset that I cried."

"I can't believe people voted for that fucking orange clown."

"Those darn deplorables. At least Heather won."

Janet glanced at Heather Miles, who sat behind the long table with the rest of the school board directors. "She won't even talk to me. The media portrays Caleb as this meek victim, but that wasn't the case. He dished it out too. He was staring at Shane's penis. What kind of person does that?"

"A disturbed person."

Janet nodded.

"Don't worry about Heather," Rachel said. "We still have her. She still listens to me. She doesn't have to know if something's from you."

Janet pursed her lips. "If she doesn't do what she's told, I'll fucking ruin her. It's her fault that Caleb killed himself. She's an awful mother. Caleb did all the cooking. All the chores around the house. He even did the grocery shopping while Heather waited in the car. No wonder he killed himself. He didn't have a father *or* a mother. Yet she has the audacity to point her finger at Shane."

Cliff Osborn's voice boomed from his microphone. "That'll conclude this school board meeting. Thank you for attending."

Much of the audience filtered out of the library. Janet made her way to Cliff Osborn, cornering him against the magazine racks.

Janet said, "When will you deal with Pruitt? The community needs change, so it can heal."

Cliff's expression was neutral, cognizant of the fact that others may be watching, even if they were out of earshot. He wore a bulky tan suit over his stocky frame and paunch. "Five of us are ready to pull the trigger now. The wheels are already in motion."

"What does that mean?"

"He can retire, or we can fire him. It's his choice. I think he'll be smart and move on without a fuss."

"When will this happen?"

"I already have a meeting scheduled with him tomorrow."

"Good. I expect to be named principal immediately, and I'd like to choose the new vice principal."

"How's Shane holding up?"

"I'm not discussing it. I need to go." Janet turned and walked away.

CHAPTER 108

Gwen and TNSILF

"Someone posted on the Watchdog that Pruitt retired," Gwen said, looking up from her phone. "It says Janet's the new principal."

Rick was near the door, bent over, lacing up his boots. "They pushed him out so Janet can have his job."

Gwen exhaled, shaking her head. She stood next to Rick, her puffy coat zipped tight, her knit cap covering her head, and her purse slung over her shoulder. "She gets the principal experience she needs, and then she'll be the superintendent when Matthews retires."

Rick stood. "Maybe. Heather Miles is a wildcard now. She may hate *us*, but she hates Shane too, and Janet's guilty by association."

Gwen shoved her phone in her purse. Rick opened the door, and they left Gwen's apartment, headed for the truck, and ultimately the football game. Inside his truck, as Rick cranked the engine, Gwen's phone chimed.

She removed her phone from her purse and glanced at the number. "Who is it?" Rick asked.

"I don't know," Gwen replied. She swiped right. "Hello?"

"This is Doris Ebersole. Is this Gwen?"

"Oh, yes. Thank you so much for calling."

"I have somethin' for you. You think you could come by?"

"Sure. When?"

"Now. My husband went to the football game, but I don't know how long he'll stay. It's so cold out tonight."

"I'll be there in fifteen minutes."

Doris disconnected the call.

Gwen looked at Rick. "We have to go to the Ebersoles."

Rick drove across town to the Ebersole farmhouse. The maples along the driveway were mostly barren, leafless monsters in the headlights. They parked close to the farmhouse. Mr. Ebersole's truck wasn't here. Neither was Greg's Nissan 350Z. They exited Rick's truck and stepped to the front door. A single overhead bulb lit the porch in a whitish glow. Gwen knocked on the door. Mrs. Ebersole answered immediately, stepping onto the porch.

"Thank you for comin'," she said.

"Of course," Gwen replied.

Rick nodded.

"I found this." Mrs. Ebersole held up a small flash drive. "I searched his room while he was at work today. I think it's what you're lookin' for." She shook her head, her face blotchy, and her eyes bloodshot. "My niece opened it for me. I won't tell youse what else we found on it. My son needs God, but ..." She paused for a moment. "Well, you can take a horse to water, but you can't make him drink." She handed the flash drive to Gwen.

They decided to forgo the game and to return to Gwen's apartment to check the contents of the flash drive. On the way to Gwen's, they passed the high school. West Lake was already up 21-0.

Rick parked his truck in a visitor spot at her apartment, and they hurried up the stairs to Gwen's place. They took off their coats and shoes and sat on the couch, Gwen opening her laptop. She slid the flash drive into the USB port. She double-clicked the drive, now looking at various labeled folders: Hard Core, Cum Shots, BBW, Gang Bang, Big Asses, Big Tits, Voyeur, Up Skirt, TNSILF, and School Shooting. "I see why Mrs. Ebersole was upset. What's a TNSILF?"

"I have no idea," Rick replied.

Gwen clicked on School Shooting, opening the folder. It was a very large video file, patched together from hallway cameras, documenting the chaos. No cameras were inside Gwen's classroom. Initially, not much happened. Then, as others were alerted by texting hostages, the fear spread like a fever. Students and staff hurried down the hallways, headed for the exits. Some fast-walked, some jogged, and some sprinted as if their lives depended on it. Throughout most of the chaos, Lewis Phelps acted as the doorman to Gwen's classroom, keeping students away from danger, and instructing them to exit the building.

Janet Wilcox appeared on-screen, chaos still around her. She said something to Lewis, but there was no audio. Lewis said something. They went back and forth, then Lewis left. Janet took Lewis's place in front of the classroom.

"Pause it," Rick said.

Gwen paused the video.

"What's wrong with her hand? Her right hand."

Gwen squinted at the screen. "It looks like her sleeve's pulled down."

"And she's holding something."

"A folded piece of paper."

"That's what it looks like."

"Let's see what she does with it." Gwen played the video.

Gwen and Rick watched closely. A large group of students passed, then she didn't have the paper anymore, and her sleeve was normal.

"Shit," Gwen said. "She waited for the kids to block her from the camera."

"Rewind it. Play that part again," Rick replied.

They watched it ten times, but the video didn't show Janet slide Caleb's essay under Gwen's classroom door. It did show her holding a folded piece of paper, then not.

"She copied it and put it under my door," Gwen said. "That's why she was holding it with her sleeve. She didn't want her fingerprints on it. It would've been nice if it showed her sliding it under my door."

"This still helps you. What she did is consistent with your story.

She'll have to answer questions about that piece of paper. We need to get this out to the public."

"But it's stolen footage."

"We could release it anonymously," Rick said.

"How do we do that?" Gwen asked.

"I don't know, but we could Google it."

"I'd have to edit the video down to the part with Janet. I don't want Caleb's death on the internet."

"Maybe you could circle the paper and the sleeve with a caption explaining what she's doing, like John Madden did."

"Who's John Madden?"

Rick smiled. "He was an NFL broadcaster who died a few years ago. He used to draw on the screen, like a coach on a whiteboard."

"That's a good idea because, if you don't know what to look for, you probably wouldn't notice it."

Rick's phone pinged. He removed it from his pocket and glanced at the screen. "I just got a direct message from Shane on Facebook." Rick tapped on his phone, retrieving the message. "He wants my email address. He says he wants to send me something."

"What do you think it is?"

Rick still tapped on his phone. "I don't know." He set his phone on the coffee table. "I guess we'll find out. I sent him my email."

"Do you think he deserves to go to prison?"

"I don't know. What he did was awful, but I don't know. I wouldn't wanna be the one making that decision."

"Me neither." She stared at the paused video.

"Did you wanna watch the rest of it?" Rick gestured to the screen.

"I'd rather not relive it, if that's okay."

"Of course." Rick placed his hand on top of hers and squeezed.

Gwen wanted to put the laptop on the coffee table and wrap her arms around him, and she would have, but he removed his hand, the signal now muddled.

"Can you go back to Greg's folders?"

Gwen frowned. "The porn?"

"Yeah, I wanna see 'em again. He had that weird acronym."

Gwen downsized the video and clicked to the folders.

"TNSILF," Rick said. "What is that?"

"Should I open it?"

"Type it into Google first. We may not wanna see what's in it."

Gwen clicked on Google Chrome and typed TNSILF. The first listing was Tnsilc.org. It was a debt consolidation organization. "There's nothing that makes sense."

"That's strange. Open the folder."

Gwen went back to the folder and opened it. Tons of subfolders appeared. "Oh, my God."

Rick shook his head. "This is *not* good."

The folders were labeled with the names of female teachers and female students. Gwen hovered over her own name and clicked. A dozen thumbnail pictures appeared along with a video.

"That piece of shit," Rick said, his jaw clenched.

Gwen held her breath as she clicked the first picture. It showed her backside in a pencil skirt. Gwen clicked through the pictures, feeling relief. They were creepy but nothing pornographic. Greg had taken pictures of her chest, her butt, her legs, her face, and a few whole-body pictures, but she was clothed. Thankfully, her work attire was conservative. The video was from Greg's office. It showed Gwen walking away from him, then looking over her shoulder.

"This is so weird," Gwen said.

"He's a creep," Rick replied.

Gwen went back to the list of teachers and students. "Janet's on here." She clicked her folder, and a deluge of images and videos appeared. There were at least a hundred thumbnails.

"Jesus."

Gwen clicked on a picture and scrolled through. The images were much more inappropriate. Lots of shots of Janet's large chest and cleavage. Even some under-the-table images that showed her uncrossed legs and her lacy underwear. Gwen put her hand to her chest. "He has students too." Gwen clicked back to the folders. "There's Ashlee Miles and Becca Ansel. I've had most of these girls in class."

"Me too," Rick replied. "We have to send this to the police."

"But we shouldn't even have this."

"We can mail it anonymously to Detective Strickland."

"But we have to get Greg out of school immediately," Gwen said. "He's around kids."

"What about his cell phone? I bet he's using the one given to him by the school. All they have to do is confiscate it and search it. Then he's done."

"Do you really think he leaves those images on his phone?"

"Maybe the recent ones. Greg takes a lot of pictures, and, from the looks of it, he's been doing it a long time. I can't imagine he downloads and deletes those images every day."

"Maybe he uses his personal phone."

"Maybe, but he strikes me as a cheap guy," Rick said. "Think about it. He has a decent job, but he still lives at home."

"If he notices that the flash drive's gone, he'll delete everything from his phone."

"We need to call someone immediately. The question is, who do we contact? Who can we trust?"

"I'll call Pruitt," Gwen said. "I know he's retired, but I trust him, and maybe he'll contact Dr. Matthews."

"That's a good idea."

Gwen tapped the Principal Pruitt contact on her cell phone.

"Hello?" Pruitt answered.

"Principal Pruitt, this is Gwen Townsend."

"Please, Gwen, call me Don."

"Of course, ... sorry."

"What can I do for you?" He sounded beaten and weary.

"I was wondering if you could get a message to Dr. Matthews."

"I still have his number, but I doubt I have much influence, if this is about your situation."

"This isn't about me. Greg Ebersole has been taking inappropriate pictures of female teachers and students in school."

"How do you know that?"

Gwen paused. "I can't say exactly, but I know for a fact that it's true, and I think he's using his school phone to take the pictures. Someone needs to take his phone and check it."

Pruitt sighed. "That place has turned into a three-ring circus. What the heck happened?"

"I'm sorry that they pushed you out."

"Thanks, Gwen, but at least I have a pension. You need to worry about yourself. I'll call Matthews and let him know."

"Thank you, Don."

"Take care of yourself, Gwen." Pruitt disconnected the call.

Gwen set her phone on the coffee table and breathed a sigh of relief. "It's done."

"I think I figured out what TNSILF stands for," Rick said. "Teachers and students I'd like to ..."

CHAPTER 109

Rick and the Real Deal

Gwen had stayed up late last night, editing the video and providing captions. Rick had fallen asleep on the couch. On Saturday morning, he let Gwen sleep in, while he mailed the flash drive to Detective Strickland. He'd left her a note, so she wouldn't worry. He wiped off the flash drive with a cloth and a little glass cleaner, just enough to get rid of any fingerprints. He wore gloves throughout the process, never touching the flash drive, the envelope, or the stamps. He dropped the envelope into a blue mailbox near the grocery store.

On the way back to Gwen's, he had stopped off at his house and grabbed some clothes. They'd been practically living together for nearly a month, holding on to each other like human life rafts, figuratively of course. Literally, they'd barely touched each other, their relationship stuck in an odd limbo. When he returned to Gwen's apartment, she was awake, sitting on her couch, her laptop on her thighs.

"Good morning," he said, putting his coat on the rack.

"How'd it go?" she asked, still wearing her flannel pajamas.

"Fine. I went by my house to get some clothes." He held up his duffel bag, set it on the floor, and sat next to her on the couch.

"You must be sick of sleeping on my couch."

"Do you want me to go home? Now that you have the video, you're gonna get your job back. It's just a matter of time."

"What about you?"

He shrugged. "If you wanted me here because you needed someone, and I just happened to be the only one, I understand. I get it." Rick looked away for a moment.

Gwen put her laptop on the coffee table and turned her body toward Rick. "I thought we were friends."

"We are, ... but we were thrown together by circumstances, and the circumstances might be changing for you."

"I don't care about the circumstances. I care about you." She reached out and touched his forearm. "We're in this together, no matter what. Okay?"

He nodded.

She removed her hand.

"What are you doing?" he asked, glancing at her laptop.

"Trying to figure out how to post the video anonymously. I think if we use a VPN and post to a site that allows anonymous posts, we'll be fine."

"What's a VPN?"

"A virtual private network. Basically, you sign on to the VPN, and it looks like you're posting from another place. I was thinking we should leave the house and post in a public place as an added layer of anonymity."

"That'd be easy enough to do."

"Have you checked your email today?"

"No, I left my phone when I went out. I know it's probably crazy, but I didn't want my phone giving away my location while I mailed the flash drive."

"I was just wondering if you received anything from Shane."

"Let's see." Rick stood from the couch and walked to the kitchen, where his phone charged on the counter. He returned to the couch, his phone in hand. He tapped his Gmail account and looked at Gwen, his expression serious as cancer. "I got something." Rick opened an anonymous email, moving his phone toward Gwen, so she could get a better look. "This has to be from Shane."

From: Flavorflav13596@hotmail.com
To: RickBarnett1212@gmail.com
Subject: The Real Deal
I posted these pictures on the West Lake Watchdog. You should put them on your page to. The Watchdog will delete them. I won't tell you where I got them.

Six images were attached. Rick clicked on the first image. It was the one that got him into hot water, the one with Ashlee kissing him in his doorway. Rick clicked on the next image. This one showed Rick pulling back from the kiss and pushing her away. The next two showed, just split seconds afterward, Rick's arms fully extended, Ashlee on the porch now. The last two showed Rick slamming the door in Ashlee's face.

CHAPTER 110

Janet and #BringBarnettBack

Janet carried shopping bags from her car into her home. She took the bags upstairs. The door to Shane's room was still shut. It was shut when she'd left this morning, and it was still shut at nearly one in the afternoon. They hadn't spoken in four days, not since Shane had signed the plea deal. She went to her bedroom, placed her purse on her dresser and her shopping bags in her walk-in closet. As she hung up her new clothes, her phone chimed. She stepped to her purse, retrieved her phone, and swiped right.

"Hello, Rachel," Janet said.

"Have you looked on Facebook today?" Rachel asked.

"No, I was shopping at the Hershey Outlets."

"Someone posted pictures of Rick pushing away Ashlee Miles, just like he said he did. Whoever posted it was obviously using a fake account."

Janet's heart pounded; her stomach tumbled. "That's impossible."

"It was on the Watchdog, but Heather deleted it."

"That's good."

"Heather's furious that everyone knows it's Ashlee now. I'm sure Ashlee's mortified."

Janet took a deep, cleansing breath. "That's Rick's fault."

"Heather thinks it's your fault."

"My fault?" Janet's voice went up an octave.

"She thinks *you* took the pictures."

"That's ridiculous."

"That's what *I* told her," Rachel replied.

"Well, I hope you set her straight."

"I tried, but she's still upset. The pictures are still out there."

"I thought she deleted them?"

"Now they're on the Truth about West Lake."

"Did you file an abuse report?" Janet said.

"I did, and I told everyone else to file reports too, but the pictures are still up. A few people didn't even respond when I texted them about filing an abuse report. Facebook probably won't do anything until Monday anyway." Rachel sighed. "Most of the comments are still on our side, but some are against us now."

Janet shook her head. "Hold on. I'm going to my laptop to take a look."

She went downstairs to her home office, her cell phone in hand. Janet sat at her desk and powered on her laptop. She entered the password, Shane12. She needed to change that password. Twelve was his jersey number, but football was over for Shane. Unceremoniously over. Janet navigated to the Facebook page. She slammed the sides of her fists on her desktop, rattling the laptop. *Shane. Why the fuck would he use his last few days to do this?*

"Are you okay?" Rachel asked, audible even though Janet's cell sat on the desktop.

The pictures were there, and they were authentic. Janet picked up her cell phone and said through gritted teeth, "I'm fine. I'm reading."

The Truth about West Lake

November 12 at 2:27 PM

Coach Rick Barnett was fired and his reputation was destroyed by the first picture in the collection. The picture portrays Rick Barnett kissing an underaged student, but it doesn't tell the whole story. To this day, Barnett maintains that the girl in the picture entered his home uninvited while he was in the shower.

When Barnett heard someone in his bedroom, he exited his shower, and put on a towel, not bothering to dry himself. He told the girl to leave, but she wouldn't, so Barnett threatened to call the police. The girl called his bluff, saying that, if he called the police, it looked bad for him.

Out of options, Barnett escorted her from his house. When he reached around her to open the front door, the girl kissed him, and Janet Wilcox was waiting outside ready to take a picture. Janet Wilcox had been tailing Barnett that evening, upset that he'd benched her son in favor of a different quarterback. She'd seen the girl park in Barnett's driveway and enter his unlocked house without knocking.

Wilcox positioned herself in Barnett's front yard, hiding behind a tree, hoping to catch Barnett in a compromising position. As soon as the girl kissed Barnett, he turned his head and shoved her onto the stoop. Then he slammed the door in her face.

This is the story that Rick Barnett has consistently told the West Lake School District administration, but they didn't have the photo evidence you see here to back up his story. Notice that Rick's hair and chest are still very wet. If this was consensual, he would've taken the time to dry off. Look at the expression on his face. At no time does he look happy.

Janet Wilcox ruined a good man's life. **#BringBarnettBack** 42 Likes 14 Shares

Roger Elkins These pictures are fake. Barnett is a scumbag. He should be arrested. **#FireBarnett #FirePruitt #FireTownsend** 8 Likes

Lance Osborn Hey dumbass, if the pictures are fake that means he didn't do it. **#BringBarnettBack** 16 Likes

Trina Grisham Where did these pictures come from? I don't trust Barnett. I heard he's in a relationship with Townsend-Walker. They are in this together. 4 Likes

Sadie Ollinger OMG. THEY LIED. Principal Wilcox set him up. 7 Likes

Aaron Fuller I knew it was a lie. I've been saying so for weeks. Principal Wilcox is a big fat hairy CUNT. She lied about Barnett, Townsend, and my brother Drew. **#FreeDrewFuller** 10 Likes

Will Gilroy This is bullshit. Don't believe it. Barnett and Townsend-Walker deserved to be fired. They might be going to prison. Drew Fuller is a piece of shit drug dealer. **#FireBarnett #FirePruitt #FireTownsend** 4 Likes

Breanna Franks I agree with you, **Will Gilroy.** 3 Likes

Janet stared at the screen in shock. She was losing the crowd. She thought about Aaron Fuller's post. CUNT. The same word that was etched into the driver's side door of her BMW.

"Are you still there?" Rachel asked.

"I have to call you back." Janet disconnected the call. She marched up the stairs and barged into Shane's room. It was dark, the shades blocking the sun. She flipped on the light. Her son was still asleep at one in the afternoon. "Wake up!"

He groaned and covered his head with a pillow.

Janet approached the bed and yanked the covers from his body. "What the hell's wrong with you?"

He rolled on his side and rubbed his eyes, squinting at his mother. "Get out of my room."

"You took those pictures off my laptop."

"I don't know what you're talkin' about."

"You know exactly what I'm talking about. The pictures you posted on Facebook."

Shane sat up, his feet now on the floor, wearing a T-shirt and boxer briefs. One side of his mouth was raised in contempt. "You lied about Coach Barnett. He got fired because of you."

"There's a lot more that you don't know. Coach Barnett has been having sex with students for a long time. He saw the camera, that's why he pushed Ashlee away."

"I don't believe you."

Janet crossed her arms over her chest. "That's the truth, which you've managed to destroy with your little stunt. It's not enough to totally humiliate me with your bullshit, you have to put my career at risk too?"

"I don't give a *fuck* about you or your career."

Janet reared back and slapped him across the face.

Shane stood abruptly, towering over his mother, posturing. "Do it again, and I'll *knock* your ass out."

Janet turned and marched from his room, slamming the door on the way out. She went back to her home office and sat behind the desk. Her hands were shaking. *This is about prison. He's scared and acting out.* Shane still had a few days to get his affairs in order before he had to report for his six-month prison sentence. Janet thought about her next move. She had to respond to this nonsense on Facebook. She tapped her Rachel contact on her cell phone.

"What do you wanna do?" Rachel asked in lieu of a greeting.

"I want you to contact anybody who's willing to post on Facebook. Tell them the real truth. You have a pen and paper handy?"

"I'm ready," Rachel replied.

"Tell them that Rick has been suspected of multiple affairs with students. He was finally caught, but he saw the camera and pushed the girl away, acting like he didn't want it. Rick Barnett is a child molester and a liar."

CHAPTER 111

Gwen and the Tide's Turning

They left their phones at home as they drove to a Sheetz gas station. Rick parked near the building so Gwen could pick up the Wi-Fi with her laptop. The gas station was sparsely populated on a Sunday night. Rick left the truck running for heat.

Gwen logged into the VPN using the free internet from Sheetz. She created a fake Gmail account, then a YouTube account using the fake Gmail account. She uploaded the edited video of Janet holding that paper on the day of the shooting. Gwen had done a good job of providing captions and still shots from the video to make her case that Janet did, in fact, have the essay and that she planted it in Gwen's classroom. After posting the video on YouTube, she spread it around in the comment sections of a few popular blogs that talked about school shootings. Gwen knew it would likely go viral from there.

"That's it." Gwen disconnected from the Wi-Fi and closed her laptop.

Rick's smile reached his eyes. "The tide's turning. I can feel it."

Gwen smiled right back. "Me too."

Rick reversed from the parking space and drove back toward Gwen's apartment. "We need to talk to a lawyer. We're running out of time to respond to Heather's lawsuit."

"With what money?" Gwen asked. "I have enough to pay my bills for maybe two more months."

"I'm not much better off, but aren't there lawyers who only get paid if you win? With the evidence we have now, we could countersue Heather and the school district for wrongful termination."

"I don't want to sue the school district. I want the truth to come out, and I want Janet gone, and I want my job back."

"So do I, but maybe suing is a way to get the truth out there. We can drop the suit if they do the right thing. Either way, we need a lawyer for Heather's lawsuit."

"You're right."

CHAPTER 112

Rick and the Lawsuit

"This is inappropriate," Cliff Osborn said. "How did you get this number?"

Rick paced in Gwen's living room, his cell phone to his ear, Gwen watching and listening from the couch. "You called me about Lance, remember?"

"But I never gave you my number. I have to go—"

"We're suing you and the school district," Rick said.

"That's ridiculous," Cliff replied.

"Is it? That's not what our lawyer says. I have pictures that show I was telling the truth about Ashlee Miles, and there's the video that shows Janet with the essay."

"It's not conclusive."

"Neither was firing Gwen. The video backs Gwen's story. Our lawyer thinks we have a multimillion-dollar wrongful termination suit. I've heard that you and some of the other school board members colluded with Janet to fire me and Gwen. We'll sue board members in civil court too. I hope it was worth it."

"Now hold on, Rick. You know I've always supported you as a coach and a teacher. I was on the board that approved your hire when you started. This is getting out of hand. We can work this out."

Rick smiled at Gwen but stayed in character with Cliff. "We want a public hearing in front of the school board to discuss the recent developments."

"I'll see what I can do."

"We won't be pushed around anymore. It's not right."

"I'll do my best."

Rick disconnected the call and looked at Gwen. "He said he'll try to get us a hearing."

"Do you think he's telling the truth?"

"I think he's scared. He knows they did some shady shit. Now he's afraid of getting sued."

Gwen had a crooked smile. "Multimillion-dollar lawsuit, huh?"

Rick chuckled. "We have a meeting with two lawyers tomorrow. They might say that."

CHAPTER 113

Janet and Mahanoy

The sky was gray, a light rain falling. Janet drove her BMW on I-81, with Shane sitting shotgun. They'd barely spoken that Wednesday morning. Shane slumped in his seat and stared from the passenger window. Janet took the exit for the Mahanoy State Correctional Institution. They were forty-five minutes early. They'd left in plenty of time. The punishment for being late was harsh.

She parked in the expansive parking lot of the expansive complex. Beyond the lot, razor wire surrounded the facility. She saw a football field in the distance. No goalposts but it looked like a football field. Janet thought about saying something positive to Shane, but she didn't have the energy, and, to be honest, she was sick of coddling him.

Janet stepped from her car and opened her umbrella. Shane lagged behind, but Janet didn't wait. Inside was a waiting area, and a small queue of damp people to talk to one of the three prison guards behind bulletproof glass. Janet stood in line. Shane entered the building, joining her in the queue. After a short wait, one of the guards motioned for them. They approached the window. The middle-aged man must've been the least-welcoming receptionist in existence. He looked at Janet and Shane, scowling.

"I'm here to drop off Shane Wilcox," Janet said.

The man didn't reply. He pecked on his keyboard for a minute, then said, "Does he have his ID?"

"Yes," Janet replied.

"Have a seat. They'll call you."

They sat in a lonely corner of the waiting room. A handful of other people sat in the plastic chairs, everyone keeping their distance from each other.

"You can go," Shane said, not looking at his mother.

"I can wait with you," Janet replied.

Shane turned to Janet, his face blank. "I want you to go."

"I know you're upset, but this was a good deal."

"For who?"

"I'm not having this discussion with you again. It was your choice."

"Was it?"

"Yes, it was. Grow up, Shane. Maybe you'll appreciate all I've done for you after spending some time here."

"I talked to Dad."

Janet's eyes went wide. "That man is an evil psychopath and a manipulative liar. I can't believe you'd go behind my back."

"He said you told him that I didn't want anything to do with him."

She put her hand to her chest, her voice going up an octave. "That's ridiculous. I never said that."

"He said you made it impossible to visit. He said you wouldn't even let him talk to me on the phone. He said he wrote letters, but I never got any letters."

"He's a liar. You didn't get any letters because he didn't send any. He could've come to visit anytime he wanted. He chose not to because he was with his whore. You don't know the first thing about your father."

"If he's lyin', why did he say he'll come and visit me here?"

"I don't see your father taking time off work to drive you to prison today. I don't see your father feeding, clothing, and housing you for the last eighteen years."

"I don't want you here." Shane said this matter-of-factly, as if he was talking about the weather.

"I don't care."

"That's the most honest thing you've ever said."

Janet stood from her seat and reared back to slap him but stopped herself, remembering where she was. She looked around the waiting room, all eyes on her. She glowered at Shane and said, "You ungrateful little piece of shit." She grabbed her umbrella, turned on her sneakers, and left.

CHAPTER 114

Gwen and a Glimmer of Hope

"I knew you guys were innocent," Lewis Phelps said through her cell phone.

"Thanks, Lewis. I think you were the only one who believed us," Gwen replied, sitting next to Rick as he drove, the world passing by in a blur. "Unfortunately, I think most people still think we're guilty. People have been posting on Facebook that Rick saw the camera, and that's the only reason he pushed Ashlee away, and they've been saying that the security footage of Janet with the essay is inconclusive."

"How did you get the video and those pictures?"

"It's probably better that we don't talk about it."

"I understand."

"How's everything at school?"

"I think Greg Ebersole's been fired."

"Really? How do you know that?"

"I saw him being escorted out by Wilcox this morning. He was in tears. It's insane. How many more people are gonna be fired by that crazy bitch? I keep wondering if I'm next."

Rick turned off Route 72 into the city of Lebanon.

"Greg deserves to be fired," Gwen said.

"Do you know what he did?" Lewis asked.

"Yes, but I can't say what or how. Trust me. It's a good thing he's gone."

"What's your next move?"

"We're on our way to meet with a lawyer."

"I'll let you go then. Let me know if you need anything."

"Thanks, Lewis. We'll talk soon." Gwen disconnected the call and turned to Rick.

He glanced her way. "I'm glad they got rid of that creep. The truth always comes out eventually."

Gwen pursed her full lips. "Not always."

Rick parked in a cramped parking lot next to a brick row house; a sign out front read Law Offices of Fischer and Ziegler. They stepped into the law office, Gwen holding a manila folder containing the legal paperwork they'd received from Heather Miles's attorney, as well as various screenshots and links to information that backed their stories. To their immediate left was an open office, a middle-aged woman sitting behind a large desk, and filing cabinets lining the walls.

"May I help you?" she asked, standing from her seat.

Rick and Gwen walked into the room, still wearing their coats.

"We have an appointment with Derrick Ziegler at two," Rick said.

"Of course. You must be Mr. Barnett and Ms. Townsend?"

Gwen smiled without showing her teeth. "Yes."

"Mr. Ziegler will be down in a few minutes. May I take your coats?" The woman hung their coats on pegs in the hallway, then led them to an empty conference room. "Please, have a seat. Would you like something to drink?"

"No thank you," Gwen said.

"Nothing for me, thank you," Rick added.

The receptionist left, and Gwen and Rick sat next to each other in cushy leather chairs. Shortly thereafter, an elderly man entered the conference room. He was thin and a little hunched, his hair white as snow. He held a pen and a yellow legal pad.

"Mr. Barnett, Ms. Townsend," the man said with a twinkle in his eyes. "I'm Derrick Ziegler."

They stood from the table and shook hands with the old man,

exchanging greetings and pleasantries. Mr. Ziegler sat at the head of the table, kitty-cornered from Rick and Gwen.

With his legal pad in front of him and his pen at the ready, Ziegler said, "How can I help you two?"

For the next hour, Gwen and Rick told their stories, and Mr. Ziegler took notes and asked questions here and there for clarification.

Mr. Ziegler put down his pen and said, "Sounds like you two poked the hornet's nest."

"That's an understatement," Rick said.

Ziegler chuckled. "Two issues are at stake. There's the Heather Miles lawsuit against you, and there's the wrongful termination by the school district. I'm assuming Heather Miles doesn't have very much money?"

"I don't think so," Rick said.

"Which means her lawyers are probably fishing for a quick settlement. We'll hit 'em with a libel countersuit. I'm assuming her attorneys took the case on contingency, meaning that they only get paid if they win a settlement, but I doubt they would continue on a contingency basis with a strong countersuit. I think there's a good chance I can make the lawsuit go away, especially if I can offer to drop the countersuit as an incentive."

"We're not interested in suing Heather Miles," Gwen said. "We just want the lawsuit to go away."

Rick nodded. "I agree."

"What are your goals with the school district?" Mr. Ziegler asked. "Would you like to be reinstated? Are you looking for a cash settlement? Both?"

"I'd rather not sue the school," Gwen said. "I want them to admit publicly that they made a mistake and to reinstate me. And I'd like for Janet Wilcox to be fired."

"Rick?" Ziegler asked.

"I agree. We also want back pay for the weeks we've been out of a job."

"I can draft a letter today to Heather Miles's attorneys, telling them of our intentions. That might be enough for them to drop the lawsuit. The bigger problem will be the school district. They have an in-house attorney and nearly unlimited funds, at least in comparison to a teacher's salary. I'd like to draft a letter to them too and see where it goes."

Gwen and Rick gave each other an uncomfortable look.

Mr. Ziegler smiled. "Provided you wish to hire me of course. My apologies for jumping the gun. I can step out of the room if you'd like to discuss it alone."

"We don't have much money to pay you," Gwen said.

"I wouldn't worry too much about that. My fees are reasonable. Eighty-dollars an hour. Sending two letters would only incur three or four hours of my time. I'm happy to give you a payment plan that fits your budget. If everything goes like I think it will, the school district will pay my bill, and you'll be back at work in no time."

Gwen and Rick looked at each other again and nodded.

"We'd like to hire you," Rick said.

CHAPTER 115

Rick and Intertwined

Rick sat with Gwen on her couch, a polite distance between them. They streamed the modern version of *Vacation* on Gwen's laptop. It was a funny distraction, not as good as the original but funny nonetheless. Rick watched her laugh. That perfect smile, the tiny dimples, the sparkle in her eyes. She was already in sweats. It was only seven, but they'd had dinner earlier, and it's not like they were going anywhere. It was still hostile outside of their bubble. Gwen had grinned and said it was too early for pajamas but not for sweats.

Her left hand rested on the couch next to her thigh. Her hands were small, her fingers delicate. His heart pounded so hard; he thought maybe she could hear it. He reached and placed his hand on top of hers. She fixed her gaze on him, her face expressionless. Rick felt the sting of embarrassment and removed his hand from hers.

"Don't." She turned her hand over and motioned with her eyes.

Rick placed his hand back into hers. Gwen turned her body toward Rick and squeezed his hand, not hard but enough to know she meant it. Her dark hair hung past her shoulders in loose waves. She had a heart-shaped face with high cheekbones and big blue eyes. Rick turned his body, intent on kissing her, but Gwen's phone chimed.

She turned her head, reached for her phone on the coffee table, and checked the number. "I don't know who this is." Gwen sent the call to voice mail. She paused the movie and shut her laptop, making her intentions known. A blush ran across her cheeks, and she dipped her head. Rick's cell phone chimed. They both looked at his phone sitting on the coffee table.

"I wonder if it's the same person who called me," Gwen said.

Rick grabbed his cell phone and swiped right. "Hello?"

"Rick?" the man asked.

"Yeah?"

"This is Dr. Matthews."

Rick sat up straighter. "Dr. Matthews. What can I do for you?"

"I think you have that the wrong way around. I was calling to let you know that we have a hearing scheduled for December 5th at 7:00 p.m. You'll have a chance to present whatever new evidence you have for the administration and the school board."

"I'm not sure I understand."

"Given recent developments, we're giving you a chance to plead your case for reinstatement."

"What about Gwen Townsend?"

"I can't discuss her situation with you."

"She's right here, if you wanna talk to her."

Matthews paused. "Uh, yes, I'd like to talk to her."

Rick handed his phone to Gwen, and School Superintendent Matthews told her the same thing he'd told Rick, with a few added details. They had a hearing in less than three weeks to determine whether or not they should be reinstated, and their cases would be decided by Matthews and voted on for approval by the school board that night. Gwen disconnected the call with that sparkling smile. They reached at the same time, embracing and hugging each other tight. Her body felt firm and soft in all the right places.

"We did it," he said.

After a moment, she let go and pulled back. He did the same, wondering if the moment was gone, if he'd crossed into the friend zone, never to return. They stared at each other, silent, their eyes wide open. Gwen made her move a split second before Rick, pressing her body and her lips against his. Her mouth parted, their tongues twisted together. His hands dropped to her hips, pulling her closer. They were breathless, their movements urgent. She straddled him, Rick sitting on the edge of the couch, his feet on the floor, her legs wrapped around him, their lips still locked together. She tasted like the strawberry ice cream they'd had for dessert. Her hands moved from his upper back to his belt. She tugged, grappling, but getting nowhere. He undid his belt, the top button of his jeans, and his fly.

Her lips moved to his neck. His hands dipped under the waistband of her sweatpants, pulling them down a few inches, exposing the top of her black bikini underwear. She stood abruptly. Rick wondered if he went too far. She answered that by removing her sweatpants and her underwear. She stepped from the pile of clothes at her feet, now naked from the waist down.

CHAPTER 116

Janet and LIAR

"A fucking hearing? You can't be serious," Janet said into her cell phone.

"We're trying to avoid a nasty wrongful termination suit," Cliff said. "Burks thinks they have a case. If we give 'em a hearing, we'll get a good look at their case, and, if they lose the hearing, they'll be less likely to waste money on a lawyer fighting the same case in court."

"And if they win?" Janet paced in her bedroom.

"They'll be reinstated, and I hope to God they don't sue."

"This is bullshit, Cliff. Townsend was negligent, and Barnett only pushed Ashlee Miles away because he saw the camera."

"That's for the hearing to determine."

"Cancel it. Let them sue. They don't have the money or the balls."

"You're lucky we're not investigating *you* for wrongdoing. That video is compelling."

Janet clenched her jaw. "*That* video doesn't show anything."

"It doesn't show anything conclusive. That's why you still have your job."

"If the board tries to fire me, they'll be in for the fight of their lives. I'll own this district before it's over."

"Relax, Janet. Nobody's trying to fire you."

"The hearing better be public. We need to build trust with the community."

"It'll be public."

"What are their chances of reinstatement?"

"They'll have to have very compelling evidence and a supportive public."

"You've seen what they have. Is it enough?"

"If it were only up to me, no, but it's not."

"You better get your people on board."

"You'll catch more flies with honey than vinegar."

Janet blew out a breath. "What do you want, Cliff?"

"Another night in Hershey."

"Then make sure the vote goes the right way." Janet disconnected the call. She tapped the Rachel contact on her cell phone.

"Hi, Janet," Rachel said, answering on the first ring, always at Janet's beck and call.

"There's a hearing to vote on reinstating Rick and Gwen based on the new evidence."

"Oh, my word. I can't believe it."

"Believe it because it's happening in three weeks."

"What can I do?"

"We need to get as many community members as possible to speak against them at the hearing."

"I can do that. I'm sure Heather will bring her people too. She has quite a following now."

"Good. Just keep my name out of it. She still hates me because of Shane."

"I think she's softening."

"We'll see." Janet paused for a beat. "We should invite Rick's ex-wife to the hearing."

"I heard he cheated on her," Rachel replied.

"Which is why she'd be a perfect guest."

"Maybe it was with someone young. I'm sure she'll have the dirt."

"Do you have her number?" Janet asked.

"No, but I know someone who does."

"Definitely invite her then and make sure she shows."

"I will. And what about the kerfuffle with Gwen's husband and that student and all those nasty rumors?"

"Unfortunately, we can't convict her based on what her husband did, and I can't talk about the rumors. She'll sue me for slander. They'll probably have their lawyer at the hearing."

"I bet the rumors are true," Rachel replied. "Where there's smoke, there's fire."

"I agree, but I have to be careful how it's presented. It could backfire and lead to a lawsuit or, even worse, sympathy." An idea flashed into her mind, and a wide smile spread across her face. "I know *exactly* what to do. I can invite—" Janet stopped midsentence, listening to an odd sound coming from outside her home.

Shhhhhh, shhhhhhh, shhhhhhh.

"Hold on, Rachel. I think I heard something." Janet went to her window and looked into the darkness. She saw the outline of a figure running away and disappearing into the black. Janet picked up her phone again. "I think someone was trying to break into my house."

"Oh, my word."

"I'll call you back." Janet disconnected the call and stepped downstairs. She peered from the bay window. Nothing. Nobody. The front door was locked. She checked the back door and the side door. Also locked. She returned to the front and stepped onto the stoop, listening, and looking off into the distance for the person she'd seen running for the woods. A cold wind whistled through the vinyl siding. She cinched her robe, feeling a chill. She looked at her concrete walkway, and that's when she saw it. The concrete had been defaced with a single spray-painted word, in all caps, CUNT.

"Fuck. Fuck. Fucking Aaron Fuller!" She turned around to go back inside, to call the police, and she saw more red spray paint. She surveyed the front fascia of her two-story colonial. In four places, the white vinyl siding was defaced with another four-letter word, LIAR.

Janet stepped inside and slammed her door. She reached into the pocket of her robe and retrieved her phone. She dialed 9-1-1.

"Nine-one-one, what is your emergency?"

"My home's been vandalized, and I know exactly who did it."

CHAPTER 117

Gwen and Good News

Gwen kissed Rick, soft and slow, her stomach fluttering. They stood next to the door, Rick in his cold-weather running gear, Gwen still in her pajamas.

"Be careful, okay?" Gwen said.

"I'll be quick. It's too cold to be out there for too long," Rick replied.

They kissed again and he left the apartment. Gwen locked the door behind him, a smile plastered on her face. She fed Buster, the cat purring as she filled her bowl. She went to her bedroom and changed into a pair of jeans and a fleece. As she dressed, her mind flashed back to last night ... and this morning. For the first time in a long time, she felt hopeful, happy even. Her phone chimed in the living room, waking her from her daydream. She hurried to the coffee table, grabbed her phone, glanced at the number, and swiped right.

"Mr. Ziegler," Gwen said.

"Good morning, Gwen. Is Rick with you?"

"No, he went out for a run, but he'll be back shortly." Gwen sat on her couch, the cell phone pressed to her ear.

"Well, I'll let you deliver the good news. Heather Miles has dropped the lawsuit against you two. I think the prospect of a countersuit scared her. Her attorneys probably told her they needed a retainer that she couldn't afford."

"That's great to hear. Rick'll be thrilled. Thank you so much, Mr. Ziegler."

"I'm glad I could help, but we're not out of the woods yet. This school board hearing is a positive development, but it's high stakes. I don't know whether they wanna reinstate you or they're simply going on a fishing expedition to see what we have."

"Do you think we have enough evidence to be reinstated?"

"Yes, but you never know how these things'll go. School boards can be very political."

Gwen sighed. "I think Janet Wilcox has a lot of influence with the board."

"She very well may, but our case isn't wholly dependent on this hearing. Speaking of Janet Wilcox, that's the other thing I wanted to talk to you two about. I did a background investigation on her, and I made a few phone calls. This woman's been married twice and has a child from each marriage. That, in and of itself, isn't unique, but I spoke to her exes, and they both had similar stories. She bled them dry in the divorce, and she plays dirty. Real dirty. She used her kids as pawns. She signed over her parental rights to her first husband in exchange for $200,000. I spoke with the daughter. She's twenty-six now, a kindergarten teacher. She hasn't spoken to her mother since the divorce. Janet tried to do a similar deal with the second husband, but the settlement was $500,000, and he couldn't raise the money. He'd been paying $2,000 a month in alimony and child support until Shane's eighteenth birthday. He'll still pay one thousand for the alimony, which he's stuck with unless she remarries. To add insult to injury, he said Janet made it impossible to see or to have any contact with Shane whatsoever. This doesn't help us, mind you, but it does give us a glimpse into the type of person we're dealing with."

"What type of person is that?"

"The type who'll do anything. The type who'll dig into your past and throw it in your face at the hearing. I think we should talk about your husband some more. I don't wanna be blindsided."

Gwen's stomach churned. She felt like she might be sick. "You know what happened."

"I'm really sorry, Gwen, but I have to ask you about the rumors," Mr. Ziegler said.

Gwen hesitated for a moment. "They're totally false."

CHAPTER 118

Rick and the Big Game

The school parking lot was lit with streetlights. School employees and community members parked around them and hurried into the building, dipping their heads into the wind and holding their coats closed. Rick and Gwen sat in his truck, parked near the rear of the lot.

He reached over the bench seat and placed his hand on top of hers and squeezed. "You okay?"

"I'm fine, … just nervous I guess," Gwen replied.

"Me too. We'll be fine. Mr. Ziegler will present the evidence. We'll back him up during the public comment."

"I don't know if I can do it."

He squeezed her hand again. "Your statement's perfect. You've practiced. You'll be great."

She nodded, but her expression was one of uncertainty.

"When I was a kid, I used to get really nervous before football games. So, I started doing things to distract myself. I'd joke around with the guys, listen to music, anything to keep my mind off the game. I found that, if I was prepared, I could just go out and play, and, once I started playing, the worry was gone."

Gwen forced a smile. "I guess I need a distraction."

"Jamar's had a helluva run through the playoffs. It's amazing how he's carried the team on his back, even after losing Drew."

Gwen nodded.

"They'll be in Hershey for the state championship on Friday. What do you think about booking a hotel room in Hershey on Thursday? We could go out to dinner on Thursday night, then we'd be down there for the game on Friday."

"Sounds like a few hundred dollars that we don't have."

"We're gonna win the hearing, and we're gonna get that back pay. It'll work out. You'll see."

"What happened to the distraction?"

"Sorry, you're right. What do you wanna talk about?"

Gwen took a heavy breath. "I don't know."

Mr. Ziegler's Range Rover parked in the lot.

"There he is," Rick said. "You ready?"

She shook her head. "No."

"Whatever happens, you have me." Rick leaned over the seat and kissed her on the cheek, lingering long enough for her to know he was serious.

They stepped from the truck, the wind whipping her hair in front of her face. Rick took her hand, and they hurried across the lot. Mr. Ziegler stepped from his SUV, wearing a suit and a long dark coat. His laptop bag was over his shoulder. He smiled as his clients approached. Rick grabbed the cardboard boxful of files for Mr. Ziegler, easily carrying it under his arm. They walked in together, prepared to take on the school board, the administration, and the community.

CHAPTER 119

Janet and Her Guests

Janet carried two Cokes and some chips from the vending machines to her office. She had stashed her guests in her office because she didn't want anyone to know that they were here. She'd bring them out at the right time, like a sneak attack. Other than her guests, the main office was empty, the lights turned off, only the glow from Janet's back office lighting her way.

She smiled at the middle-aged woman and the young man as she entered, both still sitting in the seats across from Janet's desk. "Here you go," Janet said, placing the Cokes and the chips on the edge of her desk.

"Thank you, Ms. Janet," the woman said.

The young man lifted his chin in acknowledgment.

Janet wished they'd dressed differently. The middle-aged woman wore a Looney Toons shirt and a Philadelphia Eagles jacket. People here preferred the Steelers. The young man looked like a thug. Baggy pants hanging off his ass, a huge puffy jacket, a do-rag, neck tatts. It didn't help that they were black. It's not that this town was racist. Well, maybe a little, but not sixties Mississippi racist. The residents didn't trust people who were different, and black was definitely different in this town.

"It'll probably be about an hour until I come for you," Janet said.

"Please don't wander around the school. We'll have a bigger effect if nobody knows you're here."

"We'll be fine here," the woman said.

"I hate to even ask, but, if you two could leave your jackets here, I would appreciate it."

"That ain't a problem," the man said, removing his jacket.

"And the ... ?" Janet touched her head and looked at his do-rag.

He smiled wide, showing his bright white teeth. "Wouldn't wanna scare whitey."

Janet forced a smile. "Something like that."

Janet left her guests and went to the library. It was already packed, the chairs filled, and people standing in the back. Ashlee Miles stood by herself. Lance Osborn stood with the football team. *I wonder if they're still together.* Aaron Fuller stared at Janet as she walked past. Janet shot him a glare, and Aaron grinned in response. Janet found her regular seat, Rachel guarding it like a faithful dog.

Janet sat down, a scowl on her face.

"Everything all right?" Rachel asked in a whisper.

"Aaron Fuller smiled at me."

Rachel frowned. "That little creep."

"The police are incompetent. What he did's no secret. I'd like to smack that shit-eating grin off his face."

CHAPTER 120

Gwen and into the Lion's Den

Gwen and Rick and Mr. Ziegler walked into the library. It was packed, standing room only. Rick stopped at the back table and grabbed two forms from the stack.

He looked at Mr. Ziegler and said, "We have to fill these out to participate in the public comment."

"I already submitted the forms on the website," Mr. Ziegler replied.

Rick took Gwen's hand, leading her through the crowd, just behind their attorney. People stared and whispered. A few football players and assistant coaches nodded and said, "Coach," as they walked past, Rick nodding back. Bob Schneider was notably absent. Ashlee Miles stood off to the side, her arms crossed over her chest, throwing daggers with her eyes.

Rick placed the box of files on the table. They took off their coats, setting them on their chairs. Rick and Gwen sat at the reserved table for three, front and center, facing the school board. Mr. Ziegler approached the school board. Two long tables were set up at the head of the room for the nine school board directors and Superintendent Matthews and Solicitor Burks. Each seat was punctuated with a name placard and a microphone. The school board directors were there, some already sitting, some standing and talking. The school board was all male, except for Heather Miles.

Mr. Ziegler talked to Cliff, asking about hooking up his laptop to the projector. This was prearranged, but Cliff acted dumbfounded. They eventually found the new tech guy and made it happen. A heavyset twentysomething named Wendall had already been hired to replace Greg. Mr. Ziegler brought paper copies of his arguments, just in case, but he wanted everyone in the audience to see the evidence.

A hand touched Gwen's shoulder, causing her to flinch. She turned her head.

Lewis greeted her with a small smile. "Good luck."

Gwen nodded.

"Good luck," Lewis said to Rick, his hand held out.

As Rick turned to shake his hand, his face went white, as if he'd seen a ghost. They shook hands, and Lewis disappeared into the crowd.

Rick leaned over and whispered into Gwen's ear. "My ex-wife's here."

Gwen's eyes widened. "Where?"

"Sitting in the audience, ten o' clock. Long blond hair. Pretty."

Gwen felt a pang of jealousy at that last word. She turned to look, curious. There she was, like a rose in a field of wheat. *Pretty* was an understatement. She was gorgeous. Perfect porcelain skin, with strawberry hues. A symmetrical face with a button nose and luscious lips. Honey-blond hair beyond her shoulders and breasts large enough to notice from twenty-five feet away. Rick had told Gwen very little about his ex-wife, and Gwen had told Rick very little about her soon-to-be-ex-husband. It was an unspoken agreement. Gwen did know that Rick's ex had met someone else and had moved to Virginia, but Rick didn't give specifics, and Gwen hadn't asked, not wanting to give specifics of her own.

Gwen turned back to Rick. "Why is she here?"

"I have no idea. I can't imagine she's angry with me. We haven't spoken in years. She doesn't even live here anymore."

"Everyone take your seats," Cliff Osborn said into his microphone. He waited for a moment. "Please be quiet. We're about to begin."

CHAPTER 121

Rick and Photo Evidence

The cacophony of voices quieted, and people took their seats. People in the back still stood, jockeying for position.

"Thank you," Cliff said. "Please do not shout out or heckle during the hearing. This special hearing is to determine whether or not West Lake School District will reinstate Rick Barnett and Gwen Townsend. Mr. Barnett and Ms. Townsend will be given the opportunity to present recent evidence to the board, followed by public comments, followed by board comments, followed by a vote, the majority determining the outcome. If you'd like to participate in the public comments, you must've filled out a public comment form found at the back table or submitted the form via the district's website. We'll start with Mr. Barnett, followed by Ms. Townsend." Cliff gestured to the trio sitting at the table in front.

Mr. Ziegler stood slowly. "My name's Derrick Ziegler, and I'll be representing Mr. Barnett and Ms. Townsend."

"You may approach the podium," Cliff said.

The attorney approached the podium to the right of the school board. His laptop was already there, ready to go. Mr. Ziegler moved his cursor, clicked a few times, until a photo appeared on the large screen hanging from the ceiling. The audience craned their necks to the right and gasped at the image.

Mr. Ziegler addressed the school board. "Mr. Barnett was terminated solely because of this picture." The attorney gestured to the image of Rick and Ashlee Miles kissing in his doorway. "From the beginning, Mr. Barnett maintained that the student pictured here walked into his home uninvited while he was taking a shower and stole a kiss as he escorted her from his home. The following images will prove exactly that." Mr. Ziegler went on to detail the photo evidence provided by Shane that corroborated Rick's story. He also noted small details like Rick's wet hair and chest and his look of revulsion immediately following the kiss.

Throughout the presentation, Heather and Ashlee seethed. If looks could kill, Mr. Ziegler would've dropped dead.

CHAPTER 122

Janet Turns the Tables

Janet watched the horror show. That fucking old lawyer. Now he was showing screenshots of unreturned phone calls Gwen had made to Heather Miles about Caleb. Janet thought Heather might jump over the table and strangle the old man. Then he presented that goddamn video. That lawyer went over the video in painstaking detail, pausing and showing Janet holding a piece of paper, her sleeve covering her fingers. Janet had had enough. It was time to turn the tables. She left the library, people in the audience staring, whispering, and pointing at her.

She hurried to her office. Her guests still sat in the chairs where she'd left them. Potato chip wrappers and soda cans littered Janet's desk. The young man looked like he was asleep, his head lolled to the side, his neck limp. Thankfully, he'd taken off his do-rag.

"It's time," Janet said as she approached.

The middle-aged woman turned to see Janet, then stood from her seat. She smacked the man on the back of his head, not hard. "Wake up, Elijah."

The young man's eyes fluttered. "Shit, that drive made me tired as a motherfucker."

"Language," the woman said with raised eyebrows.

Janet returned to the library with her guests in tow. People stared as if they'd never seen a black person. Rachel and another one of Janet's cronies gave up their seats so the guests could sit. They watched the end of Ziegler's presentation.

Ziegler said, "My clients are not looking to sue the school district, although I think they have a very strong wrongful termination case, and I'd be happy to represent them if they choose that route, but that's not their goal. They simply want the truth to be told, to be reinstated, and to receive back pay for the time they've missed. Thank you." Mr. Ziegler returned to the table, sitting next to Rick.

"Thank you, Mr. Ziegler," Cliff Osborn said. "We'll open up the podium for public comments." Cliff took the top form from the small stack in front of him. "Roger Elkins?"

Janet smiled to herself. Roger was on her team.

A dark-haired man—with a mustache, a gut, a fanny-pack, and a phone clipped to his belt—approached the podium.

"You have four minutes, Mr. Elkins," Cliff said.

He cleared his throat and addressed the school board. "I'm Roger Elkins. I live in West Lake, just around the corner. I went to school here. I lived here my whole life and I've never seen such disgusting behavior." He glowered at Rick and Gwen.

Gwen stared at the tabletop, but Rick glared right back at Roger.

"The fact that you're even wasting our time is disgusting." Roger looked back to the board. "They need to go, and they need to stay gone. They know what they did. Don't let them try to argue different with their fancy lawyer. The truth of the matter is that the only reason Rick Barnett pushed that girl away was because he saw the camera. He knew he was busted, and he was trying to get out of it. Rick Barnett is a pedophile." Spittle flew from his mouth when he said *pedophile*. "And Gwen Townsend-Walker's responsible for Caleb Miles's death. She knew the boy was suicidal, but she did *nothing* about it. Why wouldn't she talk to the counselor or the principal? I think those screenshots are fake. Do not reinstate these criminals."

Half the crowd clapped as Roger Elkins left the podium.

Cliff read the name from the next form in his stack. "Breanna Franks?"

It had been a long time, but Janet recognized the thin woman who approached the podium.

"I'm Breanna Franks." She had the raspy voice of a smoker. "You keep talkin' about the girl like she ain't nobody. She is somebody. She's my niece, and she's tellin' the truth. Rick Barnett tried to seduce her. She pushed him away, not the other way 'round. His face looked like that 'cause he was mad. I heard he did the same thing to other girls. It's like Jerry Sandusky all over again." She gestured to Gwen. "The other one, Ms. Townsend-Walker." Breanna practically spit out *Townsend-Walker*. "My sister is a good mother. She don't answer calls from strange numbers. You shoulda sent an email or a text. Townsend was the only one who knew Caleb was hurtin', and she didn't do nothin'. That's facts." She glared at the school board. "If you give either of them their job back, you're gonna have one helluva lawsuit."

CHAPTER 123

Gwen and the Public Comments

Gwen felt the crowd boring a hole in the back of her head. The public comments had been brutal, until now.

Jamar Burris stood at the podium, wearing slacks and a button-down shirt. He read from a single sheet of paper, his eyes never leaving the page. "Coach Barnett was my football coach and teacher, and Ms. Townsend was my teacher too. Coach Barnett's the best coach I've ever had, and Ms. Townsend cares more about her students than any teacher I've ever had. I think they're telling the truth. If you fire them, it's the students who will miss out. Everybody claims to care about kids, but they do exactly the opposite.

"I don't understand why people are attacking Coach Barnett and Ms. Townsend. It's clear from the pictures that Coach Barnett is telling the truth and that Ms. Townsend didn't cause Caleb to do what he did. Caleb Miles was my friend. Ms. Townsend talked to me about helping Caleb because she thought he was depressed. And, if Ms. Townsend says she gave that essay to Principal Wilcox, I know she did. She wouldn't lie about that.

"It's crazy that she got into trouble for Caleb doing what he did. She was one of the few people who cared about Caleb. She had tried to help him. I was in the class that Caleb held hostage. Ms. Townsend gave up herself, so we all could leave. She does that, and then you fire her?

That's so messed up." Jamar snatched his paper from the podium and walked to the rear of the room, half the crowd clapping.

"Thank you, Jamar," Cliff said. He read from the next form in the dwindling stack. "Rick Barnett."

The crowd whispered as Rick made his way to the podium. Rick didn't have a piece of paper. He was used to memorizing pregame speeches. He didn't look at the school board. Instead, he scanned the audience.

"Most of you know me. I grew up here. I went to school here. I started teaching here right out of college. At this point, I don't care what you think. I don't care about the gossip and the lies. Whatever happens tonight, I can live with it because I know I've told the truth." Rick paused for a moment, scanning the crowd again. "Many of you don't know Gwen Townsend. This was her first year at West Lake. There's one thing I know about Ms. Townsend. She's a talented and selfless teacher of the highest caliber. If you decide not to reinstate her, thousands of future students will miss out on a great teacher."

Rick turned his attention to the school board. "Ms. Townsend and I had discussions about Caleb Miles. We were both concerned. I had a one-on-one conversation with Caleb after he quit football. I thought something had happened to him, but he wasn't talking, and neither was anyone else. It was obvious to me that he wanted to move on from what happened to him, and I didn't want to humiliate him further. Ms. Townsend talked to me about calling Heather Miles and getting nowhere. She talked to me about giving the essay to Janet Wilcox. It's a travesty that Gwen Townsend's fighting for her career because of Janet Wilcox's incompetence and subsequent political bullying."

Rick turned back to the crowd. "If you really wanna make a change in this district, if you really wanna make things better, get rid of Principal Wilcox." Rick pointed across the room toward Janet's typical seat. "Wilcox is over there, sitting in her regular spot. She uses smoke and mirrors to cover up her sins and to propagandize the public against her enemies. I became her enemy because I benched her son. Ms.

Townsend became Wilcox's enemy out of circumstance and bad luck. Ms. Townsend happened to be the teacher who went to Wilcox about Caleb and his essay, the essay that Wilcox failed to do anything about. Janet Wilcox used her political clout to fire Ms. Townsend and to turn the public against her, all to cover up Wilcox's own incompetence.

"I'm sick and tired of people in this community believing lies and gossip about people without checking the source, without checking to find out whether or not it's true. Instead, they get a charge out of the juicy gossip and spread it around as if it's true, not caring for one second about the person's reputation they're destroying." Rick gestured to the room.

Faces in the crowd ranged from wide-eyed shock to narrow-eyed fury. A few nodded in agreement.

"All of you who've spread these lies should be ashamed of your-selves." Rick stepped back from the podium, half the crowd clapping.

Someone shouted, "Damn right."

Rick walked back to the table and sat between Gwen and Mr. Ziegler. He took Gwen's hand and squeezed.

Gwen had tears in her eyes. "Thank you."

Cliff waited for the applause to subside. "Lindsey Miller?"

Gwen and Rick turned in unison, looking back toward Rick's ex-wife. She stood and stepped to the podium, avoiding eye contact with Rick. She looked stylish and tall in her boots, pencil skirt, and button-down.

Lindsey adjusted the microphone down a little. She was tall but not as tall as Rick.

Gwen couldn't help but think that they would've had beautiful children.

"Hi, my name is Lindsey Miller. I used to be Lindsey Barnett. I was married to Rick Barnett for eight years. I was contacted and invited to speak by Rachel Kreider. She said that they needed to make sure Rick *wasn't* reinstated. She told me all about Rick's extracurricular activities. Rachel encouraged me to talk about what a cheating piece of crap Rick is. She was particularly interested in the age of Rick's mistress." Lindsey surveyed the crowd. "That was the rumor, right? That Rick cheated on me, and that's why we got divorced? The truth is, I hated this town. I wanted to move to the city, somewhere diverse and vibrant and growing, but this place has always been the exact opposite. I'm sorry to be blunt, but a lot of people here are petty and small and close-minded. I couldn't take it. I wanted to move, but Rick loves it here. He loves his job. He loves the kids—"

"Yeah, a little too much," a man from the audience shouted, followed by laughter.

"Please refrain from shouting out," Cliff said.

Lindsey waited for the laughter to subside. "Go ahead and laugh. That's the problem with this town. You're happy to sit in your ivory tower and judge others, but what do you do? Nothing. Nothing important. Nothing that can ever be judged. Because most of you are afraid to put yourself out there. You're content with the status quo. Content to criticize those who stand out. Rick doesn't see it that way. Rick thinks it's just a few bad apples and that most of this town really cares about their kids and each other. He sees the good.

"I didn't see it. I wanted to leave. He resisted, and I had an affair. Shortly after we divorced, I came home to see my parents for Thanksgiving. I heard from my sister that people were saying that Rick cheated. I also heard that Rick refused to talk about it." Lindsey paused and took a deep breath. "Rick and I were together for a long time. He's loyal to a fault. Do you know why he refused to set the record straight?" Lindsey paused for a moment.

The audience was on the edge of their seats, the room dead silent.

Lindsey swallowed and wiped the corners of her eyes. Her voice caught a little. "He didn't want people saying terrible things about me. That's the type of person he is." She paused again. "Do you remember when this school was awful at football? It wasn't that long ago. I remember those years. Rick built this program from nothing. He lost a lot of games back then, but he always took the blame for the losses and deflected the praise onto his players for the wins. That team that's on the way to the state championship? That's Rick's team through and through. He may not be the coach anymore, but that's his team. The coaches know it. The players know it." Lindsey turned her attention to the school board. "I wish you knew him like I do because, if you did, you'd know he was telling the truth. Do the right thing and reinstate him. He loves his students and football players more than he even loved his wife." A tear slipped down her cheek.

Applause ensued. For the first time, Lindsey looked at Rick. She mouthed, *I'm sorry.* She left the podium, grabbed her jacket from the back of her chair, and left the library, people stepping aside to let her through.

Gwen observed Rick watching Lindsey as she walked away. Gwen felt envious of the love they'd shared. She couldn't help but think of her soon-to-be-ex, Brian. If he'd never done what he did, she wouldn't be here right now.

Would Caleb still be alive?

CHAPTER 124

Rick and the Vote

Rick couldn't even look at her. He gritted his teeth as Ashlee Miles told her sob story.

"I lost my friends because of this. I've been bullied," Ashlee said, sniffling, looking at the school board but avoiding her mother's gaze. "But I'm telling the truth. Those pictures don't tell the whole story. Mr. Barnett invited me over. He told me his ex-wife, Lindsey, was gonna be there, and she wanted to see me. She used to teach me piano. We were really close. But, when I got there, she wasn't there. Mr. Barnett told me that she was running late. Then he told me how pretty he thinks I am, and he tried to kiss me. I was afraid, so I tried to laugh it off. He gave me a picture of him with his shirt off and asked if I thought he was hot. I told him that he was too old. I thought maybe that might help him to cop a clue, but it didn't. He said he needed a shower, and he even asked me to join him. Gross." Ashlee twisted her face in disgust.

"I didn't know what to do. I still wanted to see Lindsey, so I waited. After Mr. Barnett got out of the shower, he grabbed me, and I ran for the door. I opened the door to get out, and he grabbed me again and kissed me, but someone was there and took our picture. He must've seen the person because he pushed me away and slammed the door in my face. I saw someone running away, but I don't know who took the pictures. Those pictures don't show what really happened though."

Ashlee took a deep breath and surveyed the crowd. "I have a picture that'll prove what I'm saying is true." She reached into her jacket pocket, removed a photograph, and held it up to the audience and the school board.

Rick recognized the photo immediately. It was the one she'd taken from his house that pictured him after football practice, filthy and shirtless, standing with two of his college teammates.

"Ashlee, can you please bring that photo here?" Cliff asked.

Ashlee approached the stocky man, handing him the photo.

He studied the image, then passed it on to the school board director next to him. Cliff leaned into his mike. "The photo appears to be Rick Barnett, shirtless as a young man."

The audience gasped.

Rick whispered to Mr. Ziegler. "She stole it from my house."

Ashlee stepped away from the podium, applause coming from more than half of the audience. She didn't bother to collect the photograph.

Mr. Ziegler stood from his seat. "I'd like the opportunity to respond to this allegation."

"This isn't a court of law," Cliff said. "You've had ample opportunity to present your evidence."

Mr. Ziegler sat down, scowling at Cliff. The public comment forms sitting on the table in front of Cliff had dwindled to nearly none. It looked to Rick like there were only two left. One of those had to be Gwen's, as she hadn't been called yet. He worried about her. She was already nervous, and the building suspense wasn't helping.

Cliff Osborn said, "Esther Jackson? Esther Jackson?"

Gwen stiffened, her face flashing scarlet.

A thick middle-aged woman approached the podium. She walked slow, her head held high, almost regal. She wore her hair in a modest afro, like a sixties Black Panther. Despite her serious demeanor, she wore Bugs Bunny on her long-sleeved and oversize T-shirt, with the phrase What's up, Doc?

She had no notes or written speech and spoke a little too close to the mike, her voice booming. "I'm Esther Jackson." She paused for a moment. "In 1955, a fourteen-year-old black boy named Emmett Till went into a grocery store and flirted with a twenty-one-year-old white woman named Carolyn Bryant. But Carolyn Bryant told her husband that he grabbed her around the waist and said nasty things to her. Three days later, her husband and his half-brother took Emmett from his home. These two men beat Emmett, tortured the poor boy, and shot him in the head. These two murderers were brought to trial, but they were acquitted by racist jurors. In 2008, Carolyn Bryant said that Emmett Till never grabbed her or said the nasty things they said he said. You must be wondering why I'm telling you about something that happened in Mississippi in 1955."

Esther looked around the room at the white faces. "I'm telling you this because the same thing happened to my son, Emory. A few years ago, in Philly, Emory was a student of Mrs. Gwen Walker. She claimed that my son raped her, but I raised my baby right. He knew right from wrong. A mother knows her child better than anyone. I know he didn't do what she said he did." Esther looked at Gwen, her eyes narrowed. Gwen looked away. Esther shifted her gaze to the school board. "I was right too, because they tried to put my baby in prison for rape, but they found him innocent." Esther shook her head. "But that wasn't good enough. Just like Carolyn Bryant in 1955, Gwen's husband, Brian Walker, killed my baby in cold blood. He was only nineteen years old."

Gwen hung her head, staring at her lap.

Esther pursed her full lips. "I don't know about all this mess around here, but I do know that Gwen Walker or Townsend, whatever her name is now, should not be around children. She should be in prison with her husband." Esther strutted back to her seat, walking directly in front of Rick's and Gwen's table, making sure to give Gwen the evil eye on the way.

The applause for Esther Jackson exceeded all other speakers in intensity and duration. It was clear. They'd lost the crowd.

Rick shook his head, seething. "Fucking Janet," he said under his breath.

Cliff called, "Gwen Townsend."

But she didn't move. She stared into her lap, still shell-shocked by Esther Jackson.

"Ms. Townsend?" Cliff said.

Gwen shook her head, not making eye contact.

Rick whispered into Gwen's ear. "You need to respond to this bull-shit. You can do it."

But she didn't respond. Not to Esther Jackson, not to Cliff Osborn, and not to Rick.

"That's it for public comments," Cliff said. "The board will now have an opportunity to comment." Cliff went down the table from right to left, asking each school board director for a comment but all replied, "No comment." All except the director at the end of the table, Heather Miles.

"This whole thing's a show," Heather said, looking at Rick and Gwen. "It's ridiculous that we're even doin' this. Rick Barnett tried to seduce my daughter. How many other girls has there been? And Gwen Townsend-Walker's cut from the same cloth. I can't believe Pruitt hired her after what she did in Philly. It's disgustin'. They're disgustin'. We'd be stupid to let these child predators back into our school."

The audience gave Heather a standing ovation. Not everyone but most everyone. A woman shouted, "Get rid of 'em."

Cliff waited for the audience to sit down and quiet. When they did, he started the vote. Yes, for reinstatement and, no, for no action—or continued termination from Rick's and Gwen's perspective.

The vote was split four to four, with Cliff Osborn holding the final vote. He paused, his brow creased, as if he had to think about it.

Rick squeezed Gwen's hand in anticipation.

Cliff leaned into his mike and said, "No."

CHAPTER 125

Janet and Students for Change

Janet couldn't help the smile tugging at the corners of her mouth. She sauntered into school on top of the world. Students on their way to first-period classes were subdued. The school felt ... empty. Maybe not empty exactly but definitely less crowded. Janet checked her watch. Three minutes until the bell. The typical time Janet arrived. *Something's off. It's too quiet.* Janet walked into the main office. Grace Moyer didn't even look up from her laptop. She used to be Pruitt's secretary, now hers. Grace was still salty about Pruitt's forced retirement. *I'll have to get rid of her. Or at least transfer her to the middle school.* Janet continued to the back offices, passing the counselor, Mrs. Baumgartner. Again, no greeting. Janet passed her old office, and the new Vice Principal, Connor Burns. He was on the phone, but he managed a morning wave and smile. Janet returned the sentiment. He was the perfect number two. Young and dumb, loyal and eager. He already did most of the work. Janet had moved to Pruitt's office. It was a bit bigger than her old office. She shut the door, sat behind her desk, and turned on her laptop. The late bell chimed. She checked her email. One in particular raised her blood pressure.

From: wlstudentsforchange@gmail.com
To: jwilcox@westlake.k12.pa.us, cburns@westlake.k12.pa.us, vmat-thews@westlake.k12.pa.us, cosborn@westlake.k12.pa.us, hmiles@ westlake.k12.pa.us, bschneider@westlake.k12.pa.us, 7 more
Subject: Our Demands
We witnessed the disgraceful display last night, and we refuse to participate in the evil that exists in West Lake High School. Our MANY members of WL Students for Change will NOT attend classes or extracurricular activities until Mr. Barnett and Ms. Townsend are reinstated. This includes the state championship football game this Friday.
Sincerely,
WL Students for Change

Janet slammed the side of her fist onto her desk. Her desktop phone rang in response, startling her. She picked up the receiver.

"Principal Wilcox," she said.

"Janet, this is Dr. Matthews. Have you checked your email this morning?"

"I just checked it."

"I'm assuming you received the email from this Students for Change person?"

"I did."

"Does it have any merit?" Superintendent Matthews asked.

"I'm sure it doesn't," Janet replied.

"Have you checked first-period attendance?"

"The tardy bell just rang."

"I suggest you check the attendance numbers. Call me back as soon as you have the information."

"Of course—"

The line went dead, with Janet midsentence. She hung up the receiver and stepped out to the main office. Grace Moyer typed on her laptop, still not acknowledging her presence.

"Grace," Janet said, standing across the counter from the old woman.

"Hang on," Grace replied, still typing, not making eye contact.

Janet tapped her long fingernails on the counter as she waited.

Finally, Grace looked up with a fake smile.

Janet said, "I need you to pull the first-period attendance records and let me know how many kids are out today."

"My word, a bunch are out today. I could tell by the parking lot. I heard they're mad about the hearing last night."

Janet clenched her fists and spoke through gritted teeth. "I need the exact numbers. *Now.*"

"I don't know if they've all been submitted yet."

"They should've been. If any teacher hasn't submitted, call them and tell them to do it immediately. Email me as soon as you have the numbers." Janet turned on her heels and went back to her office and her emails, but she couldn't concentrate. She kept refreshing, hoping to get those attendance numbers, hoping that it was just a few bad apples. Janet could handle a few bad apples. She could give them detention, suspend them, call their parents, threaten their futures.

Twenty minutes later, an email appeared from Grace.

From: gmoyer@westlake.k12.pa.us
To: jwilcox@westlake.k12.pa.us
Subject: Attendance
Of the 460 students enrolled, 304 are at school today. We usually only have about 40 students absent on any given day. This is a lot more than normal. I looked through some of the absentees, and it is a lot of football players too.

CHAPTER 126

Gwen and Wherever You Go, There You Are

Gwen and Rick had turned off their phones since last night's hearing. Neither of them felt like fielding crank calls or even commiserating with the few friends they had left. They'd spent much of the day in bed, finding solace in each other. By the afternoon, they'd felt cooped up, so they decided to go hiking. Rick knew an isolated spot half an hour away.

On their way out, Gwen grabbed the mail. As Rick drove toward the state park, Gwen flipped through the letters. She opened one and stared at the contents, speechless.

Rick glanced her way. "What is it?"

Gwen swallowed, then sighed, shoving the folded papers back into the envelope. "I'm officially divorced."

"You okay?"

"I knew it was coming. It's for the best." She sighed again. "It's also another failure. I can't seem to do anything right."

"That's not your failure. That's bad luck. Bad circumstances."

Gwen gazed from the passenger window, watching the roadside blow by in an amalgamation of leafless trees. "I used to tell myself that, but now I wonder if we create our own luck. Good or bad. I'm at least partly to blame for my situation."

"Maybe, but none of this is your fault. Not your divorce. Not what happened in Philly and not what happened here."

She forced a smile his way. "I'd like to believe you."

Rick parked in the gravel lot. Only one other car was here on this cold Tuesday afternoon. They walked from the lot to the trail. The forest was barren, crunchy leaves underfoot. Their breath condensed in front of their mouths. To their right, the creek ran quick, white water created by rocky outcroppings. Rick held Gwen's gloved hand as they hiked the windy path. They hadn't spoken for minutes, both of them stuck in their own heads.

Rick finally broke the silence, saying what was on his mind. "It's over, isn't it?"

They stopped walking and faced each other, their hands no longer intertwined.

Gwen looked up at him, her blue eyes unblinking. "We're out of options. We don't have the money to sue the school district."

"What about us?"

She looked down. "I can't stay here, and I know you can't leave."

"What if I was willing to leave?"

She looked up at him. "Are you?"

"I don't wanna lose you."

"So, we just pack up and leave … together?"

"I was thinking that we could apply for jobs first." Rick took both of her hands in his. "Let's apply anywhere in the country. The first place where we both get hired, we'll go. We'll leave this place in the dust. A fresh start."

Gwen pursed her lips. "What if we don't get hired together? We just go our separate ways?"

Rick shook his head. "No, I don't wanna leave without you, and I don't want you to leave without me. If you get a job, I can do something else. Maybe I could start a football camp or something. Maybe I could get a job as a college coach."

She had a small smile. "This is crazy. You know that I'm nearly broke."

Rick smiled back. "If we moved in together, we'd save money."

Gwen laughed, but it came out sad. "What are we doing? Is this a business transaction? Are we together because we have nobody else?"

Rick put his arms around her puffy coat and hugged her tight. She buried her head in his chest, feeling his warmth.

He said, "I know it hasn't been the best of circumstances, but, despite everything, I'm happy with you. And, for the first time in my life, I think I can be happy anywhere, as long as you're there."

She tilted her head upward, and Rick pressed his lips to hers.

CHAPTER 127

Rick and Students on Strike

They exited the state park at dusk, barely enough light left to see. Gwen sat on the middle of the bench seat, leaning on Rick. He drove toward his house. He stopped at the end of his driveway and grabbed a week's worth of mail from the box, then set it on the seat. He parked farther down his driveway, and they walked to the front door, the porch lights showing the way. Rick keyed his way in, allowing Gwen inside first, and shutting and locking the door behind them. He flipped on the foyer lights.

"I'm gonna grab some clothes," Rick said, placing his coat on the rack. "You wanna check the kitchen? If there's anything you'd like to eat, we can take it to your house for dinner, or we can eat here if you want a change of scenery."

"Okay," Gwen replied, already walking toward the kitchen.

Rick went to his bedroom, flipped on the light, grabbed a few T-shirts, some sweats, socks, and underwear. He walked to the kitchen and set his clothes on the kitchen table. Gwen rifled through the cabinets.

She emerged from the pantry, holding a jar of sauce and a box of pasta. "I could make spaghetti." She motioned to the frozen meat she'd set on the counter. "That ground beef needs to be eaten."

"Did you wanna eat here?" Rick asked, looking under the sink.

"I think a change of scenery *would* be nice."

Rick grabbed a plastic trash bag from under the sink. "Sounds good." He shoved his clothes into the bag. "Do you mind if I go through my mail while you work on dinner? I probably have some bills that need to be paid."

Rick went through his mail while Gwen cooked dinner. Forty minutes later, the kitchen smelling like oregano and basil, Rick cleared the table of letters and bills, and Gwen set down two plates of spaghetti.

During dinner, Rick said, "My finances are worse than I thought. After paying my bills, Mr. Ziegler included, I don't see how I can pay my mortgage next month. We need to get jobs *soon*."

"I know, but can we talk about something else?" Gwen asked. "I just want to enjoy being with you. Let's pretend we're a regular couple. What would we talk about?"

Rick nodded. "You're right. Let's take a break from it. What's your favorite movie?"

Gwen smiled. "I don't know. Let me think for a minute." She tapped her index finger to her lips. "I like eighties' movies, like *Sixteen Candles* and *The Breakfast Club*. I loved *Good Will Hunting* and *Titanic*. I'm sure I'm missing a bunch of others. What about you?"

"*The Shawshank Redemption*."

"That was a good movie. I didn't see the escape coming at all."

Rick smiled. "Neither did I. Why don't we get some popcorn and soda and stream all those movies tonight? We can stay up late and sleep in tomorrow."

Gwen leaned over and kissed him on the lips. "I'm in."

"The silver lining of unemployment."

After dinner, Rick said, "I'll clean up. Why don't you find the movie you wanna watch first? Just turn on the DVD player and select Amazon Prime Video."

Rick cleaned the dishes, and Gwen padded to the living room. Shortly thereafter, Rick heard the television and Gwen's channel surfing. She stopped on what sounded like the news.

"Rick," she called out from the living room.

Rick cut the water and dried his hands on a towel.

"Rick," she said louder.

He hurried to the living room. "What is it?"

"You have to see this." Gwen pointed at the screen.

Rick stepped closer, getting a better vantage point of the television. The headline at the bottom of the screen read Students on Strike. The local newscaster, a middle-aged man with helmet hair, appeared with his likeness in one half of the split screen, Jamar appearing in the other half. His caption read Jamar Burris, President West Lake Students for Change.

"We're organized, and we're not backing down," Jamar said. "We have 114 students prepared to strike until our demands are met. That may not seem like a lot, but that's one-third of all the high school students."

The newscaster said, "We've had reports that among your members are approximately half of the varsity football team, the same football team that's scheduled to play for the state championship this Friday."

"That's true."

"And you're the quarterback. A very good quarterback from what I've heard."

Jamar couldn't help but smile a little.

The newscaster asked, "Are you and your teammates prepared to forgo the state championship game?"

"Absolutely."

They cut back to the news desk.

Rick turned to Gwen and said, "It's not over."

CHAPTER 128

Janet and Truancy

"I've already called the police," Janet said into her cell phone. "Swatara Township's sending two officers tomorrow morning. Whoever's out without an excuse will get a citation."

Superintendent Virgil Matthews sighed. "I wish you would've cleared that with me first."

Janet paced in her bedroom. "They're breaking the law. We have a duty to report truancy."

"It's a special circumstance, given the controversies."

Janet blew out a breath. "What would you have me do? Let a hundred kids take off school because they disagreed with the school board? If we let these kids blackmail the school district, what's to stop them from doing it again?"

"It looks bad. All of it looks bad. We have the national press covering us now. *The Washington Post* and the *New York Times* are running stories tomorrow. We have to be very careful about what we do. I've been in talks with Solicitor Burks and the school board. Depending on how it goes tomorrow, we may offer a settlement to make it go away."

She shook her head and clenched her jaw. "That's a terrible idea."

Matthews paused for a moment. "I didn't ask for your opinion."

CHAPTER 129

Gwen and Good Conscience

Rick and Gwen drove to the outskirts of town, passing denuded cornfields and soy fields. An upscale suburban neighborhood was planted dead center, surrounded by farms and fields. During the real estate boom, a farmer-turned-developer had made far more from selling vinyl and chipboard houses than he ever made farming the land. It was a small enclave, only twenty houses or so, each on acre lots. Rick drove through the neighborhood and parked his truck in the driveway of a stone-faced colonial. He cut the engine and the headlights.

They walked up the driveway to the front stoop, porch lights leading the way. Gwen pressed the doorbell; the chime audible even outside. Shortly thereafter, Enid Burris opened the door, looking slender and tall, wearing slacks and a sweater.

"Hi, Enid," Gwen said. "Rick and I wanted to talk to you and Jamar."

Enid nodded. "I imagine you do. Come on in." She stepped aside, beckoning them inside.

Gwen and Rick stepped into the foyer. The home was immaculate. Open floor plan. Beautiful cherry furniture. Oriental rugs.

"Should we take off our shoes?" Gwen asked.

"No, you're fine," Enid said. "Jamar and Gerald are in the dining room. We were just finishing dinner. Are you hungry? I made plenty."

"Oh, no. But thank you," Gwen said.

"We can come back if we're disturbing your dinner," Rick said.

Enid waved her hand at the air. "Nonsense."

They followed Enid past the living room, through the kitchen with the sparkling stainless-steel appliances, and into the dining room, complete with china displayed in a backlit hutch. Jamar and Gerald sat at the table, their dinner plates mostly empty. Both men stood as Gwen and Rick entered the room.

They exchanged greetings with Jamar and Gerald.

Enid said, "Gwen and Rick wanted to talk to us."

Rick nodded. "I'm sorry to interrupt your dinner. It won't take long."

"Please sit," Gerald said, motioning to the empty chairs.

They all sat around the dining room table.

"Rick and I wanted to thank Jamar for speaking out at the school board meeting and again on television." Gwen looked directly at Jamar. "Thank you. Your support means a lot to us."

Jamar shrugged as if it was no big deal. "It's the right thing to do."

"It's more than that," Rick said. "You're risking a lot. We don't want you to suffer because of us." Rick looked at Enid and Gerald. "There could be consequences for you too."

"We think Principal Wilcox will report the absent students to the police for truancy," Gwen said.

"That's means citations and fines and the police forcing kids to go to school," Rick said.

Gerald Burris nodded, his slender fingers steepled. "There comes a time when one must take a position that is neither safe, nor politic, nor popular, but he must do it because conscience tells him it is right. Those are Dr. King's words, not mine, but they're fitting for the occasion. As a family, we've spoken at length about the risks, but we can't in good conscience stand by and do nothing."

"We're prepared to weather whatever storm comes our way," Enid said.

"We have the numbers. Over a hundred kids are striking tomorrow," Jamar said.

"What about them?" Gwen asked. "Do you think those families are prepared to pay expensive tickets?"

"I hadn't thought about that," Jamar said, wincing.

"I'm embarrassed to say that I hadn't either," Enid said.

CHAPTER 130

Rick and Sick Days

"How are you able to contact the students who are on strike?" Rick asked.

"I put together a closed Facebook group," Jamar replied, "but not everyone's on Facebook, so some people are on the text list or the email list."

"How quickly do you think you could get them all a message?"

"Fifteen, twenty minutes, depending on how long the message is."

"What do you guys think about telling the parents to call the school and say that their kid's sick?" Rick glanced around the table.

"That would solve the truancy issue," Gwen said.

"I doubt they'd check the veracity," Gerald said. "That would play in our favor, if they did."

"I agree," Enid said. "Parents would be up in arms if the police went to their homes to make sure their child's actually sick."

"How long can a parent keep a child at home before a doctor's note has to be produced?" Gerald asked.

"I think it's three consecutive days," Rick said, "but I'd have to look it up to be certain."

"I think you're right," Gwen added.

"That gives people until Thursday," Gerald said. "Friday will be the fourth consecutive day."

"What happens after that?" Enid asked.

"We may not need more than three days to force a decision," Rick said. "I'm sure they're feeling the heat from the press, and West Lake's never won a state championship in any sport. They'll wanna get those kids back on the football field before this week's out."

* * *

Rick drove toward the apartment, shadows dancing on his face, Gwen in the passenger seat.

"I think I should talk to Ashlee Miles," Gwen said.

Rick glanced from the road to Gwen and back again. "I appreciate it, but she won't tell the truth. I doubt she'll even talk to you."

"I had her in class. We weren't close, but I learned a lot about her through her writing. I think I can connect with her, if I can get her alone. She does have some emotional walls I'd have to break down."

"That's an understatement."

"That picture she stole from your house gave her story credibility. It made people believe her."

Rick nodded. "I know, but there's nothing we can do about it."

"I have an idea."

CHAPTER 131

Janet and Disrespect

Janet stood in the hallway, near the main office, her arms crossed over her chest. She glared at the students as they hurried to lunch. "Slow down," she said.

Someone among a large group of students said, "Bitch," muffling it with a cough. Janet was losing control of the school. No doubt about that. About sixty parents had called in sick for their kids, a far cry from the 114 they claimed. But another thirty or so kids were no-shows without an excuse. Many of those kids got a visit from the police, and their parents received a citation. The officers were still working down the list, but they'd assured Janet that they'd get to them all over the next day or so.

It had been a brutal morning. She'd had twenty-seven kids sent to her for disciplinary reasons. A few kids refused to do anything, one laying on the floor until he was forced upright by the school resource officer. Many were insubordinate, ignoring teachers, refusing to put away their phones. One barked like a dog every time the teacher turned her back. A varsity football player called Coach Schneider "a fat fuck." In one class, half the kids started chanting, "Wilcox is a liar," over and over again. Janet had given the offenders immediate in-school suspensions. She had quarantined the degenerates in an empty classroom, Vice Principal Burns keeping watch.

Janet walked behind the students headed to lunch. She'd been dreading lunch. Usually the most serious infractions happened there. Normally two teachers had lunch duty, but today she'd made sure to have additional firepower. In addition to Bob Schneider and Lewis Phelps, the school resource officer was there, not to mention Janet's presence.

In the lunchroom, Janet was pleasantly surprised. It was especially quiet. Students talked softly, no shouting. Nobody shoved or rough-housed. They carried their trays with care. Lasagna, mashed potatoes, a dinner roll, and Jell-O, milk to drink. Maybe she'd already separated the bad apples with the in-school suspensions.

Janet approached Bob Schneider, who stood near the center of the room, keeping a watchful eye. "Bob."

He nodded, not making eye contact. "Principal Wilcox."

"I think they've finally calmed down."

Bob nodded again, still not making eye contact.

"How's practice been?"

He looked at Janet and frowned. "How do you think? I only have half my team."

"I have the police issuing citations for truancy as we speak. They'll be back for the game."

"I hope you're right."

The students went from subdued to excited. The noise level increased. Janet looked around the room. The air felt charged with anticipation. Something hit the back of Janet's head, not hard. She turned around. A dinner roll was on the floor near her. She scanned the audience. Students suppressed their smiles and laughter. Another roll hit her in the back of the head. She whipped her head around, hoping to confront the offender. That's when it erupted.

Someone shouted, "Food fight!"

Instantly, a barrage of food and half-full milk cartons flung from one end of the lunchroom to the other and vice versa. Janet and Bob stood in the middle of the melee, at ground zero. It happened so fast. The dinner rolls weren't a problem, but the lasagna, open milk cartons, and Jell-O doused Janet and Bob, along with much of the student body.

CHAPTER 132

Gwen and Parental Consent

Gwen drove her Volkswagen back from Lebanon city and Mr. Ziegler's office. He'd prepared a boilerplate nondisclosure agreement for Gwen to pick up, and he'd found an important phone number. She drove back to her apartment and dialed the number, the car still idling and pumping heat from the vents. She stayed in her car because she wanted total privacy, worried that Rick standing next to her and listening in might throw her off her game.

"This is Nathan Jameson," the man answered.

"Hi, Mr. Jameson. This is Gwen Townsend. I was your daughter's teacher—"

"How did you get this number?" He sounded annoyed.

"This is an emergency."

"What the hell is going on?"

"Ashlee's in a bit of trouble." Gwen went on to tell him what Ashlee had done.

Nathan knew about Caleb's death. Heather had hit him up for funeral expenses even though Caleb wasn't his kid. But he didn't know about Ashlee and Rick. He'd been out of the country on business over the past month. Something about a factory in Malaysia. But he wasn't the least bit surprised. He sighed and said, "Like mother, like daughter."

Gwen told him how she had planned to help Ashlee and Rick at the same time. But she needed Nathan's help. Ashlee was a minor and needed parental consent to enter into a legally binding contract.

"Ashlee hasn't even agreed to this?" Nathan asked.

"She will," Gwen replied. "I'm going to talk to her right now."

"You don't know who you're dealing with."

"I got to know her quite well through her writing. She has a logical business side. I imagine she takes after you in that regard. And, like you, I think she'll see the benefit of participating."

"Is this something I can do remotely?"

"I think it would be better if you were here."

"I really don't have time for this today."

"Mr. Jameson. We're talking about your daughter. She's standing on the precipice."

He blew out a heavy breath. "Call me if she agrees. I'm not making the trip unless Ashlee's on board."

"Thank you, Mr. Jameson."

Gwen disconnected the call and walked up to her apartment. She had Rick sign one of the nondisclosure agreements. He wanted to come with her, but she reminded him that they'll catch more bees with honey. Then she drove toward West Lake High School, hopeful to get there before dismissal.

The student parking lot was only half-full, the strike reducing the number of parked vehicles. Gwen parked with a good view of Ashlee's Jeep and waited, rehearsing her plan in her mind.

Half an hour later, students spilled from the school, entering their economy cars and beat-up trucks, and driving from the lot entirely too fast. Ashlee walked alone to her Jeep, her head bowed and covered by the hood of her jacket. Gwen followed her as she drove away from school.

Ashlee drove the short distance from school to her mother's double-wide trailer. She parked her Jeep along the street. Gwen drove past, scouting the house. The carport was empty, meaning Heather

Miles wasn't home. Gwen drove past, turned around in a cul-de-sac, and returned to the trailer. She parked behind Ashlee's Jeep and walked up to the front door, holding the manila folder filled with the nondisclosure agreements. Gwen knocked on the door several times. No answer. She knocked harder. Finally, Ashlee parted the curtains and looked from the window.

Ashlee spoke through the door. "What do you want?"

"I want to help you," Gwen said. "I know kids at school have been bullying you, and I know the comments on Facebook have been really awful."

"Like you give a shit. People keep calling me a liar and a whore on your page."

"I'm sorry about that. It's not right. I deleted the posts that called you a whore."

"What about all the posts calling me a liar, saying that I ruined Rick's life?"

"People are angry that you lied—"

"Fuck you. I didn't lie."

Gwen pursed her lips. "Mr. Barnett has a lot of enemies in this town, but he also has a lot of friends, and they'll continue to attack unless we fix it. We can fix this without anybody knowing what you did and without you getting into trouble."

Ashlee paused for a beat. "I didn't do anything."

"You and I both know that's not true, and so do all those people who keep attacking you. It'll never go away unless we fix it."

Ashlee was quiet.

"Ashlee?" Gwen said through the door. "We can fix this for everyone. Your mom doesn't have to know."

Ashlee opened the door. She stood in her socks, wearing jeans and a fleece, her dark hair hanging to chest level. Her nose was red-tipped, her eyes black-circled. "You got five minutes." She stepped aside from the threshold.

Gwen entered the trailer. A faint garbage smell hung in the air. She followed Ashlee to the living room and the couch. Plastic cups and dirty plates littered the coffee table. Ashlee slumped onto one end of the couch. Gwen sat on the edge of the other end, the folder in her lap.

"How are you gonna *fix* all my problems?" Ashlee asked, her eyes narrowed.

"I need you to tell the truth to four people," Gwen said.

"I've *been* telling the truth."

Gwen took a cleansing breath and deadpanned, "Let's cut the bullshit."

Ashlee crossed her arms over her chest.

"I could leave up those nasty posts about you. The ones that talk about your lying and your promiscuity. Some of them were incredibly detailed. I'd be mortified if I were you."

"I can't say what you want me to say."

"Because you'd be in big trouble, right?"

Ashlee dropped her arms to her lap and stared at her hands. "I just can't."

"What if I could guarantee that you won't get into trouble?"

Ashlee looked at Gwen, her eyes unblinking. "But, if I tell anyone, they'll tell the whole town, and it'll be even worse for me."

"What if I could guarantee that they won't talk?"

"How?"

Gwen opened the manila folder, grabbed the top page, and held it up to Ashlee. "We'll make them sign nondisclosure agreements, which means, if they tell anyone what you say, you can sue them."

Ashlee pursed her lips. "What about Rick? He can still tell everyone."

Gwen pointed to the signature and name at the bottom of the agreement. "Mr. Barnett already signed." Gwen made sure Ashlee got a good look at Rick's name and then put the form back in the folder. "Of course, I'm not giving you this unless you do as I ask. And you're right. If you don't do as I ask, Mr. Barnett is free to tell the truth."

"He's just one person."

"One thing that Mr. Barnett loves about being a football coach is the relationships he has with all his players. He's been coaching for thirteen years. He's probably coached close to a thousand kids. That's a lot of loyal young men who are upset about what happened to their coach. Now that Mr. Barnett's been fired, what's to stop him from telling everyone he knows?"

Ashlee looked at the carpet, no longer making eye contact with Gwen.

"In fact, he doesn't have much choice really, unless he wants everyone to think he's a child molester. What if someone lied and said you molested a little boy? Would you just let them lie about you, or would you tell everyone the truth?"

Ashlee was unresponsive.

"Ashlee?"

She turned her head toward Gwen. Her eyes were glassy. Almost in a whisper, she asked, "Who do I have to tell?"

"Dr. Matthews, two school board members, ... and your father."

CHAPTER 133

Rick and Options

A towel over his shoulder, Rick cracked eggs into a bowl, tossing the eggshells in the trash. He wanted to make Gwen a nice breakfast. It was the least he could do after what she'd done for him—all the pieces she'd put together on such short notice to make it work. All for him. She'd managed to get two board members, plus Dr. Matthews, and Ashlee's father in a room to listen to Ashlee tell the truth with the protection of nondisclosure agreements. Rick had signed one too, but what did he care? He hadn't planned on talking about it anyway. He could weather the gossip, especially if this resulted in his record being wiped clean and his reinstatement. That hinged on another hearing. That was why Dr. Matthews had been there. He had the power to call a hearing. The two board members were there to make sure the vote went Rick's and Gwen's way, if they got that hearing. Gwen figured they had four of the nine board members already, so she picked two of the five naysayers, hoping Ashlee's testimony would sway them. Technically, she only needed one to turn for a majority, but you never know. They might still vote against, so she included two, figuring at least one would turn.

His cell phone chimed as he whisked the eggs. Rick set the bowl on the counter, grabbed his cell, checked the number, and swiped right. "Good morning, Mr. Ziegler."

"Good morning, Rick. I just got off the phone with Virgil Matthews."

Rick smiled to himself, knowing what was coming. "What did he have to say?"

"Is Gwen with you?"

As if on cue, Gwen padded from the bedroom, rubbing her eyes, her hair disheveled.

"She just walked into the room," Rick said.

"Please put me on Speaker," Mr. Ziegler replied. "She should hear this."

Rick put the phone on Speaker and set it on the kitchen table. "You're on Speaker." Rick looked to Gwen. "It's Mr. Ziegler. He has news."

"Hi, Mr. Ziegler," Gwen said, sitting next to Rick.

"Good morning, Gwen," Mr. Ziegler replied. "I have good news. I received a call from Matthews this morning. They've offered us a deal. The school district's willing to let you both resign, and they'll give both of you back pay from the date you were let go until now, and they'll cover your legal fees. The alternative is to have another hearing to try for reinstatement. Of course, you both are free to make your own decisions. What you decide doesn't have to be in agreement. If one of you wants the hearing, but the other would prefer to settle, that's entirely up to you."

"We understand," Gwen said.

"The catch is, the hearing would be tonight," Mr. Ziegler said.

"Tonight?"

"Yes, tonight. Also, both of the options come with a contingency that you'll make a statement encouraging the students and specifically the football team to end their strike and to play in the state championship game tomorrow."

"What if the kids don't listen?" Rick asked.

"Matthews is pretty confident that they will. The bottom line is, the school district wants this all to go away. I think Matthews and some of the school board members are regretting that they listened to Janet

Wilcox, and now they're worried about getting sued or being thrown under the bus by the press. The community's up in arms about the football game. We have the upper hand, but we can't delay. They want an answer by noon today."

"If we're reinstated, would that mean I'm also reinstated as the head football coach?"

"I asked Matthews about that, and, if you're reinstated, they do want you to resume your duties as the head football coach, but it is not a requirement."

"Can we talk about it and call you back?" Gwen asked.

"Of course," Mr. Ziegler replied. "One more thing. If you choose the hearing, I'd like to get Victor Moretti up here. I don't wanna be blindsided like last time."

"It's really short notice."

"I know, but I don't wanna leave anything to chance."

"I'll call him if we decide to have the hearing."

"Give me a call as soon as you two make a decision."

"Thanks, Mr. Ziegler. We'll call you back." Rick disconnected the call and smiled at Gwen.

"Do you still want to leave?" she asked, turning in her chair to face Rick.

He shrugged. "I don't know. Maybe not."

"Janet will still be there, trying to ruin us."

"I don't wanna leave because of her. That's what she wants. Besides, I don't think she has the influence she once did. She's burned a lot of bridges."

Gwen pursed her lips. "What about the rumors? This admission by Ashlee isn't public. People will still think these awful things about us."

Rick shook his head. "Not necessarily. NDA or not, I know those school board members. They couldn't keep a secret to save their life. And, to be honest, I don't give a shit what these people think about me. I care about my team. I care about my students, and I care about you. The kids know us. They don't believe this bullshit for a second.

Otherwise they wouldn't've stuck their necks out for us."

"I want to move on from my past. I don't know if I can do that here."

"What's to stop someone at the next school from dredging up your past? At least here it's old news."

Gwen nodded. "I suppose that's true." She paused for a beat. "Let's say, for argument's sake, that we have another hearing, and we're reinstated. Then what? We just go back to work like nothing happened?"

"No." Rick took both of her hands in his. "We go back to work with a rededicated purpose. We're there for the kids, period."

CHAPTER 134

Janet and Dr. Matthews

D r. Virgil Matthews sat across from Janet at her desk. He was tall and thin, in his sixties, with a ruddy complexion. "We're having an emergency hearing tonight at seven to revote on reinstatement."

"How many times do we have to go through this?"

"There's new evidence. I can't say what, because I've signed an NDA, but I think we made a huge mistake firing them in the first place. We're lucky they're not interested in suing the district."

Janet glared at her boss. "It's a huge mistake to give them another hearing."

He glared right back. "At this point, I don't care what you think. You're lucky you still have a job, and, if I find evidence that you framed Gwen or Rick, I will terminate your employment immediately."

"If you do that, you and this school district will be in for the fight of your lives."

"You've made that abundantly clear. Rest assured, if we let you go, we'll have our bases covered, and we'll be more than ready for any legal action you bring. I suggest from now on that you keep your mouth shut and do your job." Dr. Matthews stood from his chair. "I better not hear about you lobbying the board."

CHAPTER 135

Gwen and Victor Moretti

The library was packed; this time more students attended. The nine school board members, plus Dr. Matthews and Solicitor Burks, listened from their seats at the long table. Victor Moretti stood at the podium, a stocky, swarthy man in his mid-forties. He wore a denim button-down shirt with Victor in cursive etched over the right breast pocket and Vic's Plumbing on the other.

"My name's Victor Moretti. I was the jury foreman on the trial that acquitted Emory Jackson of raping Gwen Townsend." He paused, letting the audience digest that mouthful. "Actually, we didn't really acquit him. It was a hung jury. The evidence was clear that Gwen Townsend was telling the truth. She'd been roughed up pretty badly and the rapist left DNA evidence. Eleven of us voted to convict, but one juror refused. Her name was Regina Trufant. We tried to convince her, but she wouldn't budge, so the judge declared a mistrial, and the court didn't bother to retry the case. The Jacksons were everywhere, talking to the media about how Emory was framed because he was black, how the system's rigged against black people. That might be true, but it wasn't true in this case. Gwen's husband, Brian, must've snapped after seeing all this in the media. To be honest, if someone did that to my wife, then went around proclaiming their innocence to the world, I would've done the same thing."

Victor paused, surveying the audience. "After the mistrial, I found out why Regina Trufant refused to listen to reason and evidence. She was a member of a black supremacy group called the BLF or the Black Liberation Front. She still is a member as far as I know. I'm gonna read you a quote from something she wrote." Victor read from the paper on the podium. "*Melanin enables black skin to capture light and to hold it in its memory mode, which reveals that blackness converts light into knowledge. Melanin directly communicates with cosmic energy. White people are recessive genetic defects who do not have the capability to be empathetic. Because of their white skin, they are not able to capture and to retain God's light. This is why, throughout history, they've committed genocide after genocide against people of color. White people should be wiped off the face of the Earth for the betterment of mankind.*"

Victor looked up from his paper and surveyed the audience again. "I don't have a lot of regrets in my life. I have a wonderful wife, great kids, and a good business. My biggest regret in life is that we didn't convict Emory Jackson. If we'd done that, if we'd done our job, Gwen's husband wouldn't have killed Emory. Not only did we deprive her of justice, we helped take away her husband from her too." Victor turned his gaze to the school board. "It doesn't surprise me that Gwen Townsend risked her own life for her students. What does surprise me is that she was fired for it. You people should be ashamed of yourselves. I hope you can redeem yourselves tonight." Victor walked back to the audience, welcomed by a thunderous applause.

Many people spoke up for Gwen and Rick that night. The fear that had kept many supporters at bay had dissipated. Word had gotten out that Janet was losing her grip on the school board and consequently losing some of her power. The opinion of the community had also turned in Gwen's and Rick's favor. Unlike the first hearing, the speakers were overwhelmingly in support of their reinstatement. Jamar and a few students spoke, pledging to end the strike if Gwen and Rick were reinstated. Lewis and a handful of teachers spoke, along with a dozen parents and community members. Ashlee Miles wasn't there.

Gwen had heard from Lewis that she went to live with her father. Janet Wilcox and Rachel Kreider weren't in their usual seats, but nobody seemed to care.

At the end of the public comments, Cliff Osborn asked each board member for a comment. They all declined, even Heather Miles. The vote was anticlimactic. Eight for reinstatement. The one negative vote came from Heather Miles, who received a torrent of boos from the audience after she voted. She was red-faced as she stormed from the library.

"Good riddance," someone from the audience shouted.

"Don't let the door hit you on the ass," another person said.

Cliff waited for the boos to subside before he said, "Gwen Townsend and Rick Barnett are reinstated effective immediately."

The crowd erupted, people standing and clapping and cheering.

CHAPTER 136

Rick's Back

The day after the hearing, Rick drove his truck toward school. Gwen was still at her apartment. They didn't have to work until Monday, but Rick had a pregame meeting with the team, and he had someone to confront. Fortunately, the district had only hired long-term substitutes for their classes, so Rick and Gwen could return, almost as if they'd never left. The long-term subs would finish off their contracts, subbing elsewhere as needed.

Rick yawned. He'd been up late last night, going over film of North Columbia High School. They were big, fast, and physical. Rick worried about his team's lack of preparation, given that they hadn't practiced all week. Rick parked in the teacher's lot and stepped from his truck. It was cloudy, the cold wind biting his nose and ears. He walked to the side door and keyed himself into the school. Rick wasn't sure if his scan card would work, but apparently they'd already reactivated it.

The hallways were quiet, faint murmurings coming from behind the classroom doors. Rick checked his watch. He still had an hour before the pregame meeting. Rick stopped at a classroom door and knocked. Bob Schneider appeared at the window, his eyes widening. He opened the door, blocking entry with his big body.

"Hey, … Rick. I didn't think you'd be back till Monday."

"Can I talk to you for a minute?"

Bob stepped back, allowing Rick to enter. His classroom was empty. Rick knew it was his planning period. Rick shut the door behind them.

"What do you want?" Bob asked, standing near the door, his chin held high, and his barrel chest puffed up.

"I wanted to talk about the football team and your employment as a coach," Rick replied.

"I've been thinkin' about it too. I might be able to offer you the defensive coordinator job next season, if you wanna come back."

Rick shook his head. "This isn't about me. This is about you."

Bob shrugged his shoulders. "That's the best I can do. What more do you want from me?"

"You're fired, Bob."

Bob's eyes widened; he creased his brows. "You can't fire me. You're not the coach anymore."

"I've been reinstated as a teacher here but also as the head football coach. You were the interim coach."

"Hold on a second. This isn't right." He walked to the classroom phone on the wall. "I'm gonna call Janet."

Rick blew out a breath. "Still on the wrong side, huh?"

Bob picked up the receiver. He pressed the keys unnecessarily hard, glancing from the phone to Rick and back again.

"There's not a damn thing she can do about it." Rick said this matter-of-factly and without emotion.

Bob still made the call. After a brief hold he said, "Principal Wilcox, it's Bob Schneider." He listened for a moment. "I have Rick Barnett here telling me that I'm no longer the head coach." He listened again. "That can't be right." He paused, his face reddening. "Sorry. Of course." Bob put the phone back on the receiver and turned to Rick. "You won't win without me."

Rick nodded. "Maybe, but some things are more important than wins and losses. I suggest you stay away from the team today. Don't make me embarrass you."

CHAPTER 137

Janet Strikes Back

She hung up her desktop phone, shaking her head. *Bob. So fucking weak. I should fire him as a teacher too, but he'd talk, and I don't have many friends left. His time will come when he least expects it. I don't make empty threats. First things first. Cliff's usefulness has run its course.* With latex gloves, Janet picked up the printed pictures of Cliff Osborn—blindfolded, naked, and spread-eagled on the bed. He looked like a beached whale, his pale gut, bulbous and bulky, making his penis look insignificant. She slid the pictures into an eight-by-eleven envelope, removed the self-sealing sticker, and sealed the envelope. She affixed the preprinted label dead center. It was addressed to Cliff's wife, with a phony return address from a faux flower shop.

CHAPTER 138

Gwen and the State Championship

It had been a tough game. North Columbia was as good as advertised. They'd trounced West Lake in the first half 20–0, but Rick must've said something profound at halftime because their fortunes had turned in the second half. West Lake had scrapped and clawed back into the football game, now only trailing by three, 27–24. Unfortunately, they were running out of time.

Gwen stood next to Lewis in the stands, bathed in the glow of the stadium lights, shivering despite her puffy coat. Jamar and the West Lake offense had possession of the football near the fifty-yard line with twenty-eight seconds and one time-out left. North Columbia wasn't taking any chances. They lined up in a dime defense with two high safeties.

On first and ten, Jamar dropped back to pass, but nobody was open, so he ran around the defensive end, streaking toward the sideline. He was pushed out of bounds after an eight-yard gain, stopping the clock at twenty seconds.

On second and two, Jamar threw the ball to Lance on a comeback near the sideline. Lance caught the pass for a twelve-yard gain, but he was tackled before he could get out of bounds. The clock was ticking.

Jamar hurried the offense to the line, shouting, "Kill, kill." As soon as the offense lined up, Jamar took the snap and threw the ball into the turf, stopping the clock with eight seconds left.

It was second and ten on the North Columbia thirty-yard line.

Lewis said to Gwen, "They only have time for two plays. I think they'll try to throw something down the middle to get into field-goal range. Then they'll kick it, but we need a miracle."

"How close do they have to be for a field goal?" Gwen asked.

Lewis frowned. "I think there's a reason they always go for two."

Jamar did as Lewis predicted, completing a pass over the middle against soft coverage for a fifteen-yard gain. Rick called their final time-out from the sideline, with three seconds left on the game clock. During the time-out, Rick trotted out to the field, talked to the offense, then jogged back to the sideline. The kicker and six other players hustled onto the turf for the game-tying field-goal attempt. Eight players ran off the field, but one stopped just short of the sideline.

West Lake lined up on the fifteen-yard line. It would be a thirty-two-yard field goal. Jamar kneeled seven yards back from the center. His job was to catch the snap, set the ball on the tee, and spin the laces outward for the kicker.

Lewis put his hand over his face. "I can't watch."

Jamar stood upright, and the center snapped the ball. North Columbia blitzed from the edges, determined to block the kick, but Jamar had no intention of holding the ball. He looked toward the West Lake sideline and threw a bomb to the uncovered receiver streaking down the field. The receiver had been lost by North Columbia, camouflaged by the crowded West Lake sideline, when the field-goal unit had subbed in and out with the offense. The ball floated through the air, carried a little by the wind. The receiver sprinted under the football, holding his hands out front like a basket. The crowd was dead silent as they watched the ball fall from the sky into his outstretched hands. As soon as the receiver tucked it in, the crowd cheered. The referee raised his hands, signaling the touchdown.

Gwen and Lewis jumped up and down and embraced, with Lewis shouting, "We won!" They disengaged, Lewis turning and hugging another friend and West Lake Wolf Pack fan.

Gwen watched Rick on the sideline, celebrating with his team. Lance and Jamar snuck up behind Rick and dumped a cooler filled with ice-cold water over his head. Gwen smiled to herself.

CHAPTER 139

Rick and Back to School

Rick put his truck in Park and cut the engine. He looked over at Gwen. "You ready for this?"

She looked back with a little smile. "I think so."

He leaned over and kissed her on the cheek. "Let's do this."

It was their first day back to work after a weekend filled with post-game celebrations. Lewis had a party at his house on Friday night, where Rick and Gwen were introduced to his many friends, including his boyfriend. The Burris family hosted a party on Saturday for the team.

Rick and Gwen walked into school together, going through the main entrance. They walked toward their classrooms, collecting students along the way, until they had a crowd surrounding them.

"Welcome back, Ms. Townsend!"

"Great game, Mr. Barnett."

"I'm so glad you guys are back."

"Are you guys dating? I heard you guys are a couple?"

Gwen blushed at that last question.

"You guys are so nosy," Rick said, laughing.

"Come on. We know it's true," a girl said.

"Yes, okay," Rick answered. "I like Ms. Townsend very much, but that's all you're gonna get outta me."

"*Aww*, that's so sweet," another girl said.

Gwen winked at Rick, as if to say, *You're not so bad yourself.*

CHAPTER 140

Janet and the Shot Heard Round the World

"There has to be some kind of discipline," Dr. Matthews said through the phone.

Janet sat at her desk, the phone to her ear. "I need to talk to my lawyer."

"Two weeks suspension without pay is very generous. If I were you, I wouldn't fight this."

"I haven't done anything wrong."

"The school board disagrees. *I* disagree."

Janet gripped the receiver, her knuckles white. "The school board's corrupt, and you're misinformed."

"There'll be a hearing next week to vote on the suspension. It'll be a closed session."

"If you attempt to suspend me, I'll bury this district. I have dirt on everyone."

Dr. Matthews sighed. "This is the problem. You act more like a DC lobbyist than an educator."

"I have no choice."

"Bullshit. I'll see you at the hearing." Dr. Matthews disconnected the call.

Janet slammed down the phone. She heard commotion coming from the halls. She left the main office, spilling into the front entry. To her right, the hallway was jam-packed with rambunctious students. She glanced at the clock on the wall. Still three minutes until the tardy bell.

She marched toward the commotion, her heels click-clacking on the linoleum. Students stared at her, whispering and smiling, and some were even laughing.

A boy shouted, "Mr. Barnett and Ms. Townsend are back!"

"Go to class!" Janet shrieked. "Stop blocking the hallway. Go to class."

But they barely moved, her orders falling on deaf ears. Some held up their phones, videoing her.

"Put those phones away! Go to class!"

Someone said, "Lying bitch."

She scanned the crowd of students, turning 360 degrees. Her glare found Aaron Fuller and his shit-eating grin. "What did you say?"

Aaron's expression didn't change.

She moved into his personal space. "What did you say?"

Aaron deadpanned, "You're a lying *bitch*."

The crowd jeered and pointed at Janet.

Janet grabbed Aaron by his upper arm and pulled, but he resisted, not moving an inch.

"Get your fucking hands off me, *cunt*."

Reflexively, Janet slapped him across the face.

The crowd went silent.

Aaron broke the silence with his laughter. The crowd joined in, their laughter blending with his in a cacophony of disrespect.

Janet reared back and slapped him again, this time harder, the smack of skin-on-skin loud enough to be heard over the crowd.

Aaron stopped laughing. His shit-eating grin was gone. He touched his cheek, pink from the impact. He narrowed his eyes at Janet and threw a roundhouse haymaker that connected with Janet's jaw, knocking her off her heels, sending her down for the count.

* * *

Janet lay in her hospital bed with a bruised face, a mild concussion, and a dull headache. The doctor wanted to keep her overnight for observation. Rachel sat by her bedside, the lighting dim.

"I still can't believe he hit you," Rachel said. "He should've been arrested."

Janet closed her eyes, trying to block out Rachel's incessant chattering.

"I'm sure he'll at least be expelled."

Janet clenched her fists, her head throbbing.

"You know? I was thinking that it never would've even happened if Rick and Gwen weren't—"

"Shut the fuck up!" Janet sat up and glared at Rachel. "*Jesus.* I'm so sick of you blabbering on and on."

Rachel's mouth hung open, her face crimson. She shut her mouth, stood from the chair, and grabbed her purse.

Janet frowned. "Don't be such a fucking baby."

Rachel left the hospital room without another word.

Janet tried to sleep in the dim light, but her mind wouldn't quiet. *He punched me. I didn't punch him. I can fix it. Aaron Fuller's a degenerate. Everyone knows that.* Her phone buzzed on the bedside table. She'd been avoiding contact with the world, but curiosity got the better of her. She grabbed her phone and checked the latest text.

Virgil Matthews: You are fired. Do not come into work.

Janet shot back a text.

Janet: You'll be hearing from my lawyer. I will ruin you
Virgil Matthews: Good luck with that. I've fired people for a lot less.

Janet hurled her phone across the hospital room, the screen shattering against the wall.

CHAPTER 141

Gwen and Justice

Gwen and Rick sat on his couch, watching the video on YouTube entitled "Principal Slaps Student and Gets Knocked Out!" In less than forty-eight hours, the video had already garnered two million views. It showed the whole incident. Janet shrieking for everyone to go to class, to put away their phones. Aaron calling her a lying bitch. Janet grabbing him, and Aaron refusing to budge, calling her a cunt. Then the slap and the laughter, followed by another slap. Then Aaron's roundhouse right, connecting to Janet's glass jaw. She fell awkwardly, her head bouncing off the linoleum. The crowd went wild, cheering and jumping up and down, as if they were at a heavyweight title bout. The video ended as Rick and the school resource officer appeared on-screen.

Gwen suppressed a smile, covering her mouth with her hand.

Rick looked at her with narrowed eyes. "What?"

She burst out with laughter.

He smiled but held it together. "I didn't know you were so mean."

Gwen eventually stopped laughing, a smile still plastered on her face. "I'm sorry. It's just … I wonder how many people wanted to punch her in the face?"

Rick laughed. "I certainly thought about it."

"Now who's mean?"

"I didn't say I was any better."

"I do worry about Aaron."

Rick shrugged. "He'll be expelled for the rest of the year, but maybe he'll do better in cyberschool, and, for the rest of his life, he'll have the best story at every party."

"I still think Janet should be arrested for slapping him."

"That's the sexism of the justice system. If a male teacher slapped a girl, he'd be serving time."

"Well, at least she was fired. Her career as an educator is over."

CHAPTER 142

Rick and Just Visiting

The drab visiting room was spruced up with nondenominational holiday decor. A life-size poster of Frosty the Snowman hung near the vending machines, 3-D snowflakes hung from the ceiling, and the tabletops each had a clear plastic centerpiece filled with green- and red-wrapped Hershey kisses.

Rick and Gwen sat on stainless steel seats attached to a stainless steel table. Shane sat across from them, wearing burgundy pants and a burgundy button-down shirt that could pass for pajamas. The room was noisy, inmates talking and laughing with friends and family.

"I was surprised when I saw you two requested a visit," Shane said.

"We wanted to see how you're doing," Rick said, acknowledging Gwen with his eyes, then looking back to Shane.

"How *are* you doing?" Gwen asked.

Shane lifted one shoulder. "It sucks, but I'm hangin' in there. They got high school classes, so I'm doin' that."

"That's great to hear," Gwen said.

Shane looked at Rick. "I saw that youse won the state championship."

Rick smiled, not showing his teeth. "North Columbia was tough. We had to run a trick play to win."

"I heard. The fake field goal where the receiver hides near the side-line." Shane forced a smile. "Everyone must've been hyped."

"We're getting state championship rings. Where would you like me to send yours?"

Shane cocked his head. "I'm gettin' one?"

"Yeah, you are." Rick nodded.

Shane smiled again; this time it reached his eyes. "Thanks, Coach. I appreciate it. You can send it to my dad. I'll tell him to email you his address."

"Has your dad been visiting?" Gwen asked.

"Every weekend."

"That's nice to hear."

"He has a construction company. They do remodels and some custom houses. He said he'll teach me the ropes when I get outta here."

"Sounds like a great opportunity," Rick said.

"I'm lookin' forward to it." Shane leaned in, putting his elbows on the table. "I saw that Lance made all-state. Is he gonna get a scholarship?"

"Division II maybe. Kutztown's interested."

"Really? I thought he'd go to Penn State or Pitt."

"For Division I, you gotta have the grades to go with the talent."

"You think Drew could've got a scholarship?"

"Maybe. Drew was one of the best linebackers I ever coached."

"You know he's here, right? Not in my cell block, but I see him sometimes."

"We visited him about an hour ago," Rick said.

Shane shook his head, a frown on his face. "He's still pretty pissed at me. I tried to tell him it was my mom who got him busted, but, you know, … I guess I'd be pissed too."

"Maybe he'll come around in time," Gwen said.

"Yeah, maybe." Shane paused, taking a deep breath. "Thank you guys for comin' to see me. It means a lot."

"You're very welcome."

Shane nodded to Gwen, then looked at Rick. "I think about football sometimes." He thought for a moment. "Man, I wish I could do it over."

"I should've moved you to wide receiver," Rick said. "You're tall. You have great hands."

Shane grinned, the alternate reality playing in his mind. "That would've been cool. We could've run a nasty double pass."

"I should've handled your situation better. I'm sorry."

"Nah, I was a douchebag. I know that now."

CHAPTER 143

Gwen and No Child Left Behind

He parked his truck in front of the rusted trailer home. Gwen and Rick stepped from the vehicle and walked to the front door. It was cloudy, everything and everyone cast in a dull gray. Gwen's breath condensed in the air as she exhaled. Rick knocked on the door, causing a dog to bark inside.

Aaron Fuller answered the door, wearing a jacket and a knit cap. A pit bull stuck his head between Aaron's leg and the doorframe. "What are youse doing here?"

"We talked to your brother yesterday," Rick said.

The dog barked again, causing Gwen to take a step back.

"What for?" Aaron stepped onto the stoop, shutting the door and the dog behind him.

Rick backed up a step to accommodate Aaron.

"We wanted to see how he was doing," Gwen said.

"Oh, ... cool," Aaron replied.

"He mentioned that he was concerned about how you're holding up without him," Rick said.

Aaron looked away, then shrugged. "It's fine."

"You sure?" Gwen asked.

"Yeah. My mom's trying to be home more."

"If you need anything, like dinner or just a warm place to be, let me or Mr. Barnett know." Gwen glanced at Rick, then back to Aaron.

"Yeah, … okay. Thanks."

"I hear you'll be back at school next year," Rick said.

"Yeah. I'm finishing the rest of this year in cyberschool."

"What do you think about coming out for football?"

Aaron thought for a moment. "I don't know. I need to make some money."

"The booster club has a lot of business owners. They like to give jobs to football players because they know you guys are used to hard work."

"Can I think about it?"

"When we went to see your brother, we visited with Shane too," Rick said.

Aaron frowned.

"It was interesting that both Drew and Shane said the exact same thing to us. You wanna know what they said?"

"You're gonna tell me either way."

Rick chuckled. "That's true." His face turned serious. "They both wished that they could do it over again." Rick paused, letting his point sink in. "I think you could be a better linebacker than your brother. And Ms. Townsend tells me that you're a bright student. This town's filled with could've-beens and would've-beens. Ultimately, it's not your potential that matters, but what you do with that potential."

Aaron nodded, his eyes downcast.

"Look at me, son."

Aaron raised his gaze.

"Ms. Townsend and I are both here to help you reach your potential, but we can't do the work for you."

CHAPTER 144

Rick ... Three Months after the Knockout

"Come on, honey." Gwen kneeled next to Buster's kennel. She tossed a few tuna-flavored treats inside the cage.

Buster meowed, then looked up at Gwen with an I-don't-know-about-this look. Ultimately, the reward must've been worth the risk as Buster entered the kennel. Gwen shut the door and latched it.

Rick appeared from the bedroom. "I did a once-over. I think we got everything."

Gwen picked up the kennel. "I had to bribe her with treats, but Buster's ready."

"You could just carry her."

"She freaks out in cars. She shredded the upholstery on my last car."

"What about you? Are you ready?"

"To save a bunch of money on rent?" Gwen smiled. "Damn straight I am."

Rick leaned in and kissed her on the lips. "You know what I meant."

"I'm ready."

Rick grabbed the cardboard box from the kitchen counter. Jamar and a few guys from the football team had moved most of Gwen's stuff yesterday. Gwen left the apartment keys on the counter for the super. Rick stepped outside, squinting into the sun. Gwen shut the door, and they stepped down the stairs and into the parking lot. A few piles of snow melted in the corners of the lot. They loaded the cargo, the box in the truck bed, and the kennel in the cab at Gwen's feet. Rick drove them to his home, parking behind Gwen's Volkswagen. They carried Buster and the last of Gwen's belongings inside. Rick took the cardboard box to the bedroom, then returned to the living room. Gwen opened the kennel door. Buster stepped out and looked around, taking in her new surroundings.

Gwen plopped down on her old couch. "I'm exhausted. I never want to move again."

Rick sat next to her. He put his arm around her, and she leaned against his chest.

Buster hopped onto the familiar couch and lay in a circle next to Gwen.

"What do you wanna do for dinner tonight?" Rick asked.

She tilted her head and looked up at Rick. "How about takeout from that Italian place?"

"Sounds good to me. I love their homemade ravioli."

A knock came from the front door. They sat upright and glanced at each other.

"Are you expecting someone?" Gwen asked.

"Nope." Rick stood from the couch. "Maybe it's the Jehovah's Witnesses."

"They'll keep coming back if you don't tell them not to."

Rick smiled, stepped to the front door, and opened it. Heather stood there, wearing a fur coat, knee-high boots, and a tight skirt. A red corvette idled in the driveway, a man behind the wheel.

"What do *you* want?" Rick said with a scowl.

Heather's mouth smiled, but the rest of her face said, *Fuck you.* "I don't want anything from you. I have everything I ever wanted."

"That's great. Now get off my property."

"My boyfriend and I are movin' to California. You know I got my settlement, right?"

"I heard."

"I'm so sick of this backward-ass town. I should've left a long time ago."

Rick nodded. "You should get going then."

"Do you know what the best revenge is?" Heather asked.

Gwen appeared at the door next to Rick and said, "Living well."

Heather glared at Gwen, then fixed her gaze back on Rick. She gestured to the corvette. "That could've been you."

"*Phew.*" Rick mimed, wiping his forehead. "I dodged a bullet."

Gwen covered her mouth, stifling a laugh.

Heather's tan face reddened. She pointed at Rick for emphasis. "You know what? You belong here with the rest of the white-trash losers." She turned on her heels and marched toward her shiny sports car.

Rick called out to her back, a big grin on his face. "Us white-trash losers prefer pickup trucks."

CHAPTER 145

Gwen ... One Year after the Knockout

Rick was loaded down like a Sherpa with his backpack, Gwen's backpack, Gwen's laptop bag, and both of their lunches.

Gwen locked his truck with his key fob. "I don't need you to carry *everything*."

"I got it," Rick said.

They walked into school together. It was still half an hour before the first bell, so the hallways were sparsely trafficked by students and arriving teachers. Gwen opened her classroom door. It was labeled with a placard that read Mrs. Barnett. Rick accompanied Gwen into her classroom, setting her gear on her desk.

"Have a good day," Rick said, leaning over and pecking her on the lips. As he leaned in, her protruding stomach brushed against him.

"You too," Gwen replied.

He touched her stomach and looked into her blue eyes. "I love you."

Gwen smiled. "I love you too."

Rick left for his classroom. Gwen sat at her desk and opened her laptop, reviewing her lesson plans. Her cell phone chimed. She fished her phone from her purse, checked the number, and swiped right. "What's up, Lewis?"

"I'm sorry to bug you so early in the morning, but could you come to the teacher's room? There's a problem you should handle."

"What's going on?"

"Rachel Kreider and her big mouth."

"I'll be right there."

Gwen walked to the teacher's room. Lewis stood at the counter, stirring his coffee. Rachel Kreider and two new female teachers sat at one of the round tables, talking and drinking their coffee.

"Oh, hey, Gwen," Lewis said.

The chatter from the ladies across the room stopped.

Lewis walked toward their table, Gwen in tow. "I heard you talking about Gwen's pregnancy."

Rachel's eyes widened. "I don't know what you're talking about."

"Really? You said that Gwen's child was fathered by her ex-husband on a conjugal visit."

The two young teachers, Ms. Windham and Ms. Taylor, looked down, avoiding Gwen's gaze.

"I didn't say that," Rachel said.

Lewis addressed the two teachers. "Did Rachel say that or not?"

Ms. Windham nodded.

"She did say that," Ms. Taylor said.

"That's what I heard too," Lewis said.

Rachel crossed her arms over her chest, her face beet red. "You shouldn't be listening to my *private* conversations."

"You shouldn't be lying."

Gwen stepped closer and said, "I don't owe anyone an explanation, but, for the record, it would've been very hard for me to have a conjugal visit with my ex-husband because I was never allowed them in the first place. Furthermore, I was divorced at the time of conception. You're welcome to do the math and to check my divorce papers. It's public record. I'm seven months along, and I was officially divorced a year ago." Gwen touched her stomach. "And, yes, our baby *was* a happy accident, and I *was* pregnant when Rick and I got married." Gwen pointed at Rachel. "If you ever spread bullshit like that again, I will sue you for slander. Don't think I won't."

Rachel's head was bowed; her eyes were glassy. She stood from her chair and hurried from the teacher's room in a huff.

"Stop lying, Rachel," Lewis called out to her back.

CHAPTER 146

Rick … Two Years after the Knockout

The library was packed. The chairs were filled with parents, press, and football players. More students, community members, and teachers stood in the back. A podium and a single rectangular table were set up in front. A camera crew filmed the scene. Rick stood at the podium, wearing a gray suit. Aaron Fuller and Jamar Burris sat at the table, also wearing suits, each of them with three hats in front of them.

Rick surveyed the audience. The Burrises sat next to Ms. Fuller and Drew, who had been released from prison earlier that year. Shane's conviction and Drew's subsequent appeal had shaved six months off his sentence, and he didn't have to register as a sex offender. Thanks to a football booster, who also happened to be the owner of the local concrete plant, Drew had gainful employment with a living wage. Rick gave them a nod. He found Gwen, who held their ten-month-old baby boy, Dylan. Rick already had visions of future football glory, but he'd promised Gwen never to pressure his son, although his crib *was* filled with cushy little footballs. Gwen grinned, the little guy bouncing in her lap. Rick returned her smile, then addressed the audience.

"Before we celebrate these two special student athletes, I'd like to thank all the members of our football team. Without that group effort, it's impossible to win a state championship, much less three of them in a row. Furthermore, I send out my grateful appreciation to our

West Lake student body and to the West Lake Students for Change for setting up the Caleb Miles Memorial Fund to Prevent Teenage Suicides.

"This effort helps bridge the gap between depressed students and school administrators. The funds collected help pay for licensed therapists for those in need. With open communication and help available to all, we hope to never lose another student to suicide."

The audience responded with a hush of silence and then a thunderous applause.

Rick waited for the crowd to calm. "Thank you to everyone who donated time and money to the Caleb Miles Memorial Fund." He paused for a moment. "Now we turn the spotlight on these two special athletes. There's never been a student in any sport from West Lake who's ever earned a Division I scholarship for collegiate athletics. This year we have two such recipients." Rick gestured to Aaron and Jamar. "I could go on and on about their on-the-field accomplishments, but I won't because their football talents aren't the most impressive characteristics of these two individuals.

"Aaron Fuller is the toughest young man I've ever coached and an extremely hard worker. He works at a concrete plant on the weekends, even during football season. After we won our second state championship, he wasn't out partying. He went straight home following the game, went to sleep, and went to work in the morning, like it was just another day. Aaron'll be successful in life because he has grit and an unstoppable will to persevere."

Rick paused for a moment. "Jamar Burris." Rick paused again. "He's a special football player, a once-in-a-lifetime talent, a leader of men, and an even better person. The worst mistake I ever made as a coach was benching Jamar. I was clearly wrong, but Jamar didn't pout. He didn't tell me that it was unfair, even though it clearly was. He stood on the sideline and cheered on his replacement as if nothing had happened. That's an example of the extraordinary character and poise this young man possesses."

Rick gestured to Aaron and Jamar. The hats in front of them displayed the university logos from the schools they were considering: Penn State, Pitt, and Ohio State for Jamar; and Temple, James Madison, and Pitt for Aaron. "Why don't you two show everyone where you'll attend college?"

They looked at each other with goofy grins; then simultaneously Jamar and Aaron picked up the blue hat from their trio of choices and placed it on their heads, the University of Pittsburgh logos visible.

The audience gave them a standing ovation.

FOR THE READER

Dear Reader,

I'm thrilled that you took precious time out of your life to read my novel. Thank you! I hope you found it entertaining, engaging, and thought-provoking. If so, please consider writing a positive review on Amazon and Goodreads. Five-star reviews have a huge impact on future sales. The review doesn't need to be long and detailed, if you're more of a reader than a writer. As an author and a small businessman, competing against the big publishers, every reader, every review, and every referral is greatly appreciated.

If you're interested in receiving my novel *Against the Grain* **for free and/or reading my other titles for free or .99 cents, go to the following link:** http://www.PhilWBooks.com. You're probably thinking, *What's the catch?* There is no catch.

If you want to contact me, don't be bashful. I can be found at Phil@PhilWBooks.com. I do my best to respond to all e-mails.

Sincerely,
Phil M. Williams

GRATITUDE

I'd like to thank my wife for her expert council on all things education as well as allowing me to plagiarize her personal narrative. Without her support and unwavering belief in my skill as an author, I'm not sure I would have embarked on this career. I love you, Denise.

I'd also like to thank my editors. My developmental editor, Caroline Smailes, did a fantastic job finding the holes in my plot and suggesting remedies. As always, my line editor, Denise Barker (not to be confused with my wife, Denise Williams), did a fantastic job making sure the manuscript was error-free. I love her comments and feedback.

Thank you to Deborah Bradseth of Tugboat Design for her excellent cover art and formatting. She's the consummate professional. I look forward to many more beautiful covers in the future.

Thank you to Olivia for her insights into central Pennsylvania culture and regional dialects.

Lastly, thank you to the truth-seekers of the world—everyone who verifies before believing, researches before trusting, and constantly questions. It's much easier to simply believe what we want to believe, and that's precisely what the liars, manipulators, and propagandists of the world rely upon.

52266340R00299

Made in the USA
Lexington, KY
10 September 2019